Praise for S. L. Viehl's *StarDoc* . . .

"Continuously surprising and deviously written and splendidly full of new characters."
—Anne McCaffrey

"An entertaining, almost old-fashioned adventure . . . the adventure and quirky mix of aliens and cultures makes a fun combination."
—*Locus*

"*StarDoc* is a fascinating reading experience that will provide much pleasure to science fiction fans. . . . The descriptions of the various sentient species are so delightfully believable that readers will feel S. L. Viehl has had firsthand encounters. . . . The lead character is a wonderful heroine. . . ."
—*Midwest Book Review*

"I don't read much science fiction, but I got ahold of *StarDoc* and just loved it—I hummed with enjoyment while reading it. Don't miss this one!"
—Catherine Coulter

"Rest easy, James White. At last there's another superlative proponent of space medicine to make you proud. With great style and panache, Ms. Viehl manages a large cast of fascinating characters, leaving no doubt that she is a major discovery in the annals of science fiction."
—*Romantic Times*

"Ms. Viehl writes a riveting tale. . . . With more than a few surprises up her sleeve, this rising star proves herself a master storyteller who can win and hold a bestselling audience."
—*Romantic Times*

ENDURANCE:
A StarDoc Novel

S. L. Viehl

ROC

A ROC BOOK

ROC
Published by New American Library, a division of
Penguin Group (USA) Inc., 375 Hudson Street,
New York, New York 10014, USA
Penguin Group (Canada), 10 Alcorn Avenue, Toronto,
Ontario M4V 3B2, Canada (a division of Pearson Penguin Canada Inc.)
Penguin Books Ltd., 80 Strand, London WC2R 0RL, England
Penguin Ireland, 25 St. Stephen's Green, Dublin 2,
Ireland (a division of Penguin Books Ltd.)
Penguin Group (Australia), 250 Camberwell Road, Camberwell, Victoria 3124,
Australia (a division of Pearson Australia Group Pty. Ltd.)
Penguin Books India Pvt. Ltd., 11 Community Centre, Panchsheel Park,
New Delhi - 110 017, India
Penguin Group (NZ), cnr Airborne and Rosedale Roads, Albany,
Auckland 1310, New Zealand (a division of Pearson New Zealand Ltd.)
Penguin Books (South Africa) (Pty.) Ltd., 24 Sturdee Avenue,
Rosebank, Johannesburg 2196, South Africa

Penguin Books Ltd., Registered Offices:
80 Strand, London WC2R 0RL, England

First published by Roc, an imprint of New American Library,
a division of Penguin Group (USA) Inc.

First Printing, January 2001
10 9 8 7 6 5 4

For Holly Lisle,
who never ceases to amaze me—
thanks for helping me handle my own
sympathy for the devil.

ACKNOWLEDGMENTS

I'd like to thank Gerry Coughlin, author of *Everyday English and Slang in Ireland,* whose on-line dictionary of the same at http://www. geocities.com/Research Triangle/8662/irish provided an invaluable linguistic resource for this novel. (And if I made a hash of it, Gerry, it's my fault, not yours.)

PART ONE:

Incarceration

Chapter One

L.T.F. *Perpetua*

"... may it be granted to me to enjoy life and the practice of the art, respected by all men at all times."

—Hippocrates (460?–377? B.C.)

Wishful thinking, Hippocrates old pal. My life was ruined, my practice was over, and I sure as hell wasn't getting any respect around here lately.

"The Hanar rules over the Hsktskt Faction." The metallic audio of the automated prisoner-orientation program droned in my ears. I'd been forced to listen to the stupid thing for days. "One maintains rank of Hanar."

The isolation cell the Hsktskt had thrown me in was small, dark, and cold. I had no clothes. No food or water. Worse, no *lavatory*, only a drain in the concave floor.

You can guess how thrilled I was with the amenities.

"There are two subHanar. Should the Hanar die, the senior subHanar assumes the rank of Hanar."

"I'll make a note of it."

I had little else to do, but sneer at the voice, and wonder what was going to happen to me.

Some of this mess was my fault. I'd been forced to surrender to the League in order to protect Joren, the homeworld of my adopted people. The Hsktskt Faction had shown up to raid Joren shortly thereafter. Again to save Joren, I had helped the Faction capture the League fleet.

My clever strategy had backfired when I learned my new husband, Duncan Reever, had not only summoned the Hsktskt to Joren, but worked for the big lizards. The final blow came when Reever revealed he'd also captured and enslaved my large feline friend, Alunthri.

That was when I'd tried to kill him.

The door panel opened once an hour, when a Hsktskt centuron counted me. I idly wondered how I was listed on the inventory. One short, bad-tempered female Terran thoracic surgeon, maybe?

The guard always flashed a light in my face. That was my cue to say something, like: "Yeah, I'm still alive" or "That you, room service?"

The ten-foot-tall, sextupedal lizards occasionally hissed something back that I couldn't understand—they'd taken my translation headgear along with my clothes—but it never sounded like *Would you care for tea, Dr. Torin?*

"No thanks." I was hanging on to my sense of humor. With a death grip. "But check back with me in an hour."

If the guard found me sleeping during these frequent inspections, I got tepid water tossed in my face. That happened a lot since what I had roughly calculated to be the end of the second day. I caught some in my mouth a few times. Gave me something to spit back at him.

The Hsktskt have zero sense of humor, of course. Whenever I made a direct hit, the guard gave me a jolt through the detainment cuff on my left wrist. The last time he'd personally nailed me with one of his thick, snakelike limbs. So far my nasty Terran habit had gotten me numerous assorted contusions, a dislocated shoulder (which I managed to fix), and a fractured left wrist (which remained broken).

My first time being a slave. Obviously I needed some practice.

"Four maintain rank for each subHanar, and each descendent rank. Thus, there are eight Akade ministers, sixty-four subAkade ministers, five hundred twelve OverLord commanders—"

"Four thousand ninety-six Lords; thirty-two thousand, seven hundred sixty-eight OverMasters; two hundred sixty-two thousand, one hundred forty-four Masters; two million, ninety-seven thousand, one hundred fifty-two OverSeers; sixteen million, seven hundred seventy-seven thousand, two hundred sixteen Seers; one hundred thirty-four million, two hundred seventeen thousand, seven hundred twenty-eight OverCenturons; one billion, seventy-three million, seven hundred forty-one thousand, eight hundred twenty-four centurons; and eight billion, five hundred eighty-nine million, nine hundred thirty-four thousand, five hundred ninety-two free citizens." I yawned. "I can multiply, okay?"

On top of the injuries, I was exhausted. Starved. Dirty. About to go berserk from the claustrophobia-inducing isolation. Funny, I'd always thought of myself as a loner, too. I tried not to brood over it. Most of the time I failed.

Imagining what was happening to the Chakacat didn't help. Had they put gentle Alunthri in one of these cells? Were they beating and starving it as well? Then came the heat of a rage that no amount of water or beatings could extinguish.

Reever did this.

Duncan Reever, who'd been the chief linguist at the colony on K-2, had done a lot to me. Besides telepathically intruding on my brain and taking control of my body from time to time, he'd also raped me, helped me cure a plague, followed me when I'd escaped the League, served with me on the Jorenian star vessel *Sunlace,* become my confident, helped me solve a series of murders, and even saved my life.

If you overlooked the rape—which wasn't exactly his fault—and the mind/body control thing, Duncan had been a pretty decent friend. I'd confided in him. Trusted him. I'd even been stupid enough to fall in love with him. My fingers curled around the metallic slave collar Duncan Reever had locked around my neck. That's how *he* felt about me.

"Congratulations, prisoner 1471428." That was what the automated prisoner-orientation program called me. "You have mastered the configurations of the Faction ranking hierarchy."

"Discontinue program and go away." My tongue had become a solid, immobile lump. Maybe I'd try swallowing some of that water next time.

"Unable to heed verbal command." The audio was piped in through the tiny ventilation duct above my head. "Orientation is requisite for all Hsktskt Faction property."

"Here's what I think of your program." I made a rather pointed gesture with my hand, yelped, then cradled my throbbing wrist. "Ouch, *damn* it."

"Do you wish to make a statement regarding your attack on OverMaster HalaVar?"

"No." Seeing Duncan Reever in a Hsktskt uniform had ripped a shuttle-sized hole through my heart. It had also completely ruined my attempt at homicide. "Want to give me another shot?"

"You attacked *your assigned OverMaster.*"

Cherijo. How could you?

What laughter I produced sounded awful—dehydration and lots of yelling had done a real job on my larynx. "I'm not assigned to him. I'm his bondmate." I thought about that for a second. "*Was* his bondmate. I want a divorce."

The drone didn't respond to my need for an attorney. "You must obey the orders of OverMaster HalaVar, and all free citizens of the Hsktskt Faction."

"Really." Another damn headache started pounding at my temples. I think it was just hearing that name. *HalaVar.* "I don't advise you to keep that circuit open."

"Acknowledge these instructions."

The pain behind my eyes expanded. I'd have cheerfully amputated one of my limbs for a syrinpress of analgesics. "Check back with me when Hell freezes over."

Or I did. They'd kept my cell temperature at about sixty degrees Fahrenheit. Too cool for comfort, too warm to induce hypothermia. At least Alunthri had fur. My thin Terran skin was starting to develop chilblains.

If Jenner had been there, he'd have kept me warm. I'd left my Tibetan temple cat back on Joren, in the care of my adopted people. I was glad he was safe, but I still missed His Majesty terribly.

Someone had programmed the drone to be persistent. Probably Reever. "Acknowledge these instructions."

"Isn't the penalty for failure to comply termination?" I could always hope.

"Acknowledge these instructions immediately."

I lay back down. I might not know what was going to happen to me, but I'd rather fight than give in. "I'd rather kiss your programmer."

"Prisoner 1471428, acknowledge these instructions or you will be disciplined."

"Maybe I wasn't clear." I put my good arm under my aching head, cushioning my skull against the hard deck. "Go fuse yourself."

The door panel slid open. Something sailed through the air and smacked into my bad shoulder before falling to the deck. Translation headgear, I saw as I picked it up. The kind the Hsktskt made all the League captives wear. I eyed the guard—guess Mr. Joviality wanted to have a meaningful chat this time—then slipped it over my limp, tangled hair. It took awhile to fit the receiver to my right ear. Not easy to do anything one-handed.

Infolded green epidermal scales gleamed over bulky muscle as the guard trained his rifle on me. "Stand up."

He couldn't discipline me. My detainment cuff had shattered when he'd broken my wrist. No, this beast looked hungry.

"What for?" I squinted as he directed an optic light in my eyes. "Got the nibbles? Think I'll go well with a nice red spicewine?"

Two of his sinuous limbs lashed restlessly at his sides. "Stand up and exit the cell."

"Right." I was in no hurry to become a canapé. "Make me."

The guard enabled the sight lock and the weapon's pulse chamber charged with an audible hum. "Comply or I will shoot you."

He wouldn't *really* shoot me. "Be my guest, you oversized scaly skinned—"

He shot me.

A single energy pulse smashed into my sternum. Impact propelled me backward along the deck until my spine slammed into the cell wall. My vision doubled, then darkened. Tremendous pain kept my lungs from expanding.

Yep, I thought, this mouth of mine just might get me killed someday. Maybe *today*.

Just before I blacked out, the guard bent over me and grabbed me by the length of my long, dirty hair. The mouthful of blood I spat hit him right between his frontal and parietal ridges.

My last thought was *Bull's-eye*.

I woke up in Medical. Some hamster-faced nurse stood over me, taking my vitals with a scanner. My tongue hurt—apparently I'd bitten it. A fiery sensation ate a continuous hole between my breasts.

The beast actually shot me.

I tested my limbs, and discovered I was still naked. Plasteel restraints immobilized my wrists and ankles. Both my bruised arms had infusers stuck in them. I could feel the monitor hookups attached to my scalp and under my breasts.

"Hey!" Flat on my back and helpless were not two of my favorite positions. "Unstrap me!"

The dark fur pelting the rodent nurse's small face bristled as she bent over me. Hamsters didn't have long, honed incisors like the ones she sported. They gleamed between twin fans of whiskery vibrissae like white blades. I heard a syrinpress clink against the slave collar around my throat.

"It takes to kill a Terran, do you know the quantity of benzodiazepine?" she asked me.

"Not much," I said. Oh, terrific. She didn't have a hamster's personality, either. "Why? Skip that class back at Medtech?"

Her blade-shaped teeth flashed as she eased the syrinpress away from my jugular. "What constitutes a fatal dose, *I* know."

"Good for you." I was such a liar. "Any chance you're going off duty soon?"

She straightened, then called out, "Regained consciousness, the Terran female has."

All at once I became very popular. Three of the *Perpetua*'s staff physicians surrounded my berth. Nurses hovered at their sides. Two Hsktskt centurons peered at me from behind them.

"Excuse me," I said, and put my polite face on. "The Terran female would like to be released now."

They ignored me. I endured a thorough examination, after which one of the nurses irrigated and dressed the pulse burn on my sternum with antibacterial pads.

I yelped while she scrubbed at another laceration. "Hey! That hurts—take it easy, will you?"

She didn't. The doctors did nothing to stop her, and discussed me as though I was comatose. A second nurse strapped my wrist in a support band, while a third scanned my swollen shoulder. The trio cleaned and sealed all my myriad lacerations, too. None of them made even a pretense of gentleness, either.

By the time they were through, I was seething. God help them if they ever worked for *me*.

"The Terran female would really, *really* like to be released now."

"Leave us," I heard TssVar say.

Those two words from the Hsktskt Commander effectively cleared the area. The towering OverLord lumbered across the deck to stand by my berth, and began reading through my chart.

TssVar would have made one hell of a doctor. Faced with the OverLord's massive physique and nightmare visage, no patient in the universe would have ever given him lip.

I could appreciate those qualities. Everybody gave *me* lip.

Octagonal keratin scales bulged over wide cords of sinew and muscle as TssVar tossed the chart aside with a grim hiss. His black tongue flickered out to taste my air as he personally examined me. Hsktskt facial muscles didn't lend themselves to much emotion, but even I could gauge the level of his contempt.

"I have seen more attractive fodder, SsurreVa."

SsurreVa was the Hsktskt name he'd given me. It translated literally to "thin-skinned." Wonder why.

One of his clawed hands lifted the edge of the dressing on my chest. When he saw the wound, he expressed even more disgust.

I wasn't falling for any intimidation tactics—this whole mess was *his* fault. Instead I glanced down, and made a *tsking* sound. "Beautiful work your guards do on unarmed prisoners."

"You Terrans are far too flimsy." He replaced the

dressing. "We will find something else to use on you besides pulse weapons."

Something that didn't damage the goods, I gathered. "That might be wise." I wasn't going to offer actual suggestions as to *what*. Plus there was something I wanted to know. "How is the Chakacat, Alunthri?"

His lower eyelids slid up, then down. "Alive."

That word covered a lot of bleak territory. "Where is it?"

"In General Detainment." He flashed some impressive enamel. "For now."

Which I'd take to mean don't press my luck. "When do I go back to my cell?"

TssVar draped a limb along the edge of my berth, and bent toward me to examine my expression. "Have you not tired of it?"

"Oh, no. I love lying naked in a dark, cold cell with nothing to eat or drink for days." I showed him some of my teeth. "First vacation I've had in years."

"Indeed." Hsktskt understood sarcasm, but rarely reacted to it. "I think you wish to hide. You did not anticipate HalaVar's actions."

Actually, I'd been stunned. During the attack, Reever had used my natural hesitation to disarm me—he knew some bizarre tricks when it came to self-defense. I remembered how I'd huddled on the deck, staring up at him. Betrayed by the one man I never would have suspected of turning on me.

You signaled the Hsktskts.

Yes. I signaled them.

That was when they'd brought Reever's leverage in: Alunthri, collared and chained. That finished any hope I had of having another go at the heartless bastard. A moment later, TssVar entered, sized up the whole sad, horrifying tableau, and had me hauled off to solitary detainment.

Reever was probably still congratulating himself at this very moment, I thought, as he enjoyed the

Hsktskt hospitality suite. I had been caged like an animal. Thank God, Alunthri was in with the other League prisoners.

Or maybe I shouldn't feel so happy about that. What if the other captives found out the Chakacat was *my* friend? Me, who had betrayed them.

I wasn't going to brood over it. TssVar wanted to keep me alive, that was pretty obvious—the Hsktskt weren't known for their patience. But my chances of freeing Alunthri and the two of us escaping were slim to none.

That didn't mean I wasn't going to try.

"We spoke of this before," TssVar said. "Warm-bloods often betray each other."

"And I said I should learn to be like you, Over-Lord, and trust in no one." I tested the plasteel restraints, which felt far too tight, effectively cutting off circulation to my hands and feet. Blasted nurses. "Take me back to my cell." Or anywhere these League staffers couldn't get at me.

"When you have recovered, you may ask Hala-Var," TssVar said. "You are his property."

My brows rose. "I don't *think* so."

One claw snapped a new detainment cuff on my uninjured wrist. Not gently, either. "You belong to OverMaster HalaVar." His lipless mouth stretched in a gruesome imitation of a smile. "Unless he decides to sell you on Catopsa."

My regenerative physiology once again had me mostly healed within a few days. Convenient, since the Medical staffers got on my nerves in as many hours.

During my recovery, I had plenty of time on my hands to observe how the League ran a medical department. Compared to the Jorenians, on whose star vessel I'd spent the last year, these staffers were undisciplined, unsupervised, and unbelievably inefficient.

At first I resisted the urge to correct one of the staff for neglecting proper procedure. Eventually I gave up and simply yelled.

"Nurse! Get a syrinpress. That man in berth nine should have had his meds *two* hours ago!

"Does the patient with the limb injury have to develop *gangrene* before you change her damn dressing?

"When does the primary physician intent to perform rounds? After all these people slide into *comas*?"

"Calm yourself, SsurreVa." A reptilian voice came over my headgear after one of my tirades. "You are provoked too easily."

I clapped my hands over the receiver against my ear and sat straight up in my berth. TssVar. "You're monitoring me?"

"We monitor all slaves."

Nice to know that now.

I decided to stop yelling directly at the staffers. It wasn't their fault no one cared enough to supervise them properly. No, I'd vent my spleen to the primary medical officer, someone named Malgat, as soon as he made rounds.

That took two full rotations.

"Where have you been?" I started in on the short, hairless humanoid when at last he appeared by my berth. "These people need some management, pronto, because . . . " I stared down at the syring press in Dr. Malgat's two-fingered hand. "*What* is *that*?"

He prepared it for infusion. "Joseph Grey Veil left instructions to administer this test compound, and several others."

"You are *not* experimenting on me!"

Malgat gave me a small, sympathetic smile.

Lazy nurses had their uses. No one had bothered to check on me or my restraints. It had taken hours, but I'd managed to work my good hand free.

As soon as Malgat leaned over me, I knocked the

syrinpress away. It went flying across the ward, dropped, and slid beneath an exam table.

"No more test compounds." Twenty-seven years of that waste back on Terra had been more than enough for me.

Malgat appeared confounded. I guess his other lab rats had never tried to bite his clammy little hand before. "Doctor!"

"Forget it." Before the primary recovered from his shock, I loosened the other three straps and yanked the monitors off my chest and head.

"No!" The little creep tried to hold me down. "Nurse! Assist me!" To me, he said, "Remain where you are!"

"In your dreams, pal." I bashed the bonesetter around my wrist into his thick neck, sending him reeling, then I rolled off the berth. Infusers ripped from my flesh. Blood trickled down my limbs. "Back off."

"Return to your berth," he said, holding a palm against his bruised flesh as he came after me. "You are not well."

I was just dandy. Sore, and naked, but not defenseless. I skirted the berth. Released the clamps on the bonesetter and shook it off. Picked up my chart and eyed his skull. Big, soft veins pulsed beneath his brown-spotted derma.

"I bet your species has no cranial bone," I said.

He stopped. "What?"

"I'd hate to rupture your brain tissue with this." I held up the chart. "Keep coming and I will."

The nurse who'd threatened me the first day came up behind Dr. Malgat. She had a syrinpress in her hand and a lovely smirk puffing out her cheek pouches. This was just the opportunity she'd been looking for. I could hear her now, explaining the tragedy. I had been struggling, trying to escape. She hadn't meant to administer an overdose, but what a shame, her finger had slipped on the calibrator.

"This patient, Doctor, shall I sedate?" she asked Malgat.

Meaning, I'd better get moving. A chart wouldn't dent the thick skull under all that fur.

I looked around. Grabbed a dermal probe off an instrument tray to my left. Held it out like a bladed weapon.

"Try it, you shrew," I said, "and I'll carve out your heart."

The nurse's broad tail slapped the deck, while she made a strange sputtering sound.

"She will do what she says."

I went still at the sound of the cold, dispassionate voice. Malgat sighed with relief. The shrew bristled, furious. A tall, light-haired man stepped around both of them.

He was a good-looking Terran male, if you over-looked the empty expression and bleak blue eyes. He moved with grace and economy for a man his size. The sinewy build and natural athletic strength helped. In fact, the only outer flaws he possessed were the thick webs of scars on the backs of both hands—for the time being. I planned to add more in other places.

"Look who's here. My husband." I smiled. The brewing hostility inside me spewed out in a geyser of scalding rage. "Hello, Reever, you corrupt, evil, traitorous, lying ass—"

"Enough, Cherijo." He took a step forward. Held out his hand. "Give me the probe."

"You mean this?" I turned the instrument in my hand so the sharp end jutted out from my fist. "Specify the artery."

He made a brief survey of my body. Not even a spark of interest glimmered in his chilly gaze. Ah, gee, didn't he want me anymore? Apparently not. Guess I was supposed to be crushed.

"If you attempt to harm me again, TssVar will sub-

ject you to much more than solitary detainment,"
he said.

Treacherous, unfeeling, blunt as always. Same old
Reever. "I'm going to do more than *attempt*, pal." I
jabbed the probe toward him. "I don't care what happens to me."

"You forget that Alunthri can be made to suffer
as well."

That did it. I lunged.

A heartbeat later, he countered my attack easily,
pushing me back and pinning me to the wall panel
beside the berth.

This was worse than his threats. "Get off me,
damn it!"

I fought, but he was bigger, stronger, and in much
better condition. He pegged my wrists above my
head with one of his strong, scarred hands and relieved me of the probe with the other. I jerked my
knee up, but one long thigh blocked me just short of
my mark. Too bad. I would have enjoyed the thought
of him speaking with a squeak for a few days.

"Stop." He used his body weight to hold me in
place. "Don't fight me."

He was touching me, and I'd sworn I'd never let
him do that again. "I'll kill you!" I could feel his
heart beating rapidly against my bare breast, and
twisted. *"Get off!"*

"When you give me your word you won't attack
anyone."

I'd tell him I'd mate with Malgat, just to get him
away from me. "Fine." I took a deep breath, let it
out. "I promise not to attack anyone."

He took the precaution of stepping out of knee-jerk
range before he let my wrists go. Like most males, he
was protective of his genitals. Smart move. One of
my immediate goals was to kick his up into his
esophagus.

He gave me the once-over again. "I will get you
a tunic."

"Don't bother." I kept my eyes on him as I grabbed a berth sheet and quickly wound it around my body. He watched my hands knot the linen over my breasts. My body had never impressed him, so why was he suddenly so interested in covering it up?

I pushed past him. Shoved the venomous nurse out of my way. Headed for the Medical entrance panel. One of the Hsktskt glared at me, then snarled something in Reever's direction. My headgear was askew, so I didn't pick that up.

"Cherijo."

I paused, but didn't turn around. "What?"

"Report to my quarters."

"Right." When I sprouted wings and could fly there.

I kept going. Another Hsktskt guard stepped out to block my path. A huge male, almost as big as TssVar, but broader and with a noticeable slope to his brow. He wore the rank of a squad commander, or OverCenturon.

"Slaves do not roam the ship unsupervised."

This was getting old. "Call off the guard dog, you jerk."

"Address the OverMaster with his proper title," FlatHead said, baring rows of discolored incisors. He smelled as good as his teeth looked.

"Sure." Now the damn *lizards* were correcting me. "Call off the guard dog, *OverMaster* HalaVar, you jerk."

FlatHead activated his weapon and targeted my face.

"She is part of the medical staff. Let her pass."

Hsktskt enamel crunched as he ground his teeth together, but the OverCenturon stepped aside.

I stalked out. In the corridor, I automatically hitched up the sheet and realized absently that I was barefoot. Good thing the deck was insulated. Wouldn't want to catch a chill before the Hsktskt scientists on Catopsa got a chance to dissect me. Might mess up their tests.

After locating the nearest glidelift, I stepped in and keyed the console for my own quarters on level six. "At last."

Reever got in the lift before the doors closed. He reprogrammed the lift to go to level nine. "I will accompany you."

"Your funeral." I didn't look at him, either. The sight of him in a modified Hsktskt military uniform still made my blood boil. "You've given the med staffers free access to the ship?"

"Within reason. OverLord TssVar is aware of your professional oath to do no harm."

That last part sounded like a warning. He didn't realize it but he'd just given me a sizeable weapon. A moment of silence passed. I amused myself by thinking of creative amputations I could perform on Reever. Minus anesthetic.

He ruined my fantasies by saying, "The Hsktskt guard you offended—stay away from him."

"I offended who? Mr. Manners?" I heaved a counterfeit sigh. "Here I thought I'd made a new friend."

"His name is GothVar." He keyed something in on the wrist unit all the Hsktskt wore. Probably a note to have me clapped in manacles later. "He has long disliked slaves, particularly Terrans."

"Considering who he has to work with?" I lifted a hand to cover my mouth. Rage was fun, but tiring. "Can't say I blame him."

"I want you to listen to me."

"Keep talking. I always yawn like this when I'm riveted."

It took a few seconds before the lift slowed and came to a halt at level nine. I walked out and down the corridor, with Reever trailing me.

"Why am I here?" I said before I crossed the threshold of his quarters.

Reever pushed me through, then closed the door

panel, but didn't secure it. Foolish man. "Continuation of prisoner orientation."

Forget that. "Send me back to my cell." When he didn't, I halted in the center of the mostly empty room. "Look, you've given me the speech. Seen me naked. Thrown me in the brig. What's left?"

"There is something I have to give you." He pointed to a circular depression in the deck. "First I must complete your orientation. Stand on the scan pad."

Another scan. They'd already done a million of them. Might as well get it over with, I thought, and stepped into the circle.

Reever crossed to the room console and keyed in a rapid sequence code. "Initiate identification scan."

A blinding white light scanned me from crown to soles while a drone voice began to recite the facts.

"Life-form identification: Torin, Cherijo. Terran female. Physician. Thoracic Surgeon. Height: 4 feet, 11 inches. Weight: 82 pounds. Hair: Black with silver streak above right temple. Eyes: Blue. Derma: Terran Caucasian."

"You forgot the freckle behind my right ear," I said.

That confused the drone. "There is no indication of abnormal pigmentation in that area—"

Reever made an impatient sound. "Disregard subject input. Results of most recent physical evaluation."

"P.E. performed by Malgat, Evo. Includes inspection, palpation, percussion, and auscultation of body and organs. General results reflect a well-developed female."

Evo had barely glanced at me, much less performed a full eval. "There was no P.E. performed. Your primary probably had to guess at my gender."

Reever didn't react to that. "Proceed."

"Neurological Assessment: Awake, alert, oriented to environment—"

"Don't start talking neuroanatomy to him," I said to the console. "He'll get aroused."

The program ignored me, too. After finishing the neuro stats, it started on the cardiovascular. "BP and heart rate consistent with intense athletic conditioning—"

"An athlete?" I chuckled. "Hardly. Wait, does whump-ball count?"

It droned on and on. "Respiratory Assessment: Respiration quiet and regular—"

"I only spit when I think of you, Reever," I said.

The automated program noted during the integumentary stats that my derma met genetic norms, but that I had no PIC.

I frowned. "What's this pee-eye-sea?"

Reever didn't answer me. During the recitation of my musculoskeletal stats, the drone stated there was little evidence of any former injuries.

I flexed my stiff wrist. "I'm still thinking about suing."

A white spot beam abruptly switched on and focused on my wedding band. "Unidentified metallic ring encircling third finger of left hand, as indicated."

I'd forgotten about that. I pulled off the ring Reever had given me back on Joren, and tossed it at the console as hard as I could. It bounced off and rolled beneath the unit. "Not anymore."

The console recited the sensory stats, noting some evidence of hypersensitivity to light, consistent with my recent detainment.

"Is it usually this obtuse?" I asked. "Or is today a special occasion?"

The drone only offered my hematological stats. At length.

I folded my arms. "Did you check between my toes, too?"

"Microbiological assessment detected no dangerous microorganisms. Augmented antibodies detected.

Unclassified genetic material detected. Origin of detected irregularities unknown."

What the hell had Joseph been pumping into me all those years? "I guess you did."

"Conclusion: this is a twenty-nine-year-old woman in excellent health."

"Bravo." I clapped twice, slow and loud. "Took you long enough."

"Hematology analysis, categorical results: CBC— 6.45; RBC—5.0; Hemoglobin—15.95; Hematocrit— 45.7; MCV—"

"Discontinue individual test results," Reever said, and the drone shut up. "Prepare the laser application."

"Application of what?"

He moved away from the console and toward me. "All prisoners must maintain a PIC—physical identification code." I jumped off the pad. "Resume your position, Cherijo."

He wanted to *brand* me. Like some agri-pharm range animal. "Not in this lifetime, pal."

Reever halted. "Permanent individual identification sequences—"

I'd almost made it to the door panel when he caught me. A hard arm snaked around my waist. The other blocked my hand just before I raked my fingernails into his face. Reever carried me back to the circle, but it took some effort. I fought him with every ounce of strength I had.

"No!" I gasped as two metallic columns rose out of the deck. Reever positioned me between them, let go, then stepped away. Before I could move, two viselike extensions snaked cold metal clamps around my arms and pelvis. One clamp undulated outward, jerking my right arm up and away from my body.

This wasn't going to happen. "Don't you dare brand me with some slaver code, you pig!"

Reever returned to the console. "Stop struggling," he said. "You will harm yourself."

"Oh, and you *won't?*"

Above me, a laser rig descended from a slot in the upper deck. I heard the power supply hum as the unit charged. My eyes went wide.

He was actually going to burn me with that thing. *"Reever!"*

Reever approached me, a syrinpress in his fist. I fought the steel embrace even harder. "This will prevent you from feeling any pain."

Pain. Good suggestion. I waited until he got close enough, then whipped my head forward and smashed it into his face as hard as I could. The instrument flew from his hand and clattered to the deck. The impact sent Reever staggering back a few steps.

I'll have a headache, too, once these spots stopped dancing in front of my eyes, I thought. A tight knot of pain began to swell just above my right brow. Well, I'd asked for it, might as well enjoy it.

I did, for about ten seconds, until the laser activated.

Searing heat rolled over my forearm. I swore at the top of my lungs and jerked at my arm, but the detainment device held. Thus immobilized, I had to watch as the laser carved a line of short, curving furrows from my wrist to my elbow. With each new mark, new pain flashed up my arm. The cauterized vapors collected in my nose, until I had to stop yelling and choke back my own bile.

Smoke. Flames. Children crying. I couldn't see where they were. Tonetka . . . the children . . . walls of fire between us . . . "Go back!"

It didn't take very long. Only forever. By the time the laser shut down, the only things keeping my shuddering body upright were the clamps.

The memories of what had happened on the *Sunlace* danced inside my eyelids.

"Why did you do that?" Reever had gotten to his

feet, and now his hands were on my face, tilting it up.

I jerked my head away and looked down. Third-degree burns, nearly six inches long and four inches wide, formed an intricate series of symbols in my flesh.

"Why, Cherijo?"

I gazed up at him, saw the icy rage with something like relief. He still cared. I could use that. "Eat . . . waste . . . and . . . d—"

I passed out before I could finish expressing my heartfelt wishes.

CHAPTER TWO

What Goes Around

I groaned, lifted my head, and squinted through decidedly gritty eyes. Too dark to tell where I was. But I could smell a hint of cinnamon and rose hips, and felt the familiar texture of Jorenian linens.

Herbal tea stores and my own bed. The old quarters I'd been assigned on level six. As close to heaven as I was going to get on the *Perpetua*.

"Bad dream." All that shrieking had brought back my sore throat. "Give me some lights."

The console didn't respond to my hoarse command. I struggled off the sleeping platform and stumbled through the dark to manually activate the controls. I felt sluggish and weak—Reever must have drugged me.

Reever did things like that.

I reached for the panel and gasped. From my right hand up, everything hurt. When I got the lights on, I saw the burn dressing encasing my forearm.

"It really happened."

I had no idea why that shocked me, but it did. *He hurt me. He really, deliberately hurt me. Why?* When would his treachery stop being a surprise and start being my reality?

That pesky inner voice of mine piped up at once. *Never.*

Suppuration had seeped through the antibacterial gel, making stains on the outer dressing. I'd unwrap it and have a look later, when I could find my med kit. A blue garment covered the rest of me. A basically transparent, voluminous robe, with only a few strategically placed opaque panels to preserve my modesty.

Reever's idea of sleepwear? Or visual titillation?

"You're feeling better."

I whipped around to find the corrupt creep sitting in one of my chairs. He looked composed and tidy, if you ignored the painful-looking bruise across his left cheekbone.

"Why?" I held out my unmarked arm. "Want to burn the other one now, you sick bastard?"

"All designated properties are given PICs." He rose to his feet. "There are no exceptions."

"Did you brand Alunthri?" It didn't bother me that Reever had used a laser on me. I was a big girl, I could handle that. But Alunthri— "Did you?"

Reever nodded once.

My jaw locked. "I'm going to kill you for that."

"No, you won't."

He had little idea what I was capable of. I had nothing else to lose. Calmly I watched as he moved to stand before me. Let him think I was subdued, beaten. The moron. "So I'm your designated . . . what? Slave-girl?"

He inclined his head. The smug gesture cost him. He didn't have quite enough time to avoid my fist when it connected with his diaphragm, or the follow-through punch I landed against the unbruised cheek. "Cherijo—"

I would have tackled him to the floor, but inexplicably, the interior lighting went off. I froze, resisting the recoil of pain stabbing through my newly healed wrist and my burned arm. "Lights, damn it!"

Before I could land another blow, Reever flung me back on the sleeping platform, then landed on top of me.

"Stop it," Reever muttered, spreading his legs over mine. I gulped in enough air to shriek, and his hand locked over my mouth to smother the sound. At the same time, his other hand encircled my throat and clenched. "Quiet."

The door panel slid open.

"Pretend you're asleep." Without a sound, Reever rolled off me and over the side of the sleeping platform.

There was someone in the room with us. I could hear the thickened breathing, the shuffling footsteps as they approached my bed. Was it that rat-faced, vigilante nurse? Through my eyelashes I watched the glimmer of tiny indicator lights as the intruder lifted a pulse rifle. The slight hum of the weapon as it activated made me stiffen.

Something Dhreen, the Oenrallian pilot who had originally helped me escape from Terra, had said to me on Furinac came back to me. *Doc, what is it with you and weapon-carrying assassins?*

At that time the Furinac First Scion had been trying to kill me, planning to later frame me for his father's murder. He'd ended up committing suicide by blowing his own head off, an inch from my face. *It's a gift, Dhreen.*

I wanted to pound something. Was there anyone left on this blasted ship who *didn't* want to beat, poison, burn, or shoot me?

This latest assassin moved in closer. The scent of acrid alien sweat drifted to my nose. It wasn't the nurse—I'd have known that smell anywhere. It took every ounce of willpower to remain motionless and let him cross those last few inches. A low, soft sound disturbed the air.

Former fleet commander Colonel Shropana was giggling.

I don't know why. Patril should have been rather upset with me. He'd come all the way to Varallan Quadrant on League orders to abduct me, had threatened to blow up Joren, and then had suffered the ultimate humiliation by falling for my Trojan horse trick. I'd turned him and his forty League troop freighters over to the Hsktskt in exchange for Joren's safety.

Considering our history? Laughing or not, he'd definitely use the rifle.

A metallic clunk came from across the room, and Shropana swung back around. I took the opportunity and rolled off the sleeping platform in the same way Reever had. I landed face-first on the deck, and cringed at the resounding *whack*. How had Reever done it so silently?

"Torin." Shropana kicked something out of his way. "I will make it quick. Come out where I can see you."

"Don't move, Cherijo." Reever's voice came out of nowhere, sounding very much in charge. "Drop the weapon, Colonel."

For once Reever had a good idea. I stayed put and covered my head with my arms.

Shropana cursed. The door panel opened a second time. The pulse rifle fired, causing a muffled explosion. A sibilant roar echoed the shot. Then complete chaos ensued. Furnishings flew over my head. Heavy objects crashed into plasteel panels. Bones snapped. Flesh ripped.

"Stop it!" I pushed myself to my feet just as the lights came on and I saw who had taken care of business.

"Shall I kill him for you, HalaVar?"

TssVar held the Colonel suspended a few feet above the deck. Shropana's broken body twitched with spasmodic shudders. Reever had the pulse rifle in his hands and was deactivating it. He looked from the League Commander to me, then made a gesture I'd never seen before.

"Very well." TssVar dropped the wounded man to the deck. The body made a distinct, wet thud.

"Oh, for God's sake." I ran to Shropana. The Hsktskt had done an excellent job, I saw as I crouched down next to the unconscious man. He was very nearly dead. "Couldn't you have just knocked him out?"

The Colonel was a mess. Deep head wound, obvious fractures in both front and back hocks. Dark purple blood spilled from the sagging flews around his mouth and pooled on the deck beneath his blunt, balding head. When I jerked aside his tunic and palpated his abdomen, I swore.

"Shattered ribs and internal hemorrhaging, from the feel of it." I checked his pulse, then jerked my head toward the room panel. "He's taching on me. Call for medevac. Now."

With swift movements I tore a piece of linen and bound it around Shropana's skull. I had no case, no bonesetters, no scanner. Unless I moved fast, I soon wouldn't have a patient.

"Well?" I glared at Reever.

TssVar nudged the Colonel with one huge clawed foot, making Shropana groan. "Isn't he dead?"

"No. Don't do that." I swatted at the Hsktskt's leg. "He needs surgery. Now. I'll have to perform a thoracotomy to see how bad it is." If his heart would stand the strain. Since my heroes evidently weren't going to signal Medical, I rose and headed for the console.

The big Hsktskt got in my way. "This one tried to kill you."

"Not my problem." I went around him. "Let me do my job, will you?"

TssVar made no indication whether he was going to grant me permission to do it, but waiting for approval was never one of my strong points. Behind me, I heard him say to Reever, "I will observe her, HalaVar."

"As you wish, OverLord," Reever said.

Like I was a bug under a microscope, doing some fascinating tricks.

"You two can stand here and chat all day," I said, and keyed in a signal. "I'm moving the Colonel before he bleeds to death."

The charge nurse dispatched two orderlies and a hover gurney to aid me. Once we loaded Shropana, I trotted down the corridor alongside him, my fingers wrapped around the pulse point in his arm. His thready heart rate had seriously weakened by the time we reached Medical.

I started handing out orders before the entrance panel slid shut behind me. "Thoracic surgical team, one minute. I need a bretyliumine infuser setup and full portable cardiac array, stat. Nurse"—the League staffer gawked when I pointed at her—"yes, *you*. Get your backside over here."

Malgat began protesting at once. I shoved him out of my face. He trailed after me, still squawking some nonsense about seniority. From the corner of my eye I saw TssVar nod to one of the centurons, who grabbed the furious physician and hauled him out of my face.

Having the OverLord around had its advantages, I thought, then looked down at the patient. Sometimes.

Between me and the suddenly cooperative nurse, we had Shropana prepped by the time the surgical team had assembled. I had an intern take the Colonel in, while the nurse and I geared up. She didn't offer to help when I changed the dressing on my burned arm before I scrubbed. She just stared at my brand, then the collar around my neck.

"Yeah, I'm a slave, too." I secured the new bandage and shook down the sleeve of my gown. "Just like everyone else."

"Doctor." TssVar walked in, looking around with interest. "This appears to be much more efficient than your center on Kevarzangia Two."

A supply closet would have been an improvement on K-2's FreeClinic. I missed it anyway.

"Here." I handed the largest set of surgical gear to TssVar. "Put this on and scrub." I nodded toward the sink, then turned to the attending nurse. "Help me."

The nurse went pale. "But—but—"

He wasn't contaminating my sterile field with all his Hsktskt germs. "Do it."

I left the two of them at the biodecon unit and entered the main surgical suite, where Shropana lay shrouded and ready for the procedure.

"Status," I said, and one of the surgical interns hesitantly rattled off Shropana's vital signs. The tachycardia had leveled out. "Okay. Let's get rolling."

League medical equipment might be better than K-2's, but it hardly compared to the Jorenian tech I had worked with on the *Sunlace*. The same main control console governed most of the surgery's various apparatus. I muttered to myself as I accessed the panel and activated one of the table scanners. This junk seemed to take forever to scan the body and chest cavity before it extrapolated a diagnosis.

"Pneumothorax, right lung," I said, reading the displayed results out loud. "Multiple fractures in both arm hocks and seven ribs. Looks like one of those pierced the gland cluster behind the cardiac organ."

TssVar was indeed very efficient.

On top of that, Shropana's heart displayed the unmistakable signs of severe coronary arterial disease. As if I didn't have enough of a challenge to deal with. I checked the other scanner.

"Head wound is superficial. No sign of subdural

hematoma." I inspected the laser rig as I powered it up. "All right, people, we're going to have our hands full. He's a myocardial infarction waiting to happen." I checked and saw the Hsktskt standing at the back of some nurses. "OverLord, you'll want to come inside the field perimeter now."

The Hsktskt quickly stepped forward. He must have remembered the last time he encountered the bioelectrical wall—also the last time he'd seen me at work, back on K-2, when I'd delivered his mate's quintuplets. At gunpoint.

The glamorous life of an intergalactic surgeon. Maybe I should have listened to Dhreen and opened a restaurant on K-2. "Activate sterile field."

The static buzz was followed by the whispered suction of the air replacement unit. I pulled down the rig and checked the settings. The beam regulator badly needed calibration, and I had to fool with the stream injector for a minute before it produced the proper bandwidth. My arm hurt, but not enough to make it difficult to handle the instruments.

"Tell me something," I asked no one in particular. "How is it that the League will waste untold millions of credits tracking down a single Terran female, but won't spend a tiny fraction of that upgrading and maintaining its own medical equipment?"

No one answered.

"Stats." When I got no answer, I glared at the nurse handling the Colonel's anesthesia. "Well? Are you taking a nap over there, or what?"

"He's barely stable," she said, muttering under her mask. "You should know."

I powered down and pushed the rig to one side. The slave brand under my gown throbbed in time with the invisible hammers on each side of my head.

I didn't really have the time to do this, I thought, as I surveyed the numerous insubordinate eyes watching me. However, that was one thing I learned in my first year of residency—if you wanted to be in charge, you'd damn well better *act* like it.

"Okay, children," I said, insulting the group at large. "Here's how it works. *I* am the surgeon. *You* are the surgical support team. *I* ask questions. *You* answer me. *I* cut. *You* mop up the blood. If you won't do that, get out and send in someone who will."

The League med pros exchanged glances. One of the male residents cleared his throat.

There's always one brave one. "You have a comment you'd like to make, resident?"

"You turned the fleet over to the Hsktskt," he said, glancing nervously at the OverLord. "Why should you wish to save the Colonel's life now?"

TssVar made an ugly sound.

Brave, and possibly suicidal. "As I recall, you people were prepared to destroy an entire world to get me. The way I see it, we're even. Got it?"

Everyone appeared to get it.

"Good. Now, can we do this, or watch him die?" I waited for the length of a heartbeat. "Stats."

The nurse sounded furious, but she rattled off the appropriate readings. My instrument nurse positioned her setup tray. The interns moved in to assist.

Hey, it worked.

I silently released the breath I'd been holding, reactivated the rig and pulled down the lascalpel. The bright optic lights made Shropana's hairy torso appear bloated and purplish.

"Here we go." I made the initial incision and pulled the beam down the median line from his chest, through the brisket and around into his upper flank. "Clamp back that subcutaneous tissue. Like that. Modify the rib spreader to clamp on the left withers only. Suction."

"Explain what you are doing, SsurreVa," I heard TssVar say.

I'm cutting open this man to repair your mess. "Standard traumatological procedure: get his lungs working, arrest the internal bleeding, then fix anything that threatens the cardiac organ. His heart is already diseased, so I have to proceed with caution. I'll do a laparotomy—that's abdominal exploratory surgery—if necessary, after that."

I didn't bother to elaborate, but continued cutting, and addressed my two resident assistants at the same time. "We'll plug the plural cavity first, then deal with the gland cluster and the ribs." To the nurse, I said, "Give me a series two chest tube. More suction. Yes. That's it."

I had to move fast. The pneumothorax compressed the Colonel's diseased cardiac organ (not a good thing), so I evacuated the air from the space between his lung and sternal plating and sealed the rupture. Once that was done, I was wrist-deep in blood.

Shropana's species possessed a network of glandular nodules—delicate-looking systemic clusters—that regulated every organ in his body. The high concentration of vessels in the clusters redefined the term "bleeder." He was a *sieve*. By the time I located and sealed off the main culprits, fluid was spilling over the table onto the deck. The nurse spent as much time suctioning as I did cauterizing micro-tears in the arterial walls.

"Doctor, his pressures are starting to red range," the vitals nurse suddenly said. "We're running low on plasma, too."

I didn't need him having an MI on me now. Why was plasma a problem? "Get more whole blood in here."

"There isn't any more," she said.

Unbelievable. "Does this flying waste station possess a whole-blood synthesizer?"

The nurse took a step back at my tone. "Of course, Doctor, but—"

I tossed a bloody instrument in her general direction. "Then have someone to whip me up a few gallons, will you?"

I rapidly completed my repairs while the residents clamped bonesetters around his arms. His shattered ribs would have to wait for another day. I closed his chest and watched his vitals monitor myself. I didn't dare move him from the surgical suite until he'd been fully transfused, but the immediate danger was over.

"Deactivate sterile field." I turned and found my nose about an inch from TssVar's surgical gear. I kinked a neck muscle as I glanced up. "Well, Over-Lord? Enjoy the show?"

"It is interesting to watch you work, SsurreVa," the Hsktskt said, stepping out of my way. Was that respect in those big yellow eyes? Surely not. I'd just ruined all his beautiful handiwork.

"Glad to hear it." I stripped off my mask and gloves. He nodded curtly, and left the surgical suite in silence. Most of the team followed. No one said a word as they passed by me.

A simple thank-you would have been nice.

I stood by Shropana and watched his vitals as one nurse, who had stayed behind, cleaned up the bloody instrument tray. A resident wheeled in a new batch of synplasma and I set up the infuser feed lines myself. The Colonel's vitals responded accordingly.

Patril might just live through this, after all.

I was still enjoying my success when the nurse jumped at me, and something slashed at my chest. "What the hell—?"

My half-turn was swift and reflexive. Fortunately. The dermal probe aimed at my heart buried itself in the flesh of my upper arm instead.

The good arm, too.

"Hey!" Through a mist of pain and fury I saw dark, glittering eyes blazing over the rim of her mask. Fury-spawned adrenaline allowed me to ignore the wound and grab her skinny throat with my hands. I took a moment to tear away her surgical mask, although I already knew who it was.

"Nurse Lucretia Borgia," I said. "What's the matter, couldn't lay your paws on any benzodiazapene?"

I didn't let her have enough air to speak. Not that I cared about what she had to say. I backed her into a plaspanel wall and held her there.

Time to use some Hsktskt tactics. To keep the lizards monitoring us from interfering, I pulled off my headgear, then hers.

"Now you *listen*." I leaned in, felt something warm run down my sleeve. Blood from the new wound. As if I needed more problems. "I've had enough of this. *Enough*. If I signal that big monster in charge, he'll put you on a tray and pass you around. Want to end up an appetizer?"

Gasping, her tail thrashing frantically against the panel, the nurse shook her head.

"Then we're going to make a deal. You don't try to kill me, and I won't feed you to them. Agreed?"

She gave a weak nod. I let go, and she dropped to the deck, choking and coughing as fresh air filled her cheek pouches.

I gave her a few moments, using the time to check out my brand. The tussle had cracked the burns open, and they were bleeding, too. I snatched a couple of sterile dressing packs, then nudged her with my foot. "Get up."

Unsteadily she pushed herself off the deck, then staggered as I grabbed her by the arm.

"Come on."

I hauled her over to the scrub unit, and stuck the dressing packs in her paws. I couldn't help grumbling as I pulled the probe from the shallow wound in my good arm and tore the sleeve away. That hurt.

Her beady eyes bulged again. "That, why are you doing?"

"*I'm* not doing anything." I held out my arm. "Clean it."

"Did you say, what?"

"You heard me. *You* stabbed me. *You* clean it up."

When she started to back away, I caught her tunic with my good hand. "I can always ask TssVar to do it."

That got me an intense look of dislike, but she retrieved what she needed and began treating the stab wound.

Maybe I should find out who wanted me dead. "What's your name?"

She sprayed a generous amount of topical antiseptic over the small gash, which made me wince. "Zella Dchêm-os."

While she worked on me, I kept an eye on Shropana's vitals. There were a few fluctuations, but on the whole the levels kept improving. Zella followed my gaze and muttered something under her breath as she wound the sterile dressing over the brand.

"What are you mumbling about?" I asked her.

"Your time, you're wasting," the nurse said. Her face resumed its usual sullen caste. "On the Colonel, that Hsktskt butcher will finish the job. A chance, as soon as he gets."

It took me a minute to figure out her backward syntax. "Oh, so *that's* why the OverLord allowed me to perform surgery on Shropana," I said, in a the-light-dawns tone. "To save his life so he could kill him later." Zella jerked and secured the ends of the dressing a little too tightly around my arm. "Now, be nice—"

"SsurreVa?" TssVar had re-entered the surgical suite, and stood looking from me to the nurse. His lower eyelids dropped in an expression I'd guess to be in the highly upset range. "You harmed the Designate."

I decided not even Zella deserved that wretched isolation cell—if she even made it that far in one piece. Surreptitiously I shoved her headgear into her hands and slipped mine over my head. "No harm done, OverLord. Just an accident. See?" I held up the arm for his inspection, and flexed it for good measure. "Works fine."

The Hsktskt ignored me. "Centurons! Attend me!"

Two of TssVar's guards burst into the room an instant later and trained their weapons on the League nurse. Time to do some fast talking, or Nurse Dchêmos was going to end up in more pieces than even *I* could sew back together.

"I never even saw the dermal probe until it was sticking out of my arm," I said, and patted my wounded limb. "My nurse kindly agreed to dress it for me."

The OverLord released a slow, suspicious hiss, then cracked a limb at the guards. The centurons retreated.

I deliberately gave the terrified nurse's narrow shoulder a shove toward the panel. "Thanks, Zel. You've done enough here."

In a blink, Zella had dodged around TssVar and darted out into Medical. I returned TssVar's suspicious gaze with my best virtuous expression.

The OverLord paced a circle around me. "Ssurre-Va, you lie."

"About what?" This innocent, who me? act had better work. "You mean this?" I patted my arm. "Why lie about someone trying to hurt me?"

He regarded me with those observant, viewport-size, yellow eyes. "This will not change their hatred of you, SsurreVa."

Too damn observant. "So it's my problem."

"Until it becomes mine." The OverLord's huge head swiveled toward the Colonel. "This one will survive?"

"He needs more surgery to repair his ribs and treatment for the preexisting problems with his heart, but with luck, yes. He'll live."

"He owes his life to you." TssVar surveyed the surgical equipment impassively. "And this is what you had chosen to devote your time and energy?"

Past tense. *Had.* Another reminder of my current predicament.

"This is it." I got busy cleaning up the last of the contaminated instruments. "Everybody needs regular medical treatment, OverLord. It's steady work."

"I am putting you in charge of this vessel's Medical Section," the Hsktskt said.

About time. "That will make Dr. Malgat and the crew happy." No, it wouldn't.

"Should the soft-skulled one object, advise me." TssVar's tongue lashed out in what I was starting to recognize as a Hsktskt expression of anticipation, then he stalked back out.

I sat down next to Shropana and watched his monitor. In one day, I thought, I'd gone from a detainee in solitary confinement to acting Primary Medical Officer.

Wonder what would happen tomorrow?

I spent the next eighteen hours in Medical, keeping close monitor on Colonel Shropana. Six more units of synplasma were required to compensate for the blood loss. Hourly doses of pentazalcine kept him quiet and as comfortable as possible. The League Commander remained in critical condition, but he made it through the night.

My vigil also provided a chance to further observe the medical staff in action. They were a busy bunch.

The night-shift nurses coming on immediately gravitated toward one end of the ward. The end with the food unit. They kept it busy preparing cups of hot beverages, snacks, and other tidbits. Three patients were forced to signal more than once before they were attended. I handled two of them personally.

Difficult to stuff your face and assist patients at the same time.

The interns worked a little harder at their jobs, but some of them scared me more than the nurses did. I watched unqualified students make rounds, treating and prescribing for patients without orders or supervision. Not good. I silently followed up on every chart. No one seemed brave enough to try to stop me when I modified the med schedules.

While fixing their disasters, I learned that the senior staffer on shift was a fourth-year intern, and he had yet to master the intricacies of galactic pharmacology.

Eventually I covered all of the inpatients and then appropriated a portable medical terminal and went through the personnel records. Well, I had to do something while I was sitting there, listening to Shropana's berth console bleep and the nurses chew.

One intrepid soul finally approached me at midshift. Basically humanoid, with one pair of arms and legs. Innumerable protuberant hemangiomas covered his body, doubtless due to the unusual distribution of blood vessels in his species' skin. He wore intern insignia on his tunic. Whether he deserved to was yet to be seen.

"I'm flavored," Strawberry the intern said, and held out a hand with three protracted digits.

I blinked. "I'll take your word for it."

"You misunderstand me, Doctor. My *name* is *flavored*." At my blank look, he typed it out on a data pad and switched it to display in Terran.

Vlaav Irde, I read. "Fourth-year intern?" He nodded. So this was the idiot prescribing overdoses. I toyed with the idea of laying into him over that, but Malgat was really at fault. "Right. So what do you want?"

Vlaav the intern went on to tell me he was a Saksonan, the senior intern onboard ship, and then promptly tried to pull rank on me. "I'm primary for this shift, you know. May I see Colonel Shropana's chart?"

An intern as primary. Mother of All Houses. "No."

I was tired and, now knowing who I was in charge of, not inclined toward tact. "Go away."

Saksonans, I would learn, had easily bruised egos. "I was just reviewing cases histories, and a thought crossed my mind—"

"Must have been a long and lonely journey. Get lost."

Blood pooled under his derma, making the countless bumps swell. "I don't see why you—"

"That's why I'm the MD and you're the intern," I said. "Take a stroll. Come back when you make resident. And keep your hands off the syrinpresses."

Dr. Malgat appeared once early in the shift, for a few moments. I got an evil look, but my predecessor wisely kept his distance. I watched as he performed rounds so fast he barely touched each patient's chart. On his way out of Medical, Malgat ignored inquiries from two nurses and an anxious patient calling after him.

I made a note to request Dr. Speedy be transferred to waste management, then went back to reworking the shift schedules.

Things got interesting sometime later, when a Hsktskt guard detachment stomped through the entrance panel. Six of them, all carrying activated weapons. A couple hissed at the nurses as they headed for the center of the bay.

I assumed they weren't here to visit a relative.

The group was lead by the biggest female Hsktskt I'd ever seen. Taller and bulkier than her male counterparts, she commanded instant attention. And fear. Something else seemed strange about her. When her massive head swung toward me, I saw exactly what it was.

Her *face.*

The sight would have made the most ambitious reconstructive surgeon weep with despair. A wide, twisted band of fresh scar tissue ran a jagged path from the top of her head down one side to disappear beneath the neck of her uniform. The wound went so deep that there appeared to be extensive skull distortion.

What had been used on her? A blunt axe? And how had she survived a wound that had torn through scales, muscles, bone, and most assuredly the frontal lobe of her brain? Next thing I knew, she was standing over me and had her weapon in *my* face.

Maybe I was going to find out. Personally.

"Hi." I blandly looked along the barrel of the pulse rifle. After enough times, I thought, you sort of got used to it. "May I help you?"

A black tongue lashed out—but half of it was gone. Amputated? "You are called SsurreVa?"

"By OverLord TssVar, yes." It couldn't hurt to mention his name, in a "we're old pals" kind of way.

That didn't awe her. "Five captives are not accounted for. You are hiding them here."

Uh-oh. Helen of Troy here was on a mission. Apparently I was *The One to Be Held Responsible.* As usual.

"I am not hiding anyone, OverSeer," I said, careful to use her rank. By now I had memorized Hsktskt uniform insignia, and displaying respect toward hers seemed prudent. "The only personnel here are staff assigned to this section, or patients who have been accounted for."

"If I find them, you die."

Not exactly fair, but completely straightforward.

She turned her mangled head and barked out a series of orders. The Hsktskts detachment fanned out and extensively searched the Medical wards, treatment rooms, and clinical services. That meant patients as well as equipment were tossed around. Nurses fled shrieking to cluster in terrified huddles. Diagnostic consoles were torn apart.

I followed after them, picked up patients, and tried to hold on to my composure.

An hour later, the last guard reported that no escapee had been found. Medical had been completely trashed, and the staff were having hysterics as quietly as they could. The female OverSeer came after me again.

I was busy rewrapping a torn dressing, so I didn't rub it in *too* much. "Does this mean I live?"

The cold metal rim of her rifle pressed against my throat. I took that to mean she wanted me to shut up. I shut up.

"TssVar values your traitorous hide," the OverSeer said. The tip of her tongue flickered so close that I could feel tiny droplets of her saliva land on my cheeks and nose. I wasn't even going to think about the smell of her breath. "But for the OverLord I would have your entrails adorning my talons. I am OverSeer FurreVa. Say it, Terran."

"Your name is OverSeer FurreVa." I had a feeling it didn't mean "good-natured."

"I am taking three of these useless females." She gestured toward the mass of frightened nurses. "They will tell me where the others are."

She might have the rifle, but I was responsible for those useless females. "Assuming they know anything, which I doubt, just how are you going to get them to tell you?" I finished the dressing and straightened. "By relying on your personal charisma?"

FurreVa's jaw dropped, maybe in surprise, which showed me every single one of her jagged teeth. There was a noticeable gap in her upper and lower palate. Most of what was left badly needed a good cleansing. Not that I was going to suggest it. Ever.

"The OverLord has given me leave to interrogate them."

Bet her idea of questioning prisoners involved inflicting serious, prolonged physical damage. "Will you allow me to speak with them first? Perhaps I can get the information from them. That way, you won't have to waste your obviously valuable time."

She stared at me for a long time. I didn't know if she was deciding if I was serious, joking, or needed salt before serving.

"Very well." At last the rifle swung away from my throat. "One minute, Terran."

I wasted no time, but went straight to the nurses. They stared at me with the usual mixture of fear and disgust. Dchêm-os emerged from somewhere and jabbed a finger into my chest.

"This, you told them to do!" she said, flinging an arm out and stamping her lower paws. "Mess, just look at this!"

I produced a chipper smile and removed my headgear. "Shut up, Zel." I scanned the faces of the other nurses. They were almost, but not quite, as scared as I was. "That big female with the attractive features over there says five prisoners are missing. She thinks one of you knows where they are. Want to guess how she's going to determine that?" The group made a collective gasp. "Exactly. Someone talk to me. Right now."

A few of the nurses exchanged glances. One finally spoke. "We'd heard about them. No one knows what happened."

Dchêm-os assumed an instant, innocent expression, while her tail thumped with agitation against the deck.

Another nurse cast a disgusted scowl at the Hsktskts. "The horrible beasts probably caught them in the corridors and ate them."

"Would you like to be the dessert course?" I didn't wait for an answer, but turned to the first nurse who'd spoken. "How do you know they escaped?" She didn't answer me. "Let me guess. Your people have already planned how to escape the Hsktskt, and these five took the first shot at it."

The nurse's eyes rounded. Another let out a small whimper of distress.

I stifled a groan. "Wonderful."

OverSeer FurreVa decided my time was up. A snakelike limb curled around my waist and hauled me back out of the group. She released me so abruptly that my legs slipped out from under me and I landed on my backside.

"Enough of this." Her troops surrounded the group, and the Hsktskt pointed to three of the nurses—one of whom had made the unpleasant joke. "Take them."

"OverSeer!" I struggled to my feet, yanked on my headgear, and reached out a hand to try to stop her. "Please, if you will wait, I—"

The big female pressed a claw to the broad unit on her wrist. Instantly a powerful jolt ran up my left arm and into my chest.

Not again.

The deck rushed up to meet my face.

CHAPTER THREE

Sharp Instruments

"Still, you keep."

Disgruntled, beady black eyes peered into mine. After riding waves of dizziness, I finally figured out I was lying on a berth in Medical. Not naked this time, but dressed in a slave tunic about four sizes too big for me. I reflexively moved my limbs, and felt severe muscle strain in my left forearm. A new support brace encircled my throbbing wrist.

At least I didn't get shot.

A paw pressed down on my shoulder. Good spot—it was the only one that didn't ache. "It, I mean!" Zella Dchêm-os gave me a look of intense dislike as she held me immobile and passed a scanner over me.

My head was still muddled, but I recalled trying to help the nurses, and the subsequently brief confrontation with the Hsktskt OverSeer. "How much damage did she do?"

"Finish first, will you let me?" She glanced over her shoulder. "For these readings, OverMaster Hala-Var is waiting."

"Space Reever." I grabbed the scanner. Plenty of contusions, but no broken bones. "He the only reason you're not sticking me with a syrinpress?"

Dchêm-os's expression changed. "Trying to help us, I suppose you *were*." She took the unit away from me.

"Does this mean we're going to be chums now?" I asked, and her vibrissae virtually stood on end. "That's what I thought." The vertigo got worse, and that had me worried. "Give me back that scanner."

"Wait." Dchêm-os took hold of my arm, where the sleeve of my tunic had slid down. She yanked her headgear off, then mine. "To your PIC, what happened? A few hours ago, I just dressed it."

Out of the corner of my eye I saw the third-degree burns had disappeared, leaving a flat, barely perceptible stretch of new pink skin.

I brought my arm down and shook the sleeve back into place. "I heal fast." And was healing faster every day.

"You, do?" She cast a glance to one side, then leaned forward and lowered her voice to a whisper. "The nurses who were taken, the beasts will maim. Make them reveal the location of the five escapees, they think it will." Dchêm-os's large incisors clattered together. "Until they are dead, that scar-faced one won't stop—but nothing they know!"

"Figures." Pointless torture. One more thing to love about the Hsktskt.

"Some of the prisoners, I'm being sent down to the Detainment Area to treat." The nurse looked odd before she added, "To help the others, can you do anything?"

I bet that hurt to ask. My respect for Zella increased by the moment.

"Let's see." I held my hand out. "Help me up." When she hesitated, I sighed. "C'mon, Zel. I can't do anything from here."

The nurse didn't argue with me. She simply

yanked. For a moment my vision blurred, then I was in an upright position. Why was I so lightheaded?

"To get them back, I'll use you," she said. "Only temporary, this—"

"Yeah, yeah, I remember. You'll still poison me the minute you get a chance, et cetera, et cetera. Save it." I put my headgear on and swung my legs over the side of the berth.

Reever appeared in front of me. "What are you doing?"

"Getting up," I said. And I did. For about three seconds. The room rocked wildly, and my knees weren't up for the ride. I crumpled forward, just in time for Reever to catch me. "Put—me—down—"

Reever turned to Dchêm-os. "I'll take her to her quarters. Resume your duties."

The long night watching Shropana combined with the pain of my bruises had sapped me of whatever smacking ability I possessed. However, the dizziness seemed to be slowly receding. I hung limp and unresisting in Reever's arms.

My mouth still worked, though. "What's the matter, get bored planning your next atrocity?"

Reever said nothing. He was good at that.

Okay, maybe I should do more than bait him. "Your pals trashed Medical looking for escaped prisoners. OverSeer FurreVa took three nurses into custody and is torturing them."

"I know." He stepped into the lift with me.

I curled my fingers into the front of his tunic, and gave it a pull. "You can have them released, right?" He remained silent and indifferent. I heaved out an impatient breath as the lift slid to a halt. "Let me rephrase. *Get* them released."

"No." He stepped out and carried me down another corridor.

I didn't argue or struggle with him—now *I* had to do some planning. Reever stepped through a door panel and into my assigned quarters. While I'd been in Medical, someone had come in and straightened up. Shropana's blood no longer stained the deck. Even the linens on my sleeping platform had been changed.

He wouldn't help me, so I needed to get rid of him.

"I never knew the Hsktskt had"—I yawned— "maid service." He placed me on the bed. "Nice job . . . you give her . . . a good tip?" I let my eyelids flutter, then faked falling asleep.

Reever hovered by the sleeping platform for a minute. I couldn't open my eyes and look at him. I was too busy pretending to breathe evenly and slowly. The subterfuge was harder to keep up than I thought. Especially with Reever close enough for me to smell.

I barely controlled a flinch when his warm hand touched my head. Fingers threaded through my tangled hair, gently brushing it away from my face. The temptation to bite him, repeatedly, became almost irresistible. So did other, less noble impulses.

No. Never. I'd rather contract Embekileen venereal disease first.

The hand moved away, and I heard him sigh. "Sleep well, wife." Some footsteps thudded across the deck. The door panel slid open and closed. He was gone.

I sat up, dizzy and shaking with relief. "Dream on, stupid." I got up, noticed the time, and automatically went to the prep unit. "Jenner? Hey, pal, time to . . ." I halted as I remembered that my cat was still back on Joren, and the familiar pang of loss made me catch my breath. "Okay. Time to get my act together."

Continual dizziness hampered my movements. What garments I found, courtesy of past occupants, were mostly sheer, feminine stuff that would fit an Amazon, a couple of Shropana's old uniforms shoved back in a corner, and a plain black robe. Since I didn't want to attract attention, I stayed in the too-large slave tunic and braided my hair out of my face.

I snorted at my reflection. Prisoner Cherijo, prepared for the search-and-rescue mission. Right. I
looked like a kid playing dress-up.

Another surge of vertigo sent me back to the sleeping platform. Couldn't pass out yet. I could sit for a
few minutes, though. While I did, I took the precaution of rolling up some bed linens and making it look
as though I was huddled under the top cover on the
sleeping platform.

Reever had left the console pass-protected, so I
played with different combinations in an attempt to
crack the protective codes he'd installed.

"What magic word did you use, Reever? Fraud?
Imposter? Villain?" I stopped, thought for a moment,
then keyed in one word.

Beloved.

The security lockout disappeared.

With a few taps on the keypad I found the deck
and a section designated "Investigation and Interrogation." The Hsktskt were practical creatures, so I
was counting on them using the existing facilities for
the same purposes.

Once I got the nurses out, I couldn't simply march
them back over to Medical. No, I'd have to find a
place to hide them.

Before I left, I searched for some kind of weapon
to take with me. There was nothing, no secret cache
of pistols, no emitter units, not even an eating utensil.
Maybe it was for the best. If things got rough, I still
wasn't sure if I could actually shoot or stab someone.

I wasn't trained to kill people. I healed them.

What about Reever? that sly voice whispered inside
my head.

"He doesn't qualify," I said.

I had taken the precaution of tucking a scanner in
my pocket, which I now used to take a reading close
to the door panel. Any life-forms within a three-
meter radius would register on the thermal sensor.

The corridor was empty. I was home free. I activated the panel.

Nothing happened. Reever had locked me in.

"For a telepathic linguist, the man has an incredibly bad memory." I accessed the interior of the panel and crossed some wires. Dhreen had taught me how to do that. I'd used it to catch Reever playing Fond Memories in a Jorenian environome once, back on the *Sunlace*. I ignored the sharp stab of pain in my chest.

Dhreen had pretended to be my friend while he spied for my creator. The Oenrallian's betrayal ranked just below Reever's on my never-to be-forgotten list.

And still I missed him.

The door panel slid open, and I stepped out into the open corridor. No one around. So far, so good. I had to go to level nineteen to get to the Interrogation Section. That was my whole plan. By the time I arrived, I'd have figured out a way to rescue the nurses.

Sometime later, standing just outside the door panel to Interrogation, I still didn't have a plan. But I could hear someone screaming and sobbing. A shame I hadn't found some kind of weapon. Shooting one of those cold-blooded monsters in there suddenly appealed to me.

Cold-blooded monsters . . .

I checked the exterior panel, and had to swallow a whoop of delight. Hail to the Allied League, those Paragons of Miserly Habits. The environcontrols for Interrogation—and every other section on the deck—were *external*.

I walked back down the corridor and accessed the main deck panel. Now, how had Dhreen said he'd fixed that problem with the nasty migrating organic cargo on the *Bestshot*? Oh, yeah. I input the setting and reinitiated the life-support system.

The effect was a blast. Literally. Ice began to form on the corridor walls as super-cooled air flooded the deck. My breath puffed out in little white clouds while I shivered and hopped from one foot to the other. Oddly, the cold made me feel more alert and cleared away the last of that bizarre dizziness.

Interrogation's door panel slid open. Something big and sluggish crawled out onto the deck and, after a moment, collapsed.

"Let it snow, let it snow, let it snow," I chanted as I stepped over the motionless Hsktskt and peered into the interior.

The smell of blood and body fluids was sharp and pervasive. I saw the three nurses, restrained against one wall. Two were conscious, the third sagging and in very bad shape. Five more big lizards lay on their bellies in various stages of stupor. FurreVa lifted her scarred head and stared at me.

Since she'd already gotten a good look at me, I waggled my fingers at her. "Hiya, Helen. I need my nurses back now."

"Kill . . . you . . ." The OverSeer slumped to the deck, unconscious.

"Not today." I stepped over her and went to the last nurse. Gently I lifted her head from where it hung limply over her chest, and checked for a pulse. She was alive, but in shock.

"Nurse." She'd been badly beaten, from the looks of the lacerations and bruises that disfigured her face. "Hey." I gave her a small shake. The swollen eyes opened to slits. "Can you hear me?" She whimpered something. "Hang on. I'm going to get you out of here."

I went to the other two nurses and checked them, then went to the console and released the locking mechanisms securing them to the wall panel.

"Help her," I said, pointing to the third, and they took positions to steady her as I released the last of the locks. "Let's go."

One stopped to pick up a pulse rifle one of the Hsktskt had dropped.

"Leave it," I told her.

The blood on her face didn't hide her astonishment. "But Doctor—"

I shook my head. "We don't need it," I said, and made a grab for the badly injured nurse, who was staggering now. "Come on, help me."

Between the three of us we were able to carry the semiconscious nurse out of Interrogation. We walked into a tunnel of white ice. Snow fell so rapidly that the insensate Hsktskt on the deck was in danger of becoming buried in the powdery crystals.

First I had to get the nurses somewhere reasonably safe to hide. "Where is the main Detainment Area?" I asked one of the ambulatory nurses.

"Mid-deck, level eleven."

"Hang on." I stopped by the main control console, and went to the panel to reverse the environcontrols.

"What are you doing?"

"Restoring the correct life-support settings," I said, and reinstated the set points.

"What for?" The other nurse sounded bitter. "Let the beasts freeze."

"They're poikilothermic, it'll kill them. No point in killing defenseless beings." I leveled a look over my shoulder at her. "That's the sort of thing *they* do. Right?"

Neither answered me. The third nurse only groaned louder. I closed the panel and felt the immediate change in temperature. "Come on. We've got to get out of here before they wake up and start looking for us."

We went up six decks before the controls were overridden from Command and the lift stopped. One of the nurses managed to key the doors partially open, and the four of us squeezed through the gap into the corridor.

On the deck above us, something large, in a hurry, and certainly not defenseless, ran toward the lift entrance.

Me and my dumb rules.

"We've got about a minute," I said. "Hold on to her and run."

We ran. Behind us I could hear the lift activating, then the booming footsteps of our pursuers. The nurses were pale beneath their bruises, and quickly losing what breath they had. So was I.

We reached Main Detention and saw a guard standing with his back to us. I raised a finger to my lips and gestured as to what I wanted them to do. The other women nodded.

We crept up to the door panel and I hit the locking mechanism. The guard whirled around just as I jumped at him. We both went down.

"I'm not going to stay in there for another millisecond!" I bellowed, pounding on him with both fists for good measure. "I want out! Now!"

While I straddled the big monster, effectively blocking his view with my body, the two nurses carried the third through the open door panel into the Detainment Area.

My playacting got me thrown back through the half-open door panel and into a group of League detainees. I landed on my back, my arms up over my head. Something fast and furry jumped on top of me.

"Hey!" I said, and got a faceful of warm fur as it sat on me.

"Be still," a familiar voice murmured against my ear. Then, to someone else, "Hurry." There was a whispered affirmative. The thing lying over my upper torso made a *hnk-hnk* sound. The only time I'd ever heard a noise like that was at the New Angeles zoo—

There was a tiger sitting on top of me?

The furry body shifted to one side, and two colorless slits peered into my face. The only other thing I saw were some fairly impressive fangs when it opened its mouth. "Cherijo."

"Oh, God. Alunthri." I threw my arms around my friend and hugged it tightly. Alunthri was alive, safe. Too thin, and badly in need of cleansing, but I didn't care. All the fear I'd been enduring since learning Reever had enslaved it dissolved. "Are you okay?"

"I am well. And you?"

Over the Chakacat's slim shoulder, I saw Nurse Dchêm-os take a length of thermal insulating cloth and unwind it above us.

"What's that for?" I asked, afraid she might answer with "A noose."

"Your head, covering," she said, keeping her voice low. "Here"—she prodded Alunthri aside and tugged me up enough to drape my head with the cloth—"your face hidden, keep."

"Why?" I glanced around, and saw we were surrounded by at least three hundred League crew members. Some were standing, a few sitting against the bare walls, but most lay huddled and sleeping on the deck. No one looked very happy. "Oh. Never mind." I gazed back at Alunthri. "You'd better get off me now."

The Chakacat made another of those *hnk*ing sounds and moved away from me. At once, the nurses I'd rescued formed a tight circle around us. Zel finished arranging the cloth and opened a narrow fold over my face.

"Talk, don't," she said. "Who are you, the minute they find out, dead you will be."

"I thought that was the general idea."

She pulled her headgear back on. "Up, shut."

Something large started moving toward us. The deck shook with every step.

One of the nurses made an urgent sound. "Devrak is coming."

Dchêm-os shoved me down on my back, and I automatically closed my eyes and played dead. The titanic footsteps halted. A sonorous, harsh voice demanded to know what the nurses were doing.

"From Interrogation, we escaped," Zella said.

"What about her?" Something nudged me. "If she's dead, dump her in the corner over there with the rest of the waste."

"She's not dead, Major Devrak." One of the nurses coughed. "Only unconscious."

"Who is she?" Devrak sounded a little *too* interested. "Why have you wrapped her brain case like that?"

Zella took that one. "A Reedol intern, she is. Their features to anyone but their mates, they don't reveal."

I wondered if the Reedols had humanoid hands, if the Major had noticed mine were distinctly Terran-shaped, and exactly when Zel's generosity was going to run out.

"Wake her up. The four of you have work to do. I'll start sending the injured over to be treated."

One of the other nurses protested. "But we haven't any supplies!"

"The beasts have furnished a few first-aid kits; do whatever you can with those." With that, the deep-voiced Major stomped off.

My eyes popped open. "Care to tell me how I'm going to pass as a Reedol, nurse? Whatever a Reedol is?"

"Than you, they're more nonverbal. Your Terran mouth closed, you keep." Dchêm-os pulled me to my feet. One of the other three nurses was still in bad shape. I prodded my unwilling assistant, then motioned to the injured female. "And rest, Bree, stay where you are. Us, Pmohhi help."

Nurse Bree gratefully sank back down on the deck. I saw a huge, League-uniformed being herding a sad-looking cluster of wounded crew members toward us.

"I take it Major Devrak is the Trytinorn?" I whispered to Zella.

She didn't have to say yes; he was looming over

us in another moment. Trytinorns make Terran elephants appear dainty and petite. Vivid yellow and black markings streaked over his dusky, wrinkled hide. Small, shrewd eyes peered at the slit in my head covering.

He was Shropana's Chief Operational Officer, I recalled. If the Major found out I was masquerading as a League captive, I'd be stomped into the deck in short order.

"Reedol, you are fit for duty?" he asked, and I nodded, keeping my hands tucked in my pockets. "Good." With one thick forelimb he urged forward the first of the injured, a small, gelatinous being with severe pulse burns on its undulating torso.

So far, so good.

A couple of small medical kits were brought over to us, along with a cargo transfer unit we were apparently to use as an exam table. I motioned for the patient to recline, and tried to ignore the Major's odorous breath as he stood over me, observing every action.

I couldn't say a word or the game would be up. I used a scanner, handed it to the nurse, and with some surreptitious hand signals was able to treat the patient with a universal topical antibiotic available from the limited supply.

"Why does the Reedol not speak?" the Major said, sending a blast of breath that ruffled my head covering.

"Injured in the fray was her larynx, from Interrogation while we were escaping" was Dchêm-os's convoluted explanation.

I injected the patient with the only analgesic on hand to help eliminate some of the pain, and received a pleasant overture of gratitude before another crew member climbed up on the unit.

We continued in that bizarre, speechless fashion. The prisoners had to be treated for everything from lacerations to broken bones, and eventually the Major lost interest and thumped off. Alunthri stalked a few feet away on all fours, then sat as though standing guard.

"Whew!" I blew out a soft breath. "That was nerve wracking." I noticed the next patient was having trouble stretching out on the table, and went to help. The willowy life-form had a few burns on his limbs, but the problem was a deep puncture wound and surrounding abdominal lividity. I frowned as I checked the injury. "We need to get this one to Medical."

"Shhhh!" Dchêm-os examined the patient herself, then removed her headgear. "Because of the incident with the guard, they have confined this section. In or out, no matter what the emergency, no one goes. Him, just stabilize."

"Not possible." I scanned the available supplies, and found a container of generic antiseptic usually used in field emergencies. "We can sterilize ourselves and the patient with this, and sedate him with what's in this syrinpress." I hunted through the rest of the case. "I need a laser."

Zel glared at me. "About, what are you talking?"

"There are no lasers," one of the other nurses said. "Nor are we likely to get one if we ask."

"Then I'll need the sharpest blade you can find, a heat source to cauterize the vessels, and something to sew the tissues back together." I thought for a moment. "Something to suction or soak up the body fluids with, too."

"Perform surgery here, you can't," Zella said. Why was she acting so agitated? "Your arm, what about?"

I flexed it gingerly. The stab wound and wrenched muscles twinged. "I can handle it. I *have* to," I said, when the nurse would have argued, "or this one won't make it."

While my staffers went to search for supplies, I walked over to Alunthri. "Why the big snarly kitty cat act?" I finally had the chance to ask.

"I have had to assume a more feral demeanor since being incarcerated," the Chakacat said. "For purposes of self-defense." It bared its fangs. "Actually, I have found it most stimulating. Dramatics are, after all, a true physical art form."

It would think that.

The nurses proved incredibly resourceful. As Zella and I prepped the patient, they went through the Detainment Area, and came back with a small garment-repair kit, a thermal braising tool, and a pile of personal hygiene sponges.

I looked over the collection and hoped it wouldn't kill my patient. "I still need a something with a blade."

"They seized all the weapons when we were boarded," Pmohhi said.

"A moment, wait." Before I could stop her, Zella took the blunt end of the braising tool and struck herself in the face with it.

"Stop—what are you doing, you idiot?" I grabbed her furry face to assess the damage, but she shoved my hands away and put a paw in her mouth.

"Take this, here." She worked it loose, then handed me a bloodstained chunk of one of her incisors. "It's sharp, be careful."

It was, I nearly sliced my hand open grabbing it. And the shock of what she'd done made me yell at her again. "God, Zel, we could have found something else!"

"Down, keep your voice!" She spat blood out onto the deck. "Use it, go ahead. Fine, I will be."

I packed her mouth with a small hygiene sponge anyway.

"All right. Sterilize everything with that antiseptic. Pmohhi, section us off with some linens and make sure you keep everyone at least three yards away from us. I'll need something undyed and as clean as possible for bandaging the patient after surgery."

Zella tugged me off to one side. "With you, I must speak."

"Okay." I bent down. "What?"

"Dizzy or nauseous, are you feeling?"

"No, I've done this thousands of times." Her fur was standing on end, why was she so damned skittish? No one was going to tear *her* into pieces. "Zel—"

"About it, forget."

I went back to the table. The sedated patient didn't flinch as I made the initial incision. Internally, the damage was thankfully restricted to the three-sided left kidney; I'd have been wasting my time if the bowel had been compromised.

"Sponge. Apply it there. Keep monitoring his vitals. That's it.

I went to work. The surgery went slowly without a lascalpel, but I silently thanked the Medtech instructor who had insisted I learn to cut with traditional as well as modern instruments. Though I wasn't sure that any surgeon in modern history had ever performed a procedure with another being's tooth. Still, the incisor was the sharpest nonmechanical implement I'd ever used.

Two hours later, I finished sewing—literally—the abdominal incision and manually checked the patient's vitals again. His signs remained weak, but steady. I had the feeling he'd make it, in spite of the crude tools I'd used to repair his body.

"He needs to be isolated," I said to Zella, checking her mouth before she could stop me. The shiny nub of her tooth looked jagged and painful. "How do you feel?"

"Fine. Grow back, it will." Dchêm-os turned to instruct the nurse, then froze.

"Very interesting work," the Trytinorn's bass voice said just above my head. "I see the Reedol intern is quite handy with a bladed weapon."

A vicious blow from behind knocked me down.

Then someone tore the covering from my head. Once my ears stopped ringing, I looked up into little, mean eyes and an extremely large, yellow-and-black striped foot.

So this is how it feels, I thought, to become a rug.

"You must be Torin," the Major said. "But Colonel Shropana told us you were Terran, not Reedol."

"Maybe he got mixed up," I said to the towering being.

The nurses all stood in place, their expressions a mixture of dismay and guilt. Dchêm-os stared at the Major, then at me, then she shrugged. Zella's compassion meter just hit empty, I thought. It had been nice while it lasted.

"It was not enough that you sold the Fleet to the butchers," the Major said. "You had to come here and do some carving of your own."

"I operated on this man"—I indicated the patient—"to save his life."

The Major turned and got louder. "The Terran traitor is here among us. What shall we do with her?"

There was some gruesome suggestions, delivered by several angry shouts. The entire population of the Detainment Area began to close in on us. God, I hoped Alunthri wouldn't have to see this. The gentle Chakacat was revolted by even the mildest form of violence. I waved a hand to get the Trytinorn's attention.

"Excuse me? Major?" When he looked down, I smiled. "Before you tear me to pieces, would you have some of your men move this patient to an isolated spot? His kidney won't take any more abuse."

"Remove him," the Major said, and the nurses helped push the makeshift operating table across the deck away from me.

Now I was standing alone, facing a ring of furious faces. Some of them I had treated only hours before. Guess League memories tended to run from short to nonexistent. No one moved, and quite frankly, I was tired, so I sat down on the deck.

The Major stepped forward. "Get up."

"No." I yawned, and rubbed my face with a tired hand. "My feet hurt."

"Terran beast-lover," someone shouted. "Stand and face your victims!"

"There's an open mind," I said to the Trytinorn. "You can feel the draft from here."

"S-s-s-stop!"

That came from someone I hardly recognized. The long, lean feline's fur was raised all along its spine. Long, dangerous-looking talons sprouted from all four paws—which it had dropped on. Sharp fangs glittered as it released a terrifying bellow.

Was that my nice, quiet, pacifist pal, Alunthri? *Roaring?* Some acting job.

Dchêm-os stepped in between the Chakacat, the Major, and me. She scanned the other crew members, her broken incisor bared in a exasperated grimace. "Me, you know. This Terran bitch dead, I vowed to see."

"I don't think that's going to help, nurse," I said. And what was this "vow" stuff? "But thanks for the thought."

"This area alive, she will not leave," Dchêm-os said. "Before we can make use of her, don't kill her."

Alunthri let out another feline screech for good measure.

"I would kill her for using my air," the Major said.

"See?" I said to Zel. "Just get out of his way, you're perpetuating his breathing problem. Take Wild Kingdom here with you."

"Up, shut!" Dchêm-os yelled at me, then turned on the Trytinorn. "The wounded, she can treat. Until she dies, it won't be long now."

"Get out of the way," Devrak said.

Finally something got through my preoccupation

with getting stomped on by the Trytinorn. Until I *died*?

"We can't trust her," someone shouted.

"In a few hours, she'll be dead." The nurse swung toward the other voice. "Makes no sense, killing her now."

"Go back to that part about a few hours," I told Zella. At the same time, Alunthri gave the little nurse a decidedly ferocious look.

"There are other doctors!" a third voice said.

Dchêm-os sent a look of antipathy in that direction. "Yes. All confined to Medical, they are."

"I'd still like to know why I'm going to die in a few hours," I said, feeling a little disgusted myself.

"Enough." The Major spat out the word. "I will hear her bones grind under my feet."

"No." Dchêm-os grabbed my good arm and hauled me to my feet. "Mine to claim, her death is. Of my people, by the right!"

"Zel, I don't think he's going to let you keep me alive until it's convenient for you personally to kill me," I murmured, eyeing the Major. The dizziness. Zel not wanting me to operate. "Or have you taken care of that, too?"

"Digitalizine," the little nurse said without a hint of remorse. "Enough to kill three Terrans, I injected you with."

That was interesting, I thought. That particular drug took a few hours to induce a fatal seizure. And all I'd felt was a little dizziness, now gone. Had my boosted immune system neutralized the toxin?

"You are League first," the Trytinorn reminded the nurse. "Step out of my way, or share her fate."

"I will sh-sh-share it." Alunthri pushed past Dchêm-os and shielded me with its body.

"Thanks, Alunthri, but I can handle this." I stepped around the Chakacat and eyed the nurse. "Get lost, Zel. Do some soul-searching. Maybe you'll locate one."

"Touch you, I won't let them." Her dark fur rose stiffly all around her nose. "Mine to kill, you are."

She was determined to protect me until I dropped dead from the digitalizine. To her, undoubtedly a perfectly logical situation.

The Major removed Dchêm-os by picking her up with his long, prehensile lip/nose and setting her down ten feet away. Others forced her away from the inner circle, which left me and Alunthri facing the towering giant being.

"I have my orders from the Colonel," the Major said as he started toward me. "You have to die."

Alunthri sprang at the Trytinorn, and landed on his broad back. I heard the Major's surprised gasp of pain when the Chakacat sank its claws into his tough hide. Devrak couldn't shake it off, not without trampling some of his people in the process.

"Alunthri." I spoke low and softly, to get its attention. "Do you remember promising to return the favor when I set you free on K-2?"

The Chakacat's tail switched back and forth as it gazed down at me. Reluctantly it gave me a single *hnk*.

I'd take that as a yes. "Enough physical art form, okay? I want the favor now. Get down from there. Go watch over the man I just operated on."

For a minute, I wasn't sure it was going to work. Then, with a slow, mesmerizing grace, the Chakacat sprang down from Devrak's back. Then Alunthri lifted a hind paw and urinated on the Major's leg.

"Alunthri," I said, trying not to grin at the gesture of supreme feline contempt. I failed.

The Chakacat gracefully padded off toward my patient.

Devrak didn't seem to be concerned about the small puddle he was standing in. Or maybe he was just trying to act nonchalant. "Now we will finish this."

"Be my guest." I sat back down on the floor and

deliberately examined the deplorable condition of my fingernails. Why was it that doctors were unable to maintain a decent manicure? I had no idea. The working conditions?

"Get up and defend yourself," the Trytinorn said.

Against a being several hundred times my size? What, was he kidding? "I've sworn an oath to do no harm to other life-forms. Do you really think I could take you in a fight, anyway? Pick on someone your own size."

"I dislike killing cringing cowards."

"I'm not cringing," I told him. "I'm sitting. And wanting to do no harm doesn't make me a coward." I raised my voice so all the mob could hear me. "Hurting people who can't or won't defend themselves—now, that's more like what a coward does."

Suddenly everyone seemed to notice how big the Major was, and how small I was in comparison. People who a minute ago wanted to stomp me into the decking now shuffled back or looked away.

"Perhaps the nurse is right," someone said. "We could use her skills, until our plan can be—"

"Silence!" The Major looked back down at me. "This is your last chance, Terran. Get to your feet."

"No. If you're going to kill me, be my guest. If you're going to stand there and argue with me all day, I'd rather take a nap. Make up your damn mind." I smiled. *"Coward."*

I knew from dealing with Trytinorns back on K-2 that the Major's species had very rigid views about honor. He couldn't bring himself to strike the killing blow. I had been counting on that. The only problem was he was League, and had learned the fine art of delegation.

"Lieutenant Wonlee!" the Trytinorn shouted.

A slender, heavily clawed being pushed his way through the crowd. He wore a specially designed uniform which allowed hundreds of thin, sharp spines to protrude. Hugging must not be big on that guy's homeworld. "Sir?"

"Kill this Terran. At once."

I watched as the Lieutenant, whose prickly species evidently had no problem at all with situations of honor, came walking toward me, his many talons extended.

Odd thoughts crossed my mind at that moment. My surrogate mother Maggie had died nearly three years ago. Kao had died in my arms on the *Sunlace*. Jenner was safe with Kao's family, HouseClan Torin, back on Joren. Alunthri, no stranger to slavery, would find a way to survive. They'd given my life true meaning, and I'd been privileged to love them all.

I kept my eyes open and my head up. I might be resigned to death, but I wasn't going out a coward.

CHAPTER FOUR

Aksel Drift Nine

Before Wonlee got within clawing distance, some interesting things happened.

Dchêm-os, and two of the nurses I'd rescued, had quietly circulated through the crowd of detainees. Now they and whomever they convinced to help them charged the inner circle, shouting for my release. At the same time, Alunthri sprang over a lot of heads and landed practically in my lap. It stayed there and bellowed at anyone who got within a foot of me.

I tried to push it out of harm's way. "Alunthri, get out of here!"

"I think not, Cherijo." The Chakacat grinned at me, then turned and snarled at an approaching crew member.

Now there was a perimeter of bodies shielding me and voices shrieking defiance. I saw the claw-carrying Lieutenant sail through the air as someone flung him away from me. The Major trumpeted his fury, but was so hemmed in by smaller crew members that he couldn't twitch, much less move in on me himself.

People, as they always do in these situations, began to brawl.

Dchêm-os worked her way over to me and snarled at Alunthri, who reluctantly allowed her to come closer. "To protect yourself, can't you even try? Of all deities, for the love?"

"It's that silly oath I took," I said, then winced as I saw two crew members beating each other senseless a few inches away. "Why are you worried? He's just finishing the job you started."

"Enough of the drug, I must not have given you," Zella said, her tail thrashing impatiently.

"Shame, isn't it?"

Two more nurses appeared out of the battling masses, both disheveled and panting. "We're going to get you out of here, Doctor," Pmohhi said.

"Unless you can override the door panel controls, that's unlikely."

"No, we have an alternate route—"

"Attention, prisoners!" a drone voice unexpectedly blared. "Cease and desist all violence at once!"

No one paid much attention, they were all busy having fun. Which quickly turned into cries of pain as their detainment cuffs started jolting them. Oddly enough, mine didn't.

A squad of armed Hsktskt entered the Detainment Area, led by none other than Duncan Reever. I pushed the Chakacat off my lap, ducked around some prisoners attempting to pry their cuffs off, and tried to hide. Reever spotted me within seconds and motioned for the centurons to head my way.

"Here come the really bad guys," I told Dchêm-os, who was crouched over, tugging at her own cuff. "Get moving."

I tugged the writhing Zel toward the open entrance panel, hoping to get around Reever and his pals before they got to us. A few more feet, and we'd have access to the corridors—

Cherijo. Reever's voice echoed inside my head.

I made a strangled sound as my body went into complete shutdown. My hands fell to my sides. Dchêm-os dropped to the deck and painfully pushed herself back up.

"Stand there . . . Doctor . . . don't just . . . "

Already too late, I thought desperately. *Come to beat me up personally, Reever?*

Reever arrived and motioned to the centurons to restrain the dark nurse. He himself swung me up into his arms, and made sure through the telepathic link that I couldn't resist.

The Chakacat sprang at Reever, but was given a severe jolt by one of the Hsktskt centurons, and fell down to sprawl senseless at his feet.

Alunthri!

It is not hurt, Cherijo.

This can't be much fun for you, OverMaster, I thought acidly. *Where's the sport in rendering your victims unconscious?*

"Shut up," Reever said quite clearly against my hair. To the centurons, he ordered, "Return the nurses to Medical. I will deal with the Terran."

Oh, and what are you? I inquired as he carried me out of the riot and into the hall.

The only hope you have, was his calm reply. *Why were you in the Detainment Area?*

I was helping those three nurses I told you about. You remember, the ones you couldn't be bothered with? I pictured OverSeer FurreVa and her cohorts, lying on the snowy deck. *I could have killed them, but I didn't. I want those nurses left alone and returned to their duty stations in Medical.*

Reever's arm tightened briefly. *What do I get if I agree to arrange it?*

I won't start another riot.

Reever took me to my quarters, and dropped me on the sleeping platform. At the same time, a signal came in over the console. He checked it, then glanced back at me. "I must return to Command. There will be a centuron stationed outside the door panel."

"What about my nurses?"

"If you agree to keep away from the Detainment Area in the future, I will have them returned to Medical."

"Okay." Finally in control of my own body again, I sank back against the pillows. "I'll stay out of Detainment."

I got up to find a scanner as soon as he left, then ran a hematological series on myself. The readings confirmed my suspicions—either Zella hadn't injected me with enough digitalizine (doubtful, she was an experienced nurse) or my genetically enhanced immunities had nullified the dose. My blood was clean.

Since I knew I wasn't going to have a seizure, and there was no getting out of my quarters anytime soon, I went back to the sleeping platform and curled up to take a nap.

Next time I might no be so lucky.

I slept for several hours, worn out by both the tension and the injuries I'd received. I woke up in darkness, because of an odd sound that shuddered through the entire deck. I'd never heard anything like it. It was a terrible, whining sound that suggested strained alloys and incredible stress.

Had the prisoners' plan included destroying the ship? I wondered. I crawled off the mattress and limped over to the room console. Reever had pass-protected it again.

Behind me, the door panel slid open. "Cherijo." It was Reever. "You should be resting."

"With all the noise? Yeah, right." I played with the console pad, trying different combinations in an attempt to crack the protective codes he'd installed. "What's the new password for this, Reever?" He stood right behind me, I could feel the warmth of his body heat reaching through my uniform tunic. "Well?"

" 'Wife,' " he said, and touched my hair.

Stone-faced, I knocked his hand away and keyed the word in. The ship's central computer came instantly on line, and provided me with full fleet status. Which was a quarter of a light year ahead of us. The *Perpetua* sat at a dead stop. "Why have we stalled in the middle of nowhere?"

He was stroking the snarled hair at the back of my neck again. "The stardrive has been shut down. One of the original crew's engineers escaped from Detainment and was successful in sabotaging the main fuel chamber. It has been completely contaminated with hydrogen ionization."

"Oh, good." I accessed main Medical, and saw fifteen new cases had been brought in from the Detainment Area. That was enough to get me on my feet. "I've got work to do."

His hands fastened on my upper arms to hold me in place. I stared at the center of his chest. "Cherijo. You cannot persist in this. The League captives will kill you."

"Why do you care?" He was right, of course. I thought of Zella, poisoning me *before* conning me into rescuing the nurses. "Don't want to risk losing whatever credits you think I'll go for, is that it?"

"Your reckless behavior has to end." He grabbed my jaw and made me look up at him. "You think it will atone for the Jorenians who died aboard the *Sunlace*? Or make amends for turning the League ships and their crews over to the Hsktskt?"

That made me blink. I had been rather careless with my own hide lately. Was he right? Was I subconsciously hoping someone would kill me?

They'd been prepared to massacre millions, just to get me, the logical side of my brain pointed out. *The League got exactly what they deserved.*

The other side got nasty. *But the League crew members didn't make that decision, did they? Shropana did.*

Reever's thumbs traced little circles on my cheeks. "I won't allow you to commit suicide, Cherijo."

"Whatever." I needed to get out from under his hands. "Can I go now?"

He put his mouth on mine, the bastard. Kissed me as if he had every right to. I stood there and did nothing. Okay, I *wanted* to do a few things, but I resisted temptation. I'd throw myself back in Detainment before I ever gave him even the slightest amount of satisfaction again.

Even my resistance had limits, though. I jerked my head back. "Can I go *now*?"

"You pretend this means nothing to you."

I let my expression match his. "It's not an act."

"Your pulse is faster." He wiped a bead of sweat from my temple. "You perspire."

"Trying not to throw up does that to me."

Whatever he was feeling melted the ice in his gaze, and he pressed me against him. Reever had a great body, and I wasn't immune to the way it felt touching mine. I was just going to make him think I was. For eternity.

His hands moved restlessly over my shoulders and back. Like he was trying to thaw me, too. "I don't repulse you, Cherijo."

No, he didn't, damn him. "You know, you really are living proof that slime can grow legs and walk."

"You are all I have ever wanted," he said.

I wasn't going to let him do this to me, with his mouth and hands and pathetic confessions of desire. "That's a rather strange motive for handing me over to slavers."

He pressed my face into his shoulder. I would have bitten it, but he was wearing that damn Hsktskt uniform, and the metal weave would have chipped my teeth.

"It doesn't have to be this way," he said in a very weird, gentle voice.

"Too late. It is."

"OverMaster HalaVar." A harsh voice came over the console.

Reever stepped around me and touched the console. "Yes, OverLord?"

"Report to the Command Center. Bring SsurreVa with you."

"At once, OverLord."

"You certainly know how to do the good soldier thing, don't you?" I said as he guided me through the door panel and out into the corridor. "Does he snap his claws to see how high you can jump?"

"He is the Commander of the Faction forces," Reever said. "And my brother."

What? "Funny, you don't look much alike. Does he take after Mom, or Dad?"

We arrived at the Command center. TssVar gave me a surly look before indicating two seats in front of a large wall display. "I have the scans on what we have discussed, HalaVar."

We sat as the Hsktskt accessed his console, and a large star chart appeared. A slow-moving cluster of dots indicated the position of the fleet, which was moving past what appeared to be the outer curve of an enormous asteroid belt.

"It will not be necessary for the fleet to drop out of flightshield and return to collect us. Your recollection was correct, as always." The Hsktskt stabbed a claw toward a wide swatch of asteroids. "Aksel maintains a significant mining operation in this region. According to scout shuttle reconnaissance, they have what we require to replace the contaminated fuel. Yet the readings indicate that material is unprocessed."

I crossed and uncrossed my ankles, and wondered if I'd get away with walking out while they were busy plotting the next raid.

Reever studied the display, enlarged a section of the vid, then tapped a fingertip on the screen. "Here. A squad of centurons can access their processing plant and convert the raw ore into fuel. We must avoid firing on the power core."

That drew my gaze to the console, and the displayed schematic of a large space station. Mining operation meant miners ran the place. "I don't think they're going to open the air locks and give you free access to their equipment," I said.

TssVar's neck scales crinkled as he turned to give me his attention. "We will attack the operation and take what we need."

"That's nice." I got up. "Excuse me, I have to report to Medical and do something meaningful now."

"Remain, Doctor." The OverLord's claws clattered against the console as he switched off the display. I stopped, pinned on a patient smile, and waited. "She demonstrates improved obedience HalaVar. Most promising."

"Perhaps." Before I could tell them both where to go, Reever turned to me and said, "You will accompany my assault team."

My smile turned into a gape. "Huh?"

"You will accompany me when we raid the Aksellan ore station."

He had to be kidding. I blinked. No, he was serious. "I wouldn't accompany you to raid a supply closet, you oblivious dolt."

TssVar's tail lashed the deck, causing a small tremor to ripple under my feet. "I see I spoke in haste. She requires more training."

Reever inclined his head. "I will see to it."

"Hey," I said, stomping my own foot to get their attention. "I'm not a pet. And for your information, doctors make lousy soldiers." Neither of them blinked. "You don't need me. I'll just get in the way."

"On the contrary." My ex-husband folded his arms

and regarded me with distant amusement. "You will go in and negotiate their surrender."

"Since when did I get elected as Faction Ambassador?"

"Your former colleague's people will find you more acceptable," TssVar said.

"Former colleague?" Bewildered now, I glanced at Reever, then the OverLord. "What are you talking about?"

Reever keyed up another image on the display. "These are the Aksellans."

All the bones evaporated from my legs, and I abruptly sat back down. "Oh, no."

The miners appeared to be large, black and green, well-fed spiders. Exactly like one I'd befriended and served with at the FreeClinic on Kevarzangia Two.

We were about to attack Dr. Dloh's people.

I'd gone from the Heroine of Joren to a Hsktskt collaborator, in the space of a few weeks. Was I happy about it? No. Was there anything I could do about it? No. But I'd be damned if I was going to take part in one of their raids, and said as much. Several times. Loudly.

Everyone ignored me, except Reever, who made it clear that I was the only chance the Aksellan miners had of surviving the assault.

The crippled *Perpetua* advanced slowly on the asteroid belt. I got to watch from command, where Reever had insisted I wait before boarding the launch.

"I want a medical relief team with me when we enter the Central Processing Station," I said to the Hsktskt Commander.

That seemed to entertain him. "The Faction does not provide rescue operations."

"It does now." When his huge eyelids dropped, I gave him a bright smile. "Think of it as a good will gesture. Patch up enough miners, they may surrender out of gratitude."

Octagonal scales gleamed as he went back to studying the monitors. "You are nothing but trouble, SsurreVa."

I played it cool and watched, too. "Does that mean I get my way?"

For a minute, I thought he was going to refuse, but then he made a sinuous gesture. "Assemble your team."

I went down to Medical with Reever and issued my orders. The League staffers were aghast, until I reminded them what the penalty for noncompliance was. Zella started getting the others busy. Reever, who stood off to one side watching me, tagged along as I herded my people out into the corridor and sent them down to the shuttle bay.

"The miners will attempt a counterattack," he said as we followed them.

"Good." I quickened my step. "Maybe they'll get lucky."

Reever kept pace without effort. "You don't want to die, Cherijo. There are too many reasons to continue existence."

"Like being your slave-girl?" I laughed. "Cross fire gets more attractive by the moment."

A corner of his mouth lifted a centimeter or two. Reever's version of a smile. Before I could slap it off his face, we arrived at the shuttle bay.

Reever bypassed the medevac team and headed for a group of Hsktskt centurons, three of whom were standing together talking in quiet hisses and clicks. One of them was the browless Hsktskt guard who had tried to teach me manners in Medical.

"OverCenturon GothVar." Reever stepped between him and his pals. All three beasts fell silent. "Is the team prepared to depart?"

FlatHead's tongue flicked out. "Yes, OverMaster HalaVar." I got the distinct impression this Hsktskt didn't like Reever. At all. And from the subtle change in Reever's voice, he was completely aware of GothVar's dislike. It wasn't the usual who's-in-charge thing, either. They actually hated each other.

I led the League medevac team into the shuttle, where we sat facing the Hsktskt centurons. No one wanted to sit next to me—naturally—so I wasn't surprised when Reever eased into the harness on my right.

"Worried I might need to hold your hand?" I asked, too aware of the memories of other jaunts at Reever's side.

"I know what you need," Reever said and secured the last strap over his chest.

"Don't hold your breath hoping I'll ask for it," I said.

The Central Processing Station maintained orbit just beyond the perimeter of the asteroid belt. Six compact, efficient-looking wheels revolved around the gigantic median core. What puzzled me was the long metallic streamers attached at regular intervals around the wheels' outer hull plates. What was the purpose of the "fringe"?

"The Aksellans use arutanium tethers to travel from the processing station to the outer fringe of the asteroids," Reever said, making me jump in my harness.

Reading my mind again, the nosy bastard. "Can they be used as garrotes?"

"The Aksellans possess five different silk-producing glands, originally used to convert excretory by-products into snarewebs to capture prey. Over the centuries of species' development, much of which was spent below the surface of their homeworld, the arachnids evolved into natural miners. They are quite capable of dealing with the problems posed by asteroid mining, and have redefined tether technology."

Even the lizards were starting to look bored. "Yeah, but can you hang someone with it?"

"Each miner ingests arutanium, which is excreted from a particular gland, along with the pseudo-silk material and strengthens the lengths of snarewebbing. The natural tethers are then attached to the exterior hull of the processing station, and the miners use them as anchor cables when traveling from the station to the outer fringe of the asteroid belt."

"So they chew up some mineral, spit it out, and use it like ropes to swing out to the rocks," I said, and yawned.

Reever leaned closer. "It is slightly more complicated than that."

"I'll take your word for it." I tried not to look at the looming image of the station through the viewport. "I want to go in alone."

That made him straighten up. "No."

"You want me to negotiate a surrender? The minute they see the Hsktskts, they won't hear a word I say."

"I cannot permit it."

I closed my eyes. "You'd better permit it, or I don't move an inch from this seat."

He didn't say anything for a long time. Then I heard, "Very well. I will go with you."

FlatHead, I noticed, was following our conversation closely. He rose out of his harness and crossed the deck to stand over both of us. "OverMaster, I will take my squad in before you and the Designate enter the facility."

"So you can kill anything that moves?" I snorted. "That should get us tons of free fuel."

OverCenturon GothVar didn't like my comment. "When you are on my tier, Terran, I will teach you silence."

I glanced at Reever. "What's a tier?"

"A section of slave chambers on Catopsa," he said. "The OverCenturon supervises the female humanoid tier."

The lizard leaned in and blasted me with his bad breath. "My slaves swiftly learn their place."

The stench of decay was making me sick. "Where's that? As far away from your mouth as possible?" I ducked just in time to avoid the blow he aimed at my face. A dent appeared in the interior panel above my head. "Temper, temper."

Reever caught the Hsktskt's limb before he could hit me again and did something that made the guard's tongue shoot out then curl down over his lower jaw. I'd guess that meant it hurt.

"She belongs to me," Reever said. "And she is mine to correct."

"He's so masterful when he's feeling stingy, isn't he?" I said to FlatHead.

Reever released GothVar, then gave me a will-you-shut-up glare before continuing. "You will not attack the miners. No weapons are to be fired without my express permission."

"TssVar will hear of this," the Hsktskt said, then backed away.

"Uh-oh, he's going to tell on you." I smirked at my keeper. "You're going to get in trouble."

Reever hauled me to my feet, then addressed the troops. "Dr. Torin and I will make the first contact with the miners. The rest of you will remain inside the access corridor until you are signaled."

The troops didn't rally to his orders. In fact, the troops appeared fairly put out by them.

The League shuttle was evidently equipped with docking overrides, as the pilot had no problem accessing the shuttle clamps. It took a minute for one of the Hsktskt to bypass the access codes, the Reever and I walked down the short passage into the main air lock.

When the interior door panel slid to one side, we faced a long tunnel of ash-colored stone. A damp, acrid odor drifted over us, and made me wrinkle my nose.

"They need to air this place out." I walked ahead of Reever, and peered at the nearest curving wall. "What is this stuff? It isn't rock."

The walls seemed to be made out of mesh or insulation material, the kind that mimicked stone. Some form of homeworld-effect decor?

"Cherijo." Reever jerked me backward as a perfectly round grey hatch popped out of the floor just in front of me.

Something black and green emerged from a vertical shaft and immediately bounced up to hang from the ceiling. An Aksellan, judging by the close resemblance to my old friend Dr. Dloh. It had no weapon, but two impressive fangs slid out from a fold in its front appendages. Dark drops oozed from the hollow-pointed tips, and sizzled as they made holes wherever they fell.

"Think they're the welcoming committee?" I said to Reever.

More concealed hatches burst open, and soon we were surrounded by twenty very large black-and-green spiders. None of them carried weapons, but all had fangs bared, and spinnerets erect and pointed at us. They knew we weren't there to say, "Hi, can we take the tour?"

"Ztay where you are!"

With that acidic poison dripping around me? I wasn't making a break for it.

Like my former colleague, the miners wore modified tunics over their exoskeletons. Each had a hard, shiny carapace marked with bright green pigmentation patterns. Tiny clusters of eyes glittered above their U-shaped mandibles. Sensory hairs on the inside of their appendages quivered, responding to the slightest air movements.

That was when I figured out the tunnel wasn't a tunnel, but a tightly woven web. And, like the proverbial flies, we had just walked into it.

"Leave thiz ztation," the largest Aksellan said. He

had the greatest amount of green mottling on his cephalothorax. A sign of age, I guessed. Or an indication he was the deadliest. Dr. Dloh had often complained about the daily chore of draining the poison sacs in his forelimbs before treating patients.

"I'm sorry, we can't do that," I said as I took a step forward and showed him my empty hands. "The ship outside your station has been commandeered by the Hsktskt Faction. Please understand, we won't harm you. Now we can do this the easy way, or—"

One of the other Aksellans spat a metallic stream of fluid at me. Reever jerked me to one side, and the snareweb fluid fell, forming a pool of hard, gleaming silver.

"—the hard way," I said, staring at the puddle. My gaze went to the leader, who was buzzing something in his native language to the spider who'd tried to snare me. "Please listen. If you don't surrender, the Hsktskt will attack."

The leader shuffled forward and peered at my tunic. Pedipalps behind his front appendages extended to brush over my face. I didn't move. Dr. Dloh's people smelled with their skin and identified everything by touch, so it was a perfectly natural thing for him to do.

"You are a phyzician?"

I exchanged a glance with Reever. "Yes."

The leader's lustrous eye clusters rotated, something Dr. Dloh had done when he'd pondered something. "The Hzktzkt want fuel ore, do they not?" I nodded. "Az I zuzpected. This ztation haz no ztrategic value, nor do my people to zlaverz."

I never got to ask why, because at that moment the Hsktskt centurons stormed through the access corridor panel, their weapons armed and humming. The spiders seized me and Reever, and suddenly I hung upside-down, dangling several feet in the air.

"Surrender," GothVar said.

"Dizengage your weaponz, and no one will be harmed," the leader said.

GothVar only swung one of his limbs up, then down. Pulse fire erupted all around us. I heard the shrieks of the medevac team, still back in the corridor.

The spiders moved faster that anything I'd ever seen. Before I could get my bearings, they had dodged the blasts, climbed down the air lock walls, dropped back into the hatches and sealed them with bursts of silk. We slid down the narrow dark passage that surfaced into another tunnel, and from there went through a more recognizable station access door panel. The Hsktskt couldn't follow us, they were simply too large to fit into the hatched passages.

"Cloze off thiz zection," the leader ordered one of the miners, then addressed me again. "You are Cherijo Torin?" Surprised, I nodded, and three of his appendages lifted. The spider holding me gently set me back on my feet. "I am Clyvoz, the fazility manager. Welcome to Akzel Drift Nine Mining Ztation."

"Nice to meet you." I made an appropriate waving gesture Dloh had taught me back on K-2. "How did you know my name?"

"The Jorenianz zent a wide-band zignal and advized all zurrounding zyztemz of your plight." Clyvos indicated a nearby com console. "We will do what we can to help you, of courze."

"I think we'd better signal the *Perpetua* and see if I can get the Hsktskt to back off. If I can't, do you have an evacuation plan?"

"Yez. What about him?" Clyvos swung a limb toward Reever, who was still being held upside-down.

"Any of you hungry?" I looked around, and the other spiders eyed Reever with distinct greed. "Though I can't guarantee he'll taste very good."

"Our digeztive juicez will render anything palatable," Clyvos said.

"You forget about Alunthri, Cherijo," Reever said, calm and unconcerned. As usual.

Damn him, I had. "You'd better not eat him yet. But if you have a detainment section, Clyvos, I'd advise stowing him in it."

Clyvos buzzed something at the spider carrying Reever, who swiftly scurried off. He and the other miners took me down another webbed, curving corridor, then through a larger passage to the center hub area of the station.

"Zeal the inner air lock panelz, and charge them," Clyvos ordered as we entered the main control room. I watched a large display as a series of protective panels slammed into place and bioelectrically charged.

"All the Hsktskt really want is fuel to replace their contaminated stores," I said as a group gathered around us.

The manager taped the monitor. "The reinforced doorz will keep the Hzktzkt buzy, long enough for me to evacuate my people to the tetherz. Once we reached the azteroid field, we can hide ourzelvez among the driftz. The raiderz' zhip cannot enter the field, and will not wazte time zending launchez to look for uz." One of his limbs touched my arm. "You can come too, Doctor."

I thought of the Chakacat, and how smart Reever had been to kidnap my friend as insurance. "I can't, but thank you. Let me run interference with the Hsktskt, and help you get your people to safety. I'll need you to make this look good."

"I underztand." Clyvos wrapped two limbs around me and carried me over to a signal array. One of the other miners sent a direct relay to the *Perpetua*. "Thiz iz Clyvoz, Ztation Facility Manager. I have captured two of your raiderz and immobilized the otherz. Ceaze fire, withdraw your troopz, and I will releaze my hoztagez."

TssVar's furious image briefly filled the display. "Hsktskt do not negotiate."

Displacer fire immediately bombarded Drift Nine's

outer hull. Clyvos didn't move, but I felt sweat trickling down the sides of my face. "Hzktzkt. You may take whatever fuel you require. All we azk iz we be left in peace once you have it."

The *Perpetua* didn't respond to Clyvos's relay. More energy blasts rocked the station.

"I don't think 'peace' translated," I said to Clyvos. "You'd better get your people out of here now."

"With the zhip firing on the Ztation?" Clyvos's appendages fell away from me. "Impozzible. The tetherz are in plain view."

I thought for a moment. Reever had mentioned something to TssVar about avoiding the main power core. "You have a central fuel system powering the entire station, right?" Clyvos pulled up a design grid for the facility and showed me their main power source.

It was fusion. Perfect.

I explained my idea. "If I can close down and seal the central exchangers and bypass the main coolant array here"—with my finger I traced the ventilation system back to the core—"the discharge will funnel back in around the main housing here, correct?"

"Yez, but the houzing will not withztand those temperaturez for more than fifteen minutez at the mozt."

"That should do the trick," I said. "Gives us time to evacuate the station. Your people should be safe in the drift tunnels. Do you have the equipment there to signal for assistance?"

The facility manager, who hadn't realized I was serious, drew back in alarm. "Yez, but if you do thiz, it will deztroy the Hzktzkt raiderz *and* the ztation."

I smiled. "Not necessarily."

One of the miners escorted me to the holding area where they'd dumped Reever. Along the way, I saw hordes of Aksellans—these without the vivid markings—busily hauling huge green nodules on their backs. They came down a separate corridor and gathered on a loading dock, where they were placing the nodules into oversize field packs. Curiosity made me comment on the difference in coloring.

"Thoze are our femalez," my escort said. When I would have walked over to say hello, he grabbed me. "Don't get too cloze to them." One of the drab-colored spiders saw me and made a low buzz that made me forget all about being congenial

"Don't they like females of other species?" I asked as I stepped back behind him.

"When they are protecting our young, they tend to regard anything that movez as a meal." He was keeping his eyes on them, too. "Even a mate."

"What are those green things? Food?"

"Egg zacs," he said. "We will not leave our hatchlingz for the Hzktzkt to devour."

"Good idea." I stopped when the spider halted at a small access panel and keyed open the hatch. Just inside the tiny space, Reever was hanging upside-down, wrapped in a metallic cocoon from his neck to his knees. Small, greyish baby Aksellans were crawling all over him.

Alarmed, I grabbed my escort by the nearest appendage. "They aren't trying to eat him, are they?"

"They can't, they're too young," the arachnid told me. "Our species doesn't develop mouth parts until after its first molting."

So he was safe, and why was I worried about it in the first place? "Hi, Reever. Having fun in there?"

"Cherijo." He didn't look amused, not with a fist-sized spider using his chin as a chair. "Tell them to release me."

I couldn't help myself. I laughed. "Say pretty, pretty please."

He shook off the baby Aksellan, and another one promptly took its place Then he sighed. "Have them release me before you get us all killed."

I might need him as a hostage, if Plan A didn't

work. "Better take him down," I told the miner, giving him a wink Reever couldn't see when I added, "you can start ingesting him as soon as I'm done."

He picked up on my joke at once. "I hope it will be zoon. I'm ztarving." With quick, efficient clacks of his mandibles, the big spider chased off the baby Aksellans, cut Reever down, and sheared off the rest of the snarewebbing.

Reever crawled out of the confining space and straightened with visible relief before giving me a cold eye. "You intend to feed me to them?"

"Why not? You made me a slave." I used my most reasonable tone. "Besides, TssVar is trying to blow up the station"—displacer blasts buffeted the hull as I said that—"and you know how competent he is at that sort of thing."

"Get me to an open console and I can stop this," Reever said.

"No, I don't think I'm going to do that." When he stepped forward, I pulled out the pulse weapon from the body-holster Clyvos had given me and pointed it at his chest. "Walk that way if you would, please."

"Joey, I can—"

"You'd enjoy having a two-foot hole in your sternum?" I asked politely, while my companion scuttled forward with a hungry sound. "You can even have your choice. Blasted, or chewed."

That shut him up. The Aksellan nudged him in the right direction, while I holstered the weapon and followed at a discreet distance. We walked down three levels until we reached the central processing unit where Clyvos had told me I could access the main fusion chamber controls.

"You are zertain you underztand the prozedure?" the facility manager asked me.

"Not a problem." I keyed the panel to open, then noticed the big spider's nervous shuffling. "Stop worrying already. Worst case scenario, I end up toasting me, Reever, and the Hsktskt." I glanced at my ex-husband. "No great loss."

Clyvoz rolled his eye clusters in apparent resignation. "Luck to you, Doctor." Then he scurried off down the corridor.

"Right." I went inside, pointed to a spot for Reever to stand, then manned the chamber control console. It was crowded with enablers fashioned for a eight-limbed being, so I had to do some fancy hand moves.

I shut down the exchangers first, which sounded an immediate alarm.

"What are you doing?" Reever asked.

"Saving the miners." I disabled the discharge feed through the coolant array. A second alarm sounded and critical temperatures began to rise. "Among other things."

"You're tampering with equipment you've never used."

"Not for the first time, either." I channeled the discharge back into the core, then altered the panel access codes.

Reever came up behind me. "You will destroy this facility." His hands were still bound by Aksellan webbing, but I kept an eye on him anyway.

"I hope not, but you never know." I signaled the *Perpetua*. "Aksellan station to OverLord TssVar. Please respond."

CHAPTER FIVE

Dire Consequences

The signal came in from the L.T.F. *Perpetua* at once. "SsurreVa. Have you and HalaVar secured the facility?"

Time he understood who was playing on his team, and who wasn't.

"Not exactly, OverLord." I programmed a chamber status report to go out with my signal. "But as you can see, I have secured the main fusion chamber, bypassed the coolant system and routed the superheated discharge back into the core. It should melt down the outer housing and cause an explosion, oh, quite soon."

There was a long stretch of silence. Then TssVar, who I had expected to detonate himself, returned the signal. "You had no intentions of negotiating a peaceful exchange, did you?"

I shrugged.

"The Terran Grey Veil was correct. You are a habitual liar, SsurreVa."

I smiled at his furious image. TssVar should have listened to Joseph Grey Veil—my creator was usually right. "If that's what it takes to keep the Aksellans from being slaughtered, you bet I am."

"I have captured a group of these miners," the OverLord told me. TssVar gestured, and a writhing Aksellan was brought before the screen. "I can kill them one at a time, or all at once. Which do you choose, SsurreVa?"

"I don't." I kept my face and voice bland. Damn, how had he managed that? "But do whatever you feel is necessary. Watch out for the females. They have awfully bad tempers."

"Very well." Surprisingly, he ordered his guards to remove the Aksellans from the Command post. "What are your terms to end this before the core detonates?"

That I could deal with. "Release the Aksellans you've captured, and allow the miners to peacefully evacuate the station. Send a small group of your centurons over to handle the ore processing. Once that's done, unload the League crew, take the fuel, leave the station, and head on your merry way."

Reever made a strange sound, but I ignored him.

Something crashed on the Hsktskt side of the link. Might have been that piece of console TssVar heaved across his office. "I will not release the League slaves."

"You'd rather be blown into itty-bitty molecules?" I spread my hands out. "Fine with me."

"You will not destroy my ship," the OverLord said. "Not when all the captives remain on board."

Bluff time. "I sold them out to you, didn't I? Watch me."

I'd been counting on TssVar's inability to feel humanoid emotion, but he'd been hanging around me for too long. "I watched you operate for hours on the League Commander after he attempted to kill you," he said. "You will not do it."

"Then it's been nice knowing you." I quickly terminated the signal. Maybe if I said nothing more, he might change his mind—

"He will not, Cherijo." Reever moved to stand beside me and examined the console. "This overload becomes irreversible in five minutes."

"I know." I gnawed at my lower lip. Surely there was some other way I could convince the Hsktskt I was serious, without actually killing anyone. Then it occurred to me that Duncan had accessed my thoughts, that we were alone, and he could do any damn thing he wanted. Especially as he'd somehow gotten his hands free.

"No, Reever." I pulled the weapon from the holster, but it was already too late.

Cherijo.

All he had to do was gently pry the weapon from my nerveless fingers and set it aside. Then he used his mind-control tricks to make me walk away from the console. I made some gasping sounds as my body mechanically followed his mental commands.

Why are you laughing? he said inside my head.

Because you don't know the override codes. Tears of strain from being unable to physically laugh rolled down my face. *So we're all going to die together, one big happy family.*

He tried to get at them for a minute, and I had to use every ounce of control I had to keep my mental bolsters in place. Finally he left the console and knelt before me. *Cherijo. You cannot do this. You cannot kill.*

He was absolutely correct, not that I was going to tell him. *Why not? I'm not too fond of the Hsktskt, or the League. Alunthri will never be free, and I know it would rather die than go back to being someone's pet. Most of the Aksellans will survive. And you—* The bitterness swamped me. *I loved you and look where it got me.*

The autodrone announced that two minutes remained before the core went to critical mass.

I can persuade TssVar to agree with everything but releasing the League captives. Reever cradled my stiff face between his scarred hands. *If I do, will you stop this?*

I had two minutes, but it didn't take that long. *Yeah. Okay.*

He kept me there while he went back to the console. "This is OverMaster HalaVar. I have negotiated an agreement on your behalf, OverLord."

"HalaVar, shut down that core!" TssVar said, in a near-bellow.

Reever's voice went low, but I still heard him. "I have never asked anything of you, TssVar, but I remind you of our blood-bond."

Another brief interval of dead silence. "Very well. Quickly, the terms."

Reever told him, and TssVar agreed to it. The next moment I was being dragged over to the console, then the mind-force controlling me disappeared. "Reverse the overload."

I worked fast. The exchangers blew open and I engaged the hull dampers to open and vent the super-heated fuel into space. The chamber sensors slowly began to inch back down out of the red range.

All the excitement was over.

The Aksellans had been monitoring the situation from their remote terminals in the asteroid field, and Clyvos agreed to provide the necessary fuel stores. As before, his only condition was that the station and the miners be left alone once the Hsktskt had what they wanted.

TssVar ordered Reever to bring me back to the *Perpetua*. "To the Command Center, brother." He appeared, if anything, angrier than he had before.

Reever nodded, grabbed my arm, and hauled me out into the corridor.

"Hey." I tugged, but his grip was like a vise. "Why the rush?"

"Have you any idea of what you have done?" Reever said as he dragged me through the station.

Not really, but I guess I was going to find out.

The launch carrying Clyvos, the miners, and another detachment of Hsktskt centurons arrived at the same time Reever and I flew back to the *Perpetua*. The Aksellan and I exchanged glances through our viewports as the launches passed each other.

I waved. "Looks like TssVar plans to keep his side of the bargain."

Reever, who was manning the launch alone, looked up from the helm for a moment. "Hsktskt rarely prevaricate. They consider it beneath them."

"Like everything else." I sat back and rubbed my hands over my face. "Will they throw me back into isolation?"

"I don't know."

That was my OverMaster, always eager to reassure me. Whatever was eating him must be suffering horrible indigestion. "I guess you're out one slave-girl. A shame. Be a good soldier and maybe he'll give you another."

Reever put the helm on autopilot, got up out of his harness, and walked back to where I was strapped in. Yeah, he was angry. I could tell from the way that little muscle ticked along his jaw.

"I used a blood-bond to keep you alive I have been holding in reserve for fifteen years." He sounded vicious, and at the same time, astonished. As though he couldn't fathom his own actions.

I felt like saying *join the club*. "So what's another blood-bond, more or less?" I closed my eyes. A moment later I was ripped out of the harness and hauled up to his eye level by my slave collar.

Okay, I thought, I should stop gloating now.

"I grow tired of your ridicule and sarcasm," he said, letting go of the collar to pin my arms to my sides. "You belong to me and you will do as I tell you."

My fear went the same route as his self-control. Out the door panel.

"I'm sick of your mouth, too." I wasn't that far off the deck—if he dropped me, nothing would break. "Despite what you think, I'm not your property, pet, or plaything. And, for future reference, I'll do exactly, *exactly* what I want, when I want, where I want."

His hands tightened, grinding into my bones. "You will say nothing of this to TssVar."

"No!" He was really hurting me now. I kicked him in the shin, as hard as I could. He didn't move a muscle. "What are you made of—stone? Damn it, put me down!"

He didn't. He shook me, fast and hard. "You will say *nothing*, Cherijo, or I will keep you suspended in a mental link. *Indefinitely.*"

"Just try it!" Could he? I fought to free myself, and kicked him a few more times. "Let go, *let go of me!*"

Unexpectedly he did just that—set me down on my feet. Before I could react, he drew back his arm and hit me. No love tap, but a heavy, openhanded slap that sent my head smashing into the cabin wall. My ears rang as I collapsed against the passenger seats.

"You will remain silent when I speak to TssVar," he said in a horrible voice. I flinched as if struck a second time. *"Do you understand?"*

"Yeah." My eyes filled with tears of hatred and pain. I slowly regained my equilibrium, pushed myself up and covered my burning cheek with my hand. "I got it."

"Cherijo." He reached out, then hesitated. Slowly his fingers curled away and he dropped his hand.

While he was preoccupied with staring at my face (and doubtless the bruise that was forming on it), I brought my right hand up and slapped him equally as hard.

"I won't say anything." I waited until he caught my gaze. "But touch me again, and one of us won't walk away breathing."

Without another word he went back to the helm.

*   *   *

An armed escort was waiting for us, and the trio of lizards didn't look very happy. They marched me and Reever up to the Command Center, where TssVar was giving orders to another group of his centurons. When the OverLord saw us, he made a single, vicious gesture that cleared the room.

Well, almost. FlatHead stuck around so he could watch the fun and games, I supposed.

"SsurreVa."

I'd forgotten just how big and scary a Hsktskt can be, especially when they stand about an inch away from you. All those gleaming teeth, perfectly designed to grab, hold, and rip to pieces. "OverLord."

Reever stepped forward, and actually put a hand on one of TssVar's upper limbs. "There is much that I must tell you, brother."

"Yes, OverMaster HalaVar." GothVar pushed away from his position by the door. He reminded me of a scavenger, moving in for whatever scraps he could get. "Tell our Commander how this Terran fodder deceived him. Tell how she conspired to betray us to the Aksellans from the moment we entered the processing station."

I noticed he didn't mention anything about his premature helpfulness, but I was going to keep this last promise to Reever. I'd keep quiet. After this, all debts were satisfied.

"HalaVar." TssVar shoved me out of his way to stalk up to Reever. "I would hear your explanation."

"Dr. Torin was held at gunpoint during the entire incident, as was I." Reever lied without twitching a blond eyelash. "She followed the Aksellan's instructions in order to keep both of us alive. I was unable to relate this during the transmission, for the same reasons."

"She did not sound as if she was under duress." The Hsktskt swiveled around to stare at me. "I would have thought her enjoying her . . . coercion."

"I had hoped you would understand our plight when I referenced our blood-bond." Reever sounded bored. "Why would I cancel such an enormous debt over the life of a few miners and one Terran female?"

"Why, indeed." TssVar's gaze roamed between us restlessly. "Yet it is done, HalaVar."

"Yes. It is."

I had no idea of what they were talking about, but now *I* was getting bored. Tempted to ask if I could go, I caught the look on Reever's face and bit the inside of my cheek instead.

GothVar had no problem with self-restraint. "HalaVar indulges this slave, OverLord." He came over to me, clamped one of his huge hands around my right wrist and nearly pulled my arm out of its socket.

"Hey!" I yanked back.

With a swipe, he shredded the length of my tunic sleeve and held out my arm to TssVar. "You see? No PIC."

My slave-brand was gone? I checked. It was. Nothing marred my flesh, not even the faint signs of fading keloids. My creator's tinkering had landed me in hot water once more. I couldn't tell TssVar that, but I wasn't letting him burn me again. "I don't need a brand, for God's sake. I'm not going—"

"See to it," TssVar said to Reever. One of his six limbs lashed toward the door panel. "All of you, get out. GothVar, assist HalaVar with this female's designation."

Even FlatHead knew when to gracefully retreat. "Yes, OverLord."

Outside in the corridor, Reever only shook his head when I opened my mouth. GothVar shadowed us from Central Command all the way to the chamber where Reever had first branded me. I began to break out in a sweat as I remembered the pain and helplessness.

"I guess you can't inject me with an indelible pigment?" I shuffled over to the circular pad. Reever said nothing. "I want the drugs this time."

"No drugs," GothVar said, and held his pulse rifle trained on my chest. "You will perform the application on her as she is, as I watch."

Reever removed his own weapon and held it on FlatHead. "Release her, OverCenturon."

Me, about to be burned, standing between two beasts with guns fighting over how to do it. Maybe I should have surrendered to Joseph the first time he'd attacked the *Sunlace*.

GothVar laughed. "You have no blood-bond to claim amnesty with, HalaVar. Kill me if you will, but TssVar will see you both dismembered for the murder of a free citizen."

The lizard had a point. I stepped between the metallic columns and held out my arm. "Do it." Reever shook his head, and I hissed out an impatient breath. "Now, Reever, before *I* end up getting shot, too."

GothVar came to stand right behind me, the best view in the house. Reever hesitated another moment, then quickly put his weapon away and went to the console.

I felt the cold, dry touch of scaled flesh on the back of my neck, and froze.

"When you feel the laser sear your flesh, scream for me," the Hsktskt said, scraping his claws against the rim of my slave collar.

"I can't decide why no one likes you." I closed my eyes when his claws slid between the collar and my throat. "However, I've narrowed it down to two possibilities. It's either your breath, or your face."

"Soon we will reach Catopsa." The claws dug into my flesh. "I will have you assigned to my tier. I will take my time with you, make you last."

Doing what? "Terrans tend to lose their appeal rather quickly," I said, then jerked as Reever activated the laser, and swallowed a shriek. "Sorry . . . to . . . disappoint . . . you. . . ."

Heat slashed through my skin as the programmed application carefully re-carved each symbol. One of FlatHead's limbs curled around my waist. Hot breath scalded my cheek. Dimly I realized he was enjoying it, aroused by the smell of burning.

Fire enveloping my suit. I was burning. Children screaming with terror. Tonetka's graceful hands, slapping at me, trying to beat out the flames. . . .

I made it through almost to the end. The last thing I heard was GothVar's tongue slithering out to taste my pain.

Reever must have kept me sedated for a day or two, because when I woke, my fresh brand was scabbed over and itching like crazy. I was on his sleeping platform, and he sat beside me, reading something on a data pad. I rolled over and got up carefully, making sure my legs would hold me.

"You're awake."

I didn't wait to have a tête-à-tête. Whatever he had fed me wanted to come back up, so I made a quick run to the lavatory. Once my stomach was empty, I spent some time under the cleanser. I couldn't rid myself of GothVar's voice, or the memory of the sick pleasure he'd taken in my branding. The nausea stayed with me even after I dressed.

FlatHead wasn't a scavenger, I decided. He was what scavengers *ate.*

I needed to do some work, so I resolved to go back to running Medical, and told Reever that. He said nothing, only examined my arm for a moment, then handed me a League physician's tunic.

"I will escort you," he said when I'd dressed and headed for the door panel.

"I know the way."

No one was running Medical anymore. Apparently Malgat had been sent to Detainment, and the nurses and residents had fallen into complete despair and equal disregard for standard procedure. I discovered a half dozen injured patients waiting who had not yet been treated, inpatients who need follow-up, and a thousand other tasks.

There was no use pointing fingers. I just called the League staffers over to the center of the Bay and laid down the law.

"OverLord TssVar has appointed me as the new Primary for this department. Senior staff will make progress reports directly to me, twice a shift. I want those patients waiting to be triaged and sorted in priority. Immediately. You"—I pointed to Vlaav, the loud-mouthed Saksonan who'd given me so much trouble after Shropana's operation—"are in charge of assessment on ambulatory patients."

The red nubbly pockets on his hide swelled. "That's a nursing slot!"

"Aren't you bright?" I wondered if those bulges ever burst, and made a mental note to keep him out of my sterile fields. "It's yours now. Show me what a good nurse you'd make, and I might let you play doctor someday."

I went on to assign the senior staff positions, which everyone objected to—even the assignees. I blocked out the protests and requisitioned a pair of the most qualified nurses to do rounds with me. Then I started walking to the first berth.

No one else moved. The entire Medical staff stood like statues in the center of the Bay, watching me while displaying varying degrees of astonishment.

This was going to be tougher than I'd thought.

I recalled something one of my own instructors had done back at Medtech, picked up a waste disposal receptacle, and banged on it a few times with an unused chart.

"*People.*" The voices hushed. "Anyone I see not working within the next sixty seconds is permanently relieved from duty. No exceptions." I dropped the receptacle so that it made a ringing *bong*. "I hear the

Hsktskt can use some extra hands in the galley. To serve or be served, I can't remember which."

That got them moving.

Vlaav began sullenly evaluating the waiting patients, while I dealt with the ones who had been ignored for days on end. They were in fairly good shape, so someone had attended to them, more or less. Still I saw infections that could have been prevented, muscle damage from lack of therapeutic treatments, and several other situations that made me very testy.

Two of the ten patients would need minor surgery, but most simply needed a doctor who actually read their chart, listened to what they had to say, and treated them accordingly.

One of my nurses was replaced almost immediately by Dchêm-os, who scurried in from the outer corridor, carrying an armful of charts. "Talk, Doctor, we must."

Zel must have requisitioned some new toxin she wanted to try out on me. "Later." I eyed the Hsktskt guard who'd come in after her. They carried a crew member between them, and when I saw who it was, I groaned. "How the hell did he get out of Medical? Can't I leave for a couple days without everything going down the sanitation duct? Vlaav, get him on a table and take a look at him."

My Saksonan intern quickly triaged Colonel Shropana. I left Zel and the other nurse holding charts as I went to evaluate Vlaav's notations. Patril snarled and tried to punch me the moment he saw me, which is why I directed two of the orderlies to put him in restraints.

Someone had gone at him with something thin and sharp. Repeatedly. His uniform hung in tatters, his upper torso and arms were slashed a dozen times. Not blade wounds, from the ragged look of the outer tears.

"Calm down, Patril. That dilapidated heart of

yours won't take much more stress." I infused him with valumine and ran a full scan series. Shropana's heart was my main concern, so after ensuring that his recent surgery hadn't been compromised, I assessed his cardiac system. "Your arteries make plasteel look spongy. Did Malgat at least start you on therapy?"

He snarled something obscene.

"Thanks, maybe later." I checked his records, and discovered that although my predecessor had diagnosed the Colonel's condition, he'd done nothing to treat it. "We're going to need to do something about those rib splinters, and talk about repairing this arterial situation." He kept quiet, so I explained what was needed, then went on to the lesser of his problems.

The gashes weren't blade wounds, they were claw marks. Whatever had attacked him had nearly ripped out his throat, too. Another centimeter here or there, and I'd be bagging him for autopsy.

"Did you and Lieutenant Wonlee get into a disagreement?"

He spat at me, but missed. "This is your fault!"

I made the appropriate chart notations while one of the nurses set up a suture tray. "Everything is my fault, have you noticed that? No matter what I do." I set the chart aside and dialed up a compound treatment on a syrinpress. "I'm going to use some topical anaesthetic on the wounds, but what I'm injecting you with will help your heart functions—for now. You need that surgery."

"I'll see you dead first," the Colonel told me.

Nurse Dchêm-os took the place of my suture nurse and assisted as I worked on Shropana's wounds.

Since Patril wasn't feeling talkative, I glanced at Zel. "Who did it?"

Zel slipped off her headgear. "Attacked him, that big cat of yours, this morning. To question it about you, he was trying."

Alunthri inflicted this kind of damage? "What did you do to the Chakacat, Patril?"

The Colonel ignored me and glared at the nurse. "You were supposed to kill it. And her." He jerked his head toward me. "Now you slave for her as well as the beasts."

Zel stopped assisting and went very still. "With digitalizine, I injected her. No effect, it had. For no one, I slave."

"Nurse." I was in the middle of a complicated suture and didn't need the patient and my assistant getting into a fistfight. "Want to shut up and swab this?"

"You see?" Patril grinned. "Next she will have you on a leash, like her domesticate."

Zel's vibrissae quivered. "Never."

"Oh, for crying out loud." Too bad I couldn't suture his lips together. I deactivated the laser and pushed it out of the way. "Zel, ignore him and do your job. Colonel, you're entitled to an opinion, but if you don't shut up immediately I'm going to sedate you."

"Won't be necessary, that." Zel turned and called to another nurse. Once her replacement came over, she stepped away from the table, her black eyes glistening with renewed malice. "Murderer, you are. From you anymore, I will not take orders."

"Crushed, I am. Taa-taa." I turned to the new nurse. "Prepare dressings for this patient." I grabbed the laser and bent back down over Shropana.

It took a double shift to get things into reasonable order in Medical, then I left. By then knots had formed in my belly, but not from hunger. I had to confront Reever again, and I wasn't looking forward to that.

Or perhaps I didn't have to. I went to the quarters that the League had assigned to me, way back when, and after a quick check to determine they were unoccupied, locked myself in.

There, I thought. Not being obligated to look at my ex-bondmate's face, eat his food, or sleep in his bed proved very relaxing. Yet when I went to the prep unit and automatically dialed up some chicken noodle soup, I still felt like weeping.

Chicken noodle soup had been the first Terran dish I'd ever made Reever.

"So I'll have asparagus bisque instead," I said, and altered my program accordingly.

When it was ready, I carried a tray over to the table and sat down. That was when I caught a glimpse of my own face in the wall reflector, and saw that the bruise from Reever's hand had darkened to a rather pretty lilac color. My appetite abruptly vanished, and I toyed with the soup until sometime later, when my door panel slid open.

"Cherijo." Of course it was Reever. It wasn't like Nurse Dchêm-os was going to drop by for some tea and a chat.

I examined the thin skin that had formed on the surface of my cold soup. "I need to reprogram those locks."

"You will report to my quarters when you have completed your shifts in Medical."

I lifted the spoon and let the thickened green liquid drip slowly from it back into the bowl. "No, I'm not going to do that." I rested my bruised cheek on my other hand, and wondered why I felt so battered and exhausted. "Go away."

He hovered. "I will not apologize for striking you."

"No one asked you to. Leave."

"I have something that belongs to you."

He certainly did. There should have been a large, oozing hole just to the left of my sternum to testify to that. "Keep it."

He sat down beside me. "You are upset."

The man was so dense that light bent around him. "Will you get the hell out of here?"

"Very well." He didn't try to touch me. "Shall I give the domesticate to the Hsktskt? They have indicated he would be considered a delicacy."

He? I finally looked at him. His bruise wasn't as spectacular as mine, and it didn't make me feel any better to see it. "Alunthri is an 'it,' and, I imagine, very stringy and tough. Don't even go there."

"I am not talking about Alunthri. I have your other domesticate. The small one."

The *small* one?

I got up so quickly that the table fell over, the server smashed into a hundred pieces and cold asparagus bisque splattered the deck. *"Say that again."*

He sat back and folded his arms. "I have your Terran feline."

I didn't stop to think about the hows or whys. "Where? *Where is he?"*

"In my quarters." He moved fast, and caught me before I could reach the door panel. "Where he will stay, as will you."

I struggled out of his grip and ran, dodging League captives and Hsktskt alike on every level until, panting, I'd reached Reever's door. My fist hit the access panel and I ran in, completely ignoring the fact that Reever had somehow kept up with me and closed the panel silently behind us.

For a moment I wondered if it had been just another game. "Jenner?" It came out in a whisper. Then, as loud as I could: *"Jenner!"*

Something small, thin, and furry flew up from the floor and landed in my arms. A hard little triangular head butted into my chin, and huge lapis eyes regarded me with extreme indignation.

Thought you'd leave me behind, you ungrateful wench. Jenner sniffed delicately at me. *After all the attention I lavished on you, too.*

I was laughing. Weeping. Burying my face in the softest silkiest fur in the universe. "Hi, pal. Oh, Lord, I've missed you."

My Tibetan temple cat slanted a sideways look at Reever. *Yeah, well, Prince Charming wouldn't let me out, or I'd have found you long before now.*

That reminded me. I sat down on the nearest surface, still holding and caressing my pet, and regarded Reever with a mixture of fury and bewilderment.

"He's been onboard, all this time, and you never told me?"

Reever nodded.

"How did you get him off Joren? Why didn't you say something?" My fingers ran over the prominent outlines of my cat's ribs, something I hadn't felt since finding Jenner as a kitten, abandoned and starving in a gutter. "Why is he so thin?"

"Adaola gave him to me before I left the planet. She hoped I could reunite the two of you someday." He walked over and stood beside us, and reached down to Jenner. His Majesty lifted his head and allowed Reever to give him a brief caress. "As for the weight loss, I have yet to discern the animal's food preferences."

"He has none. Whatever he sees, he eats." I lifted Jenner so that we were face-to-face. "Hungry, pal?"

He uttered an emphatic yowl. *Does a cat have nine lives?*

I went over to the prep unit and dialed up a dozen of his favorite dishes, then watched with pleasure as my small companion attacked the enormous meal. At the rate he was wolfing down synthetic shrimp bits, he'd be back to his old self in no time.

I sat on the floor beside him, afraid to take my hand away, certain Jenner would vanish if I did.

"Why do you call it Jenner?"

"*He's* named after Edward Jenner, the eighteenth-century English physician who cured smallpox." My fingers trailed through my pet's soft fur. "He was an

amazing man for his time. What he did altered the
course of Terran history." I went on to tell Reever
about the simple country doctor, who had noticed
that dairy workers seldom contracted smallpox, and
gone on to create the vaccine that had saved millions
from death and disfigurement.

Reever's only comment was, "He sounds much
like your creator."

"There's a big difference." Jenner had been a hu-
manitarian. Joseph, I suspected, barely rated as
human. "Why didn't you tell me about my cat,
Reever?"

"I attempted to, several times. It was necessary to
conceal his presence from the crew."

So that was why he'd been so hot and bothered to
get me to his quarters. Something occurred to me,
and my head snapped up. "You hid him because of
the League captives. You knew they'd try to hurt
him to get back at me." He didn't have to say yes. I
got up and faced him. "What's this going to cost?"

"No currency is required."

But something else was. "You know how much
Jenner means to me. What do you want?"

To his credit, Duncan didn't rub it in. He simply
said, "You will report to my quarters and remain
here when you are not working in Medical."

I'd room with GothVar, just to have Jenner.
"Done."

PART TWO:

Indoctrination

CHAPTER SIX

New Debts

So began my stint as Reever's roommate. I'd never had many. During my childhood, Joseph Grey Veil had kept me in a separate wing of the family mansion. Maggie, my "maternal influencer," had sometimes braved my creator's displeasure and slept in a chair by my sleeping platform. Jenner had been my only constant companion since her death.

Kao and I had never had the chance to live together during our brief time together on K-2, although Alunthri had shared my quarters after I'd assumed its ownership, so it would not be sold back into slavery on Chakara.

While working as Senior Healer on the *Sunlace*, I'd been forced to Choose Kao's ClanBrother, Xonea, to protect him from an unfair sentence of banishment. We'd lived together for a short, tense period, both of us the unknowing victims of aggression-enhancing drugs that had driven us both to violence.

As a roommate, however, Reever proved to be nearly invisible.

I spent most of my waking hours in Medical, getting the staff whipped back into shape and catching up with the patient caseload, and when I arrived at Reever's quarters, Jenner made up for every horrible thing that had happened since I'd left Joren.

Well, almost.

Reever invariably came in when I'd fallen asleep. The few times I'd woken up was to discover him easing down beside me on the sleeping platform. He never touched me—another bonus—and I rarely if ever acknowledged his presence.

That's how the uneasy truce went on, until captives from Detainment began to be sent to Medical, showing obvious signs of abuse.

I treated four beings with multiple fractures during the last hour of my shift, and was none too pleased by it. For once Reever was in our quarters when I came in, and I let him have it.

"What in God's name is going on in Detainment? Are the centurons playing shockball and using the prisoners for spheres?"

He set out a meal for both of us and gestured to my empty seat. "Tell me about it over dinner."

I wasn't crazy about eating something he'd prepared—he had some very strange taste preferences—but when I saw it was one of my own programmed recipes, I dropped in the chair.

"We had four new patients come in today. Three had compound fractures from severe percussion injuries, and of course they aren't going to tell me a damn thing about how they got them."

I gave him the rest of the details on each case, then finished my vegetable and synpro lasagna, and dialed an after-dinner server of herbal tea for both of us.

"Well?" I asked when he made no comment. "Is there some funny business going on down in Detainment?"

"Two of the escapees have not yet been located, and OverLord TssVar is unhappy with his managing

OverSeer's progress on the case." Reever thought about it. "It is possible someone is interrogating the slaves."

"His managing OverSeer would be the one with the pretty face . . . what's her name? FurreVa?" He sipped his tea and nodded. "Yeah, I could see her beating people to get information."

"If she is doing so, she does not have TssVar's sanction."

That might prove helpful. Getting Alunthri out of Detainment had become a top priority. I went to feed Jenner, who was hungrily prowling around my legs, then cleared the table. "Are you going to tell TssVar, or shall I?"

He set down his server. "After the debacle on Drift Nine, the OverLord has little interest in what you have to say."

"Is that right?" I propped my fists on my hips. "Then you tell him."

"TssVar trusts his centurons to follow his orders." Long fingers thrummed on the table surface. "All I have to offer are your allegations."

"I have plenty of bruised and broken patients to show him."

"They are slaves. He won't believe them." He got up, changed his tunic, and went to the door panel. "Don't meddle with OverSeer FurreVa, Cherijo." And with that, he left.

Good old Reever. Always eager to help out the tyrannized. Callous snake that he was. I thought over everything he'd said, and two facts slowly emerged.

If she is doing so, she does not have TssVar's sanction.
TssVar trusts his centurons to follow his orders.

"Does he?" I gave that some consideration. "Then maybe it's time he found out they don't."

It took half the night, but I managed to program a thermal sensor in the Detainment Area to send me an alarm whenever the ambient temperature significantly dropped, and another in the Interrogation Area to send a signal when the temperature increased.

Bodies generated heat, and took it with them when they moved.

Both alarms went off, one after the other, just as I was dragging myself from the sleeping platform. After dressing at the speed of light, I ran down to Medical.

Since Dchêm-os was on duty, I drafted her to help. "Grab a field case and come with me. We're going down to Detainment."

She took off her headgear. I noted the tooth she'd broken off for my impromptu surgery down in Detainment had almost grown back in. "In accompanying you, I am not interested. Someone else, ask."

"Who's asking? Move your tail and get that medkit together. *Now*," I told her. "Or I'll have you transferred to a sanitation crew for the rest of the trip."

Her tail whipped into a frenzied pattern of slaps. "For this, you will pay, Terran."

Yeah, like everything else. The list got longer every day. "Just shake a paw. We've only got a few minutes." I went to the console and sent three signals.

About nine and a half minutes later we arrived at Detainment. Reever was waiting for us. So was TssVar, who looked at me the way he would a smear on the decking.

"Gentlemen." I adjusted my grip on my case. "Thanks for coming."

"What is this, SsurreVa?" TssVar trudged closer, causing the entire deck to vibrate under my footgear. "No slaves are being tortured."

Low sounds of moaning and sobs echoed down the corridor, along with another set of heavy footsteps, getting progressively louder. "I hate to disagree with you, but . . ."

The surprise on the Hsktskt OverSeer's face would have been hilarious, had she not been dragging a pair of severely beaten League prisoners on each side of her.

"OverLord!" She halted in her tracks, then saw me and bellowed something my headgear wouldn't translate.

Reever took a step toward her, inadvertently placing his body between me and Helen. "Perhaps the OverSeer would care to explain how these slaves came to be in this condition?"

"Yes. Explain, FurreVa."

The OverSeer dropped both men to the deck to come after Reever, and I decided that was my cue. Zella and I edged past the furious Hsktskt and got to the injured men. One was in such bad shape I had to signal for a gurney.

"Nice work," I muttered under my breath as I packed a torn limb to stop the bleeding.

Behind us, Helen of Troy was ranting on about the escapees and how she was going to find them if she had to personally dismember the rest of the prisoners and, if necessary, the *Perpetua* in the process.

TssVar waited until she was through. "You interrogated these slaves without authorization, OverSeer."

"I— yes, OverLord." FurreVa held her bulky form in a stiffly erect pose, then dropped her head back in a bizarre manner. The stance revealed the paler, thinner scales under her jaw.

Baring her throat, I thought. To be ripped out?

"You will be disciplined accordingly. Report to launch bay in one hour."

"Yes, OverLord." The big female stalked off.

I'd done what I could for her victims, so I went back to Reever and TssVar. "I have to perform some minor surgery to repair an arm over there."

"I would know how you learned of this, SsurreVa."

"Oh, you know." I gave Reever a disgusted look. "Slave gossip, patients with multiple fractures, that sort of thing."

"I intended to investigate the matter personally."
My ex-bondmate's lips thinned. "Dr. Torin precipi-
tated my inquiry."

I pointed to the door panel leading to the Detainment Area. "I have a *friend* in there. Alunthri, the
Chakacat. It's been abused because of that friendship,
and needs to be transferred to Medical for comprehensive therapy." That lie sounded very realistic,
even to me.

"I know of this animal. The centurons consider it
extremely dangerous," TssVar said.

Alunthri was proving to be a terrific actor. "It
won't be when I get through with it. Which will
make it only more valuable when we reach Catopsa.
Let me take it to Medical." I held my breath while
he thought about it, then sighed when he nodded.
"Thank you, OverLord."

"Report to launch bay in an hour, Doctor." Off
TssVar went.

The same time Helen had been ordered to report.
I turned to Reever to ask him why, but he'd
disappeared.

One of FurreVa's victims required a substantial infusion of neuroparalyzer before I began piecing back
together his splintered radius. As some patients do,
he got chatty as soon as the medication took effect.

"I'll be okay, right, Doc?" the male told me as I
made the initial incision. He tried to get a look over
the surgical shroud. "Thought he'd tear it off this
time."

"She. OverSeer FurreVa is a she."

"No, not her." He uttered an intoxicated chuckle.
"I know her. What a face. But she's not so bad. She
pulled us out of there the last time, too."

I stopped cutting and lifted my head. "Are you
telling me that the female who was dragging you
back to Detainment didn't interrogate you?"

"No. It was the one with the flat ridges and dirty
teeth."

I finished the work on the battered prisoner and went down to the launch bay. Reever met me at the door.

"I've got to talk to TssVar," I said. "FurreVa lied. She didn't interrogate those prisoners."

He didn't look happy. "She admitted to it. There's nothing you can do now."

I went through the door. "TssVar will listen to— What's going on here?" I walked in, and saw nothing but wall-to-wall lizards. An uneasy foreboding spread inside me, coiling up in my stomach. "Reever? Am I in trouble again?"

"No. Stay back and remain silent," he said as he guided me through the crowd of waiting Hsktskt.

Why would I jump in on anything the beasts were doing? I wondered, then saw FurreVa, the position she was in, and stopped in my tracks. "Hold it. You don't mean they're going to . . ." Foreboding turned into dread. "I want to talk to TssVar. *Now.*"

Reever simply hauled me farther down the line, until we stood a few yards away from TssVar's centurons.

They'd stripped FurreVa down to her scales, and hung her upside-down on a plasteel post, the back of her body facing outward. Only one reason they'd do that.

TssVar entered with deliberate, prolonged formality, pausing to speak to some of the senior beasts before taking a position in front of the post. He didn't look at the upside-down guard; for all he cared she could have been invisible.

Four limbs rose, which brought everyone snapping to attention. "Members of the Faction. OverSeer FurreVa has submitted herself for discipline."

The other Hsktskt hissed and clicked, probably their approval. Reever finally let go of my arm, and I was briefly tempted to stomp on his instep in retaliation. Then TssVar continued and distracted me.

"FurreVa interrogated slaves without approval. No

one may overstep their rank and my authority. Discipline is required. Discipline will be administered."

"What kind of discipline?" I said to Reever, under my breath.

He grabbed me again, this time around the waist. "Shut up."

Someone brought TssVar what I thought at first was an energy emitter. Closer scrutiny made me catch my breath. Reever's arm tightened.

I twisted around to look up at him. "He isn't seriously going to use that thing on her."

"Not another word," Reever said, and held his hand up, evidently ready to clap it over my mouth.

TssVar centered the unit on the deck just in front of FurreVa. I knew what it was—an agricultural separator. Also known as a thresher. I'd seen botanical scientists using them back on K-2. The unit emitted bands of high-energy waves, which, when applied to newly harvested crops, separated the grains and rendered the remaining chaff into small, ground-up matter to be used as mulch.

Applied to the unprotected flesh of a helpless being—

"Five minutes of discipline for each damaged slave," TssVar said.

I forgot Reever's warning and bucked against his arm. "That will cut her to pieces!"

"She is Hsktskt, Cherijo. She will survive," Reever said against my ear. "Do not attempt to interfere."

Five minutes for each prisoner. I'd have to watch that thing slice into FurreVa for a half hour or more. And she hadn't beaten them—she'd saved them.

I didn't interfere. I yelled my head off. "No! Stop it! She didn't hurt them!"

An deadly hush fell over the launch bay, and every pair of yellow eyes in the place swiveled to focus on me.

So did their commander. "HalaVar. Bring the Terran to me."

Reever didn't have to drag me. Just the reverse. He ran after me and hauled me back just before I would have thrown myself at the OverLord.

"She's innocent—you can't do this!"

TssVar went around the post and looked at FurreVa. "Did you interrogate those prisoners without authorization, OverSeer?"

She didn't even hesitate. "Yes, OverLord."

"She's lying!" I fought to break Reever's hold. "TssVar, for God's sake, you'll kill her!"

TssVar activated the unit. "Restrain the doctor, brother." His tongue slid out once, twice. "Ensure she observes the entire discipline."

For the next thirty minutes, Reever held me there and forced me to watch as the thresher slowly and methodically flayed the OverSeer's back.

The displacer bands worked over her like a flail edged with a dozen individual blades, rising and falling. A rhythmic hum vibrated from the base of the unit, one that pulsed against my ears and sent my fingers digging into Reever's forearm.

Scales began to shred. Then the bands cut into the underlying tissue.

At first the Hsktskt made no sound at all. Her bulky body didn't move, either. I thought she'd fallen mercifully unconscious, until the bands falling across her raw flesh made FurreVa twist and jerk.

Bile surged up my throat, over and over. I'd never seen anyone tortured before, so I had no point of reference. My experience as a surgeon was useless; the ghastly scene was an affront to my training and a fisted blow against my humanity.

She'd lied to protect GothVar—but why? Why would she endure this to cover for him?

My outrage made me a minority of one. I jerked my head around, saw the faces of the centurons and the OverLord as they watched the thresher tear into their comrade. No one averted their gaze. No one twitched a muscle.

GothVar stood in the front row. He appeared to be enjoying himself, following the movements of the bands with intense concentration.

Perverted ghoul. Enjoying this butchering session, knowing he should have been up there, taking the punishment.

I lost it halfway through the session, and shrieked something vile at TssVar. Reever clamped a hand over my mouth and kept it there from then on. I sank my teeth into his palm, several times. The taste of blood pooled in my mouth, and I didn't know whether it was mine, or his. I didn't care. All I could do was watch, and pray it would be over soon.

Still the thresher bands rose and fell.

FurreVa started to grunt after each blow. Gobbets of shredded derma hung from her back in long peels. Rivulets of blood ran down her back and shoulders. The shreds became chunks. The rivulets became steady flows.

Ultimately, her grunts became howls.

Toward the end, Reever had to hold me caged in his arms, simply to keep me upright. Tears of rage and helplessness blinded me, but I still heard what I could no longer see clearly. No escaping the gradually weakening shrieks, the thresher's efficient hum, the sound of a body being torn apart. The nauseating smell of blood thickened and changed when the Hsktskt lost control of her bladder and bowels. A moment later, I closed my eyes, and wetness streaked over my cheeks and plopped on Reever's hand.

My conscience immediately attacked. *No. Don't shut it out. Remember this. Remember you made this happen to her.*

I opened my eyes, blinked to clear them, and made myself watch. At last, after an eternity of horror, the hum abruptly ended. TssVar had finally deactivated the unit. By then FurreVa hung loosely in her bonds, unconscious, and bleeding copiously.

The back of her body glistened, raw and tattered.

Slowly Reever let go of me, and I staggered to the nearest disposal unit and vomited as quietly as I could. Behind me, a few of the centurons made repelled sounds.

They could watch a helpless comrade be chewed to pieces, but one Terran having the heaves upset them?

Once my belly settled, I wiped my mouth on my sleeve and headed toward the OverSeer. The clinical part of my brain registered the damage: the thresher had effectively removed all the scales, subderma, and the majority of the upper muscular layer beneath it. Bits and pieces of the Hsktskt's body had fallen in clumps around the base of the post. An ever-widening pool of blood met my footgear.

I bent down to where she could see and hear me, and lifted a numb hand to her carotid. Slow and feeble, her pulse throbbed like a soundless moan against my fingertips. Then I looked up and collided with the clear, cold gaze of the Hsktskt Commander. Beside him, GothVar gave me equal attention.

"She is dead meat," he said, and flicked his tongue toward me. Wanting to taste my fear, my despair, or whatever gave his chemoreceptors a thrill.

"Not yet," I whispered, making an instant pledge. "Not yet."

No one stopped me when I got up and went to the console to signal Medical, or made Reever and two other Hsktskt help me cut her down. The medevac team arrived just as we prepared to lower FurreVa's heavy weight to the deck.

"Lift her up there. On her front, yes, like that," I said, directing the centurons as they placed her onto the grav-unit. I went over to the console again and signaled the duty nurse. "Set up a foam cradle in an isolation room. She's big, so suspend it with a couple of traction rigs." The nurse was inspecting me with visible revulsion. "What?"

"You're covered with—with—" She gestured at my tunic, and I glanced down.

Hsktskt blood and bits of tissue made splotches and stains all down the front off me.

I heaved a sigh. "I'll change. Now, *move it.*"

As we moved FurreVa from launch bay to Medical, I stayed at her side. I didn't need to scan her to know her injuries were life threatening. Then I saw her lift her head and stare up at me.

"Let me die," she said.

"You lied to your commander, and I know it." If I was going to have any chance of saving her, I needed to give her a reason to fight. "So kiss my Terran ass."

Once at Medical, we moved her into the isolation unit and sedated her. I couldn't use skin seal on such massive stretches of flesh, and there wasn't compatible synthetic grafting material available. I'd have to grow new skin and scales for her from her own cells—the database indicated her body would automatically reject any live donor tissue—but for now it was vital I simply keep her alive.

Working on the Hsktskt over the next several hours wasn't pleasant. The mess and smell were, well, without parallel. Two nurses got sick and left. Interestingly enough, Pmohhi, one of the nurses I'd rescued from FurreVa's clutches, stayed. Vlaav the Saksonan intern stuck at my side, too—although his lumpy skin turned a number of interesting colors during the treatment.

"They said you watched them do this," Vlaav said when we were finished sealing off torn vessels.

"Yeah." I changed my gloves for the fourth time. "It wasn't like I had a choice."

The nurse shifted, peering down at the big female with a queer expression. "I would have liked to watch." Then she did something even worse.

She laughed.

The front of her tunic got in my hands. Next thing I knew, she was jammed between me and a monitoring unit, and I was in her face.

"You think this is funny? Want to volunteer next time, do a little whipping yourself?" She shook her head, terrified. I shoved her toward the door. "Get out."

Pmohhi fled. Dchêm-os appeared a few moments later as replacement.

"A mess, this one is." Dark fur rose slightly around her muzzle as she stopped inspecting the patient and started on me. "Unkind to Pmohhi, you were."

"She'll live," I said. So I was snarling. The shrew could relate to that. "Get that setup tray over here."

We treated FurreVa much the same way we would a third-degree burn patient. Fragments of pulverized osteodermic matter had to be removed, then wide swaths of aerated antibacterial dressings applied over her torso and legs. I annotated what areas would require deep skin-flap transplants, and hoped there was enough flesh left on her lower abdomen and appendages to harvest what I needed.

"God, I feel like I'm piecing her together with tweezers," I said as I stripped my mask off and finished my notes.

"May I assist with the plastic surgery?" Vlaav asked.

He'd been reading FurreVa's chart over my shoulder. "Why? You want some cheap thrills, too?"

"No." His pocked, sallow face sobered. "I would like to comprehend your methods, and learn the techniques."

I carefully set down the chart and considered his solemn expression. It appeared I had a potential cutter on my hands. "Fair enough."

The damage to the back of her skull gave me justification for a full scan series, and I confirmed what

I'd suspected—someone had in the recent past tried to split her head in two with some sort of heavy, bladed weapon. The articular and quadrate bones of her jaw were crushed, with additional comprehensive damage to the structure of the dentary plate.

"See that?" I showed Vlaav the readings. "Good thing her species has a kinetic skull, or she would have starved to death. Among other things."

My main concern was the damage to the cerebral hemisphere. Reptilian life forms had small brains to begin with, and judging from localized damage, this female had lost more than twenty percent of her higher functions. That particular area of the Hsktskt brain, I discovered, also controlled personality.

"No wonder she's such a harpy."

It amazed me that she'd lived through the experience. I also discovered another, urgent reason FurreVa and I needed to have a little chat when she woke up.

If she woke up.

At last Vlaav and I shifted her to the foam cradle, which groaned under her weight, but held. I instructed two orderlies to reinforce the frame and put the intern on constant monitor.

Dchêm-os came out after cleaning up the treatment room to inquire what to do about Alunthri, who had been transferred from Detainment.

I was covered with a fresh coat of Hsktskt blood, and in no state to greet my highly sensitive friend. "Give me a minute to clean up."

I noticed Shropana's berth was empty on my way to the cleanser and grabbed his chart. "Who discharged this patient?"

One of the nurses gave me a wary look. "He discharged himself, as soon as we brought the Chaka-cat in."

Which, when I thought about Shropana's basic wimp capacity, made perfect sense. "Have him report for follow-up in the morning."

In the clean-up room, I was forced to strip down

to my skin and sluice the stains away with a sprayer. Diluted maroon blood ran down and vanished into the duct as I watched without blinking.

You made this happen.

I'd wanted the ruthless Hsktskt to get a taste of her own brutality, but not like this. Not knowing I was the cause. And my guilt had only worsened, knowing what she'd been hiding from everyone. The damage to her head would require substantial work—comprehensive bone grafts, cartilage trans-plants, and possibly open cranial repairs. . . .

I could heal her.

Mulling over exactly how I'd fix Helen's face kept me so preoccupied I never heard the door panel slide shut. Something grabbed me from behind, and I shrieked in astonishment.

Four very sharp teeth, one slightly shorter than the others, clamped on the back of my neck. "Finish this now, Doctor, we will."

Under ordinary circumstances I might have been afraid, even terrified by the assault. After watching FurreVa's discipline, however, I virtually welcomed it.

Let her tear my throat out and get it over with now.

Who really cared, anyway? It wasn't like anyone would *miss* me. Maggie and Kao were dead. Reever belonged to the Hsktskt, Dhreen had sold me out, and Alunthri would be much better off without our friendship. Joren was safer without me on it, as was my adopted family.

There was no one left who needed me.

What about Jenner? Vlaav? FurreVa?

Self-disgust instantly boiled up into the crater of shame. No, standing there and letting this homicidal shrew gnaw through my jugular wasn't an option. Not while I still had something to love, someone to teach, and a new debt to pay.

I tugged the hand sprayer up, turned the applica-tor and blasted Dchêm-os directly in the face. That knocked her off and sent her hurtling to the deck. She landed close enough for me to step on her broad, flat tail.

"Zel, this is really getting old." I could have cheerfully drowned her in the cleaner unit. No, it wasn't worth having to scrub all over again afterward. "Tell me something. Why is it so extremely vital that you *personally* kill me?"

She jerked free with such violence that she left several inches of her tail under my footgear. Her vibrissae dripped as she snarled at me. "Never stop, I will."

"I guess you won't." If it hadn't been so sad, it would have been funny. Keeping the sprayer trained on her, I picked up the piece of her tail, which was still twitching, and held it out. "Here. You detached this."

She snatched the stump and scuttled back out through the door panel. I pulled on a fresh tunic and went out to examine Alunthri.

The Chakacat wasn't in any of the berths, but it didn't take long for me to locate it. Someone had put it in a live cargo unit, from which sounds of feline displeasure were plainly audible. I released a sigh of disgust and went to let my friend out of its cage.

I crouched down next to the air slits and fumbled with the hatch lock. "Your performances have gotten pretty convincing, pal."

"Cherijo." Whiskers sprang through the narrow opening. "Is it safe to release me?"

Probably not, I thought, and my heart dropped a little farther into the black pit of depression. "You'll need to keep up the feral act, okay?"

"Of course."

I got the hatch open, and an emaciated body crawled out from the carrier. Alunthri was beyond filthy, covered with lacerations and missing patches of fur.

I sat back on my heels in shock, then took a deep

breath, and began examining it. "Who did this to you?"

"The League Colonel. Some of the others." Alunthri tried in vain to bathe some of the grime from its fur with a few swipes of its tongue. "I was compelled to defend myself."

One of the nurses approached tentatively. "Over there," I said, jerking my head toward a severe trauma room as I lifted my friend in my arms. "Prepare the berth for maximum restraint." Against Alunthri's ear I whispered, "Sorry. Have to make this look good."

I carried Alunthri in and helped the nurse treat its injuries, then stayed until it fell into a natural sleep.

No, I had all kinds of reasons to stay alive.

After I made the appropriate chart notes and mopped up my face, I went to talk to FurreVa. I took the precaution of chasing off the staffers before I sat next to the Hsktskt's foam cradle. She was barely conscious, but the sight of my face seemed to arouse her.

"You."

"Me." I sniffed back the last of my tears and scooted a little closer. "We've treated your injuries as best we can, for now. Tomorrow we'll have enough cloned tissue to start repairs on your back. Why did you lie about abusing those prisoners?"

"I want another doctor," FurreVa said, her mutilated tongue stump darting sluggishly out, then in.

Aware that what I had to talk to her about couldn't be overheard by anyone, I slipped off my headgear, then typed a question on her chart display. When I finished, I programmed it to translate my words into Hsktskt, then turned it so she could read what I'd written:

Do you know anyone else who will voluntarily agree to deliver the young?

FurreVa read the display. Her lower eyelids slid up until only a narrow rim of yellow showed. "Have you . . . informed . . . OverLord TssVar . . . of these . . . test results?"

I shook my head, then typed, *Why have you been concealing your pregnancy?*

"Unauthorized . . ."

I typed as fast as I could. *I can't judge how far along you are, but the young appear healthy and close to full development.* I'd only dealt with this situation once before, on K-2. Vicious, fully developed beings from the moment of birth, Hsktskt infants acted on one instinct only—to attack anything that moved.

"Abort . . ."

I can't perform an abortion, even if I wanted to. In your condition, it would kill you. When are you due to deliver?

Her head drooped into the cradle. "Not . . . soon."

I'm not even sure you'll survive this punishment. Which you shouldn't have been given in the first place.

"Then all . . . will be . . . resolved."

That wasn't an alternative. *I'll help you, if I can. In return, I want you to agree to allow me to perform reconstructive surgery on your face.*

She made a low, clicking sound, and tried to touch the scarred portion of her head. "Reconstruct . . . this?"

I think I can repair the damage. Will you let me do it?

Before she slipped into unconsciousness, FurreVa glared at me, than gave a single nod.

I wiped out the display record of what I'd typed, then sat with her and wondered how long "not soon" would be.

Helen of Troy proved to be as tough as a thousand Terrans put together. She survived the beating and began to heal.

It wasn't going to be that easy for me. I put in extra shifts, sat beside her berth whenever I had a spare moment, and devoted most of my waking thoughts on how I could repair the damage I'd indirectly done. It didn't erase the guilt I felt, but I wasn't sure I wanted it to. I suspected it was one of the few things that kept me from jumping out of a pressure lock.

Remember, you made this happen.

Cloning Hsktskt cells proved something of a challenge. The inner malpighian layer secreted the outer scaly derma, and also developed bony osteodermic nodules during adolescence. Once destroyed as thoroughly as FurreVa's had been, additional glandular boosters were necessary to simulate the appropriate hormonal changes required.

My Saksonan intern sputtered as he read the med schedule. "Why must we create a state of artificial puberty?"

"To regrow the subdermal nodules. She needs the support." I pulled him over to a console and keyed up a dimensional image of the Hsktskt dermis. "See these osteoderms? They reinforce the skeleton and protect the spinal cord, especially around the occipital condyle, where the skull attaches to the first vertebra. Without them, she's a walking bowl of jelly."

"She could wear an exterior brace instead," the intern said.

I raised my brows. "You want to be the one to suggest that to her?"

Vlaav made no further objections.

The trick was going to be administering the synthetic hormones without sending FurreVa into premature labor, I thought as I worked out the first phase of the grafting procedure. She had been so careful to hide her condition for months—but why? Surely violating one, rather unrealistic regulation prohibiting pregnancy wasn't that big a deal.

Yet I couldn't discuss the details complicating FurreVa's condition with my skeptical colleague, or anyone, for that matter. There was always the possibility that breaking a regulation meant more discipline, and she couldn't go another round with the thresher and live.

I'd done enough damage already.

CHAPTER SEVEN

No More Rescues

I got my answer as to why FurreVa was so determined to conceal her condition when I came off duty
one evening a week later and found Reever waiting
for me in his quarters. (I wasn't calling them ours.
Ever.) After a double shift in Medical, I was weary
and in no mood to spar with my Lord and Over-
Master.

Naturally, he was in a chatty mood.

"You have been on duty for sixteen stanhours.
Why?"

"I've been busy." I poked at my meal and sipped
from a server of strong orange pekoe. "FurreVa
needed another four dermal flap transplants, some of
Alunthri's cuts have become infected and Shropana
had to be dragged out of Detainment for his weekly
cardiac scans." I put down my utensils. "Guess I lost
track of the time."

"I will allocate more League captives to work in
Medical."

I snorted. "Please. I have enough problems as it
is." Then it occurred to me—this was the perfect op-

portunity to get more data on the female Hsktskt's dilemma. "FurreVa refuses to allow any of the male staffers to touch her, and she's petrified most of the female nurses. Are there any other female Hsktskt I could borrow to deal with her?" And, possibly, shed some light on this pregnancy taboo.

"Not on the *Perpetua*."

"There aren't many females to begin with, are there?" He shook his head. "How come?"

"Traditionally Hsktskt females remain in domestic roles on the homeworld, or serve in the civilian hierarchy." Reever allowed Jenner to jump up on his lap and absently stroked him. My perfidious cat purred and butted against Reever's hand, blissfully ignoring my frown.

"I guess it would be a problem for them to be out with the raiders, considering the nature of their species' childbirth." I gave a very real shudder as I recalled the ordeal I'd gone through delivering TssVar's young on K-2.

Reever told me exactly what I wanted to know. "Females who serve as Faction forces are prohibited from any reproductive activity."

"No sex?" I forced a laugh. This was the last subject I wanted to discuss with Reever, but I had to know how much trouble FurreVa was in. "That's pretty grim." I thought of TssVar's impromptu visit to K-2. "How did the OverLord's mate get away with being a raider and having quints? He bend the rules for her?"

"UgessVa concealed her condition from TssVar. Upon learning she was in labor, he removed her from the ship and brought her to Kevarzangia Two. It saved her life."

He needed a little reminder. "Hey, *I* saved her life."

"Had her pregnancy been discovered, UgessVa would have been put to death."

"Just for breaking the no-sex rule?" The stakes just

went from high to terminal. I tried my hardest to sound blasé. "It wouldn't be that hard to come up with a few maternity uniforms, would it?"

"If the female delivers a brood, she endangers herself and her entire command." Reever set a disgruntled Jenner down and got to his feet. "However, if she evades detection and successfully delivers, by tradition she is accorded the rank of nurturer and will not be executed." He came toward me. "Why do you ask?"

I was ready for that. "Just wondering why TssVar's mate wasn't with him now. It must be difficult to be separated." I got up and glided past him toward the prep unit.

He followed me. "Hsktskt do not form emotional bonds with their mates."

"No wonder they adopted you," I said as I programmed another server of tea. Reever's hands settled on my shoulders, and I went immobile. "What?"

His breath stirred the hair by my temple. "Do you want to have a child?"

He'd totally misinterpreted me. Not a bad thing, under the circumstances, but it still made me instantly, irrationally furious.

"Hardly." I thumped my server down and scalded the back of my hand. "Ow!" I ran cold water over the red patch, conscious of the fact he had moved his hands from my shoulders to my waist. "Forget about it, okay?"

"It is a natural, biological need." His palms slid over the lower part of my abdomen. And that felt horribly good. "I could give you all the children you desire."

"Yeah, and you could get a broken jaw in the process." I pivoted, trying to get out of his embrace, but that merely made matters worse. "Want one now?" I said, an inch from his face.

"You like my touch well enough in the night."

My cheeks burned. It was true, I'd woken up

nearly every night for the last week in Reever's arms, my limbs twined around him. I rolled away each time, but not before feeling his arousal. He'd done nothing, said nothing about it, but I still felt supremely embarrassed.

"Maybe that's the only time I can stand to touch you. When I'm unconscious."

"I think not." His long, clever fingers brushed up my throat and over my compressed lips. "I will make you pregnant, Cherijo."

For some reason, that was the most erotic thing Reever had ever said to me. And I was *not* going to whimper with pleasure, no matter how briskly my blood was pumping through my veins. "Thanks, but I'll pass. I'm not the maternal type anyway."

His breath swept over my face, warm and fragrant from the tea he'd just finished. The edge of his thumb slowly traced a crescent over my cheekbone. "You want me to touch you."

It was so tempting. My body throbbed and ached with unrelieved needs. So easy to give in to that, to take what he offered. It had been so long. . . .

Something dug into my skin as he urged me closer, and I looked down to see what it was. The OverMaster insignia from Reever's uniform. Reever's *Hsktskt* uniform.

Oh, God, what was I doing?

Even when I lost Kao, it didn't hurt like this.

I wanted him. I hated him. I also loved him. Still loved him, in spite of what had happened. Loved him desperately, passionately, hopelessly. Maybe I'd never told him how much, or how deeply, but the feelings were indisputable.

And he was tearing what remained of my heart to shreds. Slowly. Ripping a little more out of it each time we were together. Each time I saw the real monster beneath the Terran skin.

The monster was as cold and Hsktskt as if he'd been born with scales.

I acknowledged the pain of that. I still loved the monster. I would always love him. For a moment I let myself grieve over that foolish, unwise choice that had never been my choice at all.

"No." Words from the past saved me. *His* words. "No more mindless seductions, OverMaster."

Reever had said the same thing to me, back on the *Sunlace*. Of course at the time we'd both been drugged with aggression-enhancers by a psychotic bent on seeking revenge, so naturally things had gotten out of hand.

For a moment his hands tightened; then he let go of me and moved away. "Eventually you will yield."

It sounded as though he was talking to himself, not me. "I'm going to bed." And, just in case he had any ideas, "To *sleep*."

He left me alone for some time, and when he did come to bed, I didn't crawl all over him—but only because I laid awake for hours, contemplating the upper deck. Reever had a very restful night, and was still sleeping peacefully when I left for work.

I bet he wouldn't wake up with a migraine, either. Men.

My headache escalated as soon as I walked into Medical and confronted a semihysterical cluster of nurses. Once I ordered them to stop babbling and pull themselves together, one calmed enough to inform me about what had happened. Somehow, right smack in the middle of swing shift, two seriously injured patients had mysteriously vanished.

"They couldn't have walked out of here, Doctor," the nurse told me as she handed me their charts.

I reviewed the case notes. One had been in a suspension rig for spinal injuries, the other immobilized to prevent dislodging impacted bone ends in his fractured leg.

"No, not in their condition." I'd performed a surgical reduction on the second male, whose badly set femur had resulted in partial osteonecrosis. "This one's hip would have crumbled, he'd have fallen on his face after the first step." I switched off the last chart and regarded the distressed staffers. "Well? Were they removed by the Hsktskt?"

No one made a peep.

"Come on, someone *had* to see something. You weren't stuffing your faces or taking a nap, were you?"

One of the residents slithered away. The nurses scuffled their footgear and looked humiliated.

I got loud. *"You were all sleeping?"* They didn't have to say a word. My hands slammed the charts down on the nearest available surface. "I don't believe this. What is the *matter* with you people?" I didn't wait for an answer, but went to the main console to signal my Lord and Keeper. Only to discover that all signals were routed through a centuron first.

"What do you want, slave?"

To have you under my lascalpel for five minutes, I thought. "I want to speak to Reev— OverMaster HalaVar."

"Stand by."

I stood by, seething. The staff got suddenly very busy. Good for them, because I was ready to detonate. Seeing the image of Reever in uniform at the Command Center only turned the screws boring into my temples.

"Cherijo." He was pondering some data pad in his hand and didn't look at me. "Assemble on level eighteen," he said to some lizard standing there, then glanced at the screen. "I am rather busy at the moment."

Like I worried. "Too bad, OverMaster. Two of my patients are missing. What are you going to do about it?"

He glanced up. "Were they male?"

Were they? I glanced at the charts. "Yeah, they *are*."

"Report to level eighteen at once."

"I don't have time to—"

He terminated the signal.

Level eighteen was a remote storage area, seldom accessed by the crew except during loading and unloading procedures. Seven open-paneled sections had been filled with crates of redundant tech, stanissue crew gear, and other nonessential equipment. A team of centurons lead by Reever intercepted me as I got off the lift.

"Did you find them?" I paced Reever as he headed toward the end of the level access corridor.

"I don't know." He handed me the data pad he was carrying, then gave the guards orders to search every section. Only the last compartment had a closed door panel, I noted. "Do you recognize the chemical composite listed there?"

I read the list: hydrogen, oxygen, nitrogen, calcium, and phosphorous. Since the elements were listed in minute, trace amounts, they could have represented anything from a bowl of soup to hunk of plastic. The levels of hydrogen and nitrogen registered higher than the other three signatures, that was all.

"Where did you take this reading?"

"A higher concentration of the composite registered on the ship's enviromonitors." Reever activated the light panel for the last section and looked inside the panel viewer. "From in there."

Dusty and packed with junk, the storage compartment was completely silent. I would have hit the access panel and gone in to have a look, but Reever held me back. "Wait for the centurons."

"Why?" I didn't like the look in his eyes. "What are you so worried about?"

He didn't respond, and two guards came up to flank us. With a frustrated exhalation, I opened the panel and stepped inside the compartment.

Immediately the smell hit me. So sharp and dense

my eyes watered and my lungs burned. I backed out, my hand over my nose and mouth.

"Seal the room. Now." Once the panel was secured, I spent a minute coughing to clear the horrible odor from my nose and throat. "There's high levels of ammonia in there."

Reever programmed the room controls to discharge the poisonous air and replace it entirely, which took a few minutes. I wiped the tears away with my sleeve and swallowed against the searing sensation lingering in my throat.

"We'll need breathers if we go back in," I said. "It could be leaking from a storage tank." Although why the League would *want* to store liquid ammonia was beyond me. It had been used as an emergency coolant once, but had been replaced with much safer biofreon gas nearly a century ago.

One of the centurons produced the masklike units that would allow us to breathe without getting poisoned, and after we slipped them on, we went in. The interior lighting panel wasn't working, so we had to depend on Reever's emitter to illuminate the way. The stacks of crates formed a sharp-edged labyrinth, through which we walked slowly. I kept my eyes to the deck, looking for puddles, which is why I found the remains.

"Hold it. Over here." I shuffled back a step and dropped down, waving at Reever to aim his light toward my feet. A small pile of what looked like melted chalk lay in a solidified lump. I scanned it and came up with the same chemical composite. Only this time I registered something else—deoxyribonucleic acid. "There are a few viable DNA patterns in this. Reever. This was a *person*."

He told the centurons to search through the remainder of the compartment, then knelt down beside me. "Can you identify the victim?"

My scanner couldn't, but the main database array back in Medical might be able to. "I think so." I signaled the shift resident and had him send a recovery kit down to us. The remains were in such a bizarre state that nothing in my experience explained how they'd gotten that way. "What kind of weapon does this to a living being?"

"I don't know." Reever got up, and took an air sample before removing his breather. "The levels are within safety range now. Could the ammonia be used to do this?"

I could still smell it when I took off mine. "Ammonia alone, no. A few species' derma are highly sensitive to it, but not to the point of it melting them upon contact."

"Melting them?"

"I'm not sure how it happened, but that's the result." I gazed at the small, sad, white pile. "All that's left here is skeletal residue."

My postmortem only revealed two facts. One, the DNA from the remains didn't match the profile of either missing patient. Two, I was right; all that remained of the victim was a badly degraded lump of calcium and phosphorous that had once been solid bone.

I made my report directly to Reever after cleaning up.

"I want to know what happened to this person, and how the hell someone got two people out of Medical without anyone noticing," I said after I'd gone over the particulars. He nodded. "And just how did you know the missing patients were both male?"

He didn't answer, and abruptly terminated the signal.

Over the next week I spent what time I could scouring the database, but came up with no answers. Then I found myself with a whole new set of problems.

FurreVa responded well to the various skin flap

transplants and grafts I performed over her back, but the hormonal therapy was making her a bit difficult to deal with. Apparently Hsktskt adolescence is even more stress inducing than the same period in Terrans. She got loud, obnoxious, and routinely sent the nurses into panicked hysterics. Eventually I had to threaten to reveal my confidential knowledge to get her to settle down.

Either you stop hitting and swearing at the nurses, I typed, *or I'm going straight to TssVar and tell him I'm going to soon need seven crates of diapers—and why.*

"I should have snapped your spine when I had the chance," FurreVa said, turning her face toward the wall panel.

I adjusted her monitors and withstood the urge to slap her unscarred cheek. "I know exactly how you feel."

Alunthri's condition had gone from pathetic to nearly normal. Whenever one of the staff came to check on it, it continued the wildcat act, roaring, spitting, and fighting its berth restraints. Restraints I had rigged so it could release itself whenever it pleased.

Conscious that it needed more than a safe place, I had the nurse program the isolation console to play continuous loops of soothing Terran music, from classic Mozart to the B.B. King age of blues. I also altered the interior controls in order to bathe Alunthri in cool, pastel-tinted light.

Although I'd tried to keep the postmortem report quiet, it was inevitable the staff would gain access to the records. Too many of them had seen the victim's remains, and rumors began to fly.

It didn't help when I finally identified the remains as one of the original escapees from Detainment.

Colonel Shropana decided the circumstances made excellent ammunition, and he didn't waste any time in using it against me. At first he restricted himself to snide remarks about how no one had disappeared until I'd left isolation, or how convenient it was that I was in charge of injured, helpless prisoners.

Things got progressively worse. Patients began watching me with intent, leery gazes. Nurses followed up behind me, checking everything I did on rounds. I was having an argument over proper diagnostic procedure with one of the junior residents when it finally got out of hand.

"Do not listen to her," Shropana said, interrupting us from his berth. The surrounding inpatients became very quiet. "The Terran traitor will only murder more of us."

I told the resident to take the rest of the shift off, tried to ignore the voices, and went to perform my rounds. Patients started cringing or shouting at me whenever I approached. To complicate things further, all the nurses collected at the prep units and went on a mass beverage break.

"Look." I set down my charts and addressed the entire ward. Better be up front and blunt. "I didn't kill anyone. I'm a doctor. We're not allowed to do that."

"Crew members have been disappearing since you became Medical Primary," the Colonel said, his face an ugly purple color. At the side of his berth, a monitor began bleeping. "You turn them over to the monsters, to conceal your own incompetence and better your own situation!"

Patril always gave me such tempting ideas. I didn't have time to act on this one, as half of my ward began trying to leave their berths, a few with the assistance of the staffers.

I was shouting and wrestling with a patient who had tangled herself in monitor leads when an emergency signal from Command came in over the main console. "Medical Primary, report to level twelve immediately."

"I'm a little *occupied* right now!" I yelled back.

Whoever manned the Command console was nice

enough to send an armed detachment of guards to Medical. Once they had intimidated the frightened patients back into their berths, I went to Shropana. Ignoring his mouth was easy, doing the same with his readings wasn't.

"You are bordering on full arrest," I said as I pushed him back and strapped him down. He was so weak I had no problem handling him. "If you don't calm down, you *will* have a heart attack and you *will* die."

He didn't believe me—until the resident shoved in my direction saw his monitors, and started spouting the same thing.

I injected him with digitalizine—the irony of that didn't escape me—and instructed a nurse to run another full cardiac series. Before I could do anything else, one of the centurons grabbed me and dragged me out of Medical.

"Hey. Hey!" I couldn't get his attention. "I've got patients to see to back there!"

I was manhandled all the way to level twelve, where a full squad of lizards had a section of the corridor blocked off. They were wearing protective gear and looking quite grim. The guard hauling me shoved me toward the temporary barrier.

"Deal with her."

I pushed through the centurons and climbed over the four-foot panel. "Her" turned out to be FurreVa, who was on her back ruining all my transplantation work right in the center of the deck. She saw me, but still lifted a pulse rifle and fired it.

I ducked and swore. "Don't shoot!" I kept crouched over as I moved forward. "I'm here to help you!"

She fired three more times, but it was obvious she wasn't going to hit me unless I took the end of the rifle and pressed it against my chest. Her eyes appeared clouded and unfocused. Her abdomen swelled and bulged.

Mother of All Houses, I thought. Not *now*.

"OverSeer, put down the gun."

"Terran?" FurreVa's rifle sagged as she raised her head and finally recognized me. "Terran . . . the brood . . . the brood comes . . . too early."

Yes, they were definitely doing that, judging by the condition of her oviductal flaps. I looked back at the waiting centurons, all of who had trained their weapons on me. "I need some incubation units and a nurse to help me."

One of the Hsktskt threw a heavy storage container over the barrier at me. It was an empty alloy box with a sturdy-locking mechanism. "Put them in that."

"I can't. They're premature, you dimwit, they need specialized equipment." I watched the lizards exchange significant glances, but did nothing. FurreVa screeched as her belly rolled from within. "Okay, either you go *get* what I need"—I picked up FurreVa's rifle and pointed it at them—"or I do the shooting for her."

One of the Hsktskt disappeared. The others gave me nasty scowls. I kept the weapon up and on them as I knelt beside my patient.

"Why didn't you tell me you were in labor? I might have been able to suppress it." I didn't wait for an answer but rolled her to her side. Her back was bleeding freely. "Nice work. You've ruined half of my grafts, too."

"One of the young . . . emerged," she said, then writhed under my hands. "Beware . . . of it."

"It's loose?" I jumped up and scanned the corridor. Nothing in sight. No wonder they'd put up a barrier and gotten the rifles out. "Have you seen it?"

"It will not . . . attack . . . if you stay . . . close to me," she said, and groaned again.

So I could just sit back and relax? Not a chance. "Listen, Helen, I've done this before. The little darling *love* to attack soft-skinned, warm-blooded doctors who should have minded their own damn business."

She stopped moaning and lifted her disfigured head. "Helen?"

"Never mind." One of her oviduct flaps opened wider, and the curve of a miniature, sac-covered Hsktskt skull bulged out. I had no choice but to deliver it. I grabbed the storage container, shoved it next to FurreVa, then cradled the infant's crown in my hands. "On the next pain, push as hard as you can."

She did, and bellowed with maternal agony. Loud enough to make my eardrums compress.

The baby Hsktskt didn't pop out, but slid into my palms still enveloped by its embryonic sac. I guessed like most reptiles it was the first thing they ate after birth, so I merely tore a hole to check its airway, and placed the entire bloody mass in the alloy box. The infant coughed a few times, then went to work on the sac with its tiny, sharp teeth.

I should have performed a more thorough eval on the baby, but FurreVa clamped a limb around my waist and dragged me around. "More . . . come."

"Hooray." I checked her vitals with my scanner and delivered the next infant. "I can't put them together, they'll try to eat each other." Holding the sac in my arms, I glanced at the fascinated centurons. "Hey! Where's my equipment?"

Nurse Dchêm-os and two interns appeared a moment later, pushing a cluster of portable incubator units. Before I could yell out a warning, they crossed the barrier. At once something small and lethal dropped down on them from the upper deck.

"Here." I handed FurreVa the second struggling infant, who was already tearing free of the sac. "Bond for a minute. And whatever you do, *don't push*."

One of Zella's ears was half gone, and the infant was busily gnawing at an intern's throat when I got to them. I shoved the nurse to one side and grabbed the still-damp Hsktskt baby by its thin torso.

She was far too small and showing signs of respiratory distress, but her teeth worked splendidly. I got her as far as the incubator unit when she sank her teeth into my forearm. I shrieked. She kicked free and jumped to the deck to land on all sixes. A moment later she was over the barrier and down the corridor, with half of the centurons in hot pursuit.

I'd never dropped an infant before, but I couldn't exactly feel terrible about this one.

"Terran!" FurreVa still held her baby, but another had emerged halfway out her flap and was snapping at its sibling's little tail.

"Coming." I checked the intern, whose throat was a bloody mess, to make sure he'd survive. He would. The other intern was unconscious. Zel cowered when I reached for her.

I didn't have time to indulge her. "If you can knock out your own tooth, you can handle a chewed-on ear. Come on."

I delivered the fourth infant, which was in better shape than the others, and placed it in the incubator at once. Zella managed to do the same with the one FurreVa held. All that was left to do was transfer the first from the storage container to the unit, then deliver the last three.

After a minute with no further progress in the delivery, I scanned the Hsktskt OverSeer. She was panting and exhausted, but no longer experiencing active labor.

I had to tell her why.

"FurreVa. We've got three of them safe. The centurons will get the other one." I didn't want to upset her, but she had to know. "The remaining three young in your body are dead."

She turned her head and made a sound of grief.

I placed a hand on her scarred face and made her look at me. "We have to do this together. I want you to push when I tell you to, and let me take care of them. Okay?"

Delivering the stillborn proved a grim, silent task. Two were perfectly formed, but far too small. The last was huge, but from my scans possessed a congenital heart defect, which had caused the infant to die in the womb some time ago. The resulting toxic reaction within the mother's body explained the premature labor.

Unlike TssVar's mate, FurreVa wouldn't be naming this one after me.

"Let me look upon them."

Carefully I presented each one to their mother, allowing her to hold them before gently taking them from her. I carefully placed the bodies in the abandoned storage container, then attended to the cleanup.

"All right." I looked at my ravaged medical team. "Let's move them to Medical."

I stopped by Reever's quarters for a clean tunic on the way back to Medical. As soon as I stepped inside, the yowls and crashing sounds made me snap out an order for lights.

"What's going on in"—something large and solid whizzed past my face, and I ducked—"here?"

The tableau before me bordered on absolutely ludicrous. Jenner stood perched on top of the garment storage unit, his tail and back swelling with stiff, raised fur. He was peering over the edge of one side and yowling furiously.

I saw some League footgear sticking out, kicking and jerking, and strode over to confront the intruder. A familiar spine-covered being was cornered between the storage unit and the wall panel. The object of Jenner's displeasure paid no attention to me as he busily wrestled with something smaller, scaly, and quite determined to rip out his throat.

"Lieutenant Wonlee?" Then I saw what he was

clutching between his talons. "God." I looked around for my medical case. "Whatever you do, don't let go of it."

"I have . . . no intentions . . . of doing . . . so. . . ." He had to keep dodging the hungry, snapping miniature jaws.

I noted with approval that he was trying to hold FurreVa's missing infant as far away from his spine plates as possible. Then I spotted my case shoved under a chair, grabbed, and dumped the contents on the deck.

Easing the Hsktskt infant from Wonlee's sharp claws proved no simple task. A few minor lacerations later, I wrenched the baby free, thrust it into my case, and snapped the lid shut.

"There." Panting, I pushed a handful of hair from my eyes before I went to the console and reported that I'd captured the last of the infants. Then I turned to address the Lieutenant. "How did you get in here?"

"Ventilation shaft." He pointed to a small open hatch on the upper deck. "I've been using them to collect reconnaissance information for Major Devrak."

"Really." I wondered what else they'd been using the shafts for. Wonlee held out his arms and began trying to coax Jenner down from his perch. "Um, I don't think he's going to come to you."

"No, he's not." Wonlee dropped his clawed hands and gave my pet a disgruntled glower. "Ungrateful creature. I saved his life, you know."

"Did you?" I picked up the case, which was rocking back and forth from the furious struggles within. "Any particular reason why? I can't imagine it was out of fondness for me."

"I came here to . . . talk to you." Wonlee straightened his tunic.

I'd already noticed the outline of a displacer pistol standing out under his tunic. "Your nose is getting longer, Lieutenant." He gave me a puzzled frown, and I tightened my grip on the case. "You came here to kill me."

"All right." He folded his arms. "Originally, I was ordered to come here to kill you."

"Maybe next time, huh?" I tucked the case under one arm, shielding it with my body, and backed toward the door panel. "Thanks again for saving my cat."

"Wait. We need your help."

"Is that right?" My brows rose. "Why would you need help from a traitorous Terran beast-lover like me?"

He averted his gaze. "Doctor, we're going to arrive at the slave-depot soon. Many of the crew are injured, and if the slavers decide we're not worth selling . . ."

The Hsktskt would have a cookout. The irony of the situation wasn't lost on me, either. "Let me see if I follow. Major Devrak considered me unworthy of sharing the same oxygen with you people, and sent you here to assassinate me, but now you'd like me to treat the injured crew members so they'll pass slaver inspection. Have I got this right?"

He had the grace to look ashamed, then nodded.

I was tempted to tell him where to shove his weapon, then I sighed.

"I'll see what I can do." I opened the door panel, checked the corridor, then gestured toward the hatch. "You'd better crawl back there before you're missed. And do something with that pistol before they find it on you."

He patted the weapon, gave me a grin, then hoisted himself up through the narrow opening.

I thought about Wonlee's earnest request as I made my way back to Medical. Were the League prisoners in such bad shape? Shropana had likely poisoned everyone with his lies, and the sick or injured might have been too afraid to report for treatment.

Maybe I'd just *let* Patril have that heart attack.

FurreVa was back in her foam cradle and being assessed by Vlaav when I came in and placed the last of her infants into the incubator array. I did a quick scan on the babies and found them in tolerable condition.

"Schedule surfactum treatments for all of them," I told the Saksonan when he came over to report.

"Those require induction of an endotracheal tube." Vlaav peered at the infants' glittering teeth and audibly gulped. "Do I *have* to do that to these creatures?"

"If you want to create the proper spaces in the bronchial tubes and aeviolii, yeah, you do." I adjusted the incubator arrays to keep the internal temperatures warm and dry. "After you tube them, set the respirators to provide continuous positive airway pressure, so their lungs won't collapse."

"You'd better have a look at the female. The graft work has sustained considerable damage."

"Wean them off the surfactum once the lung scans clear. Remember to use gentle shaking if they experience bouts of free-breathing apnea," I told him as I cleaned up. "If apnea persists, we're going to have to keep them tubed."

Before I could go and check their mother, a familiar figure stepped forward to block my path.

I had no more patience, not even a millispec left. "What do you want, OverCenturon?"

"You have been wounded." He nodded toward my arm, still oozing blood from where the Hsktskt infant had taken a bite.

"So?"

He reached out and ripped the sleeve of my tunic completely off. Not to bandage it, of course. He jerked my arm around to display the wound. Beneath which should have been a PIC. "You have removed your identification."

"No, I didn't." I glanced around wildly. The medical staff couldn't help me. Maybe I could get to a console. "It healed. Burning me doesn't work."

His tongue touched my cheek. "I will make it work."

I should have screamed or fought or *something*, I suppose, but I was positive the nurses would carry out my orders and signal Command. Convinced, too, that Reever would come to the rescue.

After all, he *always* came to my rescue.

I told myself the same thing over and over, as GothVar marched me down the corridor to the launch bay, where the blood and gore-splattered discipline post still stood. I felt confident as he secured the door panel. I even smiled bravely when he bonded me to the post.

"Reever won't let you do this." Would be nice if he showed up right about now, too, I thought.

"HalaVar is not here. He cannot stop me." Flat-Head stretched my wounded arm above my head and lashed my wrist securely. His heavy body crushed mine into the hard, crusted surface of the post. For a moment, our faces were only a centimeter apart. His repulsive breath made me hold mine. "I will drink of your pain, Terran."

"Herbal tea is much easier on the digestion." Come on, Reever, now is the time to come charging in to save me. "I can prescribe something for you, if you'd like."

He wasn't listening, only fiddling with something on the floor.

"Why did you let FurreVa take the blame for what you did to those prisoners?"

"She will capitulate." His tail slammed into the post, just below my feet. "As will you."

What was he talking about? I leaned over to get a better look at him, and saw what he was fooling with.

"You can't use that." Sweat that had been beading

around my brow suddenly streaked down my temples. GothVar stopped for a moment to gaze at me. "Um, you have to do this with a laser."

"As long as the designation is legible," he said, activating the thresher unit, "I can use any means I wish."

"No." I said it again, louder, so he would understand. "Cutting is *not* the same thing as branding. For branding, you use heat."

FlatHead simply adjusted the unit to produce a focused, narrow beam and input something on the thresher's panel. The low hum become a high, eardrum-piercing whine. Then the OverCenturon stepped aside, and waited.

The displacer band hit my arm, and everything that had happened to FurreVa came back to me in a huge, terrifying rush of images. "Stop it!"

He didn't, of course.

The thresher began cutting into my arm. Not like a lascalpel, which was hot, fast, and efficient. No, this was more like being gouged with a cold, dull eating utensil. I twisted, digging my heels in against the post, trying to get away from the beam.

Reever, where are you? "Turn it off!"

GothVar would leave it on, I thought, closing my eyes tightly, biting the inside of my lips to keep from screaming. He'd leave it on until it dug through my skin and muscle and bone. Until my body dropped to the deck. Until my arm was left hanging by itself on the post. That was where my ex-bondmate would find me, armless, cold, and white.

Because this time, Reever wasn't coming to my rescue.

GothVar drew closer. I felt his claws hook into my slave collar, and I couldn't bear his touch and the thresher chopping into me at the same time. I opened my eyes, saw the voracious alien gaze locked on not my arm, but my face.

His mouth parted, allowing the black tongue to

slide out and trail up and down my face. Tasting the droplets of sweat and tears, I realized. Licking them from my skin as though they were wine.

My teeth stayed locked together, but I got this much out: "Get—away—from—me!"

"More, SsurreVa," he said, and ducked under the beam to crowd me from the other side. "Scream for me."

He certainly liked to hear people screaming, and looked ready to chomp down on anything I moved. I kept silent and tried to hold still. It wasn't easy. The beam had gotten through the first layers of derma and superficial tissue, and was now tearing into the deep fascia.

How had FurreVa endured this? How could I?

Like a mouth of flat-topped fangs, like *his* mouth, the thresher kept at me. The odor from the Hsktskt's mouth and my own blood choked me. I couldn't take a deep breath. The pain worsened, darkened from sharp and stabbing into profound agony.

How long, how long can I stay conscious? My ears filled with the rush of whistling sobs. *Not long, but I can't pass out—he'll leave me here to bleed to death. He'd leave me until the beam dices me up.*

GothVar's voice inched into my ears . . . telling me . . . oh, my God, he was telling me what he . . .

Something seized me by the throat, and suddenly I couldn't breathe at all. I felt my lungs burn, my larynx strain around an unreleased gasp. Yet I couldn't overcome that vise around my neck, couldn't fight it. Whatever it was held me suspended and helpless.

GothVar's repulsive presence seemed to fade away.

No, Cherijo. You can breathe. Breathe.

My pulse roared out of control. Icy sweat glazed over my face. That voice behind my wide eyes was wrong, I *couldn't* breathe. Couldn't unlock the paralyzed muscles. I was going to die here, like this, frozen, trapped, helpless.

Cherijo, breathe.

I couldn't comprehend what was happening. I wasn't having a seizure. Nothing was strangling me. The beast wasn't touching me. There *was nothing there* —

Lack of oxygen made the room transform into a shifting, vague blur. Eventually it left me, all of it, the room, the thresher, the pain. Trapped inside my own body, listening to the sound of my heart as it slowed, beat by beat, I didn't care anymore, not knowing . . .

Cherijo!

Someone pried my mouth open and filled it with something hard and round. Delicious, sweet oxygen pumped into my lungs. I drew it in eagerly, then shuddered at the resulting rawness as it left me on a ragged exhalation.

Breathe.

The voice in my head forced another breath into my lungs. I wasn't sure I wanted to do that. The other way was easy, I wouldn't have to deal with the Hsktskt or the arm he'd hacked off my body by now. I wouldn't have to be a slave.

Breathe for me.

Another rush of oxygen poured down my throat. It reconnected me with more than I wanted—the horrible pain of my arm, the wrenched, contorted muscles of my body, and the force that held me between two solid struts . . . not struts . . . arms.

Human arms.

Reever?

Old memories flashed in brief, swift sequence.

Ana Hansen, smiling. *Cherijo Grey Veil, this is Duncan Reever, our chief linguist.*

Jenner, winding in and out of Reever's ankles. *That's why they're called pet, Reever. You pet them.*

Hands that carried the scars of a terrified child. *I think of the ritual often now.*

A birthday present I'd received while serving on the *Sunlace*. *It's to keep my hair tidy.*

A list of dead and wounded, one that didn't have Reever's name on it. *What have you done to yourself?*

My own face, for once open and alive with yearning. *We belong together. I can feel it, when I touch you, when I look at you. When I hear your voice.*

Reever, the first time I'd seen him. Sitting alone, dressed in black, looking at me. The cold, handsome face that never changed. The eyes that never stayed the same.

Touch me, Cherijo. Someone pressed my hands against warm, smooth skin. *Look at me.* I opened my eyes, saw his face. *Listen to my voice.*

Gently he removed the tube from my mouth. "Breathe, beloved."

My petrified lungs slowly expanded, dragging in a shallow breath that rasped over the swollen tissues of my throat. As I released the burning gulp of air, I knew I would live.

The problem now was wanting to.

Chapter Eight

Catopsa

A few days after GothVar's attempt to part me from my right forearm (which failed), the L.T.F. *Perpetua* arrived at Catopsa.

The OverCenturon, according to Reever, had been reprimanded about his actions in the launch bay. Apparently he wasn't subject to discipline for branding me with the PIC, as that was standard Faction regulation.

Pity. I would have liked to watch him get chopped to pieces.

Reever had ordered me to remain in his quarters, but I ignored that. Work kept me busy. I made daily rounds in Medical and the Detainment Area. FurreVa and her infants were kept in an isolation chamber, and I performed a somewhat delayed postpartum. She would need more skin work, and two of the infants suffered from continued respiratory distress, which I treated.

"You would have me thank you for this," the OverSeer said as she gazed over at the reinforced incubators housing her vicious offspring.

"Not really." A ghost of my former humor emerged briefly. "After all, you're going to have to raise the little monsters."

I dealt with the rest of the caseload without much problem. Someone had assigned a pair of centurons to shadow me, and they kept the League prisoners from getting out of hand. Much was muttered about that as I made my rounds, by both patients and League staffers. None of it good.

I didn't care. I could do my job without much conversation. When someone stepped over the line, TssVar's guards made the appropriate threatening gestures. FlatHead never showed his ugly face in Medical. Reever left me alone.

As long as that remained the status quo, I'd be fine.

Why I suddenly had guards didn't concern me. Thoughts of what GothVar had done hovered on the fringe of my mind, but I didn't dwell on it. I functioned quite well in a safe, comfortable haze, and I had absolutely no intentions of leaving it.

I liked the status quo.

Shropana's former ship went into orbit above Catopsa just before I came off my shift, or so Reever informed me when I walked into his quarters.

"That's nice." I went to the cleanser and stripped. The soft support brace on my forearm was waterproof, so I didn't have to remove that. Judging from the slight problem I was having with lateral mobility, I'd have to deal with it later. For now, I was content to let it heal on its own.

Reever's voice drifted in over the hiss of the sprayers. "We will be transporting everyone to the surface."

I frowned, vaguely annoyed. Couldn't I take a shower in peace? "That's nice."

The hot jets felt good against my skin, and I stood under the port for a long time before I attended to the business of deconning. When I got out, I dried off and noticed absently that I'd lost more weight.

Weight I could put back on, of course. After I got around to fixing my arm. It didn't matter.

Nothing *really* mattered.

Reever waited until I was dry, then handed me a fresh set of garments. He always seemed to be doing helpful little things like that lately. When he wasn't bugging me.

"Cherijo, we have arrived at Catopsa and are scheduled to jaunt to the compound within the hour."

"I heard you."

I pulled on my clothes, went to the prep unit, and absently prepared Jenner's evening meal. He ignored it and started weaving around my ankles, rubbing his head against me. I gently pushed him toward the dish, then drifted over to my vanity unit.

Should cut my hair, I thought, surveying the excessive, damp length. It tangled like crazy, and was such a chore to brush out and braid every day. Where had I put my trimmer?

I searched through my storage unit until I found it, then sat down and carefully applied the comb to the mess. This was going to take awhile; there were knots upon knots.

Reever took the comb and trimmer out of my hands and set them aside. "I want to talk to you."

He wanted to start an argument. So I'd do the trim job another time. I got up and cruised past him toward the prep unit. I wasn't hungry, but a server of tea might be nice.

Hard hands spun me around and shook me. "Cherijo!"

I eased out from under his grip. Maybe I should try being more direct and polite. "Please don't do that."

He didn't let up. "What did the OverCenturon do to you before I arrived at the launch bay?"

The launch bay. No, I didn't want to think about what had happened there. I backed up a wary step.

"Cherijo?" Reever came at me again. *"Answer me."*

"Nothing." Nothing I wanted to remember. The throbbing in my arm got worse. So did the tightness in my chest. Why did he insist on continuously *yelling* at me?

"You're lying. Tell me."

Something trickled into my veins, something hot and fast. I resisted the pull of the unreasonable anger. I wanted to go back into my fuzzy, safe lethargy, and he wasn't letting me. "Leave me alone."

Instead of turning me loose, he dragged me over to the viewport. "Look."

Below the *Perpetua*, there was an immense, sparkling white sphere. At first I thought it was a dwarf star, then realized we couldn't be this close to one and remain unimpaired. A satellite? I glanced from side to side, but spotted no mother planet. No icy plume trailed from it, so it wasn't a comet. An asteroid then.

Just another hunk of space rock. "Okay. I see it."

"That is Catopsa."

Correction. Just another slave-depot.

"We leave on the first launch to the surface in one hour."

Jenner came between us and started meowing plaintively, rubbing against Reever's shins. My cat had lousy taste in men. Just like me. I lost interest in the view. "Then I'd better pack."

Reever said some other things, but I didn't listen. I floated away from the viewport and concentrated on deciding what to pack for a lifetime of enslavement.

The Hsktskt loaded as many of us as they could fit into a launch, then sent it down to Catopsa. Reever went with my group, and I spent several minutes squashed between him and Jenner's carrier. My cat swatted at the grid with his paws until I stuck my fingers through it and absently stroked what fur I could reach.

"Almost there, pal," I said.

The asteroid appeared perfectly round, like a planetary body, but wasn't really white. As the launch drew closer, I saw towering faceted structures paved the surface, and refracted light like prisms in every direction.

I squinted as the increasing brightness hurt my eyes and pierced the nimbus of indifference I'd wrapped myself in. "They built this prison?"

"No. The asteroid was discovered fully formed by the Faction centuries ago."

Untouched by scaly limbs. "Why'd they pick this ball of plas for their little enterprise?"

"Catopsa is not made of plas. It is well within Faction territory, and convenient to the bond merchant routes."

Location is everything, even in the slave trade. "If it's not plas, what is it?"

"A mineral similar to silicon dioxide, but one hundred times as hard and possessing an equally higher specific gravity."

We were close enough now for me to see tiny figures moving inside the clear pillars. "They hollowed it out?"

"No. The mineral develops natural recesses in its growth clusters."

"Okay." I didn't want to get a lecture on quasi-quartz mineralogy. I noticed no star in the immediate vicinity. "All that light it reflects, where is it coming from?"

"The Hsktskt believe it is generated from phosphorescent material near the core of the planet. The nature of the mineral mantle prevents any confirmation."

As the launch prepared to land, I saw an enormous array of artificial environment generators, which answered my only other question. Catopsa was the quintessential prison—cold and transparent, with glassy walls no one dared shatter, even if they could find a way to do it.

The Hsktskt once more displayed their efficiency as the League prisoners, now wearing prisoner uniform tunics in a disgusting shade of sickly yellow, disembarked from the launch into a portable passage, where the centurons distributed shaded eye protectors and swiftly scanned PICs using a portable database unit. Prisoners were then arranged in a line and shackled together by lengths of plasteel cable fastened to their slave collars.

Reever and I were the last to leave, which gave me time to process what I was seeing. I slid the shades over my eyes at once, suspecting overexposure to the asteroid's natural light source would cause considerable damage.

I studied the interior, mostly so I wouldn't have to look at all the League prisoners being marched in, chained like animals.

The passage ended inside an enormous chamber created by a dozen massive pillars that had grown together at different angles. More Hsktskt stood waiting, these dressed in heavier insulating uniforms. Even with the evident atmospheric enhancements, Catopsan air felt cool, barely comfortable for a Terran.

The lizards didn't bother with a prisoner indoctrination; they simply surrounded the League arrivals and began separating them into new, smaller groups to be re-chained together. Males, females, hermaphrodites, and various other genders were segregated and marched off in different directions to passages leading away from the tower.

No one who came off the launch went quietly.

"Well?" I could avoid the sights, but the sounds of weeping and despair that echoed through the icy corridors were harder to ignore. "Do you show me to my cell? Or—" I saw a blob of something ooze past my left foot and jumped away from it. "*What is that?*"

Reever prodded the moving, dun-colored puddle with his foot, and it instantly changed direction and moved away from us. "Lok-Teel fungus. They are indigenous to Catopsa."

"Moving mold." I made a disgusting sound when I spotted more of them moving along the sloping faces of the chamber. "Can this place possibly get any more offensive?"

"Centuron." Reever took Jenner's carrier from my hand, and gestured to one of the Hsktskt standing nearby. "Accompany the Doctor on an inspection of the facility, then report to me."

"Yes, OverMaster."

"Where are you going with my cat?" I asked, but he only walked away and left me with the lizard. I glanced up at my guide and sighed. "Let's get it over with."

The Hsktskt escorted me from the receiving area through the first corridor, which branched off after a few meters. The transparent walls produced double refractions that made me blink a few times until I got used to the "twinning" effect.

"Bet head counts in this place are fun to do," I said.

My companion only grunted. We passed some Hsktskt supervising small groups of prisoners wearing orange tunics in different common area sections. Finally he spoke, identifying each chamber we passed. "Depot service administration. Population regulation. Food preparation and distribution. Fluid recycling. Inedible waste disposal."

Again reality punched holes through the numbness surrounding me. Inedible? They were feeding their garbage to the prisoners? And what was this population regulation business? I started to ask, but by then we'd arrived at the first of the prisoner habitats. The tiers I'd been threatened with, by GothVar.

A hundred types of eyes peered out at me from small, six-sided cells. Five sides were composed of the quasi-quartz, the sixth barred by a huge plasteel panel. The natural walls of the structure must have been too hard to drill through, judging by the unusual clamping mechanisms that kept each cell door in place.

Prisoners appeared for the most part healthy and very unhappy. They wore the same tunics we'd been given before leaving the *Perpetua*. The hideous shade of yellow didn't look good on anyone. A few shouted some ugly words when they saw us, but the thick chamber walls muffled the sound.

All male in this tier, I noted. "Why do you keep the genders separated?"

The beast didn't answer me.

We got through the first tier and made a turn into another corridor. More exotic life-forms populated these cells, but they were just as impolite as the males had been. The only difference seemed to be a marked inactivity, something else I asked about.

He ignored that, and I noticed some commotion down the long row of cells had snared his attention. "Wait here."

He left me standing in front of an Yturi's cell. I looked in, tried a half-hearted smile. The sad-eyed creature beckoned to me.

I walked closer to the cell wall and involuntarily placed my hand against the cool surface. "Are you sick? Are you in pain?"

The Yturi took a moment to put on its headgear before it answered. Its normally strident voice barely emerged through the thick mineral wall. "Are you a physician?"

"Yes, I'm Dr. Torin." I frowned as I inspected its derma. For an Yturi, it looked very unhealthy. "Aren't you eating?"

"Yes, but the inhibitors they put in our food are disgusting."

"Inhibitors?"

"Chemicals to prevent self-propagation." It pressed a leaf-shaped appendage over its thorax. "It makes most of us sick—I should have bred months ago."

That's what the beast meant by population regulation.

By then the Hsktskt had returned, and I whirled on him. "You *drug* them to keep them sterile?"

He indicated the next corridor. "We will proceed now."

I glanced at the Yturi. "I'll be back."

It took time to tour the entire prisoner tier stockade. I tried to keep a running estimate of the number of beings, then gave up. "What's the current population?"

"As of this hour, fifteen thousand, nine hundred twenty-one, not counting the new captives arriving from Overlord TssVar's fleet."

It was a staggering figure. More surprising was the number of empty cells I saw—the Hsktskt could easily hold three times as many prisoners.

Each tier had its own administration chamber and services units, which were manned by supervised prisoners. My escort informed me that Hsktskt guards routinely prowled the corridors, so daily counts were considered unnecessary. Besides, where would anyone go? As we went along, one thing began to really bother me.

At last I had to ask. "Where are the medical facilities?"

My companion swiveled one yellow eye toward me. "There are none."

"None?" I was appalled. "What do you do if they get sick, or hurt?" He didn't answer me, only fingered his weapon. Pain began gathering at my temples as I processed that. "Right. Take me to OverMaster HalaVar."

Reever's chambers occupied a tier in an enclosed,

heavily guarded structure beyond the prisoner stockade. I found him there, deep in discussion over something with OverLord TssVar.

"Where is my cat?"

"He is waiting for you in your chambers."

Now that I knew Jenner was safe, I got right down to business. "There's not so much as an medsysbank in this place, but you're drugging prisoners. Why?"

"I see you have completed your tour of the facility," Reever said.

"Yeah, I have." I pushed a chair out of my way. "Don't you know what the side effects are from long-term exposure to chemical inhibitors?"

TssVar looked from me to Reever, who was busy inputting data on a console unit. "I remind you, HalaVar, not to neglect her training further."

"Space my training!" I thrust a hand through my hair. "You're sterilizing them!" The big Hsktskt regarded me with that only too familiar tolerant expression. "This has to stop."

My ex-bondmate indicated the only other chair in the room. "Sit down, Cherijo."

"No thanks." I paced back and forth in front of TssVar. "There's no excuse for deliberately harming these prisoners like this. None."

Reever finished whatever he was fooling with and rose. "OverLord, it would be to our advantage to have Dr. Torin administer to the needs of the slave population."

"Indeed."

The abrupt turnaround made me stop and gape for a moment. "Wait a minute. Excuse me if I looked interested. I'm not. Nor am I drugging them for you."

"Any slave found physically or psychologically unfit for trade auction is terminated," the Hsktskt Commander said.

All at once the chemical inhibitors didn't seem so

bad. "I don't know if I've mentioned this before, but you guys are real humanitarians."

TssVar was ignoring me now. "I will allow it, HalaVar. See that she is put to work at once."

I lost it as soon as the beast went out the door panel. "I'm not working for you or the Hsktskt!"

"That is your choice." Reever input one last signal, then came around the console. "Unhealthy or damaged slaves will continue to be put to death."

Hale and hearty slavery, or meaningless extermination. And all up to me. "That's not fair. You can't make me responsible for that kind of decision."

"What about the Chakacat? OverSeer FurreVa? The League captives?"

"Alunthri?" The last of the safe haze I'd been cocooned in evaporated. "Where is it? What did you do to it?"

"Come with me." Reever took my arm and guided me out the door panel.

A few minutes later we entered a chamber in the center of the prisoner tiers. There was an impressive amount of diagnostic apparatus and instruments set up, waiting to be used.

Medical equipment.

"You must have been rather confident I'd agree." I noticed the many different types of tech, jumbled together and badly in need of proper organization. "Do Hsktskt raiders routinely take anything that isn't nailed down?"

"Yes."

I thought of the avaricious traders I'd known back on K-2. "They should go into business with the Bartermen." One of the Lok-Teel blobs slid up against my ankle and I shuddered and shook it off. "First order of business: get rid of this fungal infestation."

"It does no harm." Reever took something from his pocket and tossed it on the floor. A tiny piece of dried fish—something I usually fed Jenner as a treat. The fungus immediately flowed over it and a moment later rolled off to start climbing a wall. The fish was gone. "It ingests most organic material, including natural waste products."

Which explained the lack of disposal units, and made me decide never to go to sleep in the presence of a blob. "How does it feel about living beings?"

"Touch it for yourself and see."

Curiosity would eventually kill the surgeon, I thought, but walked over to the wall anyway. I started with a fingertip, and the pleasant, warm-silky texture I encountered made me murmur in surprise.

"It feels . . . odd." Like flesh instead of a botanical.

Soon I had my whole hand pressed carefully against the blob, and jerked back only momentarily when it looked as if it was going to envelop my fingers. Instead, it gave me what felt like an amoebic version of a caress, then flowed out from under my hand.

"Very strange." Inexplicably soothed by the contact, I inspected the gear around me. "All right, I'll need a pharmaceutical synthesizer, a half dozen nurses, and more berths. That's for starters."

"I can give you everything but the synthesizer, for now."

He didn't trust me. Reever, who'd lied and cheated and betrayed me, was worried I might try something with the drugs.

"Get me a synthesizer and post a guard." Before he could say anything more, I shook my head. "It's not negotiable."

I noticed the lack of heavy equipment, thought immediately of FurreVa and gave him a few more items for the list.

"I need a reinforced exam table for the Hsktskt, and special transport for FurreVa's infants. Bring them down in those incubators, too. They should stay in them for a few more weeks."

"You intend on treating the Hsktskt?"

"Why not?" The question astonished me. "Reever,

we've had this conversation before, remember? I'll treat anyone, for anything, any time. That's what I do."

"So you have said."

The odd expression on his face annoyed me, so I picked up a data chart and began programming it to keep a running list of necessary requisitions.

"Where's Alunthri?"

"On the *Perpetua*, awaiting transport."

"Have it transported soon. Get moving, will you? I'll have to get to routine physicals for all the prisoners, but have the centurons bring the sick ones first, two at a time. And make that a dozen nurses."

Once he was gone, I shuffled some equipment around to make more work space and performed an item-by-item inventory. The numbness was gone, and my headache got worse, but I wasn't sorry about that.

It was time to get back to work.

Several weeks after I'd arrived on the Hsktskt Faction slave-depot, I'd seen nearly a third of all the prisoners, requisitioned most of what I needed, and trained my nursing staff on how to assess and triage as the patients streamed in.

Dchêm-os had been the first nurse assigned to me, much to our mutual displeasure. "For you, I will not work," she said the moment the Hsktskt guard shoved her through the door panel.

I didn't like her, but she was the best nurse on the *Perpetua*. I needed someone who could handle the patients without running to me every five seconds.

I knew what to say. "I don't want you here either, but I don't get a choice in how they punish me."

That pleased Zella, from the way her ear fur perked up. "Stay, then I will."

FurreVa reported with her brood, whose conditions were stabilized, and informed me she'd been temporarily stripped of her rank.

"I remain restricted from duty, until the young are fully ambulatory," she said as I checked over her back.

"I need you off your feet for more grafts. Once those have healed, I'll start the work on your face." I checked the database, but even here Hsktskt medical data was decidedly scanty. "How long until the kids are up on their limbs?"

"A few days, perhaps a week."

It beat the heck out of Terran infants, who took forty times that long to walk. "Get TssVar to assign someone to help you. Someone with thick skin. I'll set up a chamber for you to stick close to the infirmary." I handed her a data chart. "Study this. It details all the surgery I'm planning to do. You need to know everything before we get started."

She examined the chart for a moment. "Why?"

"Because once I cut, there's no turning back. Okay?"

She set down the data chart. "I know you arranged for TssVar to discover my unauthorized interrogations."

"Yeah, I did. Then I found out you didn't actually interrogate any of those prisoners. Why did you lie about it?"

She ignored my question. "You do this surgery to assuage your guilt."

One of us might as well be honest. "That's part of it." I did something extremely stupid then. I lifted my hand and gently touched the terrible scar. "I'm a healer. You need to be healed."

She could have taken off a few fingers with one quick snap. Yet all FurreVa did was stare down at me, hiss something, then leave.

Progress, I guessed.

Although most of the prisoners were kept in their cells, a few were allowed to move through the compound corridors without escorts. I learned that those who did had to wear the darker orange "trustee" tunics to indicate they were performing some necessary function, like the sanitation crews and meal distributors.

Not all of them performed their assigned tasks, naturally.

I noticed shadows moving behind a privacy screen in the back of the infirmary. Since no inpatients were currently assigned to that particular berth, I went back to investigate.

"Hello?" I swept the partition aside. "May I help . . . what are you doing?"

A silly question, considering the position of the two beings on the berth. Tendrils and body parts jerked apart. A feminine squeak of dismay trilled out. Then a masculine grunt of displeasure.

"Okay, you two." I crossed my arms and sighed. "Let's go. Break it up."

The male, a being of small stature, whipped his multiple tendrils as he swept a length of linen over the naked object of his affections. A beaklike orifice in place of a mouth snapped open and shut a few times, while close-set eye stems glared at me.

"Do you mind?" He slid off the berth and stepped up to me. "We were making cohesion."

Cohesion. That was a new term for it. Someone had been palming their daily ration of chemical inhibitor.

"You're messing up my inpatient berth." I tossed his trousers and orange tunic at him, then pulled the partition back in place. "Get dressed."

They appeared a few minutes later. The female was slightly larger than the male, and had a belligerent set to her otherwise softer features.

She got in my face, too. "We weren't doing anything wrong. We have made cohesion before."

I ran a scanner over her and checked my readings, which told me exactly what I'd suspected. Adolescent Forharees, just coming into their fertile phase.

Teenagers in lust.

"Okay, kids. What are your names?"

"I am Jgrap. This is Kroni." The male sounded suspicious. "Why do you wish to know our names?"

"So I can track down your parents and have them ground you both for a few revolutions."

The teenagers looked puzzled, and I sighed again.

"Want to know what the guards will do if they catch you two playing twine-the-tendrils?" Both sets of eye stems looking at me arched. "You don't want to do this. Not here. Trust me."

"We would rather die together than live apart," Jgrap said in a passionate tone, weaving his longest tendril around his girlfriend. They both fairly quivered with the dramatic conviction of young love.

I needed an antacid tablet.

"Nobody is going to die." I put aside my scanner. "Get back to your tiers, and don't let the guards see you leave together." I held up a hand when they would have hurried past me. "No more cohesion. Especially not in here."

"Very well," Kroni said as she went by. She had a sweet, lilting voice. "We will find another place."

The antacid didn't help.

I continued to work every day for as many hours as I could stay on my feet, then was escorted under guard to my chamber. It was conveniently located around the corner from the infirmary, and isolated from the rest of the prisoner population. Someone had placed a prep unit and a rather comfortable cot in the small cell, which made it tolerable.

The first day I left the infirmary, I found Jenner waiting for me. I picked him up for a joyous cuddle, and looked into his disgruntled blue eyes.

You left me alone with that cold-eyed one who never pets me.

"Sorry, pal." I buried my face in his fur. "I've been sleepwalking for a while."

Well, wake up. I'm hungry.

Alunthri was delivered back in its cage, and it took

half a shift before I could convince the guards to leave it alone. I requisitioned a separate chamber near my own and used the excuse of continuing therapy.

"You may have to keep up the wild animal act," I told my friend when I relayed the news.

"*E-e-e-e-e R-r-r-r-r,*" the Chakacat said with a yowl, then cocked its bullet-shaped head. "I'm afraid the guards no longer find me very convincing, Cherijo."

"Try to look meaner."

"How is this?" Alunthri gave me a realistic snarl, baring lots of teeth, then dissolved into purrs of delight when I took an automatic step back. "I will take that as a yes."

It became apparent that the nurses and I couldn't handle the daily caseload, so Reever allowed me to draft Vlaav Irde and two more interns. When the number of patients leveled off, then began inexplicably dropping, I didn't volunteer to send any of them back.

My earnest young intern worried about that. Constantly.

"They won't sell us if we do a good job, right?" Vlaav asked me as he scanned a patient with a low-grade fever.

Lying to him would only make it worse. "They can sell us any time they feel like it, pal."

I finished suturing my patient's multiple lacerations and inspected my handiwork. The Capel-du suture laser I had to use seemed primitive compared to League tech, but still did a fairly good job.

"How did you get these injuries?" I asked the humanoid, who had remained silent throughout the treatment.

The patient said nothing, only stared at the Hsktskt guard standing just inside the door panel.

Only a handful of prisoners had appeared for treatment that day, and I was beginning to wonder if the Hsktskt were preventing them from reporting. Making a scene about it wouldn't help, I decided, and wrote up the discharge notes.

"I want to see you back here in the morning."

He muttered something that sounded like "crying chambers," rose and then hobbled out.

Crying in his chambers? I'd done some of that myself.

The resident Lok-Teel got busy on the exam table as soon as the patient left. It had taken some getting used to, watching the blobs scour everything the moment it got dirty, but even I couldn't deny the benefits.

I'd scanned the fungus and found it exuded its waste products in a gaseous form which had the additional plus of acting as a stringent antiseptic on all surfaces.

"Who's next?"

The prisoner who would have reported was shoved aside, and two centurons hauled a third through the door panel.

"Doctor, this male has been injured."

That he had, considering the amount of blood he was dripping all over the floor. One of his limbs hung at an unnatural angle. I directed them to the exam table. Scanning revealed multiple compound fractures along the upper half of the Hsktskt's limb.

I checked his airways. "What hit him?"

"He was attacked by a slave."

"Some attack." The centurons flanked the table and got in my way. "You two can go. I'll take care of him."

"You can't help him!" someone said.

I looked around at the patient the Hsktskt had knocked aside. He was still sprawled on the floor. "I beg your pardon?"

"How can you even *think* about giving them aid?" The prisoner got up and jerked the edge of his tunic up. A big, ugly bruise darkened the flesh over his rib cage. "Look at what they did to me!"

One of the centurons shuffled forward and raised a limb with the apparent intention of adding more contusions to the angry prisoner's torso.

"Hold it." I left the exam table and put myself between them. "Centuron, I need to treat your friend over there. I *don't* need to be scraping someone else off the floor right now."

The limb dropped, and I pivoted to address the indignant loudmouth. "I understand how you feel. I'm sorry you got hurt. But you'll have to wait. Make being quiet your number-one priority, okay?"

All my warning got me was a hateful glare. "I shouldn't have come here. The League Commander was right. You'd rather make things better for yourself than help us."

The League Commander was going to get my foot up a certain portion of his anatomy if he didn't stop polluting the prison population with his waste. The centurons both looked ready to pound this guy into paté.

I scanned him, was assured there was nothing life-threatening present, then gave him a push toward the door. "Do yourself a favor. Get out of my exam room. Come back in a few hours."

The patient stalked out, muttering things not complimentary to me or the medical profession.

I went back to the injured Hsktskt, who was regaining consciousness. Heavy limbs started thrashing around. Bellows of pain erupted from the thick throat. The centurons would come in handy after all.

"Grab his limbs and help me get him into restraints. No, not the injured one, idiot." I glanced over my shoulder. "Nurse, if you're done ogling, a syrinpress would be nice."

A thorough scan reveal additional tissue and muscle damage, and I directed Vlaav to get the largest bonesetter we had prepped.

One of the centurons hovered at my elbow, and I glanced at him. "What, exactly, did this slave use to attack this male?"

"His foot."

Now I saw the outline of the wide-base sole imprinted in the flesh. No question about it, the attacker had been Major Devrak. As far as I knew, he was the only Trytinorn on Catopsa, and twice the size of the next largest prisoner. The Hsktskt had been forced to modify a launch last week just to transport him off the *Perpetua*.

"Where's the attacker?" Neither Hsktskt answered me, so I stopped working. "Don't tell me you killed him."

"The Major will be placed in isolation." Reever entered the infirmary and stood at the end of the exam table. "Will the centuron recover?"

I finished infusing the patient with a sedative/analgesic compound and helped Vlaav align the bonesetter before I replied. "He should, if he's given a week of bed rest and lets the limb heal."

"See to it," Reever told the centurons, then turned to my intern. "Can you continue the treatment by yourself?"

Vlaav's hemangiomas pulsed and darkened. "Of course, I can. But—"

Reever grabbed my medical case and my left arm. A moment later I was being hustled down a corridor.

"Hey!" I tried to get loose. "I've got work to do!"

"There are prisoners who need treatment," he said.

"So send them to the infirmary. I've been twiddling my thumbs for the past five days."

"They refuse."

I started to ask why, then recalled what the loud-mouthed prisoner had said. My lips thinned. "How many need treatment?"

"Forty. Possibly more."

We arrived at tier three's commons, where a group of male prisoners had been assembled for a meal interval. A ring of Hsktskt centurons surrounded the large group, and held their weapons ready. I saw why when I pushed past one to get a better look.

A cluster of males in bloodstained tunics were shoving and snarling at each other, while several others lay wounded or ill on the floor. Surprisingly, the injured were all female. That didn't make much sense.

Major Devrak trumpeted over the other voices, but I had no problem understanding him. "—an honorable death! It is better to die than to submit to the beast!"

Lieutenant Wonlee, I saw, was standing in front of the Major, with his claws ready to tear. Only he was holding them extended *toward* the League subcommander. Now that really confused me.

"You corrupted her!" Wonlee moved in. "She won't listen to me!"

Fists, limbs, and tendrils started to violently collide.

I turned to the closest guard. "Can you fire a warning shot off in here without making more work for me?"

The centuron glanced at Reever, who nodded. The beast pointed his rifle at the ceiling structure and activated the weapon. A moment later a huge boom shook the commons and everyone stopped fighting.

I walked over to the first prone figure and knelt beside her. She was babbling and twisting, her body temperature elevated. A red, blotchy rash covered her face and upper appendages.

I opened my case to grab my scanner. "Get a blanket or thermal covering over here."

There was absolute silence for a moment. Then someone threw a folded piece of berth linen at me. I caught it and covered the shivering female as I ran an internal series. The outer coverings of her brain and spine were badly inflamed She reacted only when I shined an optic light in her eyes, and then she tried to hit me.

"Get this one to the infirmary."

I went to the next female, who was pale and still. A quick scan revealed she had died of the same symptoms. It took a few more seconds to scan the remaining females and confirm what I already suspected.

"Reever." I gestured for him to join me. "They all have it. Two of them are already dead. I'm taking them out of here, now. We'll need help to move them to an isolation area."

Before my ex-bondmate could say or do anything, Devrak shuffled through the prisoners to stand over me. "You are not taking them anywhere."

The last patient groaned as I got to my feet and straightened my tunic. Calmly I met the Major's furious gaze.

"I said I'm taking them out of here," I said. "They're *dying*, you titanic moron."

"Doctor." Wonlee hurried over to one of the females who was curled up tightly in a fetal position, and picked her up in his arms. The insides of which, I realized, had no spines. "Can you help her?"

She possessed the same spiny exoskeletal plates as Wonlee had. They flattened to act like a prickly cushion between the two beings. A relative? I scanned her one more time to be sure, but the female was far beyond any help I could offer.

"I'm sorry, Lieutenant. It's too late."

He gently laid her down again, then hurtled up and at the Trytinorn with a furious shriek of rage. Devrak knocked him aside, but not without receiving some substantial, deep gouges on his hide.

"Wonlee, stop." I went to where he lay on the deck, and scanned him. Devrak began thumping over, and I turned my head. "Back off."

"We will not permit the doctor to remove these females." A hunched-over canine figure appeared beside Devrak. Shropana. "She will kill them. Just as she did the others, from the *Perpetua*."

"No." Wonlee spat out some blood, then propped himself up by one arm. His claws scraped over the shoulder of my tunic, but he didn't hurt me. "Take them. If you don't, they'll all die. Like she did." Despite his injuries, he got to his feet and positioned himself between me and the League officers, his spines trembling but erect. "Let her do her work."

"Very well." Shropana gave me a shrewd smile. "They're nearly dead as it is."

Meaning I'd get blamed for that, too. "I was wrong, Patril. I can't do heart surgery on you. I wouldn't be able to find it."

Reever organized more Hsktskt guards to begin transporting the females. The males watched in silence. One of the dead females was removed by a centuron, but Wonlee picked up the other before anyone could stop him.

"You will need to perform tests to identify and cure the sickness, will you not?" he asked me. I nodded. "Use her body."

Knowing how attached he was to the female, I started to shake my head. "I'd need to do an autopsy."

"I know. I want you to." The Lieutenant started limping toward the infirmary. "I want to know what killed my wife."

CHAPTER NINE

Twists and Turns

The Hsktskt grudingly transported the entire group of females to an isolation chamber near the infirmary, where I spent the next several hours treating and monitoring them. After the last patient stabilized, I returned to the infirmary to check on the injured Hsktskt and Wonlee.

I found the Lieutenant sitting alone at the end of the inpatient ward. On the berth beside him lay the body of his wife. He held her claws in his and stared down at her slack face, grief etched in deep lines around his eyes and mouth.

One of the Lok-Teel had attached itself to the dead female's leg, cleaning the encrusted bodily fluids from her cold skin. I gently removed it and set it on the floor.

"Excuse me for intruding, Lieutenant, but I need to speak with you." I sat down beside him and hoped he would confirm my suspicions without going ballistic on me. "Can you tell me what happened? How long ago did the females become ill? Why didn't your wife and the others come to the infirmary?"

"They have shown signs for several days. My wife, Mareek fell sick last night. They would have reported, but Shropana and Devrak convinced them that you would have them killed. This morning Mareek became confused, nearly incoherent." Something tore in his voice as he added, "I argued with her. Our last words to each other were spoken in anger."

I couldn't touch him, or I'd have put an arm around him. "I'm sure Mareek knew how much you loved her, Lieutenant."

He made a harsh sound. "Wonlee. Just Wonlee."

"How did the females end up in the male tier?"

"I don't know. They appeared in our commons a few days ago. We hid them in our berths at first, but the beasts are everywhere and"—he gestured toward the see-through walls around us—"our deception was discovered." He tenderly placed the female's claws on her spiny breast and got up slowly. "Last night, their temperatures spiked. They caught me trying to cool them down."

"You've had some kind of medical training, haven't you?"

"I was a medic on our homeworld. That's how I met Mareek, during one of her furloughs. I worked in the Star Surgeon's Office, and she needed a deep-space eval. We married and I joined the League, to be with her. It would be an adventure, she said." He closed his eyes briefly. "Now they've killed her."

"I'm very sorry, Wonlee." I didn't like the way he stood, favoring one side. "I should take a look at you now, okay?"

He nodded. "Doctor, I know it doesn't matter anymore, but I have resigned my commission from the League. As long as I am here, I will do what I can to aid you."

"I can always use another pair of hands." I pointed to the exam area. "First let's make sure you're going to stick around for a while."

Devrak had nearly shattered Wonlee's diaphragm

which, unlike the Terran version, was composed of bone. Had it not been for the band of cartilage that allowed it to naturally collapse under stressful conditions, his chest cavity would have been crushed. The Lieutenant's entire skeleton was similarly designed, another plus. Support braces and some analgesics for the inevitable inflammation were all he needed to remain mobile. I admitted him to the inpatient ward anyway.

"The last thing you need to do," I said when he started protesting, "is to go back to the prisoner tiers right now. So keep your promise, shut up, and get some rest."

Dchêm-os had finished the hematological workups when I emerged from the ward and offered a data pad with the results of her analysis. I didn't bother with niceties. "Well?"

"Cell levels, decreased glucose, elevated protein and white blood. Nothing, the cultures revealed."

That meant something more serious, but I'd have to do a spinal tap to confirm my suspicions. "Set up to perform lumbar punctures. Orderly." I pointed to the Lok-Teel, who were climbing up the sides of the berths. "Move those blobs away from the patients, will you?"

Later that day I lifted my face from the electroniscopic scanner and let Zella and Vlaav have a look.

"I've seen something like this before." The Saksonan peered again into the viewer. "Is it a microbe?"

"Give the intern a cigar." I shut off the scanner and rubbed my fingers against my tired eyes. "They all have bacterial meningitis."

Zella gasped. "Assassinate us, the beasts mean to."

"I don't think so." I sat down and studied the reports. "Vlaav, start the patients on the intravenous cephalosporin antibiotics, compatible with their individual species."

The nurse wasn't finished. "Poisoning us, they are—"

"Nope. It didn't originate from tainted food, or we'd all be infected. Something else did this." I decided not to tell them I'd never seen this particular microbe before, and that it didn't register on the medsysbank. Bad enough I was shaking in my footgear. No need to start a panic.

"Their side, you would take."

"If I had, poisoning you would be number one on my list." I switched off the scope. "Prep for a postmortem."

The autopsy on Wonlee's wife took nearly two hours, but I wanted to go slowly and rule out every other possibility. I knew Mareek had died of meningitis the moment I cut away the swollen meninges—mucosal exudate clogged the sulci fissures in the brain surface, and scanning revealed a massive release of proinflammatory cytokines in the basal cerebral arteries.

However, confirmation of cause of death was all I got from the autopsy. Nothing Mareek had ingested had caused the disease. Comparative scans of the survivors revealed that only two had eaten the same food within the last twelve hours. The others had been served a variety of meals, all based on their species requirements.

The worst part? I found no trace of the microbe in her corpse.

I performed spinal taps on the survivors, and verified that each of them had been infected with the bacteria. The microbe itself was very odd. The hexagonal-shaped bacteria possessed a tough outer cell hull unlike anything I'd ever seen. The dark green-colored wall darkened a few minutes after removal from the body, and completely concealed the cell nucleus. It resisted all my attempts to probe the interior as well.

Since the bacterium causing the meningitis could have been introduced to the victims through a wide variety of means, I was back to square one.

"So it didn't come from what they ate." I stripped

out of my gear, handed Zella the data pad with the forensic analysis, and yawned. "I can't think straight."

"Sleep, you go to." Dchêm-os annotated the appropriate chart. "One of the beasts for you, I will send, should they change, the females' conditions."

"Why are you suddenly being so helpful?"

"My friends, they are," Dchêm-os said.

Right. Had nothing to do with me, of course. What was I thinking?

I waved at a guard to escort me back to my chamber, but he didn't budge. "Come on, I'm tired."

"OverMaster HalaVar instructed us to allow you unrestricted movement," the Hsktskt said, and handed me a trustee's tunic.

I wondered why. "About time. I'm sick of wearing yellow."

I walked over to my room and found the door panel slightly ajar. That didn't sink in for a few minutes, until I sat on my pallet and realized who was missing. "Jenner?"

He was gone.

Since I'd been given unrestricted access to the compound, I didn't bother going to the Hsktskt about my missing pet. I looked myself, starting with all the chambers in proximity to my quarters.

I know I left that door panel shut, I thought as I peered in room after room, around and under anything that would conceal a small feline. If I hadn't, and a hungry centuron found Jenner first . . .

My pace quickened, along with my fear. I ran down the rows of prisoner cells, and pretended not to hear the angry jeers. A search of each tier's commons turned up nothing.

Where was he? What happened to him?

This was all my fault, I decided as I hurried into a corridor I hadn't taken before. If I hadn't let Jenner run loose on the *Sunlace*, he wouldn't have wandered out of my quarters here. I'd given him too much freedom, and not thought about the danger that posed.

A forbidding weight collected under my sternum. *Oh, God. If I lose him, I won't have anything left.*

The corridor arrived at a bewildering enclosure spiked with innumerable quasi-quartz columns rising from the floor. They were smaller and more tightly packed than the tower structures. It transformed the interior to a huge, glassy labyrinth.

I stopped. If I walked into the glittering maze, I might never find my way out. "Jenner?" I called out in a low voice. "Pal, are you in here?"

Something on my right made a scuffling sound, and I hurried around the pillar. And nearly stepped on the two adolescent Forharees entwined together on the floor.

"Hey!" The teenagers sprang apart and scrambled to their feet. "What is it with you two?" I looked around and lowered my voice. "Haven't you ever heard of holding hands?"

Kroni's beak arched with indignation. "We would rather die—"

"—'together than live apart.' You told me before, I know." I tossed her trustee tunic at her and made a shooing motion. "I swear, I'm going to inject both of you with chemical inhibitor myself. Get back to your tiers, *now*."

I waited until the grumbling kids hurried off, then pushed aside caution and walked into the labyrinth, calling Jenner's name again. The central pillars had grown in tightly fitted rows, which made navigating the corrugated walkway a challenge. A few times I had to squeeze through narrow gaps to continue on.

"Jenner?"

The sound of a strange Terran voice made me freeze. "Stay where you are, dope."

Astonishment left me mute. There were no other humans on Catopsa except Reever, and he barely qualified. I'd even verified it through the database. So who was this guy?

I got my answer when a slim, brown-haired Terran male dressed in a slave tunic appeared from around a corner. He had a narrow, clever face and the biggest, softest green eyes I'd ever seen. In his hands he held something wrapped in cloth, which he handed over to me.

"Who are you?" I took the heavy bundle and gasped when it moved. "Jenner?" I unwound the cloth and exposed silver fur. "Is he all right?" It took another minute to uncover him completely. He was unconscious, his regal head lolling against my breast. "What happened to him?"

"Shhhh. He tried to do a bunk through an exterior hatch and made a right hames of the job." The Terran kept his voice low as he scanned the walls around us. "Sure and I was trying to do the same thing myself." He touched my arm tentatively. "Sláinte, dope. You're the first blessed Terran I've seen in ages."

"Then why are you calling me a dope?" I wanted to know.

"*Dote*, not dope." His hand stroked my arm, then Jenner's head. "It means 'lovely little person.' Grand to see you, *dote*."

I was so preoccupied with examining my cat that it took a minute for his words to set in. What of them I could understand. "I checked the database, there weren't any other Terrans currently listed among the prisoner population." Then I noticed the stains on his tunic. "Are you injured?"

"Did it arseways, this." He tugged at his tunic, then gave me a grin so brilliant that it rivaled the crystal walls. "Coddling my own death, and the gammy thicks fell for it." He curled his fingers around mine. "Gael Kelly, from Clare."

I returned the warm grasp. "Cherijo Torin, from New Angeles. Clare? That's in the Celt Republic?"

He gave me a charming grin. "The very same.

Now, *dote*, I don't suppose you've be having any scran on you?"

"Scran?"

"Rashers and poppies. You know, food?"

"Oh. No. Sorry." I performed a visual; he was on the thin side. "How long have you been hiding here?"

"Ages." Gael kept smiling, but his constantly darting gaze made me uneasy. "Got to find myself a new kip. They'll be inspecting this section soon, and I'll have to scatter."

No one inspected my chamber, and I had enough room in my storage unit to conceal him. "If you can lead me out of here, I think I can help."

"Grand." Gael pointed in a different direction from the way I'd come in. "Follow me, *dote*."

We got back to my quarters without being stopped or questioned by the Hsktskt guards. Recalling what Zella had done for me onboard the *Perpetua*, I wrapped Gael's head with the extra cloth and had him make a pretense of leaning on me.

"Don't say a word, and they'll think you're just another of my patients."

"You're a patcher?" He sounded incredulous. "Sweet Mary, a wee *dote* like you?"

"Yep. A wee *dote* like me." His fascinating speech patterns were far too distracting. "Let's go."

There was no one to observe us as we went into my quarters, and I had Gael slide into the storage unit. Then I went to my prep unit and dialed up a substantial meal for him. I couldn't program "rashers and poppies," whatever that was, so I made some simple synpro and vegetable stew, and plenty of synwheat bread to go with it.

"Here." I handed him the tray. "Eat this. Stay out of sight. I'm taking Jenner over to the infirmary to check him out. I'll be back in a few minutes."

He was already chewing, and had to talk around

the food in his mouth. "I thank you for your kindness, *dote*."

Dchêm-os wasn't please to see me, and her ire deepened when she saw who I was carrying. "Dead, is it?"

"No." I placed Jenner's limp body on an exam table and started an internal scan series. "He got loose and ran into something that stunned him." Normal readings, and no indication of injury or trauma. Finally, I could take a deep breath.

Vlaav appeared. "Doctor, what happened to your animal?"

I repeated what I'd told Zella. "Update me on Wonlee and the meningitis cases."

"All are on the prescribed antibiotic therapy and seem to be stabilizing. Lieutenant Wonlee discharged himself voluntarily."

"Stubborn male." I made an exasperated sound. "The minute I turn my back, too. He'd better stay away from Shropana and Devrak."

"That you caused the females' illness, there are rumors." Zel's cheek pouches puffed out.

"There are rumors that I'm a Hsktskt in a Terran skinsuit, too." Vlaav's close proximity started to annoy me. "Something else, intern?"

"I've collected a number of small parasites from patients' bodies." He held out a specimen container with some tiny black things jumping around in it. "With your permission, I'll dissect them and determine if they carry the meningitis microbe."

Vlaav had one-upped me. I hadn't even considered the possibility of parasitic infection. "Excellent. Do it right away. I want a full report sent to OverMaster HalaVar as soon as you're done." I picked up Jenner and regarded my colleague. "Include in the report that I am advancing you to first-year resident status, if you would, Doctor."

The Saksonan's facial hemangiomas swelled so fast that a couple popped. Embarrassed, Vlaav blotted himself with a sleeve, then bobbed his head. "I'm very honored. Thank you, Doctor."

Zella made a disgusted sound, and I faced her. "And you, madam, will show Doctor Irde the appropriate respect." Her vibrissae quivered, but she nodded, too. "I'm going to take Jenner back to my quarters. Signal me if there is any change—"

"Remain where you are, Terran."

The sound of that rasping, insinuating tone made me cringe. I forced my spine to straighten as I confronted the two Hsktskt who had walked into the infirmary. FlatHead and one of his buddies. It was, apparently, my lucky day.

"Did you need treatment, centurons? Other than psychiatric evals, I mean?"

As GothVar advanced, I handed Jenner to Vlaav and stayed where I was, trying to look undaunted. The closer he got, the harder it became to breathe.

No, I couldn't descend into another panic attack. *I won't let him do this to me. He's nothing more than an overgrown bully. I'm not afraid of him.*

"We will escort you to your quarters." He seized one of my arms, his friend clutched the other, and they towed me out of the infirmary.

I didn't fight or say anything. Doing either would have only made it worse. No, I was going to concentrate on remaining as calm and collected as possible. Gael would hear us come in and stay out of sight.

FlatHead positioned his mouth by my ear. "Have you thought of me, Terran?"

I contrived an expression of wide-eyed confusion. "Gee, no, I haven't. But then, I haven't felt queasy lately, so that's understandable."

His grip tightened from hard to pulverizing. "You will feel more than that, soon."

I bit my lower lip as we arrived at the door to my quarters, and FlatHead yanked it open. No sign of Gael, but I thought a verbal cue might be prudent.

"Why the personal escort, OverCenturon?" I asked, deliberately loud. "Run out of slaves to kick around?"

FlatHead paused, long enough to give me hope, then addressed the other beast. "Search it."

The centuron pulled Gael out of the storage unit a few moments later. GothVar regarded him with unblinking yellow eyes.

"HalaVar will be very interested in speaking with this one. Administer standard discipline, then take him to the OverMaster. I will see to the female."

"She had no part in this business, you slimy jelly-boned bollocks!" Gael spat at the Hsktskt's feet. "Lay off her!"

"Administer special discipline for disrespect to my rank," was all GothVar said.

"You can of piss!" The Terran gave me a last, sympathetic glance before the centuron hauled him out of my chamber, leaving me alone with FlatHead.

I scratched my head, trying not to laugh. *Can of piss.* "Gee, wonder how he got in here?"

"You lie. Willfully concealing a slave makes you subject to discipline." Flathead reached out, ripped my tunic from neck to hem, then pulled it off. He didn't look at my body, only my arm. My right arm. "As I thought."

No. Not again. "Wait!"

He didn't. He flung me on the pallet, and rooted through my medical case until he found the suture-laser.

All reason left me as I rolled over, keeping my right arm between my body and the pallet. "I told you that won't work. *It doesn't work on me!*"

Claws ripped across my flesh as I was yanked onto my back. Two heavy limbs descended on my upper arm and wrist. Straddling me with a third, FlatHead activated the laser and held it an inch from my nose.

"This time, I will char your bones."

He would, too. Enraged at his grotesque determination and my own terror, I followed Gael's example and spat in his face.

The suture-laser, designed to knit together torn flesh, had a beam twice the width of a lascalpel. The first touch sent unbearable searing pain along the surface of my skin, and I tasted blood as my teeth closed together with a snap.

Why did my nerves keep regenerating? Couldn't Joseph have deprogrammed those, too?

"Watch how I mark you, Terran." GothVar slowly moved the beam over my smoldering flesh an inch at a time. "See how easily you burn."

I didn't want to look at him, at my arm. The horrible pressure of his weight holding me down was nothing compared to the gathering force squeezing the air from my throat. A whistling sound reached my ears while my vision hazed over. I could smell his breath mixing with the fumes from the beam. If I choked on my own bile—

"OverCenturon. Release the Doctor."

Reever? I gasped for air, for anything that would allow me to call out to him. The heavy weight lifted from me, and I was hauled to my feet.

"She concealed an escaped prisoner here, and removed her PIC again. I corrected this." Flathead shoved me to my knees. "She plays you for a fool, HalaVar."

"Does she?" Reever came to stand over me.

A strange Hsktskt I'd never seen before joined him. "OverCenturon, OverMaster." He gazed down at me with considerable interest. "Slave, extend your arm."

I used my good hand to wipe the blood from my mouth, then smiled with relief as the constriction in my lungs eased. "Go stick your head in a disposal unit."

The unknown Hsktskt latched his claws on to my arm and held it out so he could examine it. "You said you just applied this PIC, GothVar, did you not?"

FlatHead grunted out an affirmative.

"She heals quickly." He let go, and I cradled my wounded arm to my chest. "Have her sent to me once discipline has been administered."

The way he looked at me—who was he?

"That will not be possible, Lord." Reever gestured to two of the centurons he'd brought. "I have decided on her discipline. Confine her in the isolation pit."

I was back, right where I started, only the amenities weren't quite as comfortable this time.

The isolation pit was a deep recess in a remote corridor, down which the Hsktskt centurons dropped me via a grav-hoist. Too deep to escape—I figured they lowered me a good fifteen feet before I hit bottom—and without anything to soften my fall. Nothing in the pit, I discovered, but me, bloodstains from my injuries, and six smooth, inescapable walls.

Pain kept me from passing out, so I sat for a long time, holding my burned arm away from my body, and considering the possibilities.

Reever might just leave me here to die, I thought, which would be a fairly horrible death. It would take days, possibly weeks for starvation and dehydration to kill me. The chilly interior, like the cell on the *Perpetua*, wasn't cold enough to induce hypothermia, even if I removed all my clothes to hasten the process. Too bad.

Eventually I dozed off, the fresh burn making my sleep restless. Every time I moved, it sent a sizzling jolt of new pain through me, which brought me halfway out of slumber. The cool, white light produced by the deep layers of quasi-quartz didn't help much, either.

The hatch opened, waking me up. "Terran."

I peered up to see GothVar staring down at me. "Not you again." An image of the huge lizard being lowered down into the pit with me made me close my eyes tightly. "Don't you have anything better to do?"

He turned his head and said something to the pit guard that sounded like "not . . . rational," then slammed the hatch shut.

Rational. I was rational. Not like FlatHead was an authority on the subject.

A day passed. I took to muttering to myself, to keep awake and to stop dwelling on my thirst and hunger. Eventually both became so strong that the only peace I found was in sleep.

A small object hitting the top of my skull woke me up. I jerked out of sleep to look around, and shuddered as I remembered where I was. Then I saw it.

A small square container, the kind sojourn teams carried in their packs. I grabbed it and looked up.

Above me, a dark, furry face hung over the edge of the pit. "Doctor?"

"Zel?" What was she doing here and where was the guard? "Get back to the infirmary before you get caught!"

"Wait." She pushed something else over the side, and I tried to catch it. The burn made me clumsy, and it bounced into my lap, the weight bruising my thighs. "With more, I'll try to come back."

Before I could ask more what, her face disappeared. The thing on my lap was a large, thin plas container of liquid, the square case opened to reveal emergency sojourn rations.

Both of which Zella could have tainted, of course.

I didn't care, I thought, scrambling to open the container of liquid. It would solve my problem if she had, and I'd be a complete idiot not to drink if she hadn't.

Cool, wet liquid poured into my mouth and down the sides of my throat as I took a big swallow. Not water. Nutri-enhanced glucose and water, the kind of beverage I routinely prescribed for dehydrated patients. It slid down my desiccated throat to fill and warm my belly. Only with supreme will power was I able to close the container and keep myself from gulping it all down at once.

Can't drink too fast.

I waited for the inevitable nausea to pass, then rummaged through the sojourn rations. All Terran foods, I saw, and in sealed, nonperishable packets.

Suddenly I knew exactly what GothVar had said to the pit guard. Not "not rational," but "no rations at all."

They meant to starve me.

Don't know how long I'll be down here. Have to conserve what I can. I tore open the smallest packet and carefully ate half the contents. Simply chewing and swallowing made my jaw ache and my eyes sting. I would have wept, but I was too dehydrated.

No taste of chemicals, no indication of poison or drugs.

At last, exhausted with pleasure and the new hope it gave me, I curled over on my side and fell asleep again.

The dream I had was bizarre, without images, only sensations. For a long interval, I felt sure I'd been transported back to the *Sunlace*. The chilly, unyielding walls disappeared, and I was back on my own sleeping platform, snuggling into clean, crisp sheets. Jenner's cold, dry nose nudged me a few times, and once I thought he licked my burned arm, but it didn't hurt, so I dismissed it.

I would have gladly slept for another week, but something decided I'd been dreaming long enough.

Wake up.

I murmured something vaguely obscene and rolled over.

Wake up, woman.

The odd voice made my ears hum, and I swatted at it with one hand, annoyed by the disturbance.

Do you wish to stay here?

I opened one eye, and promptly shrieked. Or would have, if the humanoid bending over me hadn't clamped a flipper over my mouth.

"Be silent, or we will be discovered. I am not here to harm you." Gently it eased its fin-shaped hand away. It—he? she?—spoke through a wristcom, I realized, instead of the Hsktskt-issue headgear. A hooded cloak concealed it from head to toe. If it had toes. "Come, we must go now."

The cloak, I realized, was dark brown. Not yellow. Not orange.

"How did you get in here?" Behind it, I saw a gap in the wall that hadn't been there when I'd fallen asleep. A Lok-Teel scurried over my chest, and I automatically removed it and set it aside. "Where did you come from? Who are you?"

"A friend." He—taking a guess, I would say *he*—helped me to my feet, and I muffled another yelp as the days of inactivity made themselves known in my sore muscles. "You must crawl through there"—he pointed to the opening—"to reach the surface."

"I don't want to go to the surface." Did I? No, I wasn't leaving Jennifer or Alunthri behind again. Plus there were Zella and Vlaav, FurreVa, the other patients . . . no way could I go. "Take me to the infirmary."

"I take prisoners away from this place," he said in his strange, whirring voice. The wristcom translated the words, but couldn't remove the underlying hum. "Arrangements have been made. We must go now."

"No." I sat back down and reached for my liquid container. "Thanks, I'll stay." The slave-runner reached for me again, and I shook my head. "Don't get me wrong, I'm grateful for the offer. But I'm not leaving my friends behind." I thought about what he'd said. "Who made the arrangements?"

"I did." He made a disgruntled noise. Definitely a male. "Very well. I will take you to your infirmary."

Crawling through the tunnel took time, considering the shape I was in. The cloaked humanoid went first, stopping every ten feet to glance back at me.

"I'm okay. Keeping going." I disliked tight places, and the walls of the narrow passage were already starting to close in on me. "What's your name?"

He stopped for a moment at a cross section, then turned to crawl off in the right branch. "Noarr."

"My name is Cherijo."

"I know." He was silent for another few minutes, until we reached the end of the passage. "I will jump down. Wait." He disappeared over the edge, and I hurried toward it.

The tunnel emptied out into one of the prisoner tier commons. I spotted Noarr a good four meters below me. He gestured for me to jump.

I shook my head. "Too far!" He only made a more impatient version of the gesture. "Okay." I eased my legs over the side, took a breath, then pushed off. Seconds later I landed in a strong pair of arms.

"Whoa." I grabbed onto his cloak, and tore off a small piece in the process. "That was scary." The warm, dark scent of him rose from his garments, and teased my nose. I glanced up into the dark hood. I couldn't see his eyes, and that bothered me. "Thanks."

Noarr set me on my feet, then guided me to another portion of the crystal tower. We ended up at a wall, where he placed his hand on the solid surface, and pushed. An entire section silently swung inward, revealing another hidden passage, which we entered. Noarr paused long enough to shut the invisible door, and I saw my reflection on the interior.

I looked awful. My face appeared drawn and gaunt, my hair was a snarl of knots, and my tunic needed a thorough decon. But I stared at the reflection, amazed not at what I saw, but that I saw anything at all.

"How were you able to drill through the crystal?

Where did you get the mirrors to conceal the entrances to these tunnels?"

"The tunnels already existed. The Lok-Teel deposit a substance which creates the mirror effect." He urged me forward. "We must hurry."

"You're too big to be a Reedol." Hurry, my foot. "Mind showing me your face?"

He pulled the hood from his head, revealing a hairless skull half again as large as my own. "Satisfied, woman?"

I'd never seen his species before. I'd have remembered the unusual swirls of white pigmentation curving over every inch of his dark brown face. Or were they some form of tattoo? He had a large head with heavy-lidded, shadowed eyes, and a small, full-lipped mouth. More curved, white ridges followed the lines on his high-arched nose.

The eyes were veiled by the protrusion of his brow, but something less than civilized lurked in those shadows. Noarr was, I decided, not a person to be trifled with.

Neither was I.

"Where did you come from? Are you a slave? How did you get into the pit? Why do you want to get me off Catopsa? How can you do that?"

"I cannot answer these questions now." He pulled me along after him down the hidden corridor. "I will take you to your infirmary. Stay there and out of sight for now."

"I can't do that. I have to treat my patients."

He thought about that for a second. "If the beasts ask why you have returned, say it was on the orders of the Terran OverMaster."

"Right. Like they'd believe that."

"They will believe." The white spirals on his cheeks shifted as he gave me his rather startling version of a grin. "You belong to him, do you not?"

"I don't belong to *anyone*." We'd reached the end of the corridor and faced another mirrored wall.

"Hold on. Are you the one who moved those infected females over to the male tier?"

"Yes. The infirmary lies beyond." He took out a small device and aimed it toward the wall. "Readings indicate no one is in the corridor. Go, now." Noarr turned to head back down the passage.

I caught the edge of one flowing sleeve and tugged. "Wait. I want to know more about these tunnels. How you make that fungus into mirrors—"

He removed my hand and stepped back. "There is no time for that now." His full cloak swirled and he was halfway down the passage before a low "Farewell, woman" floated back to me.

CHAPTER TEN

Namesake

Nurse Dchêm-os dropped an entire tray of instruments on the floor when I finished cleaning up and walked out from behind a berth partition. "Doctor!"

"Keep your whiskers on, Zel." I spied Vlaav, who was staring at me as though I'd risen from a postmortem table. "How are the meningitis cases?"

The Saksonan shuffled his footgear, then eyed me with a nervous expression. "They weren't responding well to the intravenous cephalosporin, so I've switched them to synrifampin derivatives."

He'd done exactly what I would have. "Carry on, Doctor."

I had a great deal of work to do and probably very little time in which to accomplish it, so I gave Zella a highly abbreviated version of what had happened, without mentioning the tunnels or Noarr by name.

"Thanks for bringing me the rations," I said to the nurse, not bothering to hide the speculative tone in my voice.

She wouldn't look at me, and shoved a stack of charts in my hands. "For what I did, my family would have me torn to pieces. For my moment of weakness, do not thank me."

I put the charts aside. "Explain that to me."

"Mean, what do you?"

"Why did you make a vow to kill me?"

Zella turned and started for the inpatient berths, then stopped. Without looking at me, she removed her headgear. "They killed eight members of the crew, when the Hsktskt boarded the *Perpetua*. My genitor, one of them was." She looked back at me. "I swore to avenge him, that is why."

"I see." I'd never been told about the deaths. "I'm sorry. I didn't know."

"You responsible, I held."

I pushed the hair from my brow, and tried to think of what to say. Only the truth mattered. "I was."

"You were, yes." She retreated to the berths and began her vitals checks on the patients.

I could wallow in the guilt, or I could work. I ended up doing both.

To my utter astonishment, I discovered halfway through my first shift that Noarr was right. A Hsktskt centuron who reported for a minor laceration questioned my presence, only to accept the bland excuse completely. No one else bothered to ask.

Maybe the Hsktskt didn't run quite as tight a slave-depot as they thought they did.

FurreVa's infants had gained control of two limbs and were now confined to her chamber. The infants toddled and crawled around a "playpen" made of two quasi-quartz walls with plasteel panels clamped between them. Inhibitor webbing kept the kids from crawling out. During my house call, I checked the healing grafts on her back, then asked if she had reviewed the text data on the reconstructive surgery.

"I have." She handed the data chart back to me. "Although I am not versed in the terminology, it seems very ambitious." She looked over the web at her young. "Dangerous, as well."

"You've put your life in my hands before," I said. "I can do this procedure safely. But ultimately the decision is yours."

"I do not wish to look like this"—she touched her face—"for the balance of my existence."

I'd take that to be a yes. "Then we'll do it."

She removed several containers of what looked like synthetic, pulp-laden blood from her prep unit. "I must feed my brood." She set them a good foot apart from each other inside the "playpen."

I didn't want to watch the babies slurp that up, so I left and went on to my own chamber. Jenner was waiting for me, and I programmed a much more civilized meal for my "baby."

"Dried catfish bits for you, lucky guy." I set down the large server. I wasn't hungry, so I headed for my pallet. The chime of an incoming signal startled me— I hadn't noticed the new com console someone had installed in my quarters. Slowly I went over to answer it.

What if it's Reever, and he wants to know how I got out of that pit?

Taking a page from Noarr's book, I decided to tell my Lord and OverMaster that TssVar had released me.

Speak of the Hsktskt. TssVar's gleaming eyes coalesced onto the vidisplay, and I took an involuntarily deep breath. "OverLord?"

"Dr. Torin. You will report to Compound Command tomorrow."

"For what reason?"

"Pre-trade inspection." He terminated the signal before I could ask another question.

"Well, that tells me a lot."

"I could tell you more."

I whirled around to see Reever standing at my door panel. "Learn how to knock, will you?"

"I ordered you confined to the isolation pit for fourteen rotations." Reever walked in and closed the door. "How is it that you are released after only five?"

"Apparently OverLord TssVar needs me for this pre-trade business." It wasn't really a lie. And I could get back out of that pit, if he threw me back down in it. But if he noticed my PIC had healed and vanished again—the edge of my pallet hit the back of my legs, and I stopped shuffling away from him. "What do you want?"

"The truth."

"That's it."

"You're afraid of me," he said, as though it was some huge revelation. "Why? Because of GothVar? What did he do to you?" I gave him an ironic stare. "What did he do to you *on the ship*?"

"I have to get some sleep now." I sat down and pulled back the linens. Torn and bloodstained, I noticed, and shuddered.

"I know why you don't wish to talk about it." Reever sounded almost sympathetic. No, I was tired, and my ears weren't functioning correctly. "I endured a similar ordeal. I can help you."

I'd thought I'd felt every feasible emotion toward Reever—dislike, affection, infatuation, and abhorrence. Apparently not.

I gazed at Reever's hands. "You want to sympathize, is that it? Tell me all about your tragic childhood?" Something trickled into my veins, something hot and fast. "You enslave me, bring me to this godforsaken rock, throw me down a pit to starve to death, and now you want to *help* me?"

His brows drew together. "I ordered you be given daily rations."

I stretched out on my pallet, every muscle coiled with outrage. He genuinely expected me to believe that waste. "I need to sleep. Go harass someone else."

"I saw you after GothVar branded you here and

on the ship. This unnatural reaction you've experienced will require treatment."

The man simply had a death wish. I flung an arm over my eyes. "And when did you graduate Medtech, *Dr.* Reever?"

"I understand how you feel."

"What?" I jumped up and went after him. Both of my palms slammed into his chest, sending him staggering back. "You, *understand* me? You think you know how I *feel*? You've never understood the first thing about me. You don't feel anything. You look human, but that's all!"

"I've never been human." He seized my hands before I could hit him again. "Neither have you. That, I understand."

There was another of those long, silent intervals between us where a lot could have been said and wasn't. He let go first. I went back to my pallet. I didn't look at him again, and only when the door panel opened and closed, did I finally relax enough to bury my face in my pillow, and wish I'd let Duncan Reever die back on K-2.

I stopped by the infirmary on my way to report to TssVar the next day, only to find the entire assessment area trashed and Pmohhi treating Vlaav for a sprained elbow.

"I tried to stop them," the Saksonan said, and moaned as I took over from the nurse and assessed him. "They insisted they were here, that we were hiding them."

"More prisoners missing?" I glanced at the League nurse, who nodded. FurreVa wasn't in any shape to do this. "Which one of the lizards was in charge?"

"The one with no brow."

"That does it." I wrapped Vlaav's arm and encased it with a soft splint, then went over to the console and signaled Reever.

He regarded me with evident disapproval. "Why have you not reported to Command?"

"Because that idiot GothVar trashed my infirmary, that's why." I calculated how much damage had been done. "Half the equipment is ruined. Replace it, and get some of your precious lizards down here to clean up the mess. Then I'll report to Command."

"Report now. I will see to the infirmary."

I waited until the centurons showed up before I left anyway. Let Reever and TssVar stew about my insubordination, I thought as I stomped off to Command.

A centuron intercepted me on the way, and directed me to follow him. We caught up to TssVar as he headed to the outer perimeter structures.

"You are late," he said as soon as he saw me.

"Your guards trashed my infirmary," I said. "What is this pre-trade inspection you want me to perform?"

"The traders now insist all slaves be inspected and certified disease free before they leave Catopsa." Before I could formulate a reply to that, the OverLord cast a large yellow eye in my direction. "Do not think to falsely certify any of them unfit for trade, Doctor, or I will close down your infirmary."

So much for Strategy Number One. "What if I don't *want* to do these inspections?"

"I will close down the infirmary until you do."

And Number Two. "How many prisoners are you selling today?"

"A small group. Fifty."

There were more than fifty traders waiting in the huge trade commons when we entered. No sign of the merchandise, though. TssVar ordered the guard to take me into another chamber off the main structure, and there I found the prisoners waiting to be sold. The guard handed me a scanner and a data pad.

"Inspect them, and send them out when you are finished. Detain any who are unfit for sale."

The centuron went back out to the commons. The slaves all looked at me with varying degrees of despair, disgust, and outright hatred.

I squared my shoulders. "Do you know what happens to unfit slaves?" Several of the group made affirmative gestures. "Good. Let's get started." Since no one appeared to be anxious to volunteer, I pointed to a handful of prisoners. "You, you, and you. And you two over there. Come here, one at a time, please."

The first shuffled over. It was a Whelikkian albino, and looked on the thin side. A quick scan revealed some minor malnourishment, but no disease. "Okay." I recorded the results on the data pad. "What's your name?"

"Ska Gruv," the male said in a sullen tone. His white hide turned faintly pink. "What does it matter?"

"I'm going to make a record of your names and who they sell you to." I glanced at the doorway, then risked keeping my headgear on. "Keeping meticulous records is important. I'm going to need names, planet of origin, your last assignment, and anything else you may think pertinent. You never know who might get a chance to look at these facts."

That was the most I could say, but the Whelikkian understood as soon as I took out the other data pad I'd slipped in my tunic pocket, and copied the data over to it.

"Whelikkia, Aca Nok territories. Taken during a trade jaunt in the Hutillo Quadrant," he told me. "My ship was the *Ral Ber*. All forty crew members survived and were brought here."

I gave him a reassuring smile. "Thanks."

It took another two hours to do all the inspections, and record all the data. Two of the prisoners I asked to wait to one side while I finished with the others. Once I was alone with them, I used the data pad to translate my Terran diagnosis into their language.

I assume you know what's wrong, I keyed in. *I've altered your records and have certified you as fit. I'm sorry, but the truth is, you only have a few rotations left, at the most.*

One of the ruddy-faced Isalth-io humanoids exchanged a significant glance with its friend, then took the data pad and typed in an inquiry. *Why do you not tell the beasts?*

I don't work for them, I typed. *I figured you didn't want to die on this rock, either.*

They both nodded, touched their delicate hands to mine, then walked out to the trade platform. To the untrained eye, they both looked extremely healthy. They weren't, although they had been: for nearly four centuries, the entire length of their species natural life span. Soon—very soon—they would both be dead of natural causes—old age.

I finished saving the data to my spare data pad and followed them. What I saw made me stand in the doorway and stare.

All fifty slaves had been placed on an elevated grav-platform that was hovering a meter off the ground. The enormous stage made a slow route around the chamber, and traders peered eagerly at the prisoners standing on it.

The pre-auction viewing. The sight filled me with disgust, and I wished I could walk out. Only I couldn't. I had to fake interest so I could stay and hear every slave's destination, record it, and hope to somehow get it off Catopsa and to the nearest League Authority. The League might not want to deal with me, but they would certainly go after every one of the worlds dealing in slaves.

The bidding began as soon as the platform landed and the Hsktskt brought the prisoners forward, two at a time. A large display screen kept track of the electronic offers, and noted each final bid. I kept my eyes fixed on that as I input the same into my personal data pad.

Bastards.

Some of the prisoners wept and pleaded, and it got harder to keep my focus on the display. Centurions had to drag others off the platform to turn them over to their new "Masters." Females cringed as knowing hands ran over them. Males swore as their limbs were inspected for strength and flexibility. By the time the trading was through, I was shaking.

Alunthri had endured this. Maybe I would, too.

"Have you completed the inspection records?" the OverLord asked from behind me.

"Yes." I swiftly switched the data pads, then turned.

TssVar was accompanied by an oddly dressed, smaller Hsktskt. A female, judging by the brow markings I'd come to recognize. She returned my scrutiny.

"Here." I handed him the pad the guard had given me, and watched the traders hustling the slaves they'd purchased from the commons. "I'll get back to the infirmary now." *And throw up in private.*

"You will be required to perform these inspections at all future trade sessions."

"Be still my heart." I didn't bother to hide my aversion.

"She is punier than I remember," the female said suddenly. "But her insolence has not changed."

A clear memory of the same low, rough voice screaming at me dispelled some of my tension. "You're in a much better mood than the last time I saw you, Mom."

TssVar made an impatient sound that expressed his opinion of females. "My mate, UgessVa."

"CrreeVar." UgessVa hailed another Hsktskt coming toward us, and tapped me with the end of one limb. "Here are others you may recognize, Doctor."

A cluster of beings almost as tall as I was trailed after CrreeVar, who was wearing a male version of UgessVa's garment. Identical to Hsktskt, only shorter, they wore short, kilted tunics and were hissing and arguing among themselves. I'd seen infant Hsktskt, and the adult versions, but never had encountered the in-between ages.

Of course, my brain kicked in. These were the quintuplets I'd delivered back on K-2.

At the sight of their sire, all five came to a halt and fell into a silent, straight line.

"The brood appears fit, Nurturer," TssVar said after subjecting the kids to a thorough inspection. The largest of the brood peered at me and made a chuffing sound. "You wish to say something, ChrreechoVa?"

Oh, God, TssVar's mate had kept her promise and named the poor kid after me. No wonder the girl looked like she wanted to kick something.

The five-and-a-half-foot tall female gazed steadily in my direction. "This female is my Designate, Over-Lord, is it not?"

"Yes. This is Dr. Cherijo Torin. You may make your greeting."

The female walked out of the line and approached me, her tongue flickering constantly as she tasted my air. "There is not much to her, is there, Nuturer?"

UgessVa waved a limb. "She is Terran; they are a diminutive species."

"I greet you, Designate Chrreecho," ChrreechoVa said, and slapped a limb against my shoulder. "Your name is difficult to articulate."

Yeah, well, she was only about a year and a half old. And strong, too, judging from the throb in my upper arm. "I'm sorry they stuck you with it."

"Do I not please you?" She struck a straighter stance. "I am the Dominary among my brood-siblings. They defer to me in all things."

"You look like a nice kid." When she didn't get that, I tried again. "You please me very much."

She tried to imitate my smile, then looked up at

her mother. "Why does she bare her teeth like that, Nurturer?"

"It is an expression of approval. Her kind have an annoying mobility to their facial muscles." UgessVa turned to address me. "Our Dominary excels during her educational intervals."

Better than being lousy at school. "That's good."

"We must not detain your sire." CrreeVar, who I figured was a sort of male nanny, herded the kids along. Before she disappeared around a corner, ChrreechoVa gave me a last, lingering stare.

"Nice kids." I waved. "They look like they're thriving."

"They are." UgessVa seemed disgruntled about something. "My Dominary wishes to be a physician. That should gratify you, Terran."

I chuckled. Oddly enough, it did.

I left OverLord TssVar to play Happy Family with his brood and headed back to the infirmary. No guards followed me, which was a good thing. Halfway there a mirrored door opened into the corridor and a tall, shrouded figure beckoned to me.

"Noarr?" I glanced quickly around, then hurried into the aperture. The quasi-quartz panel swung shut behind me. "What are you, nuts? Someone will catch you!"

"I need your help." Without another word he grabbed my hand with his flipper and pulled me down another narrow tunnel. Around one bend another figure stood waiting—Wonlee.

"What are you doing here?" I looked from the League Lieutenant to my silent companion.

"There are five who must be removed from the infirmary," Noarr told me.

"Five what? Patients?"

"Yes. We need your help getting them off the planet, Doctor," Wonlee said.

"How?"

Wonlee handed Noarr a syrinpress, which the alien filled from a vial of colorless liquid then extended to me. "The guards moved them to impatient berths while you were at the trading session. Inject each of them with twenty units of this, then certify their deaths."

I stepped back, banging my shoulders into a wall. "I'm not killing anyone."

"You won't kill them," Wonlee said. "The fluid will slow their metabolisms and mask their life signs for several hours. Hsktskt use the same when preparing to enter cryogenic suspension."

"Adrenlatyne?" I snatched the syrinpress away from Noarr the moment he nodded. "Do you know how lethal this drug is?" Neither of them appeared terribly concerned. "Why risk killing them just to make them *look* dead? How are you going to get them off the planet? What's the big hurry?"

Noarr and the Lieutenant glanced at each other.

Nice to be trusted. I dropped the instrument in my tunic pocket and planted my fists on my hips. "Someone had better start talking, or I'm going to try this stuff out on one of you."

Wonlee's spines rose, but almost at once he sighed and leaned back against the wall. "I have been assigned to recycling." He inclined his head toward Noarr. "Once I retrieve the bodies, he will use the tunnels to remove them from the compound."

Time for tall, dark, and tattoo-faced to do some explaining, so I pivoted and addressed him. "What are *you* going to do with them?"

"One of the salvage merchants works for me. He will place the prisoners in suspension, relocate them to their homeworld, and see to it they receive the medical treatment they need."

I fingered the applicator. "Why these five prisoners in particular?"

"The reproductive inhibitors have created a toxic reaction in their species. Without treatment on their homeworlds with native pharmaceuticals, they will die within the next rotation."

"All right." I gave Noarr a hard look. "If you're lying to me, I swear, I will make you the most miserable being on this rock."

"That will be difficult to do," Wonlee said.

I turned on him. "Not for me, pal."

It took time to get out of the tunnel undetected and back to the infirmary. Once I was there, I had to convince Zella and Vlaav to go back to their chambers early. That required me to stage a professional temper tantrum.

"Doctor, you were a half an hour late dispensing meds. These dressings are a disgrace, nurse. And if I see one more patient developing berth sores, I'm going to find a large, blunt object and start beating you both over the head with it. Get out of here, *now*." Vlaav started making excuses, while my bad-tempered nurse began sputtering. "Shut up! Just go—*get out!*" I yelled.

They both left, justifiably upset with me. I'd apologize to them later, I promised myself. Now I had to get Noarr's five patients prepped and isolated. I pulled the charts and located them. They were grouped with the female meningitis patients. Since I hadn't performed rounds since my return, the sight of them made me gasp.

Five eight-limbed, dusk-colored bodies lay huddled beneath thermal wraps. One of the females rotated an eye cluster toward me, and buzzed something unintelligible.

Evidently TssVar hadn't returned *all* the Aksellan captives to Clyvos.

I set up privacy screens, then made quick examinations of all of them. They were uniformly battered, limbs bruised, carapaces cracked in several areas. No inhibitor drug in the world did this kind of damage.

Noarr appeared beside me. "Have you administered the adrenlatyne?"

I whirled around and jammed the syrinpress against his broad neck. "What did you do to them, you lying snake?"

A moment later I was sitting on my backside on the floor, and Noarr was administering the drug to the first Aksellan female. Whatever he'd done to me had bruised my wrist, elbow, and dignity, among other things. That didn't mean I was going to sit there and let him murder my patients.

I pushed myself up and flung myself directly at him. And found myself dangling a foot off the floor, suspended by a fistful of tunic.

"Either help me," he said, "or stay out of my way."

What he meant was, *trust* him. I had little reason to do so. Yet every instinct inside me was inclined to do just that. I swiped at the syrinpress. "Put me down. I'll do it."

He shadowed me as I infused each of the females with the drug. Another hidden door opened in the back of the infirmary, and Wonlee emerged.

"Are you done? I must report back to the centuron before I am missed."

"Go." I ran a scan on the five females and falsified death recordings for each of them. Noarr hovered, watching me. "That means you, too, Zorro."

"Zorro?"

"Another demented male with a hopeless mission. Go on. Get out of here."

Noarr and Wonlee left the way they came. I went to the console and signaled for a recycler crew to come and retrieve the not-quite-dead corpses. While I was waiting for them to arrive, I finished rounds and tried not to wonder if I'd done the right thing.

Acting nonchalant as Wonlee and two other slaves came in to remove the Aksellans wasn't easy. The Lieutenant didn't look at me, but something was wrong. I could feel it.

"Doctor."

The hair on the back of my neck rose as I turned. "OverMaster HalaVar." I gave Reever what I prayed was a convincingly snotty scowl. "Surely you don't need medical treatment. That would convince me there is a God."

"I was informed of the Aksellan deaths."

He regarded the crew removing the bodies, and stopped one litter to lift the thermal cover and inspect the motionless form. It gave me time to raise some mental walls, just in case he decided to resort to one of his mind-control tricks.

"As you see, arachnids don't respond well to reproductive controllers." I yanked the cover back over the patient. "Have some common decency and respect the dead, will you?"

He wasn't about to let it go. "There was nothing you could do for them?"

"Not a thing." Terror should have paralyzed me, made me stutter, *something*. Instead I lied my way through a concise, completely false postmortem report. "Maybe you should reconsider using chemical inhibitors on your merchandise. It's killing them faster than you can sell them," I said, as an afterthought.

Naturally he had an annoying comeback ready. "You would prefer to see small children torn from their parents and sold to the highest bidder?"

"Is that why you wanted to get me pregnant?" I smiled when I saw his nearly imperceptible reaction. Distaste? Or was it something more basic? "Think our kid would bring a good price?"

He ignored Wonlee and the others—the whole point of my provocation—and moved closer. When he would have touched me, I glided back a step. "I would never sell our child."

My face got hot again. "Let me clarify this, *Over-Master HalaVar*. We're not having a child. We're *never* having a child. I wouldn't have sex with you if you were the last Terran in existence. I'd rather mate with

GothVar. Not only would he be a better lover, but giving birth to a litter of his little monsters would be a treat versus letting you touch me."

The Aksellans were gone. The centurons Reever had brought with him had left the infirmary. It was just me and him now, and from the set of his jaw I could tell my lord and OverMaster was just a little upset. Good. Brooding over my latest rejection would keep him from interfering with Noarr. Recklessly I pushed past him and went to rescan one of the patients.

"Cherijo."

The patient's condition hadn't changed, and I made a totally unnecessary chart entry noting the same.

Reever came up behind me and tugged at the sleeve of my tunic. "Your PIC has healed over again."

He must have seen it when I'd picked up the chart. Damn it. "You'll have to brand me later," I said, unable to keep my voice from shaking. "I'm busy now."

"It doesn't have to be this way between us."

I jerked my sleeve down. "Oh, yes it does."

Several hours later, the sight of Noarr stepping out of my storage unit made me shriek and hit the door panel controls with my fist.

"What are you doing?" I looked through the wall to the corridor. "Someone will see you!"

"I wanted to see *you*."

Something touched me—a large, ridged flipper that curled over the curve of my shoulder. Then the other. Through my tunic, I felt the warmth of contact.

"Okay, you've seen me." I looked up, and the edge of Noarr's hood brushed my brow. "Noarr, please."

"You were angry with OverMaster HalaVar." His flippers slid up, and pushed into my hair. "Why?"

"How did you . . ." The clip I wore unhinged and fell to the floor. "Excuse me. What are you doing?"

"What I have wanted to, since first I saw you." Noarr spread the soft, dense weight over my back, then cradled my neck between his fins. The warmth of his breath touched my lips. I forced my eyes to stay open as his face drew closer.

"You're a very attractive male."

"I thank you."

"And there is no way I'm getting involved with you . . . like this."

He gazed at me, untroubled. "No?"

"No."

He wasn't going to kiss me. He was an alien, so he probably thought kissing was repulsive. "You're too dangerous."

"Am I?"

He didn't kiss me. He *tasted* me. Pressed his mouth to my face, and his tongue rasped over my flesh.

"Noarr?" There was something extremely unsettling about being in this position. Not the least of which was this sudden, bizarre sense of déjà vu—like I'd done this before. But when? With Kao? "Why are you, um, doing that?"

"I wish to." Both fins ran down my back and curled around my waist to support me. He lifted his mouth from my skin. Put it next to my ear. Whispered like a lover. "I like your taste, woman."

Good, I hadn't made another accidental betrothal, like I had with Kao and Xonea. Now what was I supposed to say?

"Right . . . thanks." I shook my head to clear it. The scene with Reever came back to me, and I stiffened. "No. Wait. I can't do this."

He set me away from him. "Another time."

I was in no shape to argue the point. "Sure. Right. Another time." A thousand years from now.

He slipped out of my chamber, while I sat down

weakly on the edge of my pallet and tried not to hyperventilate.

It was a rebound effect, I thought. I'd rejected Reever and Noarr had simply reminded me of Kao for a moment. That was all.

I hoped.

Pulling off Noarr's audacious scheme gave me plenty to think about. What we'd accomplished this time could work again. For the first time since I'd landed on Catopsa, I allowed myself to hope.

I decided not to confide in Zella and Vlaav, who accepted my apology for chasing them off. Not without some fuss, of course. The Saksonan worried that my attitude would get the staff sold off to traders. The nurse was simply irritated about being yelled at.

"Textbook perfect, those dressings were," she said, thumping down an instrument tray with unnecessary force.

"You're right, they were." I checked the dwindling stock of preserved synplasma and wrote up orders to produce what I hoped we wouldn't have to use. "Pardon me for venting my spleen on you."

Zella's suspicious gaze changed. "Entitled, I suppose you are."

"Gee, thanks." I saw a number of Lok-Teel crawling around the occupied berths and sighed. "Do me a favor, Zel. Take those blobs off the patients, before someone starts shrieking again."

FurreVa reported for the first of the craniofacial surgeries I'd planned. After going over the procedures with her one last time, I had Zella prep her for the initial procedure. Vlaav volunteered to assist as I performed the exploratory and neurological repairs.

"What caused the trauma?" The Saksonan asked as I carefully peeled the damaged muscles away from the underlying cranial structure.

"A large, bladed weapon, from the look of things."

I scanned her brain tissue, and wondered once more why the big female had refused to tell me exactly how she'd gotten the injury. Whatever had hit her had been a centimeter shy of killing her outright. "We'll deal with the brain damage first—that's minimal—then see if we can't fix the distortion to the cranium."

Relieving the pressure on the brain caused by scar tissue took only a few minutes. Repairing the skull itself was the real challenge.

Due to the nonunion healing of the original trauma, I had to realign and graft all the bones involved, from above the orbital rim down through the nasal arch and into the mandible. I'd never done such extensive resetting—but I'd never seen a patient survive such a wound, either. I had Vlaav attach one of the pre-adapted reconstruction plates, and explained how they would hold the rebroken bones together as the transplanted osteogenic cells took hold.

I closed the incision and carefully placed the Hsktskt female's huge head in a support halo. "Once the cranial bonesetter stabilizes the trauma sites, I'll get started on the nerve and soft tissue repairs."

Vlaav was utterly fascinated by the proposed work, and asked if he could assist on all the reconstructive procedure. "I've learned more watching you cut today than I did in my first two years at Medtech."

"Sure." I stripped off my gloves and mask to grin. "Only next time, you'll have to do some cutting yourself."

I saw Wonlee a few days after the slave auction, and he confirmed that the Aksellan females had been successfully smuggled off the planet. Since the Hsktskt didn't count how many bodies actually went into huge disposal units, he told me, no one would discover the hoax.

"Then we *can* do this again." I thought of the many

ways I could simulate death among the various species that made up the slave population. Many would only need a chemical nudge to go into a natural state of hibernation. "How do I get in touch with Noarr?"

"I don't know." The Lieutenant glanced at the hidden door at the back of the infirmary. "He has a ship hidden somewhere outside the compound. Uses the tunnels to come and go as he pleases."

Not if he was counting on using me as part of his underground. "We'll just see about that."

"Dr. Torin." Zella appeared, with one arm around the Terran who'd rescued Jenner. He swayed on his feet, and a short gash across his chin was bleeding freely down his neck. "This man needs immediate attention."

Wonlee slipped out of the infirmary as I dealt with Gael Kelly's wound. Once we'd eased him down onto an exam table, I did a thorough brain scan. From the readings, I surmised someone had swiped at him with claws or another sharp object. Sharp enough to partially sever the inferior quadratus labii muscle. Readings also indicated slight malnourishment and moderate dehydration.

"Start a glucose infusion, and get that suture tray over here, Zel." I irrigated the wound and wiped the blood from Gael's jaw and throat. As I did, I surreptitiously removed his headgear and mine. "They throw you in the confinement pit?" He nodded and grimaced as I applied the topical anesthetic. "Were you released, or do you have to go back?"

"I'm foostering, for now." His bright gaze slid to the open door panel, where two guards were lounging, then back to me while his voice dropped to a murmur. "Have you heard about this chancer? Calls himself Noarr."

There were too many centurons in the vicinity for me to have a discussion about my new ally, even without the monitored headgear on. "No, I haven't." At the same time, I glared at Gael, then moved my eyes toward the waiting guards. The suture laser hummed as I activated the beam and started repairing the muscle damage. "Don't move, don't talk, or you'll end up with an ugly profile." After I was done with the delicate work, I sealed the wound. "Okay. Now what smacked you in the face?"

"One of the thicks."

"Thicks?"

He gave me a wry grin. "An OverCenturon."

"Sloped brow, short temper, hates Terrans?"

"That's the one." Gael reached up to finger his chin, and I slapped his hand.

"No poking." I sterilized the outer derma once more, then put a small aerated dressing over the fresh sutures. "Let's get you over to a berth. You're going to be staying with us for a day or two."

As I helped him to his feet, Gael leaned forward to whisper against my hair. "Mind yourself, *dote*. The thicks have a sleeveen among the prisoners, spying for them. This chancer could be the one."

I'd learned blind trust could be lethal, I thought as I got Gael settled in. Perhaps hope was just as deadly.

A much-needed interval of calm prevailed over the next week. FurreVa's bone grafts took, and Vlaav and I continued with the reconstructive work. The meningitis patients showed astonishing, collective improvement, and I knew I'd soon be able to discharge the healthiest back to the general population. Not that I was in any big hurry to do that. Far as I was concerned, they could remain inpatients as long as they liked. Gael's chin healed without complications, and he practically demanded to be released.

"Sick of pulling me plumb, I am."

"Okay. But do me a favor," I said as I wrote up his discharge notes. "Study up on standard Terran, will you? I can't understand half the stuff you say."

"I can speak stanTerran," Gael told me, and

winked. "Only Oirish reminds me of home, and it isn't in the thicks' database."

Maybe I'd study up on Celtic dialects.

My elation over the success of FurreVa's second surgery quickly dissipated as another three prisoners were brought in, suffering from the same bacterial meningitis. Although Vlaav and I combed over every inch of their bodies, this trio carried no parasites. Nor was there any contamination of the food and water samples I had brought from their cells for analysis.

Something had to be done. I gave Wonlee a message for Noarr to see me as soon as possible, but the elusive alien had yet to reappear.

Then for some reason FurreVa decided she'd had enough of the repair work, and demanded to be released. I argued with her until she ripped the infusers from her limbs and rolled out of her berth.

"I haven't spent two shifts putting your face back together for you to go and ruin my work!" I yelled as she stomped past me. "And I still have to finish the cosmetic repairs, you stupid lizard!"

She paused for a moment. "I do not want any more fixing of my face, Terran." With that, out she went.

Furious with myself and the Hsktskt, I went over and kicked the privacy screen, which fell over.

A naked and definitely frightened Jgrap sat up and pulled Kroni into a protective hold. "You may turn me over to the beasts, but I will not permit you to harm—"

"Oh, give me a break." I turned my back and stalked off.

Finding the teenagers at it again, and my inability to stop FurreVa sent me off duty in a bad mood. That's probably why I never saw the shadow move out from behind my door panel when I closed it.

One moment I was pulling off my tunic, and silently cursing the only hope I had; the next something catapulted me face-first into a crystal wall.

"Time we settled accounts, Doctor."

Shropana.

My hands came up just in time to prevent me from cracking my skull open, but a heavy blow at the back of my neck sent me sliding to my knees. I fell over, heard Jenner yowling, and raised my head far enough to see the Colonel holding my furious, struggling cat by the neck.

"I understand this thing means something to you." He tightened his claws, and cut off Jenner's airway. "As much as my command meant to me, I think."

"No . . ." I started to drag myself up, desperate to save my pet.

Shropana stepped close enough to kick me back down onto my side, then dangled my cat above my face. "Bid it farewell."

Jenner's frantic movements slowed, and I tried again to get up. Another kick sent me spinning over into the bottom half of my console unit. I flung my hand up, hoping to hit the signal relay switch, but the Colonel only drove his foot into my abdomen once more.

"Watch, Doctor. Watch what *you* love die."

The explosion of pain made me writhe, but I wouldn't let myself black out. I kept my eyes on Jenner, on the weak, scrabbling movements of his paws against Shropana's grip. I had to get up, get to him—

"Shropana."

Pulse fire slammed into the Colonel, which sent him reeling across my chamber and Jenner's limp body to the floor. Reever appeared above me, pointing a rifle at the League commander. Gasping for breath, I crawled until I could reach my pet, then pulled him into the curve of my arm. My fingers spread over his abdomen. Hurt but breathing. Still alive. Relief made me sob as I cradled the small, warm body against my breast.

"Centurons." Reever deactivated the rifle and

came to stand over me. "Remove this prisoner immediately." He put the weapon aside and lifted me into his arms.

"OverMaster?"

Reever inhaled sharply. "I will deal with it."

I was too dazed to do more than gape back up at him. Stare at his narrowed, glittering eyes. Lips thinned to a white slash. The muscles along cheekbones and jaw were taut and flagged with a dark red tinge. I couldn't believe it. Unemotional, blank-faced Reever showed every physical indication of being completely enraged.

It didn't surprise me. It dumbfounded me.

At the same time, one of the centurons hauled a semiconscious Shropana to his feet. "What shall we do with this one, OverMaster?"

Reever glanced down at me, then turned to reply. "Execute him."

I admit, a part of me agreed. Another part wanted to watch them do it, too. But the physician within overruled both. "No. Don't. I'm okay. Jenner's still alive."

Reever's color returned to something resembling normal. His tone remained the same—as chilling as it had been after the Drift Nine incident. "I didn't ask for your approval, Doctor."

The guards dragged Shropana out of my chamber. Reever carried me over to my berth and sat down, still holding me in his arms. He ran his hands over my abdomen, and I winced as he found the two places the League commander had driven his foot into. "I'll take you to the infirmary."

"Good idea, but wait." I eased Jenner into my lap and checked him over with shaking hands. "I think he'll be all right, but I need to scan him and . . . then . . . I should check . . ."

The shock set in at last, and my teeth began to chatter. I didn't remember much after that. Reever evidently carried me and Jenner to the infirmary and left us with Vlaav. My physical reaction was of short duration, and once I re-emerged, I insisted on performing the scans on my beloved pet personally. Only when I'd verified he had little more than a sore throat did I let the resident run an abdominal series on me.

Reever signaled me later from Command. "You will be reassigned two guards at all times," he said.

Guilt made me snap at him. "Why? Shropana's dead. I'll hear Devrak coming a mile away."

"The Colonel has escaped. Report to my chamber at once."

I reported. The support braces around my bruised ribs dug into my skin as I walked through the door panel and confronted Reever. "Well? Did you find him yet?"

"No." Reever rose from his console and came around toward me. Before I could stop him, he took hold of my right arm and tugged up my sleeve. "Why do you keep removing it?"

"I don't." I wasn't going to look at my arm. I already knew the slave code was gone. "It heals by itself. What are you doing?"

"You must bear the proper designation."

This was the same man who'd ordered a prisoner executed, just for kicking me and trying to strangle my cat? "No. It won't work."

"Come with me."

Instant, nerve-shredding fear clutched at me. My lungs strained for air. "No. I won't let you do that to me again. It doesn't work, Reever." He was pushing me through the door panel and out into the corridor. "Damn you, don't *keep doing this to me*!"

Nothing I said had any effect on him. Neither did the kicking or shrieking when he grabbed me and slung me over his shoulder. He deposited me on my feet in a chamber I hadn't seen before (his?) and secured the door panel before going to a very familiar-looking console.

There was no way I could punch a hole through the plasteel panel between me and freedom. I ended up pounding on it anyway.

"Let me out of here!"

"Prepare the PIC application."

My muscles locked. No. He wasn't going to burn me, I wouldn't let him. There were no handy-dandy floor clamps in here. He couldn't burn what he couldn't hold down.

Then something stole over me, like a gentle caress. His voice, inside my head.

Why are you afraid? I won't harm you. The familiar paralysis followed.

Oh yes, you will. I fought, pushing Reever from my mind, groping for any amount of control over my body. Nothing worked. He filled my thoughts, prodding and poking at my walls, while he moved me from the door to the console and stretched out my unmarked right arm. *No. Don't burn me, please, Reever, don't, don't!*

I won't let you feel the pain. An extensor clamp emerged from the console and encircled my right wrist. Reever's mental command became imperative. *Stop fighting me.*

No no no no no no no—

A laser activated. Deep inside myself, I found an untapped source of energy and tapped into it, hurling what I found at Reever. Whatever it was drove him from my mind, and restored partial command of my body. I jerked as the heat seared into my flesh, and screamed.

The concise pattern scrolling over my forearm became blurred as I fought to pull my hand free. The clamp tightened automatically, and something snapped in my wrist. More pain, deeper and harder, rolled up my arm and into my chest.

Can't breathe. Frenzied straining and pulling only made the constriction and torment worse. *Stop it, stop you're killing me!*

A new voice hammered into my ears. "HalaVar. What is this?"

"End application program." Reever caught me as I fell, and held me with one arm as he slapped me hard across the face.

My head fell back, but the sharp impact of his palm dispelled the attack, and I inhaled a huge, rasping gulp of air. It cleared my head enough for me to regain all my senses, and put my fists to good use. I hit him as hard and fast as I could. I wasn't landing any effective blows, but the pleasure of pounding on him felt too wonderful.

Eventually he caught both of my hands—and the flaring agony of what had to be a broken wrist made me groan and stop twisting. "Merely an exercise in obedience, OverLord."

"You should conduct more of them." The Hsktskt eyed me and snorted. "She bleeds."

"Resisting PIC application. Again." Reever hauled me over to a storage unit and sat me down beside it. "Remain there, Doctor, or I will sedate you."

The audacity of the command held me suspended in disbelief. When he removed a medical case and began clumsily treating my burn, I snatched the topical applicator away from him. "I'll do it myself."

"I am pleased to find you here, Doctor." TssVar lumbered over to watch as I cleaned the burn and temporarily splinted my broken wrist. "News has been relayed that will be of personal interest to you."

"Oh?" I clamped down on my strained emotions and gave him an uninterested glance. "The Hsktskt are giving up on the slave-trading business?"

"Perhaps we will," he said, and bared his teeth at my visible start. "I believe our main resources will be required by the war effort."

I stopped strapping my wrist. "War? With who?"

"A signal was received by our border stations from Fendagal XI. It was sent by the Terran who experimented on you. He indicated the Allied League of

Worlds will soon initiate an invasion of Faction held territories."

"The *League* is attacking the Hsktskt?" How could that many world leaders descend into simultaneous lunacy? *Sent by the Terran who experimented on you.* "Joseph Grey Veil gave you this information?"

TssVar would have been blind to miss my expression. "I, too, was surprised by his actions. Until our intelligence sources on Fendagal XI reported that it was Grey Veil's speech before the Ruling Council that convinced the League to declare war."

Joseph, playing both sides of the war. Hedging his bets, or something worse? "Why are you telling me this, OverLord?"

"Your knowledge of this Terran and the League may prove valuable to me in the future."

How fast could I forget everything I knew about the League? "I'm not a military advisor," I said. "Nor do I want to be one. Remember what happened the last time I got in the middle, on Aksel Drift Nine?"

"You will not be given a chance to blow anything up this time, Doctor."

Reever released me to return to the infirmary, and I left him discussing the new threat with TssVar. My creator had instigated a war with the Hsktskt, then had warned them about it. None of it made any sense. What was he trying to do? Play both sides of the game? I knew my creator had no scruples, but this was bizarre, even for him.

"There she is."

GothVar and several other centurons blocked the corridor ahead of me. Since I had a fresh, if somewhat hard-to-read PIC on my arm, I wasn't too worried about him. "What do you want?"

FlatHead tossed a syrinpress to me, which I caught reflexively. "That was brought to me. It contains trace amounts of adrenlatyne. Explain."

Who had turned me in? Vlaav? Zella? "I don't know what you're talking about."

"Five dead Aksellans were removed from the infirmary. Yet none of the chamber monitors show them being transported to the disposal units. Where are they?"

"Like I said, I haven't a clue." I maintained my bland expression.

It didn't work. "Take her to SrrokVar."

PART THREE

Inquisition

CHAPTER ELEVEN

Crying Chambers

If I'd known then to whom and where I was being taken, I wouldn't have played the cooperative prisoner. But ignorance is temporary bliss, and all I felt as the centurons marched me through the corridors was a sort of numb relief. Whoever SrrokVar was, I thought, he wouldn't let FlatHead do anything out of line to me.

Not all the Hsktskt were pitiless sadists.

We walked past the slave tiers and through a connecting passage to another, remote structure—the one the trustees said was guarded around the clock. The two lizards posted at the entrance panel never permitted prisoners past that point, or so I'd been told.

A gesture from GothVar made one of the guards open the panel.

Inside was an area filled with strange-looking equipment. Some I recognized—examination and dissection tables. Electroniscopic scanners. A full forensic analyzer array. Was this the Hsktskt version of a morgue?

I had the feeling I wasn't here to perform an autopsy.

The main enclosure branched off into smaller, closed-panel corridors. Since the panels were closed and locked down, I couldn't tell what lay behind them. Odd stains patterned the transparent floor, due to the conspicuous absence of the efficient Lok-Teel blobs. Never a mold around when you needed one. They'd have scrubbed every surface to a pristine clarity. The faint odor of urine, feces, and blood reached my nose, and made an internal alarm go off.

Cherijo, this is not going to be fun.

Standing in the center of the consoles and rigging was the strange Hsktskt who'd been with FlatHead when he'd branded me with the hand-laser. He was dressed in a fluid-proof garment that vaguely reminded me of surgical gear.

"Dr. Torin." The Hsktskt's tail appendage curled up, then down. Probably what he thought of as a bow. Or he needed to use the lavatory. "I am Lord SrrokVar."

Which meant he was only a step below TssVar in the ranks. "Hello." I made a show of gazing around me. "Nice place you have here."

"I am pleased you think so." To the guards, he said, "You may leave us now."

FlatHead gave me a pointed snarl, then ushered the centurons out of the chamber. Why I wanted to yell for them to come back baffled me.

"I'm gratified we will have the opportunity to become better acquainted."

Maybe it was the way SrrokVar was studying me. Like I was a small, tasty hors d'oeuvre. Or maybe it was that for a Hsktskt, he was extremely erudite. The whole package gave me the creeps.

"Does OverMaster HalaVar know about this . . . visit?" It didn't hurt to throw Reever's name in the ring. Just in case Mr. Erudite intended more than a getting-to-know-you session.

"If he knew you were helping slaves escape, Hala-Var would have you placed in permanent solitary confinement."

There was that. "I didn't help anyone escape, Lord SrrokVar. I tried to explain that to the OverCenturon, but"—I lifted my shoulders and rolled my eyes—"GothVar is not exactly fond of Terrans."

"Only too prevalent an opinion among my kind, I fear." SrrokVar indicated a bare metal chair. "Sit down, please, Doctor."

Gingerly I lowered myself into the seat. "Am I here for discipline?"

SrrokVar actually laughed—an eerie sound, coming from that inhuman throat. "No, my dear Dr. Torin. Like you, I am a physician. My field of study in xenobiology. I thought we might talk and . . . exchange experiences?"

He simply wanted to chat. And I was a Larian flatworm. Still, what could I say? "All right." I pretended to relax in the seat while I studied his equipment array. The treadmills and spinal traction rigs started to bug me. "We could use some of this stuff over in the infirmary. Can I borrow a few things, when we're through?"

"I have been informed that you treat slaves and Hsktskt alike."

"Someone's got to do it." I tapped my fingers on the narrow plasteel chair arm. "If you're a physician, why aren't you attending to your people?"

"My aspirations require me to confine my efforts to research, Doctor. According to your records, you have worked on both a League colonial world and a Jorenian star vessel. I should like to hear about those experiences."

He was *definitely* too well-spoken for a lizard. I wasn't inclined to share fond memories with a Hsktskt. "That would take awhile."

"We have sufficient time, once we clear up the matter for which you were brought here." He tested, then adjusted the clamp on a grav-hoist. "You can do so by relating exactly what happened to the five Aksellans removed from your infirmary."

"Far as I know, their bodies were taken to a disposal and incinerated."

He extended a limb and pressed something on one of the consoles. A bright white light swept over me, and I got to my feet. "Don't be alarmed. It is merely a body scan."

I stayed on my feet and cradled my injured arm. "I've been scanned before. Why now?"

He studied the resulting display data. "Two minor carpal fractures. How did you injure your wrist?"

Before I could reply, a door panel slid open, a centuron dragged a motionless prisoner into the central chamber. "Lord. This one has expired."

"As I expected." SrrokVar picked up a data pad, made a brief entry, then flicked his tongue at the guard. "Take it to disposal. Bring another of its kind to replace it."

The guard dragged the dead body out to the connecting corridor. I began slowly inching over in the same direction.

"Well, it's been great meeting you," I said. "And much as I'd love to stick around, I really have to get back to the infirmary."

"Oh, no, my dear." SrrokVar had two limbs around me before I could blink. "You're not leaving. Not until you give me all the information I require."

I refused to panic. Panic got me broken bones and burned arms. "Like I said, Lord SrrokVar, I didn't help anyone. Those five patients died as a result of toxic reaction to the inhibitors they were given. I have *living* patients I need to attend to."

"Until you give me a satisfactory explanation, you will remain here." He picked me up like a doll, trudged over, and placed me back in the metal chair. This time two half-circles of plasteel slid out and clamped around my abdomen and thighs. Through the door panel the guard had come from, I heard the faint sound of someone weeping.

Crying . . . where had I heard that . . . ?

Crying chambers, one battered prisoner had said.

Xenobiologists studied off-world species—not that there was a big demand for that career field on Terra. The distant memory of an infamous war criminal from a mid-twentieth century conflict came back to me. A doctor. It was discovered he'd been experimenting on interred prisoners at an infamous concentration camp.

The stains on the floor and odd collection of equipment suddenly made sense. And me furious.

"You're experimenting on prisoners, aren't you?"

"I am determining the range of physical endurance limitations among non-Hsktskt species." SrrokVar returned to his console and began inputting more data. "It is vital to know which slaves have the highest physical endurance ratios, so that an appropriate trade value can be assigned to them."

"And how do you determine these ratios?" My hands knotted into fists. "By torturing them?"

"I prefer to think of my trials as testing." He swiveled around, and calibrated a syrinpress as he approached me. "The few Terran trials I have conducted in the past have not yielded significant endurance factors in your species. However, your personal display of superior healing ability has intrigued me. I am looking forward to exploring it fully."

I told him what I thought of his monstrous work as he infused me. It got harder to swear as my tongue thickened, and the too-familiar lethargy of sedation seeped into my limbs.

"You will change your mind," he said as he released me, caught me before I fell, and began stripping my tunic from my body. "Let us begin with what happened to the Áksellans."

"Ak . . . sel . . . lans . . ."

Everything got hazy from there. I broke through the drugged stupor several times to find myself naked, strapped down, and being subjected to a thorough physical examination.

Have to stay awake. My bleary eyes wouldn't cooperate. *Have to know what he's doing.*

When the sedative wore off, I realized I had been moved from the main chamber into a smaller section. I glanced down. My tunic had been replaced, and my arm throbbed. The support strap on my wrist had been augmented with a bonesetter. As for the PIC, it was healing. So fast I could almost feel the edges of the burn pulling together.

I had no clue as to what SrrokVar had done. Had I told him about Noarr? Had he used other drugs to force information out of me?

A broad strap of alloy across my chest manacled me into a sitting position against one wall panel. Another had been fastened to the back of my slave collar. I wasn't alone. Prisoners of many different species lined the three sides of the chamber. A few were unconscious, the rest awake, all staring directly at me.

"How long have I been out?" Sounds of distress and despair erupted around me. I repeated the question to the prisoner closest to me. He didn't respond. No headgear. "Does anyone understand me?"

"I do," a listless, feminine voice said. "Two hours. Perhaps a little longer."

I craned my head over and saw a League Ensign's tunic. A humanoid female was shackled three prisoners down from me. Dark fluid made matted patches in her pale hair, and her face was distorted by a dozen oddly shaped lumps.

I didn't recognize her species, but at least she spoke my language. "Were you on the *Perpetua*?"

"No. The *Stephenson*." The thin, weary-looking female rested her bulbous head against the transparent wall. "Why are you here? I thought you were an ally of the beasts."

"No, I'm not. I never was."

Her lips spread into a cynical grimace. "You will be now."

"Not me." I tested the strength of the straps. I wasn't going anywhere.

The Ensign closed her three eyes. "You'll do anything they want, Terran. It won't get you out of here, but you'll beg them to do it."

Before I could find out more, the chamber door panel slid open and SrrokVar entered, along with three guards. He pointed to me, the female Ensign, and the emaciated figure of a badly injured humanoid. "Bring these three."

The League female cringed. The other being was too far gone to offer more than a low whimper. I lifted my gaze to SrrokVar's, and saw the avid interest glowing there.

I'd seen that look before. It made me want to empty my stomach on his footgear. "You don't need them. Take me."

"Your observations will prove instructional," he said. "Perhaps after the trials, you can offer more enlightened opinions on the methods I employ."

I really was going to vomit. "I don't need to see you in action, thanks."

The guard had to carry the injured humanoid, but the League Ensign fought them. In the end, they resorted to dragging her by the arms down the corridor. I walked behind them without protest. Watching for a chance to escape allowed me to focus on something besides the coming horrors.

Only there were no chances.

"Doctor, if you will resume your position there"—SrrokVar pointed to the metal chair I'd sat in before—"I can begin the latest test trials."

He actually expected me to seat myself and calmly

observe this sickening abomination. "No. Put them back. I can be your test subject for today."

"You are."

The centurons shoved me in the chair, and one stayed to keep his rifle trained on me while SrrokVar briefly examined the first humanoid.

"Hardly worth the time or effort, in this case. Still, I prefer my trials to be comprehensive. Put him there." He indicated the treadmill, which had twin support clamps to hold the sagging prisoner in place. The half-dead alien's body twitched spasmodically as he became aware of what was happening. That was worse than hearing him scream.

"I have information!" The League Ensign clawed at SrrokVar's gear with a desperate hand as the guards lugged her over to one of the traction rigs. "Good information—you'll be pleased this time, I promise. Please, please, don't do this to me again."

My teeth sank into my lower lip as I turned my head away. I couldn't watch her, couldn't be a witness to this. Not like this. Not helpless. "Lord SrrokVar, release these prisoners, and I'll jump through whatever hoops you want me to. I swear I will. Just let them go."

"In contrast, this species is most resilient." SrrokVar said, as if he hadn't heard me. He even patted the Ensign's head with absent affection. "Today we will thoroughly test her structural limitations."

He was going to tear her apart. "You're insane!"

As the centurons forced the now sobbing League female's limbs into restraint cuffs, it distracted the one watching me. I gripped the chair's cold plasteel arms and searched the immediate area for anything I could use as a weapon. The only thing within reach was a data pad, sitting near me on a utility tray. I took it and tucked it under my arm.

"Observe, Doctor." SrrokVar activated the tread-mill and placed a monitor patch on the heaving chest of the stumbling humanoid male. He motioned to one of the guards, who positioned himself behind the male. "Fracture one of his lower appendages."

The guard swung one of his limbs back. I was halfway to the treadmill before I heard the whipping sound and subsequent bone shatter.

"No!" Let them shoot me. "Stop!"

SrrokVar barred my path with his bulk. "You must not interfere with my test subjects, Doctor. All I require now is your clinical observation."

"Get out of my way." I tried to go around him, but he was bigger and faster. The Ensign's shrieks increased in intensity as the traction rig gears whined. I saw that counterweights had been programmed to pull her body in four different directions. "You can't do this to them!"

"I'm a scientist." SrrokVar folded two limbs across his broad chest. "Surely you can appreciate how valuable the knowledge I gain is for the Faction. Now, if you'll observe the Unohew male, he manages to support his entire body weight on a single appendage. Quite well, as it happens. However, his species has no natural endorphins, which creates—"

I jammed the corner of the data pad into one of SrrokVar's eyes, darted around him and saw the humanoid male's unconscious body being dragged backward by the treadmill track. I lunged for the control panel to the traction rig, and managed to slam my fists into the keypad before the first pulse burst over my back.

SrrokVar had me removed to the general holding cell, and left me there for an undeterminable amount of time. The Unohew male never returned, and the newly battered League female sat curled over and wept incoherently.

I was furious. Sick. Frantic to find a way to prevent this animal imitating a physician from continuing his revolting work. I wasn't going to sit there, stare at my footgear, and wonder how long it would take to die, like the others.

No, I had to stop this madness. But how?

The sight of two new prisoners being brought in snared my attention, especially when SrrokVar directed the centurons to manacle each on either side of me.

Wonlee—and Gael Kelly.

"Up your swiss, you caffler," the Terran said as he fought the claws restraining him. Once the Hsktskt had departed, the rage faded from his narrow face and concerned green eyes met mine. "How's the form, *dote*?"

The ache in my back was nothing compared to the vile taste in my mouth. What was SrrokVar using on me? "The form hurts, Irishman. How did you two get thrown in here?"

Wonlee's spines grated against the restraints as he tested them. "Someone informed the beasts of our escape attempt."

"The Lieutenant here and I tried to do a flit to the surface. Snared rapid, we were," Gael said. "Scabby thicks were already there, by God, waiting for us." He shook his head sadly. "And after I warned your hardchaw friend here to whist—"

"I *had* to tell my comrades, in the event we failed." Won's clawed feet tapped an impatient rhythm against the quasi-quartz floor. "They wouldn't betray us."

"Someone did, boyo." Gael banged his head back against the wall. "This place makes me want to bolt. What manner of mortaller are they inflicting on these poor knackers?"

I wasn't looking forward to telling him. For a moment, I closed my eyes and tried to think. Did Reever know I was here? Would he even care? "The one in charge is called SrrokVar. He's torturing slaves and calling it research."

Wonlee made a strangled sound of frustration. "How do we get out of here?"

I watched as guards reappeared and one of them came toward me. My stomach solidified into a cold, clenched knot as my restraints were released. "I wish I knew."

Most of the drugs in my system wore off over the next hours as SrrokVar conducted his first series of tolerance tests on me.

The tests appeared deceptively mild at first. The Hsktskt compelled me to run the treadmill at various speeds, then stand in a tiny envirodome while the internal temperature went from arid to freezing. Uncomfortable, but not painful. Not until the guards removed the bonesetter and strapped my wrists into two small rings suspended from a grav-hoist. SrrokVar raised me a few feet off the floor, and my own weight put immediate, searing stress on my broken carpal bones.

"Tell me about the Aksellans, Doctor."

"I've told you what I know." I wouldn't give him the satisfaction, I thought, sweat pouring down my face. "By the way, are we nearly done? I'm rather tired of hanging around."

SrrokVar looked up from his console. "Humor as a pain-management device, Doctor?"

"A nap"—I clenched my teeth against the strain— "works better."

He walked over and clamped two more restraints around my ankles. Apparently they were hooked up to some kind of winch, because they began pulling, and the rings around my wrists grew tighter. Something inside me made an audible *pop*. I screamed. Fresh pain expanded through my right leg.

"Discouraging, these fragile joints of yours," SrrokVar said as he scanned the knee and hip that now throbbed in unison. They hurt more than my broken wrist—not that I was going to tell him that. "Altogether very simple to dislocate."

"Is . . . two . . . enough?"

"I'm not concerned with the number, Doctor." He completed the scan and circled around me. "How they heal, however, is of great interest to me."

Knowing that didn't make it easier to keep quiet. "You're . . . a . . . maniac." Blood welled from the inside of my cheek; I'd bitten through it trying not to shriek. Something else popped, and my vision narrowed abruptly. I'd pass out now, I thought, grateful for my body's response to the unbearable abuse. My head sagged for a moment, then I choked as a splash of icy water hit me in the face.

"You will remain conscious, Doctor."

"Don't . . . think . . . so . . ."

"I have the proper stimulants, once dousing you fails to work."

I shut out his face and voice, and pulled back deep within myself. He could keep me awake and all my senses working, but my mind didn't have to stay connected with them. The dark, hidden place I'd fallen into once before beckoned, and I rushed to it, grateful for the respite.

About time.

Maggie's voice drifted from the edge of that safe abyss, and I halted, wary of what that meant.

Am I dead again?

The sound of a faint snort. *Get your skinny backside in here, Joey. Pronto.*

Eighteen years of obedience sent me hurtling into the nameless haven, and I tumbled down the long passage until I landed in the featureless blackness that held only the sense of the woman I'd thought of as my only mother.

Maggie?

You're in big trouble, kiddo. C'mon, we've got some serious talking to do.

The last two times we'd done this, I'd landed in

the tavern district back on Terra, then my own bedroom. So when colors and sounds bloomed around me to form my Medtech freshman anatomy class, I wasn't exactly surprised.

What shocked me was seeing Maggie up in front of the empty classroom, instead of Professor Larson, who'd taught me to know and recognize every inch of the human body inside and out. She wore an educator's tunic one size too small, and clattered over toward me on the high, thin-heeled footgear she'd always loved. The locket I'd given her for her last birthday gleamed around her neck.

"Things are not looking good for you, baby," she said as she pulled an illegal cigarette out of her breast pocket and lit it by bending over one of the Bunsen units. She drew the smoke in and released it with a long, slow sigh before smiling at me. "I'm glad you found your way here, though."

I put the student pack I was carrying on the nearest table and sat down on a stool. My nose wrinkled. "Is this where I get to spend eternity? Back in Medtech, listening to Professor Larson recite the number of muscles in the maxillary region?"

Maggie coughed out a lungful of smoke, gave me an irritated glare, then stubbed out the cigarette. "Not according to the plan, Joey."

"Oh? And exactly what *is* this plan?"

"For me to know, and you to find out." She winked. "Now, let's deal with the nasty situation at hand. How the hell did you end up with Dr. Mengele out there? Never mind, I already know. Time to make some tough choices, kiddo."

I heard distant, agonized screaming and knew it was coming from me. Not in any hurry to get back to that, I crossed my legs and regarded my surrogate mother patiently. "Such as?"

"He's going to find out he can't kill you." Maggie went over to the wall panel and activated the instructional display. A full Terran female anatomical chart appeared on the screen. "Look at all these weird names. Christ, how do you pronounce that one? And check the rest of this out. Who knew these people had all this junk packed under their skins?"

"Maggie." I waited until I had her attention. "Why can't he kill me?"

"Oh. Yeah." She switched off the display and gave me another brilliant grin. "It's the same reason those disgusting PIC burns keep healing up and disappearing."

"My immune system."

"You've got the motherlode when it comes to immune systems, baby. It's what makes you immortal."

"Immortal." Well, I was hallucinating, what did I expect? "Cute, Maggie. Nothing is *immortal*."

"You are. Think about it, Cherijo. Why didn't you die on K-2? You contracted the core virus from the cat-fellow Karas. What about while you were on the *Sunlace*? You died twice on Tonetka's table. That's not even counting the times you overdosed, got burned, stopped your heart, and took all that radiation, remember?"

She'd told me before, during a dream I'd had on the *Sunlace*. *You won't die, baby.* "So you're saying I *can't* die? Ever?"

"Nope."

I sat in silence for long time. Then I asked her, "Does my fa— my creator know about this?"

"Sure. Joseph tried to kill you a couple of times himself." Maggie shook her head sadly. "I kept telling him it was hopeless, but did he listen to me? Noooooo . . ."

"You didn't try and stop him." Why it didn't anger me was a total mystery. I was too busy rearranging certain events over the last two years in an entirely new order. "I'd wondered how Joseph convinced the League to come after me when everything he'd done was illegal. He told them about this."

"You're his blueprint for everlasting life, Joey.

Which brings us to our other problem—if the lizards do figure out you can't be killed, that would be bad."

Yes, it would. "So how do I get out of this?"

"Duncan is coming for you." Maggie shook her head. "Late, of course—he's just discovered you've been taken—but he'll come. You do whatever he says, Cherijo."

I laughed. "I don't think so."

My former hired companion exploded with rage. "You *want* to let that animal out there torture you for weeks, months, years? Because that's what will happen, Joey. He'll keep you for as long as it takes to satisfy his curiosity—and that's endless. You'd choose to live like that, just to spite the one man who can protect you?"

"Some protector. He's a traitor and a liar. He *sold me out*, Maggie."

"He's *all you got!*"

Now it was my turn. "What about you? Aren't you ever going to tell me the truth about all this? Who I am? What did you and Joseph Grey Veil do to me?" I looked up at the screen, then back at her. "You won't even tell me who you are. Are you my mother? My *real* mother?"

"No, Joey. I'm not." She went very still, and groped in her pocket for another cigarette. Her fingers remained hooked there, and for some reason my gaze stayed riveted to the sight. What was wrong with her hand?

Then I saw. Saw what I'd never seen in all the years we'd spent together. It made me jolt off the stool and back away. "No. It's some kind of trick."

With a sad smile she lifted her fingers—each with five articulated joints—to her face, and passed it over the care-worn, lined features. They smoothed out as her flesh took on an outlandish luminescence. Red-tinted curls straightened and darkened to black. Both ears receded into flat slits on either side of her elongating skull. Her brown eyes narrowed and tilted up at the corners toward her brows, which disappeared beneath an thin band of sparkling gems that stretched across her forehead.

I'd never known anyone with such a serene, beautiful face. What I did know was this woman wasn't human. She didn't belong to any other species I'd ever encountered, either.

The Maggie I had grown up loving wasn't dead. She'd never existed. As I processed that, an irrational fury surged through me. I'd loved my surrogate mother. She'd been the only part of my life on Terra that I could bear to remember. Now she'd taken that away from me.

"No tricks, Cherijo." Her voice had transmuted from the familiar husky rasp to alien octaves. The sheer clarity made me cringe. It felt as though my head was stuck inside of a huge, multitonal chime as it rang. "This is who I am."

"You pretended to be human? Why? What world are you from?" The questions rushed out of me in an irate succession. "Why did you come to Terra? Why did you get involved with me?"

"Duncan Reever is not your only protector. I waited centuries for your birth, Cherijo." The terrible beauty of her voice deepened, and her features blurred back into the false visage of the woman who had stood back and let my creator try to kill me. "You have to go back now, Joey. He will come for you."

"No." I resisted the urge to move back into reality. "Whoever you are, you owe me some answers. I have to know more."

"You will."

SrrokVar must have injected me with enough stimulant to keep an entire squad of League troops awake and aware. After my abrupt and unwilling trip back into reality, I discovered my body was on the brink of systemic overload. Nerve cells sent ceaseless transmissions of the multiple afflictions I'd endured, and the pain pushed beyond anything I'd ever experienced. At the same time, my heart and blood pressure careened at levels that would have killed an ordinary human. Sweat and cold water coated every centimeter of my skin.

It hurt to blink, so talking only upped the ante. "Aren't . . . you . . . finished . . . yet?"

SrrokVar's eyelids peeled back in evident astonishment. "Why, Doctor, welcome back. I was certain you had retreated for the duration. Yes, I'm quite finished for today."

He lowered me back to the floor, where I added to the various stains on the mottled surface as the centurons released my limbs. SrrokVar had them place my broken body onto one of the exam tables, where he efficiently dealt with each dislocated joint. There were twenty of them altogether, including two veterbrae in my lower spine.

"Your reactions were not as I expected in the high tolerance ranges." The Hsktskt finished manipulating the last bone—my left femur back into the hip socket—and scanned me once more. "According to my data, tissue inflammation should not set in immediately. I am quite sure you will be able to stand and walk without support."

"Yipee." I pushed my abused body from the table and landed on my feet. The floor seemed to rock under me for a moment as my violated joints screeched in protest. "We'll have . . . to do this . . . again . . . sometime."

"After you've had time to think about the many variations I can use to gain information from you, we will." SrrokVar gestured to the waiting centurons. "Take her back to the holding cell."

"Disregard that order."

I turned my head. Just as Maggie had predicted, Reever entered the central chamber, accompanied by more Hsktskt.

He wasn't pleased. "Why have you requisitioned this Terran without my authorization, Lord SrrokVar?"

"I did not *requisition* her, OverMaster." The Hsktskt set down his data pad with a distinct thump. "She was brought here to be interrogated over the disappearance of five slaves."

Colorless eyes narrowed under the bright lights as Reever studied me. "What have you learned?"

Some protector he was.

"Nothing yet. You are familiar with my methods, HalaVar." The Hsktskt scientist beckoned to his personal guards. "This will take some time. Remove her."

"No." Reever came at me and tugged me off to the side. "I will speak with her."

He knew. I clutched at him when my knees started to give out. *Reever knew everything that was going on in here.*

Agree with whatever I say, Cherijo, and I can free you.

What was he talking about? Free me? What about the others? I started to shake my head, but my neck was stiffening up and I could only turn it to one side. By then Reever was talking to the head monster again.

"I have spoken with the OverLord and have his permission to take this one as my mate. Under the circumstances, the unity ritual will have to be held at once."

"What?" I gasped and staggered away from him.

"She does not display a great deal of enthusiasm, HalaVar." SrrokVar crossed the space between us and placed his claws around my jaw. Some of what I felt must have shown on my face, for SrrokVar dipped his head close to mine. "Does the prospect of coupling with the OverMaster appeal to you, Doctor?"

I didn't care what Maggie said, I wasn't doing this. I'd rather take my chances and hope Noarr could find a way to free us. My eyes fell to the sidearm Reever wore. "No thanks . . . rather be . . . lab rat."

"You will give your consent. Eventually." The Hsktskt addressed Reever. "I'd prefer to continue my interrogation, but perhaps you'd allow a study of any resulting progeny. I believe the genetic enhancements would be somewhat diminished by the second generation, but a detailed analysis would still prove beneficial. Your species' gestational period is three cycles, is it not?"

"Yes." Reever tried to take hold of me, but the Hsktskt refused to turn me loose.

He had no problem with allowing the scaly sadist to experiment on a child. Not just any child. *Our* child. Nausea surged through me. At that very moment, whatever residual feelings I had for Duncan Reever died a swift, miserable death. It had to end, now. Maybe I couldn't die easily, but I could try. I could kill him, too. Maybe by doing so I'd save an unborn child from living hell.

Adrenaline poured into my veins as I made a grab for Reever's weapon, and whipped it from his belt. "No more!" My hand shook as I raised it and fired directly at his chest.

The pulse sent Reever flying into the traction rig. Before I could shoot myself, a huge limb knocked me aside and the weapon went flying. I remained conscious as one of the centurons snatched me up and shook me like a rag doll. Out of the corner of my eye I saw Reever slowly getting to his feet. Blood stained the front of his uniform, but he was alive, breathing, and staring at me with wide, colorless eyes.

I'd failed. I hadn't killed anyone.

"Escort the OverMaster to the infirmary." SrrokVar peered into my tear-filled eyes. "Attacking any member of the Faction requires an interval of discipline, Doctor." To the centuron, he said, "Put her on the table."

I didn't care what he did to me. He could use the thresher or yank more bones apart. Maybe Maggie was wrong and I would die. Maybe I should start praying for that.

The sound of a beam activating made my blood run cold. I lifted my head and saw SrrokVar coming at me with the same kind of hand-laser FlatHead had used on me.

"Yes, the OverCenturon's report was most expansive," the Hsktskt said as he tore the front of my tunic open. "I will begin here, where the flesh is thinnest."

Helplessly I tried to beg, but there wasn't any air left in my lungs to carry the sounds.

Heat, burning into me. Pummeling hands ripping. Smoldering fabric tearing. No gloves on my hands. Black, charred tissue. White gleam of bone —

SrrokVar etched something into my right breast, then forced an endotracheal tube into my throat when I wouldn't breathe on my own. He took a moment to administer more stimulants, which prevented any hope of unconsciousness. The hand-laser's beam trickled down my abdomen, melting through the layers of skin, branding a path from sternum to navel.

Whatever pain receptors I had were so overloaded that they no longer functioned. Fear seized control and for a long period I was only aware of the stench and the soft puffs of breath from the Hsktskt's partially open jaws.

I realized dimly when it was over, when they took me from the table and stapled my limbs into some upright pylons just beyond the equipment. SrrokVar jabbered something, but I couldn't make it out. I only roused briefly when I saw Gael and Wonlee dragged into the center chamber. I moaned something, tried to clear my head.

SrrokVar removed the tube and waited until I breathed naturally before speaking. "HalaVar will be displeased, I fear, unless I gain your willing confession. Tell me what happened to the Aksellans, and I will release you."

"Drop . . . dead."

"Begin with the Terran."

He kept me awake and made me watch as he tortured my friend on the traction rig. Gael was trough, but even he couldn't hold out against the merciless counterweights. In the end, he screamed and begged anyone to make it stop.

"Well, Doctor?"

Through Gael's shouts of agony, I saw Wonlee staring at me, and the small shake of his head as they hooked him up to the grav-hoist.

I couldn't do this anymore. *Noarr, forgive me.* "Y-y-y-yes, I'll tell you everything."

"Good." He gestured to the guards to continue, then caught my incredulous gaze. "In the event you are considering deceiving me."

It was harder to hurt the Lieutenant. SrrokVar marveled over the flexibility of his infrastructures as the hoist and rings jerked and pulled at his limbs. Won never made a sound, even when the splintered end of one arm bone pushed out through his spiny flesh.

"An amazing creature," the Hsktskt said as the centurons hauled the two unconscious males from the chamber. "Now, give me the information I require."

Tears streamed down my face as I opened my mouth to explain what we'd done.

"Lord SrrokVar." A detachment of centurons surrounded me. "OverMaster HalaVar has directed we remove the Terran and place her in solitary confinement."

Despite SrrokVar's protests, they took me from the crying chambers and through the main compound to the confinement area. I was lowered down into one of the pits, where I collapsed and stared at the hatch above me for hours.

This particular pit was even wider and deeper than

the last one, but lit from below with a soft, diffused glow. No handy escape tunnel hatch to be found this time, either. One of the guards lowered food and water twice a day to me, but I hoarded half of every nonperishable, just in case they decided to forget about me again. One of the water containers served as an awkward, though welcome, waste receptacle.

Stimulants wear off eventually. In my case, it took three days. During the endless hours of forced wakefulness, I remained as still as I could and tried to rest. Tried to forget what I'd endured. And yet my eyes continued to return to the hatch, wondering when Reever or SrrokVar would send someone to take me back.

On the third day I finally threw off the last of the drugs, and slept. Faceless voices whispering wordless wounds of comfort filled my dreams.

CHAPTER TWELVE

Arena Games

I could have slept for a week, but judging from the number of ration caches dumped around me, it was more like two rotations. Hunger and a certain amount of nameless relief caused me to eat my way through three of them before remembering I was saving food. Reluctantly I put aside what wouldn't spoil from the last cache and relieved my pressing physical discomfort.

"I could use a couple of blobs around here," I muttered, and jumped when my voice echoed around me. *Whoa.* That hadn't happened the last time I'd been in confinement. Though this pit was at least twice as deep, I decided, eyeing the distance to the hatch. Perhaps that explained the sound effects.

As if answering my summons, one of the small fungi appeared, inching down the side of the pit.

"Hi there." The mold crawled over my leg. I reached over to stroke it—the satiny soft texture was irresistible—then opened the top of the waste container. "Hope you're hungry."

Lok-Teel were *always* hungry. As if presented with

a treat, the voracious fungus scurried over, enveloped the container and began absorbing the contents. For the first time I noticed it seemed to expand as it digested the waste products. When the slightly larger blob moved from the empty, sterilized container, and started toward my hoard of food, I yelped and grabbed the supplies to protect them.

"Nope, sorry, this is mine."

Once more, it acted as if it understood me. For a moment it hesitated, then changed direction. The blob trundled over my leg and back up the wall. I watched it crawl up all the way to the top, then disappear out under the hatch.

"What do you know? Smart mold." I said it out loud, letting my head fall back against the quasi-quartz wall. It had to be intelligent, otherwise it would have crawled over me to get at the food. Interesting.

A small sound pinged next to my ear, then another. Then a third. The trio of echoes sounded like words.

"What?"

"Know. It's. Food."

I turned my face so that my ear was pressed against the cold surface. Not a sound. When I lifted my head, something vibrated between my cheek and the wall. "Hello?"

Another series of pings. "Lo . . . can . . . hear?"

I spoke without thinking. "Can you hear me?"

The sound grew fainter. "Just . . . echo."

"No!" I yelled, and pressed my hands against the interior of the pit. Beneath it, the surface seemed to be humming. "I hear you! I'm here!"

There was a moment of silence, then louder pings, as though someone on the other side was speaking slowly and carefully.

"Can you hear me, woman?"

Noarr. "Yes. Noarr, it's Cherijo. I can hear you. Where are you?"

"In the tunnels. Are you injured?"

Yes, but there seemed no point in telling him. "No. Can you get me out of here?"

"I am trying to find a way." Noarr went on to tell me he was in one of the hidden passages that ran parallel to the isolation pits. Apparently some quality of the mineral in the deeper layers allowed transmission of sound waves. "You are scheduled to remain in the pit for three weeks."

"Good thing I have one of these blobs down here."

"I sent the Lok-Teel to you."

He *sent* the fungus? What does that mean? "Mind telling me how you did that?"

"I will be back soon."

"No, wait." I thought of Gael and Won, and panicked. "Go back to your ship. You may be in danger."

I called him a few more times, but heard nothing more. Frustrated, I slumped back against the pit, and resisted the urge to pound my head against it. *Three weeks.* I couldn't sit here that long. I had to get back to the infirmary; I had to find a way to stop Srrok-Var's barbarous experiments.

I was so busy brooding that when the hatch opened and my daily ration cache dropped down next to me, I yelped.

"Hey!" I squinted up at the guard. "I need to speak to OverLord TssVar, right away."

The centuron thrust his snout over the edge. "Why?"

"Lord SrrokVar is torturing and killing prisoners in the crying chambers. It has to stop." I knew what upset the Hsktskt. "Think of all the credits you guys are losing."

"I will relay your request to OverMaster HalaVar."

My fists clenched. "No, not him. Tell TssVar. He's in charge of this dump. Don't wait, either. Tell him now!" I yelled as the hatch closed, then I curled into a miserable huddle. "Please, please tell him now."

* * *

TssVar never showed up, and the centuron refused to respond to any more of my shouted questions. Days passed. I started talking to the Lok-Teel, who paid me frequent visits. Better them than the walls.

"How many Hsktskt does it take to change an optic sensor?" I said to the mold as it sat on my lap and flowed over my fingers. "Give up? Two. One to hold the pulse rifle—"

Above me, the hatch opened again. That was odd. I'd just gotten my daily rations. A dark figure on a rope swung over the edge of the pit and rappelled down the wall. Only when I saw the scrolled dark cloak did the tension in my limbs ease.

How had he gotten past the pit guard?

He dropped lightly to his feet and stood towering over me.

"And the other to terrorize the slave changing it."

"Noarr." I jumped up and threw myself at him.

Large, warm flippers ran over my shoulders and arms as he shook back his head covering. The white spiral tatoos and lack of hair on his skull didn't bother me.

The chance he was taking did.

"Are you out of your mind?" I pushed his flippers away and got huffy. "What are you doing here?"

"I told you I would find a way. You look well." He examined me and my small collection of supplies.

"I am. Now leave. And move your ship while you're at it." My glare turned sorrowful as I told him about SrrokVar's torture chamber. "Gael Kelly and Wonlee have probably confessed to everything by now. They'll be looking for you."

"I do not think they are. They have more to occupy their time, if these rumors about the invasion are true."

"Huh?"

"The Hsktskt have been receiving long-range intelligence reports. It is said the League has sent three planetary fleets to liberate the slave-depots."

TssVar's revelation about my creator came back to me, and I frowned. More likely the League was sending its fleets to attack the Faction territory worlds. "Is there any way you can transmit a message to the Jorenians? They may be able to help us."

"Perhaps." The Lok-Teel climbed up Noarr's cloak and tried to get into his hood, and he gently set it down. "SrrokVar is a powerful Lord. He has already petitioned the Faction Hanar to conduct further experiments on you."

"Marvelous." I sat back down. "That should be entertaining." Bravado didn't keep me from hugging my knees to my chest, or trembling violently. "I can't go back there."

"OverMaster HalaVar wants you as his mate. He will intercede on your behalf."

Reever might. An image of him handing a tiny Terran baby over to SrrokVar made me choke on a sob. "I don't know which is worse."

Strong, muscular arms came around me. Noarr sat there and held me, doing nothing more than stroking my matted hair and murmuring softly in a language I didn't know. Finally, I knuckled the last of the tears away.

"Reever giving our child to SrrokVar or SrrokVar torturing me for the rest of my life. Some choice, don't you think?"

A ferocious expression passed over his features. "You're a physician. Make sure you don't get pregnant."

The callous practicality of his suggestion made me recoil. "God, don't you get it? He'd still be touching me! The thought of it makes me—"

"Ill." A flipper settled over my mouth. "I know. The thought of anyone else sharing intimacies with you does the same to me." A corner of his mouth quirked as he examined my face. "You're surprised?"

Yeah, I was.

"I'm Terran," I said, suddenly aware of the intimacy of our positions and the possessive way he was holding me.

He brushed my hair back from my brow. "Does it matter?"

In some ways, it did. Why couldn't I develop feelings for someone of my own species, like Gael? My relationships with non-human males had wrecked my life. I'd killed Kao. Xonea had nearly killed me. And Reever—only technically human, to my mind— had made me a slave.

Yet being with Noarr, I felt that same sense of déjà vu, as if I'd come home after a long, exhausting journey. Who cared if we came from two different worlds?

"You do not answer me, woman."

I was getting tired of the "woman" thing. No. To be honest, I wanted to hear him say my name. Just this once. "Cherijo. Call me Cherijo."

He put his mouth at the curve of my throat, and slid his tongue against my skin in a slow, sensual caress. "Does it matter, Cherijo?"

Not every species indulges in kissing. So for an answer, I leaned forward and brushed my lips against his cheek. His grip tightened briefly, then he gently set me aside.

"I would take you with me if I could." He grabbed on to the cord and pulled his hood back over his head. "I'll come back as soon as it's safe."

"Yes. All right." I needed desperately to believe him, so I summoned up a confident grin. "You know where to find me."

He nodded. "Always."

Oddly enough, it wasn't Noarr who released me from the pit, but my former patient FurreVa. The retrieval clamps tugged me out of the pit before I saw her, so I wasn't prepared for the grim visage and gave a startled cry.

"Doctor." She removed the clamps and surveyed me. "You appear to be healed from your ordeal."

"So far, so good." I glanced around and saw no other Hsktskt in the immediate vicinity. "Why are you letting me out?"

"I wish to undergo the final reconstructive surgery." She gave me what could be called an appealing look, if you ignored the bared fangs and lashing tongue.

I frowned. "I thought you weren't interested in getting your face fixed."

"My decision was too hasty. I now have an opportunity . . . if I am to secure a mate for my brood . . ." Her claws traced over the still-visible groove in her scales.

I'd been experimented on, terrorized, and thrown in a pit, and Helen was only worried about what her new boyfriend thought of her face. Good to know I meant something to my friends.

Not that FurreVa had ever considered me a friend.

"You have someone in mind?" Not that it was any of my business, but if the groom was FlatHead, I was going to talk her into staying single.

"Yes. Can you make me appear as a normal female?"

I gave her an ironic glance. "That was the whole idea in the first place. Come on."

My long absence hadn't stopped the medical staff from functioning. I saw when I walked in with the Hsktskt female. Good to know they could work on their own now.

Pmohhi turned, screamed, and dropped an entire batch of newly sterilized instruments. "Creation, she's still alive!"

Zella's tail knocked over an infuser array. "Doctor!"

"Cherijo—I mean—Dr. Torin—" Vlaav's hemangiomas turned a bright, vivid scarlet, and he gave me a sheepish grin. "It's good to see you're intact."

"Reports of my dismemberment have been greatly exaggerated," I said, and glared at the nurses. "And since when did you two turn into clutzes? Pick up that gear, Pmohhi. Zella, I want you to prep for surgery. You too, Vlaav."

I made quick rounds. Most of the meningitis patients had been discharged. Those patients I recognized from the crying chambers I noted to remain on indefinite inpatient status. I wouldn't willingly allow any of them to go back if I could stop it.

"Are you sure you are feeling well enough to perform this procedure?" Vlaav asked me at the cleansing unit.

"I'm okay." Mostly. The burns on my arm and chest had healed, and my wrist was sore but flexible. "Any problems while I was gone?"

"Some. More prisoners have escaped. A pair were discovered in the sanitation room by OverCenturon GothVar."

Trepidation set in. "Two Forharsees? The young ones?"

"I believe so. They were taken to the restricted area."

Jgrap and Kroni, in the crying chambers. Neither of them would last very long. This had to be stopped. I used my knee to switch off the biodecon port. "When we're done with this, I'm going to see TssVar. I may not come back, so you may have to handle the follow-ups. Pay attention."

"But—but—" The Saksonan looked appalled. "I've never done any reconstructive procedures before."

"You will now," I said with a grim smile. "Welcome to Plastic Surgery 101."

FurreVa stretched out on one of the exam tables, and I scanned her thoroughly. The bone grafts and soft tissue repairs had healed well, and near-total brain function had been restored. All that remained was cosmetic work, but that was in some ways the trickiest part.

Hsktskt facial derma contained the same muscle and mucosal tissues as warm-blooded life-forms, but hardly any fat layer existed. Also, the arrangement and pattern of scales presented a problem—the markings destroyed by FurreVa's injury had to be restored to a near-natural appearance, or she would never appear "unscarred" to other Hsktskt.

Vlaav observed as I reopened the keloid groove from brow to jaw and checked the muscular and neuro-repair sites.

"I'm using small, deep-epithelial grafts from appropriately shaded markings here, like this"—I made the first cone-shaped incisions on her right lower appendage, lifting the scaled-topped plug and placing it directly into the open granulated facial tissue—"and transferring them, one by one. The missing subcutaneous fasciae will be filled in, and the scale patterns reestablished."

"That will take hours."

"I work fast, Doctor. So will you." I handed him the spare lascalpel and pointed to the other appendage. "You can do the neck area. Match the markings on the opposite side as closely as you can. And keep your arm joints out of my way while I work on her face."

Vlaav's angiomas purpled. "I can't perform this procedure. I've never excised grafts this small before."

"Don't start popping those pustules in my sterile field." I softened that with, "Just be careful, and start cutting."

Doing this on a smooth-skinned being would have been out of the question, given the inevitable postoperative dermal contractions. On a Terran, visible bumps would be left wherever a plug had been placed. FurreVa's surface scale layer, however, would camouflage the effect completely.

"Why are you doing this for her?" my resident asked me after we'd been working for an hour.

"Everyone deserves a chance for a normal life, Vlaav." I centered a graft plug and lifted my head to check the match. "Even a Hsktskt."

Vlaav did a remarkable job in repairing the damage to the neck patterns. Once I had the face and outer jaw finished, I sterilized the outer surface of the grafts and had the Hsktskt female moved to an isolation area. Zella agreed to keep her sedated and under constant monitor.

As we stripped out of our surgical gear, I went over the prognosis with Vlaav and discussed the possible postoperative complications to watch out for.

"The dentary implants look like they've taken, but how stable are they?" he asked as we shrugged into fresh tunics.

"It will take a couple more weeks for them to take completely. She'll be on a soft diet until then."

Zella reappeared, her vibrissae quivering. "Back, that slope-browed one is. Kill her, he says he's going to."

Great. I slipped a syrinpress into my tunic pocket. "Come on, Vlaav. Let's go deal with this beast."

FlatHead stood over the unconscious FurreVa, his rifle pointed at her new face.

"OverCenturon." I dried my hands and stared at his ugly face with bland indifference. "Come to volunteer your time as an infirmary aid?"

His tongue shot out, then slid back with a hiss. "She released you from the confinement pit."

"Yes."

"Without any authorization. To do"—he gestured toward her face—"this."

"Actually, I talked her into it." What had FurreVa gotten me into now? "You know, I really can't stand to go a week without performing some kind of surgery. Call me obsessive-compulsive."

He activated his weapon. "This time she dies."

"Do *you* have authorization for that?" One baleful eye swiveled toward me. "No, I suppose that's not important right now. All right. How can I persuade you not to ruin all this nice work I've done? Do you want to take me back to SrrokVar? I'll go. Just put the rifle down."

"No." He moved a step back from the berth. "Not to SrrokVar. To the arena."

"And this arena is . . . ?" All he did was raise the weapon again. "Fine. Whatever it is, I'll do it. Leave her alone."

FlatHead didn't give me time to leave instructions with Zella and Vlaav, and I hoped my resident would remember everything I'd told him about FurreVa's case.

"I heard you took a couple of kids to SrrokVar," I said as I walked out of the infirmary. "What's the matter, couldn't find anyone your own size to pick on?"

"So it is true. You have some pathetic affection for them."

I turned around. "Who told you that?"

"They're fodder now." He shoved me forward. "Keep walking."

I could still hear Jgrap passionately vowing to die rather than live without Kroni. Oh, God. "They were just kids, you repulsive scum."

He gave the small of my back a vicious jab with his rifle. I bit my lip against the sharp pain. Somehow, some way, I promised myself, I was going to see him in the same shape.

I was marched out to a section I knew was the guards' barracks, another place I'd never visited.

"Mind telling me what this arena is for?"

"Slave challenges. I will enjoy watching you bleed."

I bet he would. "What kind of challenges?"

"Physical combat. One species against another."

He gave me his version of a leer. "The thin-hided ones don't last long."

Behind the guard barracks an enclosure lined with high, plasteel walls had been erected. GothVar led me into it through a narrow, guarded opening and secured the panel behind us.

"Fresh skin," he called out.

Hsktskt guards sat in rows on eating benches pushed back against the walls. They were hissing and shouting at two slaves who appeared to be strangling each other. One was an aquatic life-form with suction-padded tendrils; the other a gargantuan insectile being with sharp, gleaming mandibles. Old and fresh blood made spattered marks on the crystal beneath their feet.

Minutes passed. Then the larger combatant wrestled the aquatic under his thorax and collapsed on top of it. Inky fluid oozed out from beneath the victor's carapace. GothVar added his voice to the guards' clicking cheers, then pushed me into the center of the arena.

"New fodder for the champion!" he shouted.

Some of the other guards yelled their protests. From what they said, apparently I wasn't expected to present much of a challenge.

The huge insect creature stared at me, and from the glaze over its eye clusters I could tell it was in pain. As it hauled itself off the aquatic, I saw a crack in the underside of its abdomen, and the protruding end of something black sticking out. The aquatic lay motionless.

"Do you speak Terran?" I asked, and the big bug cocked its head. "No, I didn't think you did."

I didn't move as it came closer, rubbing its mandibles together as it scrutinized me. One snap of those and some vital part of me would end up next to the wounded aquatic.

What to do now? I held out my hands, palms up, and took a step forward. One of the life-form's legs lashed out and swept my feet out from under me. I landed on my back, and looked up to see it positioning itself over me. Planning to squash me, too. Now I could see the nether wound clearly. The aquatic had lodged some kind of spine into the victor. A poisonous one, I'd bet—most of them were.

It didn't sit on me. It just stood there.

Maybe it didn't understand Terran, but it could have recognized my physician's tunic. I stopped thinking about dying and lifted my hand to touch the undamaged carapace, and gently probed the wound.

"Have to get this out," I said, and curled both hands around the protrusion. A humming roar emerged from the mandibles as I extracted the short spine and tossed it aside. Copious bleeding commenced, and I tore a handful of fabric from my tunic, wadded it up and used it to staunch the flow.

My opponent released a high-pitched sound that hurt my ears, then lost its footing. I rolled out from under it just before it collapsed completely. By the time I got to my feet, centurons were dragging both the dead aquatic and wounded insect being from the arena.

FlatHead stood watching me, his tail curling and lashing with agitation.

"Take it to the infirmary, they may be able to save it." I straightened my tunic and folded my arms. "Is that all?"

"Send out the Husras."

The Husras turned out to be an amorphous protean creature who extruded itself from an aperture and remassed in front of me. In its own way it was beautiful—transparent cellular walls displayed a glittering, protoplasmic interior with a fascinating arrangement of internal organs. Sensory organ pseudopods sprouted from different areas as it took a look at and smell of me.

For a moment I simply admired the being, until it arranged the majority of its bulk into a burly, multiplelimbed form that mimicked the Hsktskt upper torso. This lion had no thorn for me to pluck from its paw, and it didn't speak Terran either.

Time to move.

As I skittered away from it, my opponent flowed its lower portion across the arena to pursue me. The guards began shouting again, calling out suggestions that ranged from ridiculous to obscene. I saw GothVar watching intently, and decided I'd have to resort to the syrinpress. I reached into my pocket and calibrated what I needed by touch.

This had better work.

A snaking pseudo-limb caught me by the waist and started dragging me toward an enlarging pit in the transparent surface. Before it could ingest me, I thrust my hand into the newly formed mouth, and shuddered as cold, viscous flesh closed over it. I triggered the syrinpress, and hoped the large dose of muscle relaxer would do the trick.

For a moment the Husras simply remained there with my arm in its mouth; then it slowly began losing control of its shape. The Hsktskt guards voiced their fury as the being melted into an unconscious puddle around me.

I caught GothVar's furious gaze, and assumed a pleasant demeanor. "*Now* can I go?"

Not yet, Doctor.

The Hsktskt came at me with his rifle poised to fire, but I had no more ability to move, than I had to get Duncan Reever out of my skull.

"OverCenturon. Release the Terran."

GothVar didn't. He threw down his weapon, lifted a limb, and smacked me off my feet. Before he could do more damage, Reever's guards hauled him back away from me. I found myself sitting calmly back up and lifting my hand to take Reever's outstretched fingers.

I was handling this on my own, OverMaster. Get out of my brain.

No, Cherijo. I'm not going to do that. Reever kept tight reign over my body as he helped me out of the puddled Husras and enfolded me in the curve of one arm. Out loud, he said, "Dr. Torin has agreed to become my consort."

The guards fell silent and looked at me. I heard my own voice emerge from my throat. "Yes. I have agreed to this." The words were spoken without inflection. Reever could make me talk, but he couldn't instill any faked enthusiasm.

The hell I have, I thought with a shrill shriek of fury. *You're the last man on Catopsa I'd even consider consorting with, you self-absorbed butcher. What are you doing?*

Saving your life.

The Hsktskt didn't have marriage ceremonies, they had unity rituals. Reever maintained his mind control over me during the whole thing. It took the rest of that day to go through the stark, solemn series of vows and commitments, all of which we both had to utter in front of TssVar and every Hsktskt who could be spared from duty.

By the time we were done being "joined," I was exhausted. I'd tried ceaselessly to break free of Reever's control, but he had superior ability and experience backing him up. He not only controlled my body and voice, but somehow got past my walls and started hammering at my mind with each vow we spoke.

His promises were simple. "I will provide for, protect, and promote you and our young."

Mine were slightly briefer. "I will nurture and protect you and our young." *As long as you don't fall asleep for the next seventy years, you cold-blooded bastard.*

That was it. It was the ritual joining and recognition phrases that had to be uttered by the other Hsktskt that took so long.

TssVar gave a sonorous speech about the Faction

hierarchy and the place Reever had occupied in it. This involved naming everyone in TssVar's immediate family, their current assignments, and unities made with other Hsktskt lineages. He then formally recognized our "unity" and gave me the rank of OverMaster's Mate.

Then everyone else had to repeat basically the same thing. I noticed GothVar wasn't present; maybe Reever hadn't invited him to the wedding.

I knew Reever couldn't maintain control over me forever, and bided my time. When we left the Over-Lord's chamber, Reever made me walk to his quarters and closed the door panel. I expected him to end the link then, but he removed the syrinpress from my tunic pocket and calibrated it.

Oh no. I realized what his intentions were. *You aren't drugging me.*

He pressed the applicator tip to my throat and injected me with something. *Until you're ready to accept this, I have no choice but to sedate you.*

The familiar lassitude of valumine slipped into my bloodstream, and Reever released his mind and body control a moment before I fell into a heap on the floor. He picked me up and carried me to his berth.

"Now you will listen to me."

"No." The tranquilizer made my tongue feel thick. "Why should I? You're a . . ."

"GothVar's arena slaves don't leave until they're dead. One of the others would have killed you eventually. SrrokVar has also expressed his desire to continue experimenting on you, to both TssVar and the Faction Hanar. This is the only way I can safeguard you now. You must agree to act as my consort."

I made a silly sputtering sound with my lips.

"You refuse to see the truth." Reever stretched out beside me and gathered my limp form into his arms. "I am attempting to protect you."

My eyes rolled. Protect me. I'd love to see how he treated someone he didn't give a damn about.

"If you fight me on this, you will be returned to SrrokVar."

Then you'd better get more drugs, and develop insomnia while you're at it.

"You're late."

I shut the door panel and headed straight for the cleanser. "Things got busy."

My new husband watched me from the table littered with the remains of his solitary meal. I turned my back on him, stripped off my stained tunic, and stepped in under the heated jets. The past two weeks had re-established some of our old routines. Like his penchant for nagging. And mine for pretending he was invisible.

Once I was dressed, I sat down and picked at the meal he'd warmed up for me. Yet another of his vile alien concoctions, I deducted from the taste, and dropped my utensils with a clatter.

"I don't know what you ate for the first three decades of your life—dirt, probably—but I like food. Simple, nourishing food. As in something I can actually *swallow*." I shoved the plate away. My voice had risen to a near-shout, not that I cared. "If you're going to waste your time preparing our meals, for God's sake use the Terran recipes I've programmed for my stuff."

Reever sat back. "You lost another patient."

"Two of them." My lips drew back from my teeth. "Cerebrovascular complications, attributed to bacterial meningitis. Then your cretinous lizard pals removed the bodies before I could perform autopsies. *Again.*"

Whatever was killing the handful of prisoners I lost each week remained unidentifiable. I'd run microanalysis on everything they ate, drank, or touched. I tested prisoners in adjoining cells. I'd found exactly zero.

I wasn't as angry about the patients I'd lost as I

was over their bodies being removed without my authorization. There was also the last signal I'd received before going off shift. "TssVar disapproved my request to vaccinate all the prisoners. For the fourth time. Why?"

"He does not believe it is merited. There have only been twenty deaths."

"*Only* twenty deaths. I see." I took a sip from my server, then threw it across the chamber and watched it burst against the wall. "So, what you're saying is, only when hundreds of prisoners die of meningitis will I be allowed to start vaccinating the live ones. That's logical. Let a contagion spread out of control, then try to contain it. Gee, I can relive the K-2 epidemic all over again."

"What happened on Kevarzangia Two was vastly different, Cherijo."

"Just for your information, I reported GothVar's private little sporting arena to the OverLord, too."

"The Hsktskt regard physical challenges as a form of recreation. TssVar will likely wish to attend some of the bouts."

"That's pretty much what he said." I went over and flopped on the berth we shared. "Have I mentioned lately how much I hate these lizards? And you?"

"You said something to that effect this morning, before leaving for your shift."

"Oh, good." I closed my eyes. "Thought I'd forgotten."

"I arranged to have someone come here tonight to see you."

Probably one of his Hsktskt pals who didn't want to report to the infirmary. "I'll see he, she, or it in the morning. I'm going to sleep."

Exhaustion sent me into dreamless sleep. It didn't last very long, though. Reever woke me up by shaking my shoulders and whispering my name.

"Knock it off," I said, yawning as I rolled away from his hands.

My husband didn't roll me back over toward him. He shoved me off the side of the berth. I hit the hard floor with a screech.

"Reever! Are you crazy? What—"

"Listen."

I shut my mouth and heard a low hiss a few feet away. The sort of hiss a Hsktskt infant made when it was hungry.

Scampering claws clattered across the chamber toward the other side of the berth, where Reever was crouching. By my reckoning there were three of them. That didn't make sense, the only baby Hsktskt on Catopsa belonged to FurreVa, and she . . . was still recovering from surgery in the infirmary.

"Someone let FurreVa's young loose in here." I edged backward until my shoulders hit the wall. "You're the expert, Reever. Talk to me. How do we handle this?"

"Keep them away from your face and throat."

"Oh, good advice." I concentrated on the odd, hitching noises coming from the infant near my feet. Respiratory distress syndrome, from the sound of it. Premature infants often had recurrent bouts of breathing arrest and apnea, and this one was no exception. I doubted it would go into respiratory arrest before it tore my heart out, however. "Whatever you do, don't kick or hit them. Their lungs won't take that kind of abuse."

"Climb."

I reached back for a handhold, and that's when the first infant jumped at me. Underdeveloped as it was, it still had plenty of teeth to use while tearing up the front of my tunic. I pushed it away as lightly as I could, whirled, and started climbing up the crystal outcroppings until I reached the top of the chamber's dome.

Two of the infants appeared at the base of the wall,

and looked up at me with large, hungry eyes. Small claws extended and encircled the lowest crystal outcropping.

"Um, Reever"—I shifted my grip and looked along the wall toward my husband—"looks like they can climb, too."

Alunthri chose that moment to walk through the chamber door panel.

"Get out of here!" I yelled. "Secure the door!"

The Chakacat saw the infants, dropped onto all fours, and went into its fake-ferocity act. That drew the three infants' attention, and they moved away from the wall and toward my friend.

"Alunthri, don't hurt them—they're just babies—" Quickly I inched back down the wall, spied my medical case, and made a run for it.

The big cat yowled and hissed as one of the infants jumped at its face. Reever grabbed another before it could do the same. I retrieved a syrinpress and made a dive to clutch the third. The tiny claws swiped at my face, then sagged as the tranquilizer I injected it with took effect.

Reever's hands and wrist bled but held firm as I took care of the one he held. He had a small cut on his cheek, but otherwise had survived intact, so I went to aid Alunthri.

The last of FurreVa's brood had latched on to the Chakacat's throat with its small jaws, and was now trying to bite through the thick silvery fur. Alunthri struggled to loosen the tiny reptile's grip, then with claws sheathed, knocked it away. The infant landed on its chest and released a squeal of distress.

"Damn it." I knelt beside it, eased it over, and placed a palm on its heaving torso. "Signal the infirmary, Reever."

Alunthri crouched beside me and gazed at the little Hsktskt with a grave expression. "I am sorry, Cherijo. I tried not to harm it."

I pressed finger to my lips in warning, then swiftly

examined the Chakacat. The small Hsktskt had done a good job, I saw, and put a temporary pressure dressing on the neck wound it had inflicted. Since Reever was at the console, I dipped my head down next to one flickering ear. "It wasn't your fault, my friend. We'll talk later."

Alunthri uttered a single *hnk*.

CHAPTER THIRTEEN

Fully Restored

FurreVa's daughter required cardiac surgery, which I performed immediately after placing her two siblings in reinforced incubator units and dealing with an extremely angry mother lizard.

"Terran!" FurreVa left her berth and stomped toward me, sending my nurses scattering. She saw her young and activated her weapon. "You took my brood from my chambers."

"No, I *found* your brood in mine." I put myself between her and the infants. "Put down the gun, we need to talk."

"They were in your chambers?" She scanned me from crown to ground. "Who placed them there? Why are you not injured?"

"Yes, I have no idea, and pure luck." I wasn't going to tell her about Alunthri's timely intervention. "Power down that rifle. I've got to get one of them into surgery."

She complied and went from outraged straight into classic maternal panic. "Surgery? On my female? Why?"

I gave her an abbreviated diagnosis, including the fact that if I didn't perform the surgery, it was unlikely that the little female would survive another rotation.

"I will wait here until this surgery is completed." FurreVa took a position beside the incubator units. "You will save her, Terran."

She didn't have to say *Or else.* "Right."

Vlaav and I prepped the tiny Hsktskt, and moved her into surgery. My resident had identified the source of the cardiac distress, but was unfamiliar with the treatment.

"Premature infants sometimes have PDA, a heart duct that remains open. I initially treated this female with indosyne in small doses to protect the kidneys," I told him as I made the midchest incision and exposed the tiny heart. "Unfortunately in this case, it didn't close the duct, so I have to try PDA ligation. Surgery is always the last-resort treatment in these cases."

The procedure was successful, and after reassuring FurreVa she had no further reason to shoot me, I turned the critical, but stable, infant over to the nurses for postop care. From there I went to check on Alunthri, who was occupying a berth in an isolation chamber.

"Nice acting job," I said as I scanned its throat.

The Chakacat began to say something, then turned it into a patently false yowl as Wonlee appeared at my side.

"Don't worry, he's a friend." I turned to the Lieutenant. "Were you able to get in touch with Noarr yet?"

"No." The fierce scowl drooped. "I have other information I must relay to you."

"You can talk in front of Alunthri."

Won nodded. "There were several recent direct relay transmissions received by the Hsktskt that we've been able to access. You should know that the

Terran doctor—Joseph Grey Veil—is enroute to attack Catopsa and to free the League captives."

"He *transmitted* this?" I asked. Wonlee nodded.

"Why would he *tell* the Hsktskt they were coming
to raid the slave depot?"

Won shrugged. "He's one of their collaborators.
It's said they have many among the League worlds."

"No." I realized what my creator was doing, and
it appalled me. "He's trying to make a deal with
TssVar—information in exchange for something he
wants."

"What could be that valuable?"

"It might sound conceited, but"—I finished dressing Alunthri's wound—"he wants me."

"HalaVar won't allow him to take you."

I thought about the consequences of a League attack. "One Terran in exchange for an entire slave-
depot. He won't have a choice."

The partition separating Alunthri from the rest of
the inpatient ward was suddenly jerked aside. Reever
stood there, holding his bloody wrist and looking
highly peeved.

"If you have a moment, Doctor?" He held up his
wounded arm.

"Sure. Excuse me, Lieutenant."

I cleaned and dressed the bite, which required no
sutures. Reever questioned me about FurreVa's injured infant, and I gave him a concise report on the
cardiac surgery.

"I have to stick around for a few hours and monitor the baby," I told him. "Don't wait up for me."

"I will not be in our chambers when you return."
He stood and flexed his arm. "Secure the door before
you go to sleep."

"Aye-aye, Master." I watched him go, then sagged
back against the exam table with a sigh of relief.
Won reappeared.

"Did he hear what we said?"

"I don't know. I don't think so." I was tempted to

tear out a handful of hair. "Get in touch with Noarr, Won. We need some help, now, before this situation gets out of hand."

I never went back to Reever's quarters that night.

A few hours after the Hsktskt infants' attack, I saw the back of the infirmary wall move slightly. Without hesitation I slipped behind a partition and into the hidden tunnel.

A tall, dark-cloaked figure pushed the crystal hatch closed behind me.

I didn't wait to say, "Hello" and "How are you?" "Where have you been? Do you know how long I've been trying to get in touch with you? Have you ever thought about checking in once in a blue moon?"

The hooded head turned toward me. "There are no moons around Catopsa."

"Hmph." I tried to sound disagreeable, but I was too relieved and happy to see him. "I've got problems, Noarr."

"You are not the only one, woman." He took my arm and started walking me away from the infirmary. "Come. We will talk along the way."

"Along the way to where?"

"I have something I want you to see."

As we made our way through the tunnel labyrinth, I filled him in on what I'd learned since FurreVa had released me. He didn't seem surprised to hear about the League's plans, or my creator's latest treachery.

"This Terran, does he have that much influence with the Allied League?"

"He does if he's promised to give them the secrets of an indestructible life-form." That made him stop and stare. "Oh, I don't know if it's true. All I know is, I'm not aging anymore. Also, my immune system seems to get stronger and more aggressive every time I'm wounded. Take this stupid PIC they keep burning into me"—I jerked up the sleeve of my tunic to show him the unmarked skin—"the marks don't last more than a few hours lately."

He gently rolled down my sleeve and grasped my forearm with his flipper. "That would be enough to convince the League to attack the Hsktskt Faction."

"Yeah, promise them immortality and they'll jump through plenty of hoops to save one genetic freak."

Now he touched my face. "You are not a freak, Cherijo."

I could have stood like that for several years. "Okay. An immortal genetic construct. Now where are we going?"

"I will show you."

He steered me through to the last passage. A pair of odd-looking garments and helmets sat by the final access panel. Some kind of envirosuit, I decided, and climbed into the one he handed me. He switched on an oxygen pack and donned the other suit, then opened the panel.

The tunnel led directly onto Catopsa's surface.

Despite the suit's thermal regulators, cold instantly seeped through my skin. I shivered as I walked through the opening onto the irregular surface of the asteroid, then glanced at my companion.

"Noarr, it's freezing out here!"

"We are not far from the field." The comunit inside the helmet made his voice sound slightly distorted as he raised one glove and pointed to a clearing beyond a range of free-standing crystal growths, several hundred yards beyond us. "There it is."

It was slow going. The asteroid had less than one-sixth the gravity I was used to, and the effect made every step into an awkward sort of bounce. By the time we passed through the rows of transparent towers, I felt more than a little disoriented and slightly nauseated by all the jolting.

Then I saw what Noarr had brought me to look at, and forgot to breathe. "How . . . ?"

"I don't know." He led me out to the clearing, and

to the first of the growths emerging from a fissure in the asteroid's surface.

It wasn't transparent, or symmetrical like the crystal towers occupied by the Hsktskt. Enormous, solid black spirals jutted in beautiful, erratic eruptions that flowered far above our heads. The smallest was at least fifty meters tall and had a variated diameter ranging from twenty meters to a half centimeter. Some of the formations reminded me of clouds; others resembled intricate veils of lace. It didn't glitter like the crystal, either. It glowed with a faint oily sheen. I'd never seen anything so beautiful or so strange in my life.

"Have you scanned it?"

"Yes." He reached out and placed one flipper on the surface of the black formation. A more intense glow surrounded his glove. "It absorbs heat, produces random vibrations, and is incredibly dense. So much so that I cannot take a sample of it back to my ship for analysis."

"Okay." An irresistible urge to touch it made me lift my glove and place it next to his. The icy atmospheric temperature leaking into my suit seemed to intensify. I snatched my hand away. "God, it almost feels like it's—it's—"

"Drawing the warmth from your body?"

I looked at him, and nodded slowly.

"I think it does." He dropped his flipper and turned to sweep one arm around the entire clearing. "Whatever it is, it is ancient. Readings indicate most of these growths are more than a billion years old."

"Noarr. Why did you bring me here?"

"I found more of these. Inside the compound. They've started appearing in some of the outer tunnels."

I had no idea of what to say. It was possible the black growths were some kind of seismically generated magma, which had frozen upon emerging onto the surface. But logic dictated that the oldest would have crumbled millions of yeas ago. There wasn't even regolithic dust on any of them.

And no magma I'd ever heard of absorbed heat from a living being.

We returned to the compound, removed our suits, and went to the tunnel where Noarr had discovered the first of the new growths. They were smaller, but just as bizarre and stark and mysterious as the ones on the surface.

I should have thought they were beautiful, but all I could summon up was a steady sense of aversion.

"The Lok-Teel seem to dislike them," I said as I watched one of the busy fungi give the growth a wide berth, and went down to give the little house cleaner a fond caress. "You're worried they'll collapse the tunnel network."

"Yes." Noarr didn't touch the Lok-Teel, but paced around the growth. "At the rate they're appearing, the tunnels will be destroyed or rendered impassible in a few weeks."

That meant no more slaves would escape Catopsa. "I'll see if I can figure out what's causing it. Now I have to get back, or I will be missed."

"Woman." His cloak swirled around me as he put an arm around my waist. "When I leave Catopsa, you are coming with me."

My jaw nearly hit my chest. "What?"

"You can no longer remain here. The Hsktskt will either kill you, or turn you over to the League."

"I can't just fly off and pretend none of these people exist," I said, trying to step out of the embrace.

"And me? You have no attachment to me?"

That was the whole problem. Somehow I'd managed to transfer all those disastrous emotions I'd had for Reever to this slave-runner, who I knew next to nothing about.

"Don't be an ass," I said, not sure if I meant him, or me.

Noarr pressed his mouth against my throat. "You're coming with me."

He had a very talented tongue. "No, I'm not."

The fabric of my tunic bunched as he ran one rough fin up from my waist to the nape of my neck. I felt the edge of his teeth, the strength of his grip. When he bit me, it didn't hurt. Somehow I understood the inexplicable need. Marking me as his, I thought. His woman. Kao had done the same.

Kao, I realized with a start, would have liked Noarr. A lot.

"Look. I'm flattered, but we hardly know each other," I said. "Stop nibbling on me."

"Why?"

"Because . . ." I couldn't think of a single reason. I couldn't think, period.

Noarr stripped my tunic away, spanned my waist with his long fins, and lifted me up. His tongue caressed the stiff peaks of my nipples, the lines of my ribs. My breasts felt painfully full, and swelled even more as he rhythmically stroked them with his flippers.

"Noarr." I took in a deep breath as he pressed me against his full length. We fit together, without a single gap between us. "Much as I would like to . . ."— God, would I have liked to—". . . this isn't the time or place."

"Very well, *Waenara*," he said, then replaced my tunic and let go of me.

"What's that mean?"

He hesitated. "A term of affection."

"What's the corresponding term for a guy?"

"*Osepeke*."

"I'm taking a raincheck on this, okay? Don't worry, we'll figure something out." I smiled. "*Osepeke*."

Noarr led me back to the infirmary, where I made final rounds before leaving to get some sleep. True to his word, Reever was gone, which suited me fine.

I was exhausted, worried about the threat to the tunnels, and ready to bang my head against the nearest hard surface. Surely nothing else could go wrong.

Before I could drop onto the berth, however, Gael Kelly slid out from under it and gave me a cheerful grin.

"Pull your socks up, *dote*. Haven't seen you in donkey's years. Howya?"

"Gael." Guilt over leaving him behind in the crying chambers rushed back over me. "Did SrrokVar release you?"

"Won's recycler crew smuggled me out of there a few days ago." He glanced around and rubbed his flat abdomen. "I could use some scran, if you can spare it."

"Of course." I rushed over to the prep unit and quickly prepared him a meal. He didn't bother to sit, but devoured everything in short order.

"Ah, that's a gift. I'm knackered." He rubbed a hand over his weary face. "Barreling about dodging the thicks has me flah'ed out, *dote*."

I didn't need a translation of that. "These are Over-Master HalaVar's quarters. Not exactly the best spot in the compound to lay low."

"Eejit won't be finding me." Gael put down the servers. "I can have a kip in the back of one of the storage units. . . ." He glanced at the berth. "Unless I'd be intruding on you and your old man."

"Please." I snorted. "The only thing you'll be listening to is the sound of me and the old man snoring."

A signal came in over the console, and I motioned Gael to hide. He dropped and rolled back under the berth. Once he was out of sight, I answered the signal.

"Doctor." It was TssVar.

"Change your mind about vaccinating the prisoners?"

"I require your presence in the guard barracks."

He motioned to someone, and I thought I saw Reever walking past one edge of the screen. "You will accompany me to the arena games."

"Can I refuse?"

He didn't bother to say no. "A centuron will escort you."

I terminated the signal. "Stay out of sight, Gael. I've got to go watch helpless prisoners beat each other to death."

The Terran's muffled voice drifted out from under the berth. "Don't be letting them get you up to ninety, *dote*."

"Up to ninety?"

"Ready to explode."

"Too late." I was way past ninety already, and speeding out of control.

OverLord TssVar and I were given deferential seating in the makeshift arena's gallery, and I sat beside him in absolute, stony silence. GothVar, I noticed, was busy handpicking which of the assembled slaves would fight each other, and seemed to be having a good time.

Reever was nowhere in sight.

"The first match should be of great interest." TssVar sat back as someone led a huge figure out from another chamber.

Devrak.

Someone pushed a mild-looking humanoid female from the group of slaves GothVar was currently terrorizing. She wouldn't last long against the Trytinorn, I thought, and leaned forward, my hands gripping the chair. "OverLord, does anyone even *care* to make these challenges equitable. Look at her, she's too little. That jumbo bully will flatten her in about two seconds."

"Appearances are deceptive, SurreVa." TssVar's tongue flickered out. "Observe."

GothVar and the guards cleared everyone out to

stand beyond the quad parameters, and someone shouted for the combatants to begin. Devrak stood looking down at the small female, obviously unwilling to step on her.

Good to know he wasn't a complete bastard, I thought, slightly startled.

In contrast, Devrak's opponent only waited a moment before snarling and launching herself at the Trytinorn. She must be suicidal, I thought, until I saw two whiplike extensions shoot out from the sides of her abdomen and slash across Devrak's sensory organs. She completed her attack with a flawless vault up onto his broad back, where she clamped powerful legs around the Trytinorn's neck.

The League Major trumpeted his pain and fury, and began stomping around the quad, trying to shake her off.

"Uh-oh." Now I sat back. "This isn't going to be pretty."

TssVar made a hiss of agreement.

The Major and his tiny opponent fought on. I cringed as the female's whipping appendages cut into the Trytinorn's thick hide. Much as I disliked Devrak, my hands still clenched the edge of my seat until my knuckles bulged under my skin.

"OverLord." A centuron appeared beside us. "We have received a signal from SubHanar HssoVar."

"Excuse me, Doctor." The Hsktskt lumbered off out of the arena with the centuron, leaving me alone in the gallery.

For about ten seconds, anyway.

Quietly I rose and picked my way through the shouting, cheering crowd of lizards, until I stood on the edge of the quad. Devrak was starting to weaken, and his shuffling steps pounded slowly in front of me. I waited until the pair were on the other side of the arena, then crawled under the plasteel cords and up onto the quad platform.

"Hey. *Hey.*" I waved my arms to get the female's

attention. A reptilian limb made a swipe at me, and I skittered forward to avoid it. "Down here."

The female paused long enough to peer over the dome of Devrak's skull. She yelled something that sounded like, "I'm not finished with him yet," just in a completely alien tongue.

I inched closer. "Devrak, are you okay?"

"Do I appear *okay* to you, Terran?" The Trytinorn lifted his long nasal appendage, but stopped short of grabbing the female. "I don't wish to harm her."

My cue to be brave and bold. I walked over and placed a gentle hand near one of Devrak's lacerations, then squinted up at the female prisoner. "He needs medical attention," I said, and used my hands to convey my meaning. I pointed to the medical insignia on my tunic. "I'm a doctor. Let me help him now."

The centurons weren't amused. One of them fired a warning shot from a pulse rifle close to my legs.

"Get out of the quad, Terran."

Devrak lowered his head, and carefully knelt down on the quad. I assumed a sitting position, and held my breath as his female opponent sat very still, her legs still clutching his neck. Then, with a soft sigh, she slid down and off the Major's back, and sat on the quad beside me.

I raised my palms in the universal gesture of peace. "Good for you, lady." What we needed here was a good, old-fashioned Terran sit-in. I turned so all the other slaves could see my hands, and made the appropriate motion. "You don't have to fight, any of you. Sit down. Don't let them bully you."

Enough of them got the message, and murmured to each other. Slowly, one by one, they began sitting down wherever they stood. After a minute, there wasn't a slave left standing.

The Hsktskt didn't like that. The lizards began shouting and prodding the prisoners, making threatening gestures with their weapons. I was counting on the fact that no one would actually kill the prisoners for not fighting—they were valuable merchandise, after all. Okay to lose some, but not the whole shipment.

It worked.

I didn't have time to crow over my victory. GothVar clambered over the quad boundary cords and yanked me to my feet.

"You have interfered for the last time, Terran!"

Someone fired another pulse blast, but this one came very close to hitting FlatHead's lower extremities.

A low, savage growl erupted behind us. "Release the Doctor, OverCenturon."

I glanced over FlatHead's broad shoulder to see OverSeer FurreVa standing at the entrance of the arena, flanked by six heavily armed centurons.

"Hi, OverSeer." I yelped as GothVar dropped me, and I landed on my backside. "Boy, am I . . ." The big Hsktskt female reached up and tore the surgical dressing from her face, and I stared at the results. The corners of my mouth tried to reach my ears. "Am I *glad* to see you."

What had once been a grotesque nightmare now had become a balanced, appealing visage. She'd never meet humanoid standards for charm and allure, but to me, FurreVa simply looked beautiful.

Every Hsktskt around me had their gazes riveted on her new face. You could have heard a dust mote land.

I do good work.

"As you see," FurreVa said, "I am fully restored."

I opened my mouth to tell her she should have spent another week in her berth recovering, but I realized she wasn't talking to me. She advanced on GothVar, who stood there gawking like the rest of the guards.

"You cannot resume your rank. You have a brood

to nurture," FlatHead said, then took a step back as she got closer.

He was afraid of her, I thought. Which proved he had some brains, much to my disappointment.

"My young return to the homeworld with TssVar's mate. She agrees to nurture them." FurreVa activated her weapon and raised it, aiming directly at Goth-Var's nonexistent brow plate. "Stand down, Over-Centuron."

For a few seconds it looked like someone was going to the infirmary with a big, ugly wound. At last FlatHead pivoted away, lumbered into the crowd, then disappeared.

FurreVa turned full circle as she addressed the guards. "There will be no more arena games, now or in the future." When a cluster of four males grumbled out loud, she whipped her new face around to stare at them. "I shall administer discipline personally to the first centuron who disobeys my order."

If Hsktskt could pale, every guy in the place would have been flat white. Almost in unison, every male in the arena area dropped his head back slightly, in effect bowing to her will.

"Doctor, my personal guard will return these prisoners to their cells. I will assist you in moving the Trytinorn to an area suitable for treatment."

I bent down and picked up her discarded dressings, and tucked them into my tunic pocket. When we were back at the infirmary, I'd yell at her for removing her own bandages. Right now supporting her dignified return to duty was more important. "Thank you, OverSeer. I would appreciate that."

Devrak's injuries required some creative suturing techniques, which I carried out in one of the equipment storage areas in a corridor adjacent to the infirmary. FurreVa stayed to observe, and permitted me to rig a support harness for the Trytinorn to stay in for a few days until his wounds healed.

"If I hear you've twitched an inch from this harness, I will sedate you and string you up from the ceiling myself," I told Devrak. "Understand me?"

The analgesics I'd given him took over, and he mumbled something nasty under his breath.

We left the Major with a pair of centurons guarding him, and I insisted FurreVa let me perform a skull series before she reported back to her post. Happily, no complications appeared to be setting in, but I gave her the usual lecture.

"Wash the graft areas three times per shift with lukewarm water rinses, and keep applying that dermal emollient I prescribed for you."

"Hsktskt do not bathe daily."

"As far as you're concerned, they do now." I set down my scanner and patted one of her limbs. "Thanks for rescuing me, and shutting down that damn arena."

"I did not *rescue* you." She rose to her full ten-and-a-half feet and glowered down at me. "I merely instituted measures to protect our merchandise." Her tail appendage curled as she said this, which (according to Reever) indicated she wasn't being completely truthful.

I gathered up my instruments and shook my head. "Whatever you say, OverSeer." The end of a limb landed on the front of my tunic, and I peered up at her.

"Stay away from the OverCenturon, Terran. He is mine to deal with."

Before I could ask why, FurreVa departed. I was brooding over my meningitis cases when my resident careened through the infirmary entrance. Hemangiomas had burst over his face and arms.

"They've just brought in more! Hundreds!" He pointed back toward the prisoner reception structure, and spattered me with some fluid in the process. "Maybe a thousand!"

I caught his arm, sat him down on the closest stool, and gave his shoulders a little shake.

"Whoa, Vlaav. Settle down and catch your breath for a moment." He breathed in and out deliberately while I mopped both of us up. "Okay, now tell me all that again. Coherently this time."

Turned out a new group of Hsktskt raiders had arrived, their ship holds filled with recently captured beings to be sold at the compound. Beings captured while traveling through the border territories, just outside the Pmoc Quadrant.

It wasn't good news, but it could have been worse. "At least they didn't decimate an entire planet this time. What species are the prisoners?"

"All kinds—Darmarek, Ramperilii, Caffors, even some Tingaeleans. Someone said they were all working on some new planetary orbital station project when the raiders attacked."

A terrible feeling of dread stole over me. Two years ago I'd heard one of my neighbors talking about that project. Back then it had been in the planning stages. "Were there any Terrans among them?"

"I think I saw one, a male—"

"Where did they bring them in? Where we were?" I didn't wait for more than his nod. "I'll be back. Hold down the fort."

I raced down the corridors until I reached the enormous, empty chamber situated below central command. All those big pillars came in handy—I hid in a small recess between two of them and watched the Hsktskt march in the last of their newly acquired prisoners.

Scanning faces, I quickly located the only Terran male among approximately six hundred captured construction workers and technicians. Of average weight and height, with nondescript coloring, he was easy to overlook. His smile and personality would have made him stand out, but at present he wasn't a happy man. No grin appeared on the face of the small, multilimbed alien standing beside him, either.

No, I thought, my heart sinking. Not *both* of them.

The two I'd recognized joined one of several clusters of males—there seemed to be a predominance of them—then were directed by a centuron toward the appropriate corridor.

I couldn't stand there and do nothing, so I put on my best fake-furious face and went after them.

"Centuron!" I pointed at the group of males I needed to stop. "Detain these prisoners."

The Terran's brown eyes widened, and he opened his mouth to speak to me. I gave him a tiny shake of my head, then a wink. His mouth snapped shut on a grin.

I turned on the unfortunate Hsktskt and began reading him the riot act.

"Why wasn't I informed of these arrivals? Have you forgotten that med evals have to be performed on every single one of these prisoners?" I planted my finger in the center of his uniform. "Am I supposed to be psychic and *guess* when you're polluting the general prisoner population with these unevaluated individuals?"

"A signal would have been sent after they were segregated—"

"You'd have waited *that long*? Have you even a clue as to how many germs they're carrying?" The harassed centuron grunted something incomprehensible. "Well, don't just stand there griping at me. I'll have to take the first group to the infirmary and schedule the others. You"—I pointed to the Terran—"and the short one standing beside you. Yes, you. Come with me."

I swept off in the direction of the infirmary, and didn't glance to see if the two males were following. I walked around the first pillar, stopped and waited.

Paul Dalton and Geef Skrople appeared two seconds later.

When the two men would have spoken, I lifted a finger to my lips. "Follow me."

Only when we were far from the unloading area did I stop again and plant my hands on my hips. "Well, this is a fine mess, Paul." Then I laughed and gave them both a hug. "God, it's good to see you, Hi, Geef. Are you okay? Either of you hurt?"

Paul exchanged a glance with Geef and started laughing. "We're fine, Doc. Though I doubt you'll take our word for it."

"That's right." I took each by the arm and started them toward the infirmary. "Gentlemen, prepare to be thoroughly examined."

Geef kept an eye out for centurons while Paul filled me in on some rather staggering facts behind the raid.

"We got a signal from some friends of yours. They'd tracked Hsktskt raiders headed for the new station we've been working on. When they asked us to voluntarily surrender, I thought they were crazy." Paul shook his head and chuckled. "Until they told us they intended to liberate Catopsa, with a little inside help."

"So you just let the Hsktskt capture the station?"

"Once we'd stripped out all the vital tech and shipped it off station, yeah, we did. Since the engineering crew were the only items left of any value, they took us all."

I still didn't get it. "What can you do here, as prisoners? You don't have any weapons." I gave him a dark look. "Do you?"

"We don't need weapons. Our friends will be here soon."

I thought of the League. "Just who are these *friends*?"

Paul grinned. "You know how Jorenians feel about someone who attacks a valued member of their HouseClan. The miners on Aksel Drift Nine also happen to be just as obnoxious, especially after learning that same female saved the lives of five of their female engineers."

"The Jorenians *and* the Aksellans." I closed my eyes briefly as I imagined it. "Mother of All Houses."

"Combined invasion forces will be here within a week, Doc. We don't have much time. Can you help us?"

"I'll have to, won't I?" I grumbled, then regarded Paul. "How many ships?"

"Not many." His grin stretched. "Just every one available from Joren, and Aksel Major. Maybe two, three thousand."

That would do the job. Unless they ran into the League on their way. "How are they going to know where and when to attack?"

"After Geef and I put the word out to the prisoners, we're going to escape to the surface." Paul tapped his forearm, where I could see a small bulge under the skin. "Signal beacon. They'll send a shuttle down to retrieve us, then we'll give them the layout of the compound."

"If this is going to work without weapons, we're going to need some way to disable the Hsktskt centurons."

Geef glanced at me over his shoulder. "We were hoping you could help us out with that, Doc."

"Disable several hundred, ten-foot tall, armed lizards. Sure, no problem." I wanted to knock both their heads together. "All right, I'll figure something out. Tell me something—before you were captured, did you hear anything about this insane decision the League's made to declare war on the Hsktskt Faction?"

"I watched the transmission from Fendagal XI personally of the Allied League Council debate over the Hsktskt problem." Paul made a face. "Your father makes a hell of a speech. Toward the end, the entire assembly got out of their seats and demanded a first strike invasion."

"Yeah. Sounds like him. He's had practice." It was time for me to make a stop at my quarters to check on Gael and feed Jenner, so I told both men to wait for me to return before reporting to their assigned cells. "This will just take a few minutes."

Well, it *would* have taken a few minutes, if I hadn't be so preoccupied by what the two engineers had told me. If I hadn't missed the shadow waiting a few yards down from my chamber as I entered it. If I'd remembered to secure the damn door panel behind me once I'd closed it.

"Gael?" I opened the largest of the storage units and peeked inside. A brown-haired head nearly bumped into mine as the Terran emerged from behind the racks of garments. Jenner climbed down from where he'd been sleeping on the berth, took one look at Gael, and darted underneath it. "Don't mind him, he's shy. You'll never guess who—"

The door panel slid open, and I tried to close the storage unit, but Gael was halfway out. We were caught, and by the last Hsktskt I wanted to catch me doing anything.

"Dr. Torin and . . . Kelly, is it?" SrrokVar strode in and surveyed us with visible satisfaction. "My two missing Terrans."

Chapter Fourteen

Truth Hurts

SrrokVar had his guards take both of us back to the crying chambers. I went quietly, but Gael kicked up quite a fuss as soon as he saw the entrance to the special corridor.

"Plonker, get your gammy claws off!" he yelled, and fought the centurons so wildly that one of them resorted to a sharp cuff which promptly knocked the Terran out.

"Leave him alone, damn it!" I grabbed Gael as he fell and flung one of his arms over my shoulder.

SrrokVar had us both clamped into restraint chairs and spent a good deal of time questioning and scanning me. I refused to speak to him, and he warned me my lack of cooperation would lead only to more discipline.

The thought of being burned again made my stomach heave, but I kept my mouth shut and my eyes focused on the door panel past his shoulder.

"Really, Doctor, you of all people should understand the importance of my research. After all, you were the subject of an extended experiment most of your life. I can't fathom why you would even attempt to counter my orders. Unless by doing so, you hope to conceal the more miraculous qualities of your unique physiology?"

So he'd somehow figured out the big secret. Or Reever had figured it out and told him. Or Joseph Grey Veil. Not that it mattered. I wasn't going to budge an inch.

"Perhaps there are other means to persuade you."

I kept my resolve until SrrokVar began walking over toward Gael Kelly. The terror in the Terran's eyes made me shout at the Hsktskt to stop.

That didn't get his attention, but the sight of TssVar and Reever entering the main chamber did.

"OverLord. OverMaster." SrrokVar sounded pleased. "I was just preparing to begin a new series of interrogations."

"Release the female," Reever said.

"I fear I cannot." SrrokVar heaved a rather human-sounding sigh. "I discovered her concealing this escaped prisoner. In your chamber, OverMaster." He turned around and flicked a limb toward me. "I'm sure you were unaware of her illicit activities—or did you know she consorts regularly with this Terran male?"

"That's a lie!" I jerked against my restraints. "I was just helping him, for God's sake!"

Reever ignored SrrokVar and spoke directly to his commander. "This female was joined to me, and our unity recognized by the Faction. I will not permit Lord SrrokVar to damage the future nurturer of my young."

"She's not breeding, OverMaster." SrrokVar held out a data pad as evidence. "Perhaps due to her refusal to consort with you?"

TssVar faced me. "Is this true? You refuse him?"

A huge force slammed into my mind. *Tell them you have been willingly intimate with me.*

Go to hell.

Which naturally led to me being turned into an instant puppet.

"I've never refused to consort with my husband," I heard myself say in a monotone. "I do so, willingly and frequently."

"Then why isn't she pregnant?" SrrokVar pretended to look askance. "I should run reproductive viability tests on the female, to assure she is capable of providing ample young."

TssVar gazed at me. "It would be advisable, HalaVar."

"I assure you, OverLord, Cherijo will breed, very soon. Now release her."

"Very well." SrrokVar reluctantly removed my restraints, and pulled me out of the chair. Reever used his mental control to force me to walk to his side, then lift my arms and embrace him. His hand stroked over my disordered hair.

"You see? She is uncommonly affectionate." He dropped a kiss on my brow, and I swore silently that I was going to rip his lips off the very moment he dropped the link. His voice changed as he looked at SrrokVar. "Should you attempt to experiment on my mate again, I will petition the Hanar to strip you of all rank at once."

Reever walked me out of the crying chambers, and before the door panel closed I heard Gael Kelly start screaming again.

This has to end, Reever. You can't keep lying to them about me. And while you're at it, get out of my head.

I wasn't lying, Cherijo. You're going to carry my child.

Before I could react to that bald statement, Reever did something that made my mind go hazy. Before I'd gone another step, I fell forward into unconsciousness.

I woke up in the infirmary, with Paul and Geef watching over me. I groaned and clapped a palm to my aching brow.

"What did he do, hit me with something?" I eyed the nearest console and sat straight up. I'd been out for nearly twelve hours. "Who drugged me?"

"No one, far as I know." Paul edged off the chair he'd been sitting in next to my berth and helped me up onto my feet. "You okay, Doc?"

I felt like I'd been run over by a platoon of Hsktskt. "Yeah, I'm fine. Long story."

"If you are, then Geef and I should be released. We have to get things started."

I signed the discharge orders and wished them both luck. "Talk to a League Lieutenant named Wonlee, he'll help you."

After I sent my friends on their way, Pmohhi informed me that a signal was waiting for me on the infirmary console. I accessed it, and found a prerecorded message from SrrokVar.

"My congratulations on an excellent performance, Doctor. You were most convincing."

Too bad he couldn't hear me. "I didn't have anything to do with it."

"I also wanted to inform you that your other Terran consort, Kelly, will be executed in two rotations. My condolences."

"No. No!"

Throwing caution to the winds, I ran back and slipped into the access tunnel and went to find Noarr myself. More of the black crystal growths had sprung up in the passages, making navigation even more difficult. After an hour of wandering, I was tired and ready to admit defeat.

I was also completely, totally lost.

I sat down next to one of the gleaming black flows and rubbed an idle hand against it. "You're beautiful to look at, but as a landmark you leave a lot to be desired."

"You do not."

I should have decked him, but I was too relieved.

"Where have you been? I've got so much to tell you! Two of my friends are here, and—"

"There's no time. I've arranged to have you transported from Catopsa. The ship must leave at once. Come." He pulled me toward another passage.

"Wait. I can't go anywhere. Gael Kelly is going to be executed tomorrow. We have to get him out of the crying chambers and off this rock. Now."

"Kelly." Noarr halted. "I know him. He has been here a long time."

"Then you know what he's been through. You have to help me."

"Cherijo." He slid his flippers up to cradle my face. "You are in danger here. You must leave. I will free Kelly after you go."

"I'm not going. We've been through this before." He couldn't make me go. Not until I shut down SrrokVar's operation, and took care of a few other things. "Is there a way to get into the crying chambers from here?"

He dropped his flippers and made a frustrated sound. "Possibly, if the tunnel has not been cut off by the black growths."

"Show me."

It took time, and some climbing at certain points. As we passed through the tunnels, I noticed that the Lok-Teel clung in droves to some of the growths, while others remained bare.

At last we reached the tunnel that led directly into SrrokVar's main chamber. Through an unglazed aperture, I spotted Gael in the holding cell. Blood stained his tunic, but he was speaking to one of the other prisoners, so his injuries must not have been too bad.

"How do we free him?"

"Watch." Noarr brushed past me and crawled down into a small side corridor too low to walk into. Minutes later, the crystal behind Gael swung inward, and he uttered a short cry as a cloaked arm pulled him back into the rock. The other prisoners showed little reaction to what had happened, and suddenly I realized why. No wonder all those severely injured prisoners had walked out of SrrokVar's hands and over to my infirmary. Noarr must have been pulling them out of the cell all along.

But why hadn't SrrokVar raised the alarm when he found them missing?

"*Dote.*" Gael gave me a hug, then grabbed his arm and groaned. "Uh, forgot, I'm a bit flitters. My thanks for pulling me out of that perishing hole." He gazed around at the tunnel. "Grand, this is."

Noarr towered over him. "We do not have time for a tour."

"Yeah, he's right." I smiled at Gael. "I've got a one-way ticket for you to get off this place. Are you game?"

"Bejappers, you have?" Gael chuckled, then sobered abruptly. "My thanks, but I'm not bolting from here just yet."

Noarr pointed to the corridor that led back to the main compound tunnels. "Let us discuss this when we move out of this area."

In a hushed voice, I argued with Gael the whole way, but was unable to get him to agree to leave Catopsa.

"If it was just me, I would, *dote.* But I have skin here, and I can't be abandoning them."

"Skin?"

"Friends."

The sincerity in his voice made me glance at Noarr. "See? I'm not the only one."

"Jesus, Mary, and Joseph." Gael studied the latest outcropping of black growths. "Clearing this muck out should come first."

"Your offer is appreciated," Noarr said. "But I prefer to work alone."

We had arrived at the access panel to the infirmary, and I made both males slip inside with me. "I have more to tell you," I said to Noarr as he closed the panel. "And I want to do a thorough scan of Gael for his injuries."

The concealment of the partition vanished, and a huge Hsktskt shadow fell over us. It was FurreVa. Probably reporting for that follow-up exam, I recalled, and silently groaned.

"How did these males get in here?"

Gael didn't move. I stepped forward, groping for some rational explanation. Noarr decided to be cute and make a grab for the Hsktskt's rifle. FurreVa fired it, and the pulse smashed into his side. Dark blood soaked his cloak, and I gasped. The alien tossed a tray of instruments at FurreVa, who threw her limbs up to protect her new face. Before any of us could blink, Noarr dropped down onto the floor. By the time my eyes went from where he'd been standing to the floor, he had vanished.

FurreVa searched the entire infirmary, then took me and Gael into custody.

"Where are you taking us?" I asked her as she marched both of us out into the corridor.

"To OverLord TssVar." The weapon she held on us never wavered. "He will decide what discipline is required."

During the short walk from the infirmary to Central Command, I decided I'd take whatever discipline was involved. Gael had already displayed an distinct aversion for torture, and letting TssVar work him over might jeopardize Noarr's safety.

"How did they know we would be doing a bunk there?" he said as we approached TssVar's chamber.

"Huh?" I'd been busy pondering the sort of discipline TssVar would administer, and took a moment to process the question. "You mean FurreVa? She was reporting for a follow-up eval."

"I'm thinking she has a sleeveen working for her. One of those patchers you work with."

I tried to imagine Vlaav, Zella, or Pmohhi spilling

the beans to the Hsktskt. Zella might have, before she and I had worked out our little difficulties. Pmohhi had no love for the Hsktskt. Vlaav . . . perpetually nervous, pacifistic Vlaav . . . "I don't think so."

FurreVa pressed some keys to request permission to enter, then gestured for us to go in as the door panel slid to one side. TssVar sat behind a new, strange-looking console I hadn't seen before, and rose slowly to regard me and Gael with glittering eyes.

"What has she done now?"

"I caught her hiding two prisoners. I detained this one"—FurreVa nodded toward Gael—"but the second escaped. He is injured, I will track him."

"Carry on." TssVar waited until FurreVa left before stomping around his new toy. "Members of the Faction do not harbor runaway slaves."

"I guess someone forgot to give me the Faction rule book. This whole thing was my idea." I ignored Gael's incredulous stare. "Prisoner Kelly had no choice but to do as I told him."

"An effort to deflect blame, Doctor?"

"No. Just taking responsibility for my actions."

"SrrokVar indicated you were most reluctant to see others suffer in your place. A telling revelation about your character, he said." TssVar scrutinized Gael for a moment. "This prisoner is a habitual problem. HalaVar will not be pleased to learn of this."

"HalaVar can go skating on the surface without a helmet." I smiled as though the thought amused me. My tunic started getting damp between the shoulder blades.

"I will allow prisoner Kelly to return to the general population," the Hsktskt said. "In return for your information and cooperation."

I had no idea where Noarr was, or where he regularly hung out, other than his ship. And he'd moved that. "Sure. Whatever you want."

"You may go, Terran." TssVar flicked a limb toward the door panel.

"OverLord . . ." Gael sent a panicked glance at me. "This bit of skirt is not—"

"You heard the OverLord, Kelly." I shoved him toward the door with exaggerated impatience. "Get out of here. Shoo."

A centuron was waiting outside. I watched until TssVar secured the door panel once more.

"So what information am I supposed to have?" I asked in a deliberately skeptical tone, then crossed my fingers behind my back. "This was only my second shot at slave concealment, you know. I've decided I'm terrible at it, and promise I won't do it again."

"You are still a habitual liar. Come around here." TssVar resumed his seat behind the console, and pressed his claws into two Hsktskt-shaped palm pads. I circled around in time to see the dimensional simulators flicker into operation, and a large star chart take shape over the surface of the unit. "Do you know this region?"

Of course I did. I'd lived there for a year. And he knew it—his young had been born there. "No." I scratched my scalp. "Doesn't look very familiar."

"Observe."

Tiny holo ships began creeping in diagonal waves across the binary solar system. I'd seen a Hsktskt planetary invasion force—some three hundred star vessels in orbit around Joren—but this fleet had fifty times that many ships. I bent over to study one of the tiny holos, and bit the inside of my lip before I straightened.

"League troop freighters."

"Yes. Seventeen thousand of them, we estimate, originating from more than thirty different systems." TssVar pressed another pad, and the star chart shrank to a wide-view chunk of galaxy. The specs of light representing the fleet now barely inched through the simulation. "Notice their path, Doctor." He highlighted one small white speck on the other side of the chart. "Catopsa's present position."

I didn't have to draw a line with my finger to see that unheard-of forces were heading straight toward us. "You'd better think about relocating to a new neighborhood, OverLord."

"Hsktskt do not retreat, Doctor." He turned off the simulation and regarded me steadily. "Now you will tell me everything you know about League troop movements and tactics."

Recalling he'd said the same thing when he'd told me about Joseph's transmission, I exhaled a grateful breath of relief. "Which is practically nothing." I thought about what I'd observed while on the *Perpetua,* and related the most harmless details of what I'd seen, ending with, "They will probably send their most experienced commanders, their seasoned troops. One doesn't take on the Faction with trainees." An idiot would tell him the same thing. "That's all I can tell you—pure speculation, at best."

"How does Joseph Grey Veil fit into this equation? He calls for an invasion, then informs the Hsktskt of the same. I understand warm-bloods and their penchant for betrayal, but this man has another agenda."

Did he know he was sitting next to it? "Joseph Grey Veil is manipulative, but that's like saying Catopsa is shiny." I decided to be partially honest. "He's obsessed with perfection, has no morals or conscience, and will do whatever it takes to get what he wants. That includes inciting the League to war one minute, and collaborating with the Faction the next. His goal is as much a mystery to me as it is to you." No, it wasn't. "But whatever he wants, he gets."

"Except you."

I let my mouth curl. "I don't think even Joseph could convince thirty-some odd worlds to send that many ships after one individual. I'm not that important a lab rat."

"Perhaps you are."

I started sweating again.

TssVar kept me at the console for the rest of the day, as he showed me possible attack scenarios and questioned me about Joseph, the League, and what I thought might happen. I tried to sound stupid, without sounding stupid, and committed everything I saw and heard to memory. I couldn't do anything to help the Hsktskt, but perhaps Noarr could use the information to assist the invasion and free the prisoners.

A centuron finally interrupted us with an urgent request for me to return to the infirmary.

"The escaped League Commander has been recovered."

I found what was left of Shropana strapped to a berth. His generally demented state didn't concern me as much as the condition of his diseased heart did. I'd soon have to operate on him, with or without his permission. Then I ran the rest of my scans as he raved incoherently. He kept shrieking something about his eyes being put out.

I checked, of course. They were still intact, but milky cataracts had formed on the surface of his corneas.

"Patril. *Patril.*" I held his thrashing head still between my hands. "What happened to your eyes?"

"Couldn't see, they blinded me, they shot me in the face from every direction. . . ."

"These aren't pulse burns." When he didn't respond, I huffed out an impatient breath and turned to the waiting centuron. "Where did you find him?"

"On the surface, Doctor."

He shouldn't be blind, I thought, only dead. "Where?"

"In the clearing beyond the compound perimeter. The one with the black outcroppings."

Shropana tore one arm free of restraints and grabbed the front of my tunic. "They kidnapped me! They dragged me out there, the beasts, to sacrifice me! But I fooled them." He chuckled, then started sobbing. "I fooled . . ."

"Well?" The centuron didn't blink when I glanced at him again. "Is that how he got out there? Did one of the guards dump him on the surface?"

"It is unlikely, Doctor."

I considered sedating Shropana, but opted for a mild tranquilizer and kept him on close monitor. After an hour, the centuron seemed satisfied that his escaped prisoner was incapable of making another break for freedom, and left me alone with him.

"Patril." I leaned forward as he opened his eyes to stare at me with no small amount of confusion. "How do you feel?"

"Tired." He gazed around, his eyes widening. "Don't let him take me out there again. Don't let him."

"Who? Who took you? What did he do to you?"

"The low-browed one, he took me. Him and two of the other beasts." Patril's gaze darted as he frantically searched the room. "He tried to kill me. I saw. I saw everything."

"What did you see?"

For the first time Shropana seemed to focus on my face, then his expression turned cunning. "You know. You help him. You've always helped them, you *bitch*."

"I need to speak with you, Doctor."

I turned to see Reever standing beside the partition. He'd want to lecture me about Gael, no doubt. "Not now."

"It is important."

I adjusted a monitor that didn't need adjusting. "So is my patient." When he touched me, I stood up and glided away. "Okay." I stepped around the partition and folded my arms. "You've got a minute. Start talking."

"FurreVa reported she discovered you concealing two escaped prisoners." Reever removed a data pad from his tunic pocket and switched it to display. "The Terran Kelly and an unidentified humanoid male."

"So?"

"As a member of the Faction, you—"

"—aren't allowed to harbor runaway slaves, I know. So?"

He didn't prepare me for the next bombshell. He simply dropped it. "Lord SrrokVar has filed a protest against OverLord TssVar's decision to recognize our union, and a request to have it terminated."

I controlled my expression. Barely. "How do you terminate a Hsktskt marriage? Does someone kill you?"

"No."

"Pity."

"The SubHanar has granted SrrokVar permission to continue conducting his research involving Terrans, specifically on you."

"Has he?" I resisted the urge to collapse on the nearest berth. "When do I report for torture?"

"He cannot conduct his research if you are pregnant."

It didn't take ten seconds for that to sink in. "Oh, no. *No.*"

He inclined his head politely. "Then you must falsify your medical records. I would suggest having your resident sign off on the positive pregnancy scan, to avoid difficulty in convincing the Lord you are actually carrying my child."

Suspicion settled over me. He was being nice. Too nice. "Why would you encourage me to deceive the Hsktskt when you could force me to do something much more fun for you personally?"

"We will discuss that at length another time." He

handed me the data pad. "A large group of prisoners in tier nine have been reported to be suffering from an outbreak of a new disease. I am ordering them to be kept sequestered in their chambers until you can verify that the pathogen infecting them is not contagious."

"That's smart." I studied the guard's report. "Looks like it could be some kind of food poisoning. I'll have to go and examine the victims." I grabbed my medical case and headed for the door panel.

I learned from the guard that the latest batch of new arrivals occupied tier nine, and that Paul Dalton and Geef Skrople were among the infected prisoners. Friends in trouble again, as they'd been on K-2. What could be causing it this time?

I located Paul and Geef in the prisoner commons, with about two hundred other males who had been captured in the border territories. I knelt down beside Paul, listened to his broken moans, and studied the speckled condition of his face.

He looked awful. On death's doorstep. And it was all I could do to swallow my laughter.

"Nice job." I pulled out my scanner, and reached a hand toward his artificially flushed brow. "Whose bright idea was this?"

"Mine," he whispered, and lolled his head to one side in an excellent imitation of fever-induced delirium. "Don't touch, Doc. The stuff we used for the fake rash rubs off."

I nodded toward the other spotty, moaning prisoners. "The rest of them, too?"

"Yeah. Pretty smart, huh?"

"Pretty reckless." I played worried doctor and performed a completely unnecessary examination. "So why the performance?"

"We needed to get you out of that infirmary so we could talk. Met a friend of yours as soon as we were brought over here." Paul moved his eyes to the left, and I looked down to see Wonlee lying in a state of counterfeit delirium. "He's going to rally the rest of the prisoners to help us."

"And in the meantime?"

"Geef and I need to get to the surface. That's why we thought we'd fake the contagion. Can you get us out of this tier and into the main complex? We can take it from there."

I'd have to get TssVar to agree to set up some kind of quarantine ward. "I think so."

One of the centurons appeared in the entrance to the commons, and I lunged to my feet. "Don't come in here! These prisoners are highly contagious. I'm instituting an immediate level-one quarantine."

The centuron backed out and sealed the door panel at once.

"I love it when they jump like that." I turned back to Paul. "You'll need help to get to the surface. But let's get you out of here first."

It took a bunch of shouting and striding around looking frantic, but I convinced TssVar to move Paul and the other two hundred "contagious" new prisoners out of the slave tiers and into an unused cargo storage area. During the move, I released Won, who promptly went back to his own tier to start recruiting prisoners for the cause.

I set up Zella to run the ward, after confiding what the real story was and threatening to dismember her—slowly—with a lascalpel if she breathed a word of it to anyone in a thermal uniform. Geef asked me to spread the word about the coming rescue forces, and I briefed prisoners I trusted from each tier as I made rounds of the entire compound to check for any other cases of the "contagion."

It was during these rounds that one of the prisoners on Gael Kelly's tier informed me the Terran had been slated to be sold at auction. The same auction I was summoned to the next day.

"Perform standard pre-trade inspections," TssVar instructed me. "Pay particular attention to any members of the Isalth-io species. A trader complained he lost two of them a day out from Catopsa."

"Is that right?" I gave him my best puzzled look. "Gee, wonder what went wrong."

When I entered the holding area, I saw Gael among the prisoners, and went to him first.

"Hey, pal." I tugged him to the far side of the chamber, away from the guards. "Are you okay?"

"Nawful, *dote*, but I'm not letting on, am I?"

"No." He was lean but otherwise healthy. There wasn't much I could do, now that TssVar suspected about the two Isalth-ios, and it frustrated me. "I'll make sure I record who you're sold to, and once we're liberated, I'll do everything I can to recover you."

"Liberated?" Gael glanced around, then lowered his voice. "What's this about now?"

"Long story." I took out my scanner and activated it. "Hold still, and let me at least look like I'm evaluating you."

"I hoofed about, looking for one of them grand tunnels, but no luck here." Gael gnawed at his lower lip. "That rapid skin of yours, Noarr, could he help me to bolt outta here?"

"I'm not even sure where I can find him." I finished the scan and noted the results on the data pad. Then I saw the determined glint in his eye. "Don't think about doing something stupid and getting yourself shot."

"If someone's coming here to millie up, I'd like to be in on the ructions." He smacked his closed fist into his other palm. "I've foostered longer on this rock than most of the knackers here. I'm gummin' to lose the head."

He was right. "Okay, let me see if I can track Noarr down somehow. Just don't start losing the head with the guards until I get back."

I used the excuse of the contagion to postpone the slave auction, leave the trade area, and return to the infirmary. The only quick way I could find Noarr was by using my friend Alunthri to track his scent through the tunnels, so I had the Chakacat brought to me on the pretense of screening it for the contagion.

Alunthri acted suitably feral until the centurons departed, then dropped the wildcat pose at once. "What is wrong, Cherijo?"

I took the small swatch of robe from my tunic pocket—okay, I'd been saving it for stupid, sentimental reasons—and handed it to my friend. "I have to find this male. Can you track him down for me?"

Alunthri sniffed the fabric, then the hard surface of the floor. "Most scent-paths have been eradicated by the Lok-Teel. I cannot track him in this manner."

Which meant we'd probably get lost in the tunnels, even if they were still passable. I thought for a moment. "What if you were able to smell the prisoners? He may be wearing a disguise when he works inside the compound, but he'd still smell the same. Would that work?"

It would.

"Are you sure your nose is working right?"

We had spent a day going through the prisoner population, with no luck. If Noarr had been in the compound, Alunthri would have tracked him down. The only place it scented Noarr was in the infirmary, and outside SrroVar's central chamber. Those recent scents hadn't yet been eradicated by the ever-busy Lok-Teel, it told me, but they were still very faint.

I'd taken the precaution of tallying up the prisoners we checked, and discovered the prison population matched the current statistics on the Hsktskt database. Which meant Noarr wasn't currently posing as a slave, or there would be a one prisoner difference between the figures.

Since I had no evidence that the fake contagion had spread, TssVar ordered the slave auction to continue and for me to get the inspections finished.

I knew Gael was depressed by the news, but he simply thanked me for trying.

"I can get in touch with your family on Terra, as soon as we're out of here," I offered. "At least they'll know you're still alive, until we can free you from whoever buys you."

"That'd be murder," Gael said, and got an odd look on his face. "Ma and Da did a flit from Clare with the rest of the Kellys. Thick as ditches, they were, barreling from Terra to an agri-colony. New-Eire, they meant to call it. Planned to be culchies, raise sheep and crops, the dense bollocks." He made a harsh sound. "Made a right hames of it. The thicks belted our ship, banjaxed it. Everyone died but me."

Blast my thoughtless tongue. "I'm sorry, Gael."

"They were plonkers, thinking they could scrap with the thicks." He stared past me at the wall, then shook his head. "Sorry, *dote*. I'm being annoying, aren't I?"

"Be as annoying as you like." I pressed my hand over his. "We'll find a way to set you free, I promise."

Just before the auction began, I took my usual position behind one of the pillars so I could record who went where. That was where Noarr found me.

A warm flipper descended on my shoulder. "Cherijo."

I nearly dropped my data pad and whirled around. "Noarr!" I lowered my voice to a murmur. "God, don't *do* that, you scared me." I peered into his hood. "Are you okay?"

"I have been better." He appraised the sight of the traders bidding for a pair of Cordobels for a moment. "I am told you need my assistance moving some prisoners off Catopsa."

"Yes. Paul Dalton and Geef Skrople have to get to the surface to signal the rescue forces." I quickly explained the approaching invasion fleet and what the two engineers needed. "There's also a Terran,

Gael Kelly, the one we rescued from the crying chambers. We could use him to help move the prisoners out of the compound. But he's up for auction today."

"I remember him." Noarr's humming voice grew harder. "You care for him."

"Yeah, I do." This was all I needed. A jealous slave-runner on my hands. I lifted my scanner to check the injury I knew was on his side and his flipper caught my wrist. "Don't be a baby, let me do a quick scan."

"I am fine." He pushed my hand away. "Dalton and Skrople can be moved. Kelly I can do nothing for. There is no access to this area of the compound, and what tunnels I have in the proximity are completely blocked off by black growth."

"Okay." I wasn't happy about abandoning Gael, but there was only so much we could do. "We'll track him down after the liberation."

"Kelly will not be sold, I think."

"Why, because he's a troublemaker?"

"No one will offer for him. I must go now." Noarr stepped back, but I reached and latched on to one sleeve. "There is more?"

"Yeah, there is." I slipped my arms around his waist and rested my head against his chest for a moment. "Thanks, *Osepeke*."

His flipper touched my hair. "Be careful, *Waenara*."

The only other good thing that happened that day was watching Gael Kelly stand on the platform, and seeing the instant looks of dislike pass over the faces of the assembled traders.

Noarr's prediction came true. No one offered a single credit for the Terran. Gael's notorious reputation as a habitual escapee had actually saved him.

CHAPTER FIFTEEN

Persuading the Pel

We managed to keep up the facade of the contagion for another week without the Hsktskt becoming suspicious. Paul told me Noarr had contacted him to make the arrangements for the move to the surface as soon as he detected the Jorenian/Aksellan forces approaching Catopsa.

"The Hsktskt will pick them up on their scanners, too." I was worried this rescue attempt would end up starting another war. "How are you going to deal with that?"

Paul gave me a mysterious smile. "We've figured out how to handle that, too. Don't worry, Doc."

" 'Don't worry, Doc.' 'We'll handle it, Doc.' Oh sure. Then it's 'Can you sew up this hole they blasted through my belly, Doc?' " I snorted. "You'd better make sure you can handle it."

Gael Kelly came to see me in the infirmary toward the end of the week. He had been returned to his tier, and had managed to get into another fight with a guard. I sutured his gashed abdomen and lectured him on being more cautious, too.

He was quiet—a little too quiet for my liking. "What's wrong? Are you in pain somewhere else and not telling me?"

"Doc, I heard . . . a bit of news." He looked miserable. "You need to be wide about this. Dog wide."

I dressed the wound lightly and helped him back into his tunic. "I'll be a bridge, if you like. Just tell me in stanTerran, Gael."

"Okay." He wiped the sweat from his brow with the back of his hand and eased off the exam table. "I've been listening in on the thicks' gobbing, uh, conversations. Trying to learn if they know anything about the liberation plans." He dropped his gaze. "I heard three of them talking about a meeting SrrokVar was having with a special prisoner on the tier.

"I slipped down to the tier controller's office and listened at the door panel. SrrokVar was talking to someone. He said pretending to help the knackers do a bunk from that feck hole of his was brilliant, and it was too bad the tunnels were mucked or they could keep using them to taking the knackers to the execution grounds." Gael's voice became very gentle. "Then I heard the sleeven say he would find another way to do it. It was that skin of yours. The tall one."

"No." My throat dried up. "You're wrong. He must have been talking to someone else. It's not Noarr."

Gael looked at me then. "God forgive me, *dote*, but it was. I know his voice." As I sat numbly down on the chair next to the exam table, the Terran pulled the partition closed and came to me. "I'm so sorry."

So Noarr had lied to me, and was working for the lizards. How could I have trusted him? Believed in him? "I'm an idiot. A complete, blind idiot."

"No." Gael pressed a kiss on the top of my head. "You're an amazing bird, you are."

I lifted my face and found Gael's mouth on mine a second later. I froze, burning with humiliation and embarrassment. Because I felt sorry for him, I let him kiss me. It soothed my shattered nerves, but I felt nothing beyond that.

Gael's body pressed into mine. He was breathing hard, his heart pounding, his limbs trembling. His hands stroked up my back and moved around to caress my breasts. The ridge of his erection pressed lightly against my stomach.

"Slagging bastard. It's mortifying, how he's had you on." He buried his mouth against my neck. "I won't let him make a hash out of you, *dote*. Not ever again. I'll look out for you."

I couldn't do this, I thought, and carefully stepped away, out of his embrace. "I'm sorry, Gael."

Gael's face reddened. "Even knowing what a caffler he is, you—"

"No. This isn't about Noarr." I let my sorrow and sympathy show through. "I'm sorry."

"Right jibber, you are. Or a brasser. I can't decide which." The Terran strode out of the infirmary.

I was voting for complete fool myself.

Alunthri was waiting in Reever's chamber when I went off shift. It took one look at my face and started preparing a server of tea for me.

"Hey." I peeled off my outer tunic and dropped onto a chair. "I thought we agreed you wouldn't do that."

"We're both slaves now." Alunthri calmly padded over and placed the server on the table before me. "Something has happened. Something that hurt you."

I took a sip and winced as the hot liquid scalded my tongue. "You're psychic."

"I'm your friend. I know you."

Tears spilled down my face as I buried it in my arms and let go. I felt Alunthri's palm stroking my back as I wept, and thanked whatever God or fate had brought one true friend into my life. Ultimately, I pulled myself together. "Sorry."

Alunthri mopped me up, made me more tea, and listened as I related what Gael had told me.

"The worst part is, I swore I'd never trust anyone again. Then Noarr comes along, and seems like everything good and fine in a man, and crash, there go my walls." I finished the tea and blew my nose. "It was as bad as that moment I saw you on the *Perpetua*, and knew Reever had kidnapped you from Garnot just as leverage against me."

Alunthri sat back in its chair and made an odd noise. "Cherijo, there is something you are not aware of. Reever did not kidnap me."

I put my server down and had to quickly right it before it fell over. "What are you talking about?"

"Reever did not kidnap me. The Garnotans are not artists, Cherijo. There is no artists' colony on that world." All around its neck, silvery fur rose. "They are slavers."

"What?" I got to my feet. "Alunthri, I went down there. I saw those people. They were all . . . they weren't really artists?"

"I am sorry to say they are not. Their pretense draws the unsuspecting to the planet. It's all a sham. Garnot is a slaver-depot. Just like this one." Alunthri bared its teeth in a silent snarl. "They had me chained and in a holding pit before the *Sunlace* left orbit. One of them said I would fetch a good price from Chakaran traders."

"I left you there. I should have checked that place out more thoroughly, damn it." My brow furrowed. "So Reever . . . what, bought you?"

"I do not know if credits were exchanged. Hsktskt centurons removed me from the slave pits and brought me directly to Joren and the *Perpetua*. By the time we arrived, Reever and the Hsktskt had gained control of the League fleet."

Which I'd helped them do. Willingly. *Cheerfully.*

"You carry much blame for the actions of others, Cherijo. What happened to me on Garnot is not your fault. Nor is the betrayal of someone you thought a friend."

"I have no friends, except you." I laughed bitterly. "Isn't that awful? But it's true. I can't trust anyone. Not Reever, not Noarr." I wiped the last traces of tears from my face as Reever walked through the door panel. "A blinding example of my own lousy judgment."

"I beg your pardon?" Reever said.

"Never mind." I got up and trudged over to my sleeping platform. "Alunthri is staying with us tonight." I glanced back at the big cat. "You don't mind sleeping on the sofa, do you?"

It knew I didn't want to be alone with Reever now. "Not at all, Cherijo."

I silently cried myself to sleep that night, and several nights following that. Reever made a few comments, but otherwise left me alone. Noarr didn't attempt to make contact. The moment he did, I was going to add a few more swirls to that face of his.

Everything seemed to decelerate to slow motion as we waited for the Jorenian/Aksellan forces to reach Catopsa. The days dragged while the tension mounted. Prisoners avoided congregating in groups to prevent the guards from overhearing any plans being made. We simply had to hold on until help arrived.

Someone got suspicious anyway.

I was summoned by FurreVa early one morning to slave tier six, where she and her guards had started making a surprise inspection of the prisoner chambers. I found her standing in front of an access door that had been smashed. Shards peppered the floor around her.

For a moment, I simply stared. What had happened to the quasi-quartz to make it break like this? No one had been able to make a scratch on it for months. None of the Hsktskt had any unusual devices or weapons. Then I saw black streaks running through the bits all around my feet, and peered into the tunnel.

The black growths were gone. They'd somehow gotten into the walls.

"We discovered this passage. What is it?" FurreVa asked me.

"I have no idea." I looked as confused as I felt. "What broke the wall?"

"Her." FurreVa pointed to a large, muscular female prisoner being held by three centurons. "And him." An injured centuron lay on his side, clutching a certain vulnerable portion of his anatomy. Dozens of transparent shards gleamed, imbedded in the thick scales along his outer arm.

I seized on the medical problem to avoid dealing with more questions about the crystal. "Let me get him to the infirmary."

TssVar ordered his centurons to search the entire compound, of course. Once I'd finished removing the quasi-quartz from the injured guard's hide, I was summoned to accompany one of the teams sweeping the tiers for more hidden passageways.

I didn't want to go. Didn't want to find the Hsktskt dragging Noarr out of some hidden corner. I ended up on Reever's team, which only made things worse. He positioned himself at my side and watched my every movement. Keeping up a bland, indifferent expression while I watched the guards smash their weapon butts into the prison walls was a real challenge.

FurreVa's team joined ours. Then GothVar and his squad. No one looked very happy to see each other. Something bad was going to happen. Really bad. I could feel it, like a palpable force, tightening around me.

Another tunnel was exposed, right in front of my eyes. I spotted the barely noticeable dark veins, and tried not to react. The centuron must have noticed them, too. He heaved the end of his rifle into the center of the thinly webbed surface. The mirrored panel didn't crack. It shattered, spilling tiny, black-shot shards all around our feet. Centurons disappeared into the small tunnel, searching for concealed prisoners.

Reever stared at me. I shook some shards from the top of my footgear and didn't return the favor. GothVar trudged over and planted himself in front of me.

"She knew about this," he said, stroking the pulse rifle's trigger with two claws.

"You think so?" I gave him a thin smile. "Prove it."

The centurons called to Reever from the tunnel, and he gave me a final glare before stepping through the entrance. A moment later, he came out and beckoned to me. "Cherijo, I need you to look at this."

Was it Noarr? My bruised heart turned over in my chest. Was he hurt, had someone—"Right. Coming."

Reever disappeared into the dark ahead of me. More veins laced the inner tunnel surfaces, creating shadows that thickened several feet in until they solidified to form an impenetrable expanse of solid black. With all the light gone, I felt my way by walking with one hand against a wall. A centuron outlined in the frame of another shattered access door curled a limb toward me, and I headed in his direction.

The tunnel emptied out into an equipment storage area, and a strange sense of déjà vu swept over me when I saw Reever kneeling next to something small and white.

Suddenly I flashed back to the incident on the *Perpetua*. Level eighteen. The sharp, poisonous smell of ammonia. A lump of what appeared to be melted chalk.

I slowly removed my scanner, passed it over the residue, and recited the readings. "Hydrogen, oxygen, nitrogen, calcium, and phosphorous. Minute amounts of deoxyribonucleic acid."

Reever sent the bulk of the guards on to continue their sweep. "The same as we found on the *Perpetua*."

GothVar came over to peer at the remains. "It is filth, nothing more."

"No, OverCenturon." I deactivated the instrument. "This was a person."

"So was this." FurreVa entered the chamber, carrying the partial remains of another prisoner, and placed them next to the skeletal residue. What she'd brought in was gruesome, only a portion of a torso and one limb. It was bundled in a transparent material of a type I hadn't seen before. "I found it in an adjoining compartment."

GothVar stepped aside, as if offended by the sight of the bundle.

I unwrapped the material and examined the bloodless remains. "This appears to have been a female Tingalean." I bent closer to study the unusual striations on what was left of her right lower appendage. "She was dismembered, but not very efficiently. These look like gnaw marks." I glanced up at GothVar as I carefully replaced the material. Interesting, the way he'd reacted to the corpse. Wonder why?

"There are dozens more like this." FurreVa hitched her weapon up on one shoulder. "All dead. All *escaped* prisoners, from the look of them."

"They didn't escape far. The pattern of the wounds suggests a large, sharp-toothed assailant." I turned to Reever. "I'll have to do a postmortem to be positive, OverMaster, but from the marks I'd say one of your friends here got hungry. And this"—I indicated the chalky pile—"is what couldn't be digested."

"Hsktskt no longer consume lesser-evolved beings," FurreVa said, her gruff voice almost soft and thoughtful. She wasn't talking to me, I saw. She kept her gaze fixed on GothVar.

"I've heard plenty of Hsktskt threaten to eat prisoners," I said, even as I realized I'd never seen a Hsktskt eat anything, other than the synthesized glop FurreVa had fed her brood.

"We threaten, yes. Perpetuating your ignorant assumptions provides an excellent means of control." FurreVa took a step toward GothVar. "No Hsktskt would in fact devour a live being. That would violate Faction law."

"Someone violated it. I need to see where you found them, FurreVa. With that many bodies, I'll have plenty of saliva traces to identify who killed these prisoners."

But I already knew.

I went still as an odd sound rushed in my ears. The sound of a low, monstrous voice . . .

For a moment, I was back in the launch bay on the *Perpetua,* my arm being gouged by the thresher. He had come up behind me. He had told me what he planned to do to me.

"I will take you on the tiers, Terran. Piece by piece, I will devour you. A small part of you each time. First your fingers . . . then your ears. . . ."

He had told me exactly how he'd planned to eat me. I hitched in a breath at the thought of what these poor beings had suffered, then swiveled around slowly and stared at the one responsible for doing it.

GothVar must have realized I'd remembered, for he chose that moment to go completely insane.

"Move against the wall." He gestured to two of the centurons who tended to hang around him, and the trio leveled their weapons at me, Reever, and FurreVa. Reever and I slowly backed against the specified wall. The big female stood her ground and hissed with what I could only call satisfaction.

"At last, you rankless son of a worm. I have you in violation."

GothVar lifted the rifle and pointed it directly at her face. "Your new visage will not be so easy to repair this time."

"He did this to you?" I asked FurreVa, hoping to distract FlatHead long enough for someone to do something.

"Tell her," GothVar said. "It does not matter if they know. None of you will leave here alive."

"This *worm*"—FurreVa took great pleasure in enunciating that—"attacked me while we were on a planetary raid. He wanted my position, and sought to take it."

I looked at her once-distorted face, then GothVar's oddly sloped brow. "You did this to each other by fighting over how much junk is on your uniforms?"

"I would be interested in hearing more on this."

TssVar and several heavily armed guards came into the storage area, which abruptly got rather crowded. There wasn't even a question of a fight this time; GothVar and his cronies lowered their weapons and were swiftly disarmed.

"OverLord." FurreVa made her report about the bodies she'd discovered, and implicated GothVar and his two pals as the perpetrators. "Dr. Torin believes she will have enough evidence to prove their guilt."

"I claim reprieve as brood sire," GothVar said at once.

"Indeed." TssVar turned to gaze at the OverCenturon. "You claim it now, yet you are not joined."

"I'm definitely not following this," I said to Reever.

"Hsktskt males can assume the higher rank of a female, if they join in a unity ritual. The female is reduced to the rank of Nurturer until she delivers her brood."

"Yes, but OverSeer FurreVa refused to join with me." GothVar's tongue flickered rapidly. "Thus I persuaded her to cooperate."

"He rendered me unconscious so he could sire my brood," the Hsktskt female said. "When he told me what he had done, I refused the union. That is when he did this." She touched her reconstructed face.

"Why didn't you tell someone?" I demanded.

"As soon as my superiors discovered my state, GothVar and I would have been required by law to join." FurreVa lifted her head, and her eyes resembled small, raging suns. "I preferred to be executed."

"You are still required by Faction law to join with me. I offer it to you again," FaltHead said, as though conferring a great honor.

TssVar hit him then, driving him back into a cluster of console units. "She does not accept. Once it is proven you violated Faction law by devouring these prisoners, you will be executed."

"As sire of her brood, you cannot execute me, no matter what my crime is. I claim sire's amnesty."

"So be it," TssVar said.

"Wait." I looked from Reever to TssVar. "Let me understand this correctly. FlatHead beat and raped FurreVa, in order to take over her rank and force her to marry him. She refused, he tried to murder her. He didn't succeed. She's had to hide her pregnancy, avoid him, and wait all this time to nail him for some other violation of your laws. But when she finds out that he and his friends have been snacking on prisoners, he says he wants to get married and play Daddy, and you're saying you can't kill him because of that?"

"In a sense, yes, that is correct."

"And she still has to marry him?" FurreVa hissed. TssVar nodded. I held out a hand. "I can solve this problem. Give me one of those rifles."

"There is an alternative, brother." Reever stepped forward to tug me away from the OverLord. "I remind you of the sire's right of protection."

GothVar sneered. "TssVar did not sire this female."

If TssVar could have smiled, his lipless mouth would have stretched from brow ridge to brow ridge. "You forget, OverCenturon. We are at war with the Allied League of Worlds."

FurreVa gaped for a moment, then performed a low, respectful bow. "I am honored, OverLord."

GothVar, on the other hand, said nothing, but suddenly seemed to be shrinking a few inches.

"Escort them to the arena," TssVar said to his guards, then watched them depart. "Doctor, I will need that forensic evidence immediately." He walked out, and FurreVa followed.

"They lost me again," I said to Reever.

"TssVar claims a sire's prerogative—to defend his female young from a rank challenger. Something he can do only in wartime."

"Why only then?"

"Mobilization during military conflict prevents FurreVa from returning to the homeworld and petitioning her sire to defend her. As her commander, TssVar may act *in loco parentis* and will fight GothVar for the right of protection over FurreVa."

Which meant one or both of them was going to need my services immediately thereafter.

I had to transport the remains of thirty-seven dead prisoners to the infirmary, where I set up a temporary morgue. I performed five scans before I found enough DNA evidence to convict GothVar and the other two guards of Faction law violation. When I signaled the same to Command, TssVar ordered me to report to the arena.

"I don't want to watch," I said. "I've got thirty-one more autopsies to perform."

"FurreVa has no comrades. No one to stand as witness." The OverLord studied me for a moment. "Except you."

"All right, all right." He certainly knew what buttons to push. "I'm on the way."

Every Hsktskt who could be spared entered the arena to watch the OverLord defend FurreVa's honor. I managed to stay back out of the way, until Reever saw me and made me squeeze through to the front of the crowd.

"I really, really don't want to see this," I told him.

"FurreVa—"

"I know. FurreVa needs a pal." I saw the big female standing beside the quad, looking distinctly isolated. No one came near her—probably another weird taboo of theirs—so I inched my way in her direction. When I got there, I saw the fine tremors of rage and worry running through her limbs.

"Hi." I took position at her side and studied the gore-spattered panels in front of us. "Should we get some popcorn?"

She turned to me. "Some what?"

"Popcorn. It's what Terrans eat when they watch holofilms. Sort of goes along with entertainment."

"I think not." Her perfectly proportioned head swung back toward the quad. "Even now, you seem determined to provoke me."

"No. I'm determined to be your friend."

"You are Terran. I am Hsktskt. We should not be friends."

"Shouldn't we?" I saw the crowd part on either side of the arena. "Here comes the main event."

TssVar and GothVar entered the quad. Both were stripped down to minimal garments and displayed fairly awesome physiques. As far as size went, TssVar held the advantage, but GothVar had more bulk. It looked to be a fairly even match.

The crowd fell silent as TssVar stepped into the center of the quad and held up two of his limbs.

"My people. I come here defending OverSeer FurreVa, with sire's right of protection." He turned to indicate GothVar. "This male has violated her, attempted to kill her, and now tries to force unity. He is a coward, undeserving of the honor of broodsire's rights."

Now it was FlatHead's turn. "My comrades. I have but wished to join with my mate. She has delivered the brood I sired. By law she is to be mine. OverLord TssVar claims sire's right when none is necessary. She will be mine."

"Now they beat each other's brains out?" I murmured to FurreVa.

"Yes."

And with no further speeches or ceremony, that's what they did. I'd seen hand-to-hand combat before, even participated in some myself. It paled in comparison to this.

Hsktskt use all their limbs in the quad—upper, lower, and even their prehensile tail appendages. The results ranged from bone-cracking grappling holds to violent impacts of limbs into torsos and heads. TssVar sent GothVar sprawling to the surface of the quad over and over. GothVar ripped huge gouges in TssVar's hide.

The blood and brutality made me sick. "How long will they keep this up?" I yelled to FurreVa over the shouts of the crowd.

She never took her eyes from the quad. "Until one of them dies."

For a short time I thought that might be TssVar. FlatHead sank his teeth into one of the OverLord's upper limbs and held on, tearing and pulling at the joint until with a horrible cry TssVar went down.

The limb, however, stayed in GothVar's mouth until he removed it and threw it from the ring.

"No." I ran over to where the limb had landed and grabbed it. Reever appeared. "I need a cryo-unit to preserve this," I said. "Get the infirmary to send one down at once."

Exhausted and bleeding copiously now, TssVar launched himself from the quad surface to wrap his remaining limbs around GothVar's torso. He planted his huge feet, contracted his limbs, and bones began to snap. GothVar screamed.

I'd had enough of this, I thought, and reached up to climb into the ring. Reever pulled me back down. When I started arguing, he pointed toward the grappling pair. "Watch. He will finish it now."

TssVar kept tightening his limbs, GothVar kept

bellowing. The crowd fell oddly silent. I stepped back as I heard tissues tear and blood spill between the two Hsktskt. There was a loud, final snapping sound, then GothVar sagged limp and motionless in TssVar's lethal embrace.

The OverLord released the body, which fell like a sack of broken servers to the quad. "It is done."

I didn't have time to applaud. I raced under the cords and over to the tottering Hsktskt, who was now reeling in a pool of GothVar's blood, and contributing a lot of his own to the same.

"Congratulations." I tore the sleeve from my tunic and used it as a temporary tourniquet over the jagged stump. "You're a mess."

"I will leave you to deal with the repairs," he said, then sat down heavily.

"That's what they all say." I moved my foot to avoid a stream of GothVar's spreading body fluid, then squinted at it. Like Terrans, the Hskskt had red blood. So there was no reason for GothVar's blood to have streaks of black . . . unless . . .

A feeble strand of black lifted out of the congealing red puddle and started to elongate toward TssVar.

I jumped away from the fluid pool, trying to pull the Hsktskt with me, then yelled at two nearby centurons. "Help me!"

Without hesitation the two guards assisted me as I dragged the OverLord away from the contaminated plasma.

The black streaks subsided, and began to crystallize.

I didn't have time to celebrate what I'd discovered. The OverLord's condition required immediate surgery. I ran in front of his gurney to the infirmary, shouted for a scrub team to move faster than the speed of light, and checked the still-twitching limb in the cryo-unit.

"I need full text on Hsktskt limb replantation," I

said as I scrubbed. "If they're not in our database, signal Command and tell them to relay them *now*."

A nurse brought them in on a data pad as I geared up, and I studied the data carefully. Had GothVar torn off TssVar's tail, it wouldn't have been a problem—Hsktskt regenerated those naturally. But the limb was going to require some very special, fancy cutting, especially in areas where the ruptured vessels were not as easily accessible, in and around the major shoulder joint.

"Plan on being here for a few hours, people," I said as I walked into surgery, gloves up to prevent accidental contamination. TssVar's vitals were weak, but gratifyingly steady. "Power up the laser, and remove the tourniquet. Clamp."

The microsurgery turned out to be no picnic. GothVar, obviously a pro at rending a victim limb from limb, had done extensive, serious damage.

I clamped off the bleeders and started prepping the stump, then the end of the limb for reconnection. Blood vessels and nerves had to be accurately rejoined in order for regeneration to occur, so I worked with a scope in my face for the rest of the procedure.

I rejoined the major vessels first, then watched the scanner display as circulation was reinstated. "Okay. Six vessels down, twenty-four to go."

Seven hours later, I stripped off my mask and deactivated the sterile field. "We're done for now. Wheel him out into recovery." I turned around and nearly ran over Duncan Reever, who was also dressed in surgical gear. "What are you doing here? I thought surgery made you sick."

"He is my brother," Reever said.

"Whatever. I want GothVar's body brought over here for an autopsy," I said as I went to the cleansing unit. "Make sure whoever handles it uses a hazardous waste transport and wears an envirosuit."

"Why?"

"His blood has been contaminated." I peeled off

my surgical gown. "I'll let you know by what as soon as I get it under a scope."

"I'll see to it. You performed well today." Without another word, Reever turned and left.

That might have been a thank-you, I thought, then went to scrub TssVar's blood from my hands. I'd have to think about it, though.

Two fully suited centurons delivered GothVar's body in an enormous, sealed receptacle, and I pulled Vlaav off the ward to assist me with the postmortem. What I'd suspected showed up a moment after I'd made the median incision.

Hundreds of solid black growths encrusted his internal organs.

"I've never seen a disease like this," my resident said as he handed me a clamp.

"It's not a disease, and yes, you have seen it before."

The growths couldn't be detached, I discovered, after practically burning out a lascalpel. Taking a sample required the excision of an entire lymph node. I had to modify the electroniscopic scanner to accommodate the over-large specimen before I could examine it from the molecular level up.

Vlaav had completed the brain examination and brought a slice of GothVar's outer cerebral tissue over in a specimen tray. "You're not going to believe this, Doctor, but he was—"

"Infected with meningitis?" I glanced at the mucus-covered sample. "Yes, I believe it. He wouldn't let the Lok-Teel near him."

Vlaav appeared totally confused now.

"The meningitis was the body's natural reaction to the bacteria, which isn't a bacteria, by the way. It's minute particles of this black crystal."

I adjusted the scope's magnification and had Vlaav take a look at it.

"Those cells resemble the microbe we found in all

the spinal fluid samples." He lifted his head, confused. "But these are transparent, and there are no nuclei present."

"It's not bacteria. This mineral seems to have two forms: liquid, and solid. Heat seems to be the factor. The pseudo-bacteria solidifies when the body temperature cools."

"But why didn't we find any of them in the autopsies we performed?"

I spotted one of the blobs ambling along the side of a wall, and gently picked it off. After pulling the organ sample out from under the scope, I set the mold beside it and stepped back.

The Lok-Teel instantly flowed over the encrusted node and began contracting and expanding. A few minutes later, it moved off and revealed a normal, crystal-free specimen.

"The Lok-Teel ate it. These little guys make penicillin look practically useless."

"So that must be the reason the others didn't die!" Vlaav's arms flapped with excitement. "I remember, I kept picking the mold off their berths—it must have absorbed the mineral directly through contact with their flesh."

"Yep. That's it." I cleaned up and went to send a signal to Central Command.

You'd think reattaching the limb of a Hsktskt OverLord and curing a toxic plague would make the powers that be just a tad grateful to you, wouldn't you? I thought so, too, until I was seized and dragged back to the solitary confinement pits.

Well, it really wasn't TssVar's fault. SrrokVar had been responsible for the entire mess.

It happened a few days after the battle over FurreVa, while I was on duty. Dr. Mengele showed up at the infirmary and demanded to see TssVar. I let him, mostly because I was busy. Next thing I knew SrrokVar was arguing with my patient about the tunnels, and the informant who had seen me using them.

"How many slaves has she declared deceased, only to smuggle them through these passages? How many have escaped Catopsa?"

I came to the berth and regarded the Hsktskt scientist with extreme exasperation. "The OverLord can listen to your allegations later—when he's recovered. Leave."

"Such audacity," SrrokVar said. "I will leech that out of her, TssVar—"

That's when the OverLord summoned his personal guard, and sent me to sit in an isolation pit until further notice.

I should have been furious, but an hour into my confinement I realized something. By putting me in the pit, TssVar had actually protected me. Without his intervention, SrrokVar would have certainly taken me back to the crying chambers.

So he does care what happens to me, in his own cold-blooded fashion.

Since they'd placed me in one of the deeper shafts, I tried communicating with other prisoners. Either no one spoke Terran, or I was the only lucky occupant of the confinement pits.

I leaned back against the crystal wall, still fighting frustration. *I have to get out of here, before the liberation forces reach Catopsa. Can't trust Noarr. Maybe Gael . . . ?*

An odd sensation passed over the back of my neck, and I sat up to rub it. That was when I felt the first, barely perceptible trace of another presence, and turned toward the crystal.

"Hel . . ."—my eyes widened as glittering black veins flowered inside the transparent surface—
". . . lo?"

The wall of the pit began to crackle, and I edged back away from it. A tiny shard fell down by my right hand. Then another. Then four more. Suddenly the entire wall was crumbling, and I had nowhere to go.

Stop!

As if it heard me, the wall stopped disintegrating. No hidden passage appeared, much to my disappointment. Just more of the black-shot toxin. Before I released my breath, I felt the presence again.

Then I *heard* it.

you

I waited. That was it. Not audible sound, more like a vibration, traveling up my arm and into my head. "Me what?"

*you*can*

Some kind of telepathy? *What do you want? Who are you?*

*you*can*be*you*can*be*trus*

I can be a truss?

*ted*you*can*be*trus*ted*

Some instinct made me reach out and press my palms to an intact part of the wall. "Noarr?"

*not*the*way*we*are*

It was some sort of echo . . . or not. *Of course it's some kind of weird echo.* I dropped my hands. *Or wishful thinking. What else would it be?*

The vibration shot up through my legs and made my ears ring.

pel

The presence became stronger. As I shook my head, trying to clear the muddle caused by the odd effect, something moved inside the wall. Something large. Very large. And it moved very fast.

"Noarr?" The name burst from me before I could control myself. "Noarr, if this is your idea of a joke, it's not funny."

*no*no*arr*pel*

An oozing mass of clear, thick fluid spilled over the shattered edge of the wall, and I scrabbled backward to avoid it. It didn't puddle around me; it froze in mid-spill, then backed up a few inches. Not much

more than a huge mass of quivering, colorless glop.
I could almost swear that if it had eyes, it would be
staring at me.

pel

Why do I keep hearing that— I saw the glop extend
an arm-sized mass that wrapped around my ankle
before I could move. The cool, satiny texture of the
stuff against my skin didn't scare me as much as
astound me.

That's exactly what the Lok-Teel feel like. I placed my
hand on the top of the mass, and it threaded itself
around my fingers.

PEL

The vibration was so strong I yelped in pain, and
reflexively shook the glop off my hand. It didn't spat-
ter, but hastily retracted back into itself.

Geez, you don't have to yell at me.

That's when it really astounded me. *for*give*

Can you hear me? I crawled forward, and watched
the goo shrink back against the wall. *Can you understand what I'm thinking?*

*don't*have*to*yell*

"Great. Glop with a sense of humor." I sat back
and tried to control the intensity of my thoughts. *Can
you understand me?*

yes

I had to find out where it had come from, how it
had gotten through the quasi-quartz. *Are you a prisoner here?*

*pel*is*here*

It didn't understand me. *Yeah, I know you're here.
Were you in a confinement pit? How did you get through
the wall?*

It didn't respond. I sat back down with a thump
and pressed my hands to my head, which was starting to ache. *Strange, you feel just like the Lok-Teel.*

*lok*teel* It seemed to think that over for a minute.
*pure*keep*all*

That's all it does. Keep things pure and tidy. Including my patients, thank God.

*keep*pel*tid*y* A small stream of goo came out of the solid wall and joined with the larger blob, increasing the mass until it was equal in size to me.

You're not hungry, I hope.

*hun*gry*

The vibration had a faint intonation to it this time, an uprising change in intensity. Evidently the pel could pick up some of the nuances of human thought and make an echo into a question. *Never mind. You're not big enough to eat me.*

*pel*big* More streams of glop erupted from the wall and added to the massive blob.

I don't need proof! I had to chuckle. The sound seemed to mesmerize the creature. *Besides, if you fill up this space, I'll suffocate, and they'll shoot you or something. If they could tell the difference between you and the quasi-quartz.*

*quas*i*

It seemed to ponder that for a moment, then reversed, and slowly ran up along the cracked surface of the wall. I gasped out loud when I realized what it was doing—repair work. Whatever it touched solidified back into its former state. A few moments later, the wall was completely whole again.

You didn't bust through the quasi-quartz, you ARE the quasi-quartz.

*pel*is*not*pel*is*

An image of the sentient crystal that had saved two lives back on the *Sunlace* formed in my head. And I wasn't generating it. *Is this one of your kind?*

*yes*pel*

How many of you live on this asteroid?

*pel*is* It didn't try to echo the last word. Instead, it swiftly formed a sphere, and solidified its outer surface into perfect, six-sided hexagons.

pel

The sphere split in half, revealing the center, swirling and undulating.

pel

This entire asteroid is pel?

It resumed its blob form. *is*pel*

If this entire world was actually a colonial mass of sentient beings—

Pel, we need to talk about a few things.

It took time. The pel didn't altogether grasp the intricacies of humanoid communication, and seemed to have a problem understanding certain ideas and phrases. It understood that its surface was occupied by other beings. It could even differentiate between species, but the contrasts made it think we were "impure"—covered in dirt, I realized.

Learning that the Lok-Teel fungi was actually a cooperative symbiot that cleaned and consumed impurities from the pel surprised me. Impurities . . .

Is that why your center is black? Because the Lok-Teel can't reach it and purify it?

*black*not*pel*

What is it?

tul The thought/vibration transmitted a deep ache into my limbs.

Of course, the physician in me responded at once. *Is tul a sickness? Is the pel sick?*

*tul*not*pel*

It didn't understand me. *Why does it grow in the pel? Is it infecting you?*

*tul*kill*pel*

Maybe it was some kind of mineral parasite. Or enemy life-form. *So we're not the only ones with problems.*

*tul*pel* The glop settled for a moment. *hskt*skt*slave*

I grinned and patted the blob. *That's it. The tul is to the pel what the Hasktskt is to the slave.*

*lok*teel*kill*tul* The glop enlarged abruptly. *slave*kill*hskt*skt*

No, I had to backtrack. I thought once more of the

separated chunk of crystal on the *Sunlace*, and felt a tremor of something odd. *Do you miss that part of yourself?*

*yes*mine*taken*

That's what the Hsktskt did to us. I formed a mental image of the NessNevat world, where the Hsktskt had nearly wiped out an entire race. *What the Hsktskt did to these beings.*

The clear glop suddenly shot out in a gleaming, sharp column, and smashed into the opposite wall. More shards sprayed all over me.

*pel*help*slaves*

Yes. I resisted an urge to hug the glop. *We could use a little help like that.*

The pel stayed with me as I explained. Over the following hours, it slowly grasped more understanding of my thoughts, which allowed me to communicate exactly what kind of help the prisoners would need, once the liberation forces arrived.

I sent it back into the wall when I saw the hatch slide open, and the retrieval clamps lower into the pit. *Go now. Wait for me to contact you.*

*pel*wait* The glop funneled itself into the wall and disappeared.

SrrokVar was waiting up top, and personally removed me from the retrieval unit.

"What's the matter, Lord?" I tried to free myself, but he wasn't letting go. "Get tired of harassing my patients?"

"Greetings, Doctor." He stared down, then nodded his head. "As I suspected."

My PIC had healed over, but that didn't matter now that I was a member of the Faction. I told him that, too. Loudly.

"I neglected to mention your union with OverMaster HalaVar has been rescinded, didn't I? No matter. We will make restoring your designation our first priority."

PART FOUR

Insurrection

CHAPTER SIXTEEN

Table Turns

I made it to the crying chambers without pleading, but I fought the centurons every step of the way. Cold sweat ran down the sides of my face as they wrestled me into a suspension rig, then hoisted me off the floor upside-down.

"You're not going to get away with this!" I shouted, trying to free myself, knowing it was hopeless. All right, Cherijo, calm down. It will all be over in a few minutes. "As soon as Reever finds out I'm here—"

"HalaVar will not be removing you on this or any other day, Doctor." SrrokVar activated the laser array and targeted my right forearm. "You see, he believes you are still in solitary confinement."

My heart rate sped out of control. Incongruously, time seemed to slow down. The beam flashed, then took forever to reach my arm. Scalding heat spliced my flesh, but it didn't move. My throat locked when I realized SrrokVar had calibrated the laser to the lowest speed.

This wasn't going to take a few minutes.

I fought the mind-scrambling panic. "No! Just do it and get it over with!"

"Calm yourself, my dear." SrrokVar drew closer, observing and tapping notes into a data pad. "Or can't you?" He peered at my face as I gasped for breath. "No, I don't believe you can. You've been burned before, haven't you, Doctor?"

The Sunlace. *Trying to rescue Tonetka and the children. The fire between us—*

"Is that why you're so afraid of the sensation? Have you been fighting those memories? Or reliving them?"

I couldn't answer. Pain and hysteria descended, corroding my breath, my control, my sanity.

Before everything spun out of coherency, I saw the Hsktskt shake his head, heard him say, "Subject displays severe phobic reaction to . . ."

Strangling terror slammed a wall between me and my surroundings, leaving me imprisoned in an airless pocket of fire. I saw my fingers shred as I climbed over the rubble, felt the veils of flame drape over my body. Blackened, charred bodies, the memory of those I hadn't saved, crowded the smoke-stained deck of the *Sunlace*. Bile surged up, but even that remained trapped. Nothing would unlock the frozen muscles of my throat.

I wasn't going to save anyone this time. . . . I was going to burn and burn and burn. . . .

Before I could black out from lack of oxygen, a cruel hand forced an endotracheal tube into my throat. The now-familiar burn of pure oxygen billowed down into my chest, pushing my lungs out, keeping my body alive.

No . . . I fought to dislodge the tube penetrating the swollen tissues of my throat. *Just let me die. . . .*

Something stung the side of my neck. Drugs entered my bloodstream, speeding through my veins into my heart, which began hammering faster and faster. Stimulants. SrrokVar wasn't going to let me miss a single moment.

There was no place to go. I tried to cower behind a mental wall, but the pain swelled over it and found me. In a haze of convulsive shudders, I heard some-one calling to me.

Joey.

I raced to find the path to the inner place. *Maggie, help me!* Yet the wall I'd erected had begun to close in around me, imprisoning me in a mental confine-ment pit. A pit lined with razor-sharp teeth. *Maggie, for God's sake!*

The memory of my surrogate mother's voice came to me with another, suffocating wave of torment— *He'll keep at you for as long as it takes to satisfy his curiosity—and that's endless.*

Endless. No. I couldn't take this.

Maggie's voice took on a beseeching tone. *Call him, Joey. Call to the one who loves you. The one who can save you.*

Two faces merged in my mind. Reever. Noarr. I loved them both, but only one would save me.

Reever!

At the sound of his name, the walls collapsed, and agony began tearing me apart.

I don't know how long SrrokVar worked on me. I didn't care. The pain had thrust me into a tight, dark, airless chamber. No doors. No windows. Just me, agony, and the sound of my own screaming.

With or without SrrokVar's special treatment, I knew I would scream in that chamber forever.

Yet eventually the pain stopped. It didn't dwindle. It was there one moment, gone the next. Or perhaps my awareness of it had discontinued. I remained, huddled, terrified, my throat raw, my muscles unresponsive.

I really, really wanted to stop screaming. I just couldn't.

Slowly the darkness came alive with sound. At first a mere hum, passing through the unyielding walls to whisper against my hypersensitive flesh. I squeezed myself tighter, smaller, still shrieking mindlessly.

The hum became a voice. The voice called out a word. No, not a word. A name.

Cherijo.

It knew me, it was coming for me, and it promised no more pain. A trick, I decided, and kept yelling without words, hoping, praying that would be enough to drive it away.

It wasn't. *Cherijo, I am here.*

The chamber disintegrated, and I was left alone in the boundless dark, trying to fold in upon myself, fear stealing what little air remained. I didn't have enough breath to scream anymore; all I could do was hope it wouldn't find me.

Hands touched me, then came a coolness so soothing that I wept. And still I couldn't unlock myself from that little ball of misery.

Look at me.

No way was I doing that. If I did, I'd see SrrokVar. I'd see my severed hand dangling from the suspension clamp. I'd see the truth of where I was, what had put hands on me, and what was coming next.

"Cherijo." A gentle caress on the side of my face. "Look at me, *Waenara*."

I didn't possess the strength to fight anymore, and yet the sound of that last, whispered word terrified me beyond anything SrrokVar could ever do.

Flippers, not hands, stroked my cheek, my throat, my hair. "You do not have to be afraid."

Oh yes, I did. Noarr had left me, betrayed me, abandoned me. I clung stubbornly to my terror, which had done many things, but had never, ever deserted me.

He made a sound—a terrible, helpless sound—then gently placed something over my body and head. I felt myself being carried over a distance; cold seeped into my limbs.

I knew what was going on. Noarr had taken me from the crying chambers. He had brought me out onto the surface. Noarr, who had led so many others through his tunnels, only to turn them over to GothVar and his pals. It didn't matter that FlatHead was dead. There were plenty of Hsktskt on Catopsa; Noarr had doubtless found replacement monsters hungry for slave meat.

Maggie didn't need to tell me the obvious. No immune system, no matter however aggressive, could counter the effects of being torn up, eaten, and digested.

So this is it. This is how it ends.

A disturbing sense of calm settled over me. Ever since Reever's betrayal, I'd been prepared for this. I'd courted it and found it with equal amounts of determination. But now that the moment of my death was upon me, I felt rather peaceful.

If nothing else, I hope I poison them.

The cold went away. Noarr said something in that strange, strumming language of his, then lifted me up and onto a soft surface. I kept my eyes and mouth shut, and didn't fight him as he uncurled my stiff limbs.

I'd had an exceptional life over the last couple of years. No regrets, then, I thought, and waited for them to start ripping into me.

"Cherijo. Open your eyes for me."

He *wanted* me to see, to watch what they were going to do. The bastard. Clean, purifying anger pumped into my veins, devouring the serenity I'd been enjoying. He could have simply done it, but no, he wanted more. He wanted me to go out shrieking.

Not without a fight, damn it. My eyes snapped open in time to see Noarr remove the envirohelmet from his head and place it aside. My muscles sang with strain as I curled up and began to roll over off the platform.

"Cherijo." Noarr came and blocked my path with his body. "Be still. I must—"

"*Judas!*" I couldn't make a fist, so I slammed my good arm into the side of his body. New, clean pain shot up into my neck as I rolled the other way. Noarr flung himself on top on me and pinned me facedown into the sleeping platform.

Sleeping platform?

Agitated breath rushed by my ear. "Do not move. I must examine your burns."

"Why?" The linens muffled my voice, so I lifted my head. "Don't they like their meat cooked?" It didn't help. All that yelling must have badly strained my larynx.

He rolled off me, flipped me over, and pinned my arms down so fast I didn't have time to get my hands up. "What are you talking about?"

"You. GothVar and his buddies. Prisoners à la carte?" I spat in his face. "And I thought Hsktskt were animals." His weight pressed on my burned forearm, and tears welled into my eyes. "Just kill me first, will you?"

Gently he released his grip and sat back. "I never helped GothVar or the other Hsktskt. Every prisoner I've liberated has left Catopsa." He brushed my hair out of my face. "You must believe me."

"Stop playing with me." I couldn't get my voice above a whisper now. "Finish it."

"Let me examine your arm."

I didn't fight anymore. He tugged off my tunic, revealing a burn deeper and more severe than any I'd had before. Noarr gently cleansed it, then wrapped it lightly. For once I didn't give directions. Besides, he did a fine job.

"Thanks." I flexed my arm and marveled at the lack of pain. "What did you shoot me up with?"

"Morphinol. It should last until your body repairs

the damage. There is nothing I can do to counter the stimulant."

"It'll wear off." I reached for my tunic, then stopped. "Too late for modesty, I guess." I got up and walked on unsteady legs around the small compartment. "So this is your ship."

He cleaned up the med-kit supplies and put them away. "Yes."

I peered out the viewport. "You hid it in the tul growth field."

He came up behind me. "As the hull is black, it seemed the most logical place."

I counted the number of growths, and was surprised to see the Lok-Teel had cleaned up nearly half of them. "So if you're not planning to serve me to the beasts, why am I here?"

Flippers landed lightly on my shoulders. "I could not leave you there, *Waenara*. Not another moment." The silky webbed appendages moved down my bare back. "I could not be without you."

"And that's it. That's all. You simply expected me to trust you?"

"Yes."

He left me there, and left the door panel unlocked. After a moment, I got up from the sleeping platform and went looking for him.

Noarr's ship was small, and stripped down to only the bare essentials. It only took a moment to locate the helm.

He sat at the com console, where he was relaying a message.

"How fares my ClanSister?"

My jaw dropped as I heard the familiar, warm voice of my ClanBrother, Xonea Torin.

"I retrieved her from the compound. She was injured, but will recover."

"I have spoken to the Ruling Council. They have ruled to break the Choice between her and Duncan Reever."

"I will let her know." Noarr sounded angry.

Xonea wasn't done being a pest. "Do you intend to Choose my ClanSister?"

I held my breath as Noarr paused. "If she will have me," he said at last.

"Good. She needs a strong protector. I will welcome you as a ClanBrother, Noarr." Zonea made a fluid gesture, reserved for adopted members of the HouseClan.

Noarr nodded. "How close are you to transitioning to this region?"

"Seven rotations. Possibly less. The Aksellans will arrive before we do. Will you be ready to evacuate the facility when we arrive?"

Noarr turned around and gazed at me before answering. "Yes."

I went back to the room he'd given me, and felt like a complete idiot for the better part of the night. How was I going to apologize for what I'd said to him? Would he understand? Or had I destroyed everything between us?

The darkness parted as the door panel opened. "Are you feeling better, woman?"

"Not really." Relief made me slide from the sleeping platform. "I owe you an apology. I'm sorry."

"I know." He stood in the doorway, staring at me.

"I had no idea you'd contacted the Jorenians." I gestured to him. "Come in. We need to talk."

"If I come in, Cherijo, I will stay."

I knew what he meant. And I wanted what his voice promised. Not only to soothe away the pain and helplessness. Noarr's voice called to my blood. Such a strong response, simply from hearing the sound of my name, those words . . .

Everything became absolutely, entirely clear to me.

I had a million questions, of course. Who wouldn't? Yet it was time to let go of the doubt. To trust myself and him. To surrender to what had begun that moment we'd met.

"Come in."

He came to me without another word. In silence I lifted my hands, felt his fins curl around my finger.

"I thought you'd betrayed me."

"You don't trust easily."

That was the truth. "No."

"Neither do I." His flippers brought my fingers to his mouth, and he licked each one. "Do you trust me now?"

I didn't have all the answers, but I'd take a chance. "Yes."

"I knew, the first time I saw you."

I frowned. "Knew what?"

"We would be together." His tongue curled around my little finger. "Like this."

Fascinated, acutely aware of the symbolism, I stared at him. The space between us became unbearable. I sensed it was my move, so I stepped forward. Pressed my body along his long, muscular frame. His strength against my softness made me release a low, delicious sigh.

Noarr's voice spilled over me again.

"You want me." Surprise and satisfaction blended in each word.

"Yeah, I do." One word that opened a passage to a terrifying new world. His hand moved up my arm, and stroked it. I laid my head against his chest. "I always have."

"I have wondered. How you would feel, how you would taste. I have tried to ignore it, yet you are always in my thoughts." His flippers threaded through the long strands of my hair as he wound the soft mass around his fist. "I need you, woman."

"Noarr." A few brain cells were still working; I had to be responsible. Even if it meant turning away from him when he needed me the most. "I'm not protected."

"I don't want you to be," he said.

And suddenly, neither did I.

Noarr's expression remained hidden. Under my cheek, his pulse beat, heavy and rapid. My hand moved blindly to the fastenings of his garments. The warm skin I exposed was as hairless as his head. I stood on my toes, pressed my lips against his throat. Tasted his flesh with my tongue. Sucked lightly.

His entire body went tense. "Stop."

I laughed a little. "No." Reckless with new knowledge, I pulled his tunic off. The muscular surface of his chest under my palms only made me greedy for more.

He turned slightly so that the light fell on me, and proceeded to deal with my tunic. I watched him as he cupped one breast. "Pretty."

A muted sound came from my throat as Noarr lowered his head. His mouth touched the swelling curve, the edge of his teeth scraped down, raking over my nipple.

Reality was on the way out the door. Fast. Too fast. The room suddenly tilted as his arm went under my knees and my feet left the floor. "Noarr—"

"Tell me later."

"This is important."

"Look at me," he said.

The light from the corridor fell across his face. I looked. Hunger stared back at me, so dark and naked and deep that it took my breath away.

"Do you understand?" he asked me.

I understood. Noarr wanted me. Had to have me. Would have me, unless I said "no" right now. No one else, nothing else mattered to him.

I nodded.

He carried me with him to the sleeping platform. I brought one of his fins to my mouth, and delicately traced the edges with the tip of my tongue. His scent changed, grew darker as it blended with heat and perspiration. It created new, uncontrollable impulses

that spread like wildfire. The emptiness I had ignored for so long now clamored with aching intensity. My hands fisted against his chest.

"Yes," Noarr said against my hair as he lifted and
placed me on the mattress. "Give it all to me."

Dimly I heard my trousers rip as Noarr tore them
from me. It didn't frighten me. Excitement flashed
bright strobes behind my eyes. Hard fins took and
twisted my hair, used it to tug my head back, baring
the sensitive zone below my jawline.

The abrasive caress of his teeth on my throat shook
me to my heels. I muffled a cry of pleasure as he
caught the delicate skin and bit down. His teeth left
a wet, stinging patch behind as they moved to ravage
and brand another spot. Then another. And another.

He lifted his head once to gaze down at me. "Your
taste intoxicates me."

Before I could respond coherently, his tongue ran
from my chin to my breast, where he bit me again.
Immediately he laved the stiff nipple with rough,
slick strokes of his tongue.

"The light," I gasped.

"Light?" His flippers were doing things to my
body that I'd never imagined possibly.

"I want to see you. Watch you touch me."

"No." He hesitated for a moment. "I am shy."

Him, shy. It made me smile first, then I laughed.
"All right. No lights."

His warm, hard body stretched over mine, and
strong arms drew me in. "Do you care for me,
Waenara?"

"Care for you?" After everything we'd been
through? I hit him. "I *love* you, you stubborn, unman-
ageable idiot."

Flippers cradled my face, tilted it up to his. "You
are all I have ever loved, the only one I will ever
love."

"Then show me," I whispered against his mouth.

He licked my lips. It made my blood heat, my toes

curl, and my arms slide around him. A sense of relief and safety came over me, along with the deep, wrenching throb of desire.

This is where I belong. Where I've always belonged.

Urgency made us fumble; Noarr became endearingly awkward and I wasn't much better. We got better, though. His warm, smooth flippers seemed to flow over me, sculpting my body into a writhing mass of aroused nerves under flushed, damp flesh. His mouth trailed over my breasts, which seemed to fascinate him. He certainly bit them enough.

"Don't do that," I said, when the emptiness I needed him to fill became nearly unbearable.

"Very well." His mouth traveled south. "May I do this?"

"I don't . . ." A low moan came out of nowhere as he settled between my thighs, and suckled at a different spot. "Yes . . . oh, yes."

The darkness blurred, everything rushed away, and my entire focus remained on the building pulse beneath his tongue. My hips lifted off the platform while my hands knotted into the linens.

He lifted his mouth for a moment, easing the emptiness temporarily by using the edge of his flipper to penetrate me. "Do you like this?"

"Wait." Panting and trembling, I curled around him, my hands running down his smooth, hairless abdomen. I found what I wanted, and bent my head. "Better."

Now he groaned against me as I explored how we fit in this juxtaposition. His limbs trembled as I took him deeper.

"Cherijo." He pulled me around, separated my thighs, and came halfway into me with a slow movement. My vagina stretched, and I took in a quick breath. He went still at once. "Do I hurt you?"

"No." I moved my hips up, trying to lodge him deeper. And still he wouldn't move. "If you stop now, I'll strangle you."

He moved, pushing deeper into me. "I won't stop."

My hands clutched at his shoulders as he kept his word. I came almost immediately, bearing down on him as I cried out, and still he stroked my flesh with his. It seemed to go on forever. Then as I hurtled toward my next peak, he held me tightly and made a low, guttural sound. Liquid heat pulsed into me, and I shattered once more.

CHAPTER SEVENTEEN

Holding the Fort

I never appreciated how soothing the darkness could be, I thought, before I came to Catopsa. It was never dark in the compound, not with all that glowing quasi-quartz around. Here I felt safe for the first time in months.

Someone was being a little too quiet, and I stroked my palm over his back. "What are you thinking about?"

"What it will be like, when we leave this place."

"It'll be *better*." I yawned, then snuggled closer. "God, a life sentence shoveling swamp mud on Ichthora would be better than living on this rock."

"Is that so?" He gave my bare backside a gentle tap. "And what if I am Ichthori, woman?"

I spent the next minute laughing too hard to talk. Finally, I recovered my self-control. "Sorry. I've been there. You, um, don't fit the native profile."

A signal chimed, and Noarr reluctantly left me to answer it. I wrapped some bed linen around me and padded after him to see who was signaling.

Jgrap's face appeared on the viewer. "Is she all right, Noarr?"

He was still alive! I stumbled over a fold of the linen and careened into the console.

Noarr grabbed me and held on until I regained my footing. "Yes. I believe she is." He terminated the signal.

"So you got the Forharsees out of the crying chamber, too." I thought of the despair I'd felt, thinking they were dead.

He waited there, not moving. "Yes."

"GothVar told me they were dead."

"They appeared to be, when I removed them. As have all the others I took from there. With the exception of you and Kelly. The drug I used on the Aksellans is very effective."

I thumped him on the upper arm. "Why didn't you tell me?"

"You were not in a state to listen to anything I had to say."

"Try harder next time." I sat on the edge of the sleeping platform, and listened to the sounds of Noarr dressing. Irritated as I was, I didn't want to be left alone. "Are you going somewhere?"

"No. I expect we will shortly have some"—the door panel chimed—"visitors. Come in."

The panel slid open, and a familiar tang filled the air. My lover switched on the lights to reveal the Forharsees, tendrils all over each other, beaming at both of us.

Being naked and in Noarr's bed didn't make me much of a role model, I decided. "Not you two again."

"Doctor." Jgrap skipped over, dragging Kroni with him. "We have news. You will never guess what has happened."

"I wouldn't wager credits on that." I ran an experienced gaze over Kroni's plump form. "Finally got yourselves pregnant, right?"

The male Forharsee gawked. "How did you know?"

My mouth curled. "Lucky guess."

Kroni giggled and hid her face against her lover's tunic while the proud papa-to-be relayed what had happened since Noarr had taken them from the crying chambers. They'd spent the last week hiding here on the ship, waiting for the trader to return to take them to freedom.

"Was a little crowded at first, with those others, so Kroni and I volunteered to stay behind and wait for the next vessel."

"Plus you got to have a mini-honeymoon in the meantime." I was too relieved to see them breathing to work up a good stern look. "She'd better be on prenatal supplements and getting enough rest. I'll have a look at you myself later, Kroni."

Noarr didn't say anything after the couple departed. I knew what he was thinking, though, and sat up.

"Okay. I was wrong. I apologize."

"There is no need." He came to sit beside me and brushed the tangle of hair from my brow.

I pulled him down beside me. "Oh yes, there is."

"We're as bad as those kids," I said several hours later, pleasantly exhausted. "You know that, don't you?"

"You are wrong." Noarr's flipper traced the outline of my lips, then he used it to tickle me under my chin. "They are adolescents. We are experienced adults. Perhaps we should instruct them on the variety of methods one may employ to achieve mutual satisfaction."

"I wouldn't have pegged you as a closet exhibitionist." I bit the edge of his fin-shaped hand. "Okay, enough. We need to talk."

"Not yet." He pushed me onto my stomach and pressed over me. "I need to keep you in my bed for a cycle." Despite what we'd nearly exhausted our-

selves doing, he was aroused again, and nudged me.
"Are you weary?"

"I don't need"—I uttered a single sound as he pen-
etrated me—"to sleep. . . ." I couldn't think, not with
his flippers lifting me up, positioning my knees, cup-
ping my breasts. Not with the way he was moving
inside me. "After we . . ."

It took another hour to get to the *after-we* stage. By
then I'd fallen asleep in my lover's arms. Even when
I woke up, it was to a sense of total satisfaction.

*This is much better than sitting in that damn solitary
confinement pit.*

The pel. I sat straight up and disengaged myself
from Noarr's embrace. "Enough fooling around,
pal." I swung my legs off the platform and groped
for a tunic. Since my garments were in shreds, I went
to his storage unit and rummaged through his supplies. "Get up. Get dressed."

"You need to sleep."

"You need to hear about the visitor I got in the
solitary confinement pit." I went on and described
my encounter with the pel, and what I'd asked it to
do. "We had a chunk of this crystal on the *Sunlace*.
I knew it could access other life-forms' thoughts telepathically, but I had no idea I could carry on a conversation with it."

"It cannot, or it would have communicated with
others long before this."

"It has. Me. I need to get in touch with the *Sunlace*
and talk to Xonea."

"It will take time to encode the transmission."
Noarr switched on the lights and regarded me with
that hooded, enigmatic gaze of his. "Your Clan-
Brother will ask if you have made your Choice."

"I'm sure he will, nosy as he is." I rolled my eyes.

"Do you Choose me, woman?"

He actually sounded *nervous*. I could make him
suffer, a little bit, considering what he'd put me
through. "Since the Ruling Council has given me a

divorce, and premarital sex is forbidden among my adopted family—" I grinned. "Stop thinking what you're thinking. Of course I Choose you."

"You didn't tell me you were a telepath."

"I'm not." I reconsidered that as I pulled on a pair of his trousers and rolled them up until my feet emerged. "Okay, maybe a little." I concentrated. "Though I was just guessing. I can't seem to pick up what you're thinking."

"Let me know when you can."

I gave him an ironic glance. There was a *lot* I needed to let him know.

Noarr took some time to encrypt the signal transmitters against Hsktskt detection, then helped me to signal the *Sunlace*.

Xonea gazed at me, first with relief, then with a large grin. "You appear to have made your Choice, ClanSister."

"Oh, stop it." I swiped a hand over my disheveled hair and turned pink. "Yes, I've Chosen Noarr. Enough about my personal life. I need to talk to you about the plan to liberate the compound."

I filled Xonea in on what I knew, and sent messages of affection to the entire ship.

"I look forward to meeting your Chosen," my big brother said. "Until then, walk within beauty, Cherijo."

As for my Chosen, well, when we weren't making love, we argued. For the next two days, ad infinitum, until I strained several muscles, then threatened to bash Noarr over the head with a blunt object.

"I'm not leaving Catopsa and that's final!" I shouted, causing Jgrap and Kroni to get up from their half-finished meals and scurry out of the galley.

Noarr tried the fierce, glittery look that I already knew as mostly bluff. "You know what will happen if I take you back to the compound, woman."

"So don't take me back." I drained my server of

tea and shoved myself away from the table. "I'll stay on your ship. But I'm not abandoning those prisoners, not with the Aksellans and Jorenians about to arrive. And don't call me *woman*."

Right on cue, Jgrap popped back in through the door panel. "Incoming encrypted message for you, Noarr. From the commander of the Aksellan fleet."

My lover gave me a dark look before sweeping out to deal with the communication.

I cleared the table and wondered how hard it would be to sneak back into the compound without Noarr's assistance. I knew two of the outer access hatches, and there had to be a schematic of more around the ship somewhere. Maybe I could break into the main database through the prep console.

"Might as well give it a shot."

An hour later, I had produced nine different types of vegetarian lasagna, twenty-two varieties of synthetic herbal tea, but had completely run out of swear words.

"Cherijo."

I stopped trying to reroute my bogus access code through the recipe submenu. "The spider calvary has arrived?"

"In a manner of speaking." Noarr came to stand beside me. "You are thirsty?"

"Ha. Ha. Ha." I shut down the unit and swiveled my chair around to face him. "So? What's the plan?"

"I must go back to the compound and pass the information to Wonlee."

I got up. "I'm going with you."

He pushed me back down. "No, you are not."

"But—"

"TssVar has doubled security since I took you from the crying chambers. If I am captured, you must take my place." He handed me a disc and closed my fingers over it. "Plans and signal encodes for the liberation forces, and a diagram of all the viable pel tunnels."

I wanted to throw the disc across the room. "Don't ask me to do this. Please."

"*Waenara.*" His flipper stroked my arm. "You are the only one I can ask."

"All right."

He kissed me, then left me alone at the prep unit to stare at the rapidly cooling servers around me.

I only spent a few minutes feeling sorry for myself. Since I had the disc, it would help to review it. I placed it in the prep console and switched the display to view. Encrypted data scrolled onto the screen, shifted, then became readable text.

According to the data, nine Aksellan scout ships currently maintained a position on the opposite side of Catopsa, matching rotation with the asteroid to keep it between them and the Hsktskt perimeter scanners. Eighty more were due to arrive within the next day or so, and they wouldn't be hiding. They planned to offer a frontal assault, to draw the Hsktskt out into open space.

That's when the Jorenian fleet would transition into orbit directly behind the Hsktskt, and box them in.

"Yikes." I skipped over the specific orbital battle attacks and went on to the information and maps Noarr had designed of the prison compound. He'd not only mapped every tunnel in existence, but had indicated the current number of tul growths and where they rendered the passages unusable. Over half still remained blocked, which wouldn't make the liberation any easier.

Jgrap and Kroni emerged from their chamber complaining of hunger a short time after I'd memorized the data. I fed them, and decided to give Kroni her first prenatal exam. Jgrap insisted on using their chamber and staying to watch the procedure.

"You're about nine weeks along, Kroni." I stripped off my gloves and made some notes on a data pad. "I'm outlining a nutritional plan and I want you to follow it." Jgrap was practically hopping up and down with excitement, and I frowned. "What?"

"Look." He pointed to the scanner display, which showed the internal view of Kroni's reproductive system. "Twelve, my love, at least twelve!"

"What?" I peered at the scanner. "No, pal, there's only one fetus in there."

"Oh, Jgrap." Kroni sighed, her eyes dreamy. "I would want nothing more than that." She smiled at my perplexed look. "What my darling one means, Doc, is the number of upper limbs. Females have ten, males have twelve or more."

"So it's a boy." I grinned, too. "Congratulations."

"A bit premature, Doctor."

I turned my head to see Reever step into the chamber, then flinched at the clatter of the data pad that had slipped out of my hands and hit the deck.

After locking the Forharees in their chamber, Reever escorted me to the helm so we could, in his words, "discuss the situation."

"What situation?" I dropped into a control seat and crossed my arms. The rifle in his hands made me angry. "You caught us. We surrender. Put the damn gun away."

He deactivated the weapon and placed it on a sensor console near his side. "The Forharee female is expecting a child. How is that possible?"

"Lousy planning on the part of the lizards." I smirked. "Forharee physiology requires oral doses of the chemical inhibitor—infusions don't work. Those kids haven't been swallowing their pills."

Reever studied me. "And you refused to terminate the pregnancy."

"Refused? No. I just found out about it. But even if I had know, I wouldn't have even considered it."

He leaned closer. "You know what the Hsktskt do to breeding female slaves."

"She's not a slave anymore. The Hsktskt won't get

their claws on her." I rubbed my fingers against my temples. A squad of Hsktskt centurons might be on their way. "Unless you turn them over to the centurons, and I'll kill you myself before I let that happen."

You don't want me dead, Cherijo.

My teeth clenched against the familiar voice speaking behind my eyes. No, I didn't. "Get out of my brain, Reever."

He did exactly that, then gazed around him. "You plan to use this ship to transport the Forharees off Catopsa as well?"

"Probably."

"Be sure to stay on that safe world when you arrive, Cherijo. Do not return."

That was it. He started to walk back toward the air lock.

So that's how he's going to play it. My initial amazement faded and I went after him. "Reever, wait. We need to talk about this."

He stopped, and looked over his shoulder at me. "My presence is required back at the compound. I cannot delay my return." He reached for my hand and held it between his for a moment. "Good luck, Cherijo." He reached for the air lock controls.

"Duncan—" I started to tell him what I knew, then saw the indicators go red. "Hold on, don't open it!"

Someone had accessed the outer hull panel in order to enter the ship. And I knew it wasn't Noarr. Without another word I ran back to the Forharees' chamber and released the door panel to stick my head inside. "Jgrap, take Kroni and hide in one of the storage containers. Whatever you do, don't make a sound."

I darted back across the small corridor into the galley, and tried to find a place to conceal myself. Within seconds, the centurons blasted through the secured panel and cornered me against the cleansing unit.

TssVar lumbered in through the ruined panel, and

regarded me with faint disgust. "I suspected as much. Put her in a suit and take her back to the compound. Inform SrrokVar I have apprehended both Terrans."

"Gael." I struggled as the guards hauled me out of the galley. "You leave him alone, he's done noth . . . ing. . . ." My stomach lurched when I saw two more guards holding Reever between them. "What's going on here?"

TssVar ignored me and went over to Reever. "You knew the location of the vessel, and concealed it from me."

Reever inclined his head. "Yes, OverLord."

"For what reason? The life of a female?" The Hsktskt flung a limb toward me. "Is she worth your rank, your connections, your life?"

That scared me. "No. I'm not."

"She is." Reever simply wouldn't shut up. Half the time I'd known him I couldn't get a word edgewise out of his mouth, and now he spilled like a defective infuser line. "Of all those I have ever experienced, she remains the only one I have ever loved. She deserves the right to her work. Her freedom. Her life." His eyes turned a beautiful, haunting shade of blue. "She is worth all of that, and more."

TssVar hit Reever, hard enough to send him to his knees. "This will be your last betrayal, HalaVar. Our bond is broken. Your membership in the Faction rescinded." He paused, then spoken to one of the guards holding Reever. "Place him in the slave tiers."

The party wasn't over yet. When the Hsktskt escorted me and Reever back to the compound, SrrokVar was waiting for us.

"OverLord." He made the obligatory bow. "I demand this Terran male be executed, for crimes of treason against the Faction."

TssVar was in no mood to grant something as quick as an execution, judging by the way he was stomping past SrrokVar. "File your request with my assistant."

"Prisoners Wonlee and Kelly must be executed, as well."

"Why?" Once more I tested the grip of my escorts' claws. "Are you having all the torturing equipment cleaned and recalibrated?"

"Take her to my chambers," SrrokVar said, and then stepped back as TssVar whirled suddenly.

"I will not permit further *research*, Lord." TssVar turned to address his centurons. "Remove the slaves being held in SrrokVar's chambers, and confine them to the auction holding cell until further notice."

"TssVar." I waited until he looked at me directly. "I need to treat those prisoners."

He paused for a long moment, then inclined his head. "Allow the doctor to see to them."

I mouthed a silent thank-you as I walked past him. One echoed many times by the battered, pathetically grateful prisoners I later treated in the holding cell.

Gael Kelly came to me the moment I was thrust into the cell and produced a med kit. "I think you'll be wanting this, *dote*."

I gave him an enthusiastic hug, glad to see his winsome grin had returned. My smile tightened as I thought of what SrrokVar had requested. "Give me a hand with these people, will you?"

The Irishman made a good assistant, mostly by keeping my patients distracted and calm. Everyone settled down as we took care of the last of the injured and discussed the situation in low tones.

"He'll not sell these knackers, not as they are." Gael scanned the twenty prisoners and sighed. "Bushed, the whole gang of them. I'm gobsmacked they didn't do away with them on the spot."

That reminded me. "Gael, I need to tell you something important." I relayed the standoff between TssVar and SrrokVar, then the sadist's requests for execution.

He didn't say anything for a long time. "As thick as two planks, I am. Should have expected it. Letting on like I was going back to Clare." He sat back against a wall and closed his eyes. "Pisses me off, it does. Can't scatter from this one. Unless . . ."

I nudged him with my elbow. "Unless?"

"You could give up the sleeven and save us all."

"The sleeven." It took a moment to recall what that meant. "Oh, no, Gael, not Noarr. He didn't betray us."

"Didn't he?" Gael swept his hand around the cell. "I begged him to help me get these knackers to safety, Doc. Scaldy chancer said no."

"But that's only because—" I stopped. I couldn't exactly blurt out the details of what I knew, and the coming attack. "Trust me, Noarr had his reasons for refusing."

"Away on." Gael got to his feet. "I'll not give out to you about Noarr. You'll see what he is, when they come for us."

"We're not going to die," I said, not totally convinced I was right.

"Everyone dies, Doc." He gave me a strange smile. "Some poor bastards a little sooner than others. This time, you get to pick when."

I didn't get to pick anything that happened after that. I barely got the details, and those left me stunned.

TssVar's stubborn refusal to execute me, Reever, Gael, or any of the injured prisoners created a rift straight down the center of his ranks. Half the centurons apparently agreed with SrrokVar's demands to rid the compound of the unhealthy and the perennial troublemakers. The other half were intensely loyal to the OverLord and supported his decision.

In the end, it didn't matter whose side anyone was on. SrrokVar directly petitioned the Faction Hanar, the supreme ruler over all Hsktskt, and demanded TssVar be replaced immediately.

In a completely unexpected, stunning move, the Hanar agreed and sent back orders to do just that.

SrrokVar was promoted to the rank of OverLord and given full command over the Catopsa facility. After being publicly reprimanded and demoted to Lord, TssVar was to return to the Hsktskt homeworld.

As his last official act, TssVar had me removed from the holding cell and returned to the infirmary. There he brought his mate, FurreVa's brood, and the quints just before they were scheduled to leave the compound.

"OverLord." I nodded to his mate and gave the kids an encouraging smile. "I was sorry to hear you're leaving." Sorrier than he could ever know, now that I faced the prospect of the sadist running things on the rock.

"I regret it has come to this absurdity."

"SrrokVar will do a lot more than that." I lowered my voice. "We may not have much in common as people, but what he's doing to these prisoners is insufferable. Is there anything you can do to get your ruler to prohibit this research of his?"

The huge yellow eyes blinked. "Even now, you do not try to plead for yourself."

I lifted my shoulder in a helpless shrug. Pleading for myself wouldn't do anything.

TssVar glanced at his brood, then drew me to one side and bent his massive head down. "I will go before the Hanar when I return, and inform him of the damage being inflicted on Hsktskt property. That is all I can promise, Doctor."

"That should be plenty." I curled my small hand around one clawed appendage end. "Thank you."

Before they made their dignified exit, my namesake tugged on the edge of my tunic. "I will continue to work hard at my studies. You will find no fault with me when I become a physician, Designate."

I couldn't exactly hug her, but I gave her an affectionate stroke on one limb. "I know I won't."

TssVar and his family left without looking back. I made unnecessary rounds and swore under my breath every time I sniffed.

We waited to hear when the first of the executions was scheduled to take place. I kept my fingers crossed, hoping the Aksellans and Jorenians would be ready in time to stop them.

No one quite knew what to do when SrrokVar announced that he had cancelled every single one of the executions.

Paul Dalton came in for treatment the next day for a wrenched back that was perfectly fine.

"You tried to get out of work on K-2 doing this, if I remember correctly," I said as I scanned his back, keeping the display averted from Zella's sharp gaze. "Nurse, prepare a therapeutic bath. Make it nice and cool."

She eyed Paul, then me. "Seems very minor, this male's injury."

"When I need a consultation, you'll be the first to know," I said, which made her stomp off toward the treatment room.

I removed our headgear as soon as she was out of sight.

"You haven't told your staff yet?" Paul asked as he feigned stiffness and reclined on the treatment table.

"Not a good idea." Now that I knew Noarr wasn't the Hsktskt informant, everyone looked suspicious to me. "Tell me what the status is on your preparations."

My engineer friend quickly related how he and Geef Skrople had rallied support among the population, including the League prisoners Wonlee felt could be trusted.

"We've created a grid of the entire compound, and planned escape routes. The guards should be no problem, if you can pull off your end of the plan."

"I've almost got enough supplies synthesized." Which hadn't been easy, especially with the League staffers constantly underfoot. "I'll need a couple of trustees to handle the distribution from here—food prep would draw the least notice."

"We'll start moving it, then." He smiled up at me. "Don't look so worried, Doc. This will be a piece of cake."

"Be cake, it will not." Zella appeared beside me and tugged off her headgear. Her tail slapped the floor beside my feet a few times. "To move the drugs, what containers do you plan to use?" Her teeth glittered as Paul and I gaped at her. "That happens in this facility, the nurses know everything. You had us fooled, you didn't think?"

"Who else knows?"

Zella nodded toward Pmohhi and the Saksonan resident. "Be trusted, they can. To help, we want."

Paul stayed quiet as I considered what I saw in the nurse's keen black eyes. "I'm not so sure I trust you, Zel."

"The feeling, I know." She helped Paul up into a sitting position, then slapped his chart in my hands. "No choice, you have."

She'd forgotten a vow. Maybe I could do the same. "All right. Let's get Pmohhi and Vlaav to give us a hand, and I'll fill you all in."

I was astonished to find out how much of our plans the nurses and resident had pieced together. They seemed eager to help, too.

"Those drugs need to be infused, not ingested," Vlaav said. We'd kept our headgear off, and the sound of the therapy bath jets concealed our voices. "We do not have nearly enough syrinpresses for our own use, much less this."

"Since we're not dealing with intravenous infusion, we're not going to use instruments. Intramuscular will work just fine." I told them what we planned to resort to. "Wonlee has been hoarding them every since we got here."

"That's . . . barbaric," Pmohhi said.

"If the shoe fits," I said, and turned to Paul. "Stop relaxing, pal. You've got to get back to the tiers and spread the word."

"Maybe I'll sprain my ankle tomorrow," the Terran said, grumbling as he climbed out of the bath.

Pmohhi and Vlaav helped Paul into a support brace he didn't need, while Zella and I cleaned up the therapy room.

"Someone has been working as an informant to the Hsktskt," I said as I drained the tub. "I need to know who."

Her fur rose around her neck. "One of us, you think it is? Impossible, that is."

"Don't be so sure. This place makes even the most virtuous souls desperate. Someone might be trying to earn back their freedom."

"Coming for us, they say the League is." Zella disposed of the used linens and gazed at me. "Will be over if they do, your freedom."

Joseph would see to that. "Maybe I'll stay."

"Testify to help you, we will."

Like the colonists had on K-2. I let out a single, sad laugh. "It's been done before. Didn't help. Thanks anyway."

A paw touched my arm. "Why you are so driven, that is. For you, there is no freedom."

"No." It struck me again, hard. If the Jorenians and Aksellans arrived first, I'd get a headstart. But Zella was right. I'd never be free, not as long as the League thought I was alive. "There never will be."

"A way, there could be."

I listened as Zella described her idea, then shook my head. "Won't work."

"Unless you attempt this, you'll never know." She

seemed a little ashamed when she added, "As a slave forever, I do not wish to think of you."

"Me neither." I sterilized my hands and picked up Paul's chart. What she'd said made me feel better than I had in weeks. "Let's get moving on rounds. We have a lot to do before the food prep team gets here."

"Doctor." Pmohhi stood in the open door panel, looking rather flustered. "The female Hsktskt is here."

CHAPTER EIGHTEEN

Abrupt Offerings

Shortly after I began FurreVa's final postop evaluation, she informed me that she was getting married.

To *SrrokVar*.

It took a minute to comprehend what she'd said. "You're going to *what*?"

Pmohhi had been standing between me and FurreVa while I performed the final postop evaluation. She squeaked and darted out of the way.

The big female Hsktskt glowered at me. "As I indicated, SrrokVar desires to unite with me. I have agreed."

I wanted to put her face back the way it was. With a blunt object. "When did *this* happen?"

"SrrokVar has expressed interest in me for some time now. GothVar threatened to harm my brood if I returned the OverLord's favors." Her tail smacked the base of the table, making it rock. "He used the same intimidation to compel me to discontinue the reconstructive surgery."

That explained why she had refused the work and stomped out of the infirmary. "He was a genuine maniac, FurreVa, and put you through hell. Wasn't that enough? Why get involved with another one?"

"OverLord SrrokVar is an honorable male." She pushed the magniviewer arm aside and slid off the exam table. "You are welcome to attend the ritual."

"Has your brain leaked out of your ears?" I blocked her path. "An honorable male. Mother of All Houses. He's a monster!"

"SrrokVar will not harm me. I must join, or my young will never attain rank." With one limb she picked me up and set me out of the way, then awkwardly patted my shoulder. "His status makes him a desirable mate. He will ensure my young realize their place in the Faction."

I finally broke out of my slack-jawed trance. "Fine. Marry the perverted brute. You have to live with him, I don't."

She left, and I performed rounds in complete silence. Zella eventually got up the nerve to approach me, and slapped her tail on the floor to get my attention.

"*What?*" I caught myself and grimaced. "Sorry. What do you need?"

"Upset, I know you are. In a position to help us, she will be." The nurse said. "His mate, being."

"You're probably right." I sighed as I wrote up a schedule of antibiotics for a patient with infected lacerations—inflicted by the prospective bridegroom. "Just don't expect me to throw rice at them."

Pmohhi, who was standing nearby, started to ask me why Terrans pelted newlyweds with grain, but Vlaav interrupted her and asked to speak with me privately. Since his angiomas looked ready to pop, I handed the nurse the chart I was working on and walked over to the empty side of the infirmary.

"What's the problem?"

"Lieutenant Wonlee asked me to relay a message—"

That was as far as my resident got, because the

walls around us began to shake. Huge, booming explosions went off above the compound. Nothing shattered, but I didn't like the way the rock was trembling under my footgear.

"What is that?" Vlaav began trickling all over his tunic. "Seismic tremors?"

I handed him a square of linen. "I think HouseClan Torin has arrived."

The Hsktskt had been smart enough to get their ships out of firing range, which obliged the liberation forces to begin the surface assault. Trustees with access to Central Command told me the Aksellans and Jorenians weren't firing on the compound itself, only bombarding the area around it. Still, it was enough to mobilize the Hsktskt centurons, who immediately began herding all the trustees back to their tiers.

No injured were reported, but the guards may have been keeping them in lockdown. We made the patients as comfortable and safe as possible, then began our final preparations to aid the assault teams. Since we'd reached zero hour, I briefed the remainder of the medical staffers on the details of our inside job.

"If Paul Dalton and Geef Skrople manage to get a food prep team in here, give them the last of the synthesized stock," I said, after checking what we had in the drug storage unit.

Pmohhi exchanged a troubled look with the other nurses. "We may need it to treat the injured."

"We can get everything we need on the Jorenian and Aksellan vessels," I said. "Or we won't need it at all."

"Doctor." The Saksonan kept glancing at the centuron guarding the entrance to the infirmary. "We should prioritize by location."

"Absolutely." I gave him an encouraging slap on the shoulder, then had to wipe my hand on my trousers. "Just do the best you can, Doctor."

The signal from tier nine came in, and I left Vlaav in charge and went to find Wonlee. A couple of centurons stopped me in the main corridor, but they all believed my story about being summoned to the tier by the new OverLord.

The Hsktskt should really learn the fine art of falsehood.

"I need to see prisoner Wonlee," I told the guard on tier nine. He showed me to the cell and opened the panel. I wasn't terribly surprised to find it empty, but he was.

"I'll report the escape to OverLord SrrokVar," I said when he had finished throwing his tantrum. The shaking and explosions had stopped, which had me worried. "He can't go anywhere, not with those ships firing on the surface."

"They will not be firing much longer." The Centuron displayed his toothy pleasure over that. "The enemy's attack was reflected back at their own ships."

Great. I needed to talk to the pel, too.

I made my way through the tiers, but no Won. As I crossed the prisoner commons on tier fifteen, someone called my name from the depths of the labyrinth.

"Gael?" I whispered, then nearly jumped out of my skin when Alunthri and Jenner crept around a corner. "God, what is it with everyone sneaking up on me?"

"Forgive us, Cherijo." My eternally patient friend looked calm, but my poor cat was frantic. "Will they destroy the compound before we can escape?"

"No. Hey, pal." I picked up Jenner, then curled my arm around the Chakacat and gave it a hug. "Don't be afraid, we'll get out." By my estimate it was time to get to the pits. "Come with me. I could use your help."

Alunthri followed me to the isolated corridor which led to the solitary confinement area. Before it entered, it came to a shocked halt. "Cherijo, we can't go in there. The guards—"

"Are taking a nap." I pointed to an unconscious centuron huddled beside a deactivated console. "Trust me, it's safe."

Jenner went over to sniff at the Hsktskt, while my friend eyed the small spot of blood on the guard's tunic. "What is this thing in his chest?"

"One of Lieutenant Wonlee's quills." I plucked the spine from the lizard's chest and held it out for Alunthri. "See? It's hollow. Won sheds them like hair; he's been hoarding them for weeks."

"But how does it make the beast unconscious?"

"It doesn't." I tucked the spine in my tunic pocket. "The neuroparalyzer we filled it with did. Over here."

The big cat accompanied me as I went to open the hatch to one of the deep pits. Jenner, who had apparently appointed himself guard dog, paced back and forth between the entrances. "Who is in here?"

I pried the hatch off and pushed it aside. "Reever."

"We are freeing Duncan?" Colorless eyes regarded me with renewed alarm.

"Yep." I got up and went after the grav-hoist. "He's handy to have around when the world is coming to an end."

"He could cause trouble for us."

"Don't worry." I had a few scores to settle with Duncan. "If he gives anyone any grief, I'll shoot him myself."

I couldn't see Reever, mostly because there were about a hundred Lok-Teel clinging to the six walls of the pit. I called down to him as we lowered the retrieval clamps, and felt the tug of weight when I reversed the hoist. Reever's naked body appeared suspended in the clamps a moment later.

"Thank you." I handed him a prisoner's tunic, which he swiftly pulled on. "The liberation forces have arrived?"

Alunthri stared. "How did you know about that?"

"The Hsktskt thought it so much slave gossip. I did not."

I was busy being miffed. Of all the prisoners on the rock, only Reever looked good in that awful yellow. It just wasn't fair. I secured the hoist, picked up Jenner, then turned to my former Lord and OverMaster.

"Yeah, well, they're here. The Jorenians *and* the Aksellans." I scratched the fur around Jenner's ears, knowing it would soothe him. "They're having problems."

"If we can reach the slave-runner's ship, I can help."

"That's just what I was counting on."

Reever helped us escape the compound by putting the three of us in envirosuits—my cat in an airtight sojourn pack—then had us climb in an inorganic waste disposal unit. Before he climbed in, he programmed the waste management system to dump the cube a few meters from Noarr's ship.

"And nothing is going to compress or crunch us once we get out there, right?" I asked as he closed the top panel.

"Nothing, unless the Jorenians renew their surface bombardment." Reever stepped in and then handed me the squirming bundle containing Jenner. "That would not be a favorable situation."

"There's an understatement."

Sitting in the disposal unit wasn't much of a joyride. The transport drone seemed to take forever, and before long we were all cramped and cold. Alunthri huddled close to me and Jenner while I talked through chattering teeth to Reever.

"I can signal the Jorenians from Noarr's ship. Now what are you planning to do to help?"

"Once you and the cats are safe, I will return to the compound and help the League prisoners organize against the guards. I must pay Lord SrrokVar a visit as well."

I shuddered, thinking of the hours I'd spent in that maniac's hands. "Why bother?"

"He has some information that I want."

I snorted. "I don't see him giving it to you."

Reever put his hand on the pulse weapon he'd taken from the unconscious guard. "I feel confident I can persuade him to cooperate."

The disposal drone dropped the cube exactly where Reever had programmed it to, and we waited until it was out of visual range before climbing out of the unit. Luckily the ships above us weren't firing, or things could have gotten very hairy.

"God, it's cold." I rubbed my gloved hands over the case containing Jenner, and was relieved to hear a faint but imperative yowl. "Come on, let's get into the ship."

Reever didn't come with us, but headed back on foot toward the compound.

"Duncan."

He turned, and looked at me.

There was more to say—a lot more—but now was not the time. "Thank you."

He lifted a hand, then continued on.

I helped Alunthri up the entrance ramp and into the pressure lock. Once inside, we deconned thoroughly, then entered the main cabin as soon as Jgrap released the internal locks.

"Any signal from Wonlee?" I asked as I let my cat out of the bag, but the Forharsee only shook his head. "Damn. All right, prepare to leave this rock. I've got to send some signals."

An hour later, a group of envirosuited beings mounted the entrance ramp, and filed into the pressure lock. I scanned them before completing the decon cycle and opening the hatch.

The tallest one took off his helmet, and held out his arms. "ClanSister."

"Xonea." I ran over and let him swing me up for

a rib-bruising hug. Over his shoulder, I grinned at the other relieved, sapphire-skinned faces. "What took you guys so long?"

Salo made a grumpy gesture. "I would have come after you the day the fleet left orbit." He bent down to touch his brow to mine. "It is good to see you join our path again, Healer."

"Same here." I gave Xonea another squeeze, then he placed me back down on my feet. "Darea." I held out my hands to Salo's bondmate. "How is Fasala progressing?"

"Very well, Healer. Her hair has grown back, and she shows no ill effects from the bone marrow transplant." The big Jorenian female's eyes shadowed. "Salo and I still have some difficulty with the memories of what happened to us."

I didn't blame them. Darea and Fasala had very nearly been victims of the serial murderer on the *Sunlace*. Later, during the surgery I performed to save Darea's life, an injured and irrational Salo had hurtled through a surgical suite viewer and tried to kill me.

It seemed appropriate, so I reached up and gave Darea the traditional Jorenian kiss of peace. "It takes time, lady. Give yourself that."

The rest of the Torin landing party made their less-than-formal greetings, and my sides ached by the time I got through all the hugs. They were happy to see Alunthri and Jenner, and warmly greeted Jgrap and Kroni.

"We must not linger, Cherijo." Xonea was already at the ship's controls, scanning for Hsktskt. "Our launch will not remain undetected for long."

Noarr. Reever. I closed my eyes for a moment. Then I nodded. "We're ready. Let's go."

The launch left the surface shortly after that, carrying all of us away from the crystal asteroid up to a familiar sight. A huge, elegant star vessel, shaped much like a Terran nautilus shell, spiraled slowly as it maintained orbit above Catopsa. Gyrlifts whirled busily around the hull, transporting crew members from one level to another.

With a small sinking feeling, I noticed the newly installed weaponry. Until they broke off relations with the Allied League of Worlds, the Jorenians had never bothered much with armament. They were primarily a race of nonviolent explorers.

Had been, until they'd gotten involved with me.

"The *Sunlace* looks good," I said to Xonea. He had invited me to sit by him at the helm, and I enjoyed watching him pilot the launch. He made it look so easy. "Everything go well with the retrofit?"

"Yes, although it took some time to correct the problems with the buffer and damage to the stardrive."

I let a little ice enter my tone. "I see you finally got all those big sonic cannons you wanted."

"I will not quarrel with you over the upgrade of ship's defense systems, ClanSister." He gave me a wry glance. "On the last occasion I did so, I suffered no small amount of humiliation, and lost the argument as well."

"All right. For now." I sat back and relaxed. "In any event, I'm too glad to see everyone to be debating defense systems."

"They eagerly await your return." He glanced at me and smiled. "You should know our entire HouseClan volunteered as crew for this mission."

My brows rose. "Did you fit all the Torins on the ship?"

He laughed. "I tried."

We flew directly into the launch bay, where a huge assembly of Jorenians stood patiently waiting. Once we had deconned, Xonea took my hand and led me to the hull doors.

As they opened, I gulped. It sure looked like the entire HouseClan was out there. "I don't have to make a speech, right?"

"I do not believe you will have the opportunity, ClanSister."

Everyone started shouting and smiling and laughing, and I found myself doing the same. I was embraced everywhere I turned, by every member of the crew. Jenner and Alunthri were equally adored. It took awhile to get through that. At last I saw one face that was definitely *not* blue, and excused myself to head in that direction.

His blue-and-white tunic looked good on him, in spite of the fact he had bright pink skin. The beard-like mass of white tendrils around his mouth were straight and solemn, but there was affection and relief glowing in the round, dark eyes.

"Senior Healer," I said, and awkwardly made the formal Jorenian gesture of greeting.

"Doctor Torin." The Omorr inclined his head.

We stood like that for maybe ten seconds. Then my successor hopped closer, curled his membranes around my hands, and grinned.

"It's good to see you, Cherijo."

"You too, Squilyp."

"On second thought, perhaps not." He frowned as he caught sight of the dressing on my arm, and extended it for inspection. "What have you done to yourself now, you demented female?"

"Just a little present from the Hsktskt." I suppressed a grin, remembering all the other times the Omorr had been forced to patch me up.

"She will tell us all at the reception in the galley," Xonea said.

"She will go straight to Medical so I can examine her properly first," Squilyp said in his most authoritative tones, his gildrells flaring. He directed a scowl at me. "Do not even think of arguing about it, madam."

I was so proud of him I felt like crying. "I wouldn't dream of it, Squid Lips."

Xonea and the crew promised to hold off on the

formal reception for an hour, so I could make the Senior Healer happy. Squilyp personally escorted me to Medical. I passed my physical, although the Omorr did some ranting about the injuries recently inflicted on me.

"Animals. Have they no regard for the sanctity of the body?" Despite the fact the wound was healed, he scanned me from head to toe. "Have you been experiencing any abnormal psychological effects?"

I thought about the severe phobic reaction I'd had to the many PIC applications, and decided to tell him the truth. "I've been having panic attacks, probably due to a form of pyrophobia."

"You're afraid of fire?"

"No." I tapped my arm. "I'm afraid of being burned."

He checked my eyes with an optic light. "How severe are the symptoms?"

"Pretty bad. Hyperventilation, palpitations, severe anxiety, derealization. Some postattack depression." I met his gaze. "I've gone into respiratory arrest a few times."

"We can treat it," he said in a brisk, professional tone. "Psychotherapy, perhaps antidepressant drugs, if they're required. Why are you grimacing like that?"

"I don't like admitting I have a problem, I guess."

"Cherijo." He put the chart aside and got serious on me. "It is nothing to be ashamed of."

"You're right, of course." Fond as I was of Squilyp, I had little tolerance for my own weakness. "Well? Aside from the pyrophobia, do I pass?"

"No. You are underweight and moderately malnourished." He wrote up a nutritional plan and handed it to me to read.

"I don't like half the stuff on here," I said, scowling.

"I will hand feed you myself, if I must. Don't be belligerent." He double-checked my hands, then had me demonstrate my dexterity. "Incredible. Not a trace of the original injuries are present. Not even a scar."

I had penty of those. Just not where he could see them. "What's the latest news from Joren?"

"The Captain held a briefing this morning." Squilyp infused me with some vitamins and had me recline for a second, full series of scans. "According to reports received from systems beyond Varallan, a massive League invasion of Hsktskt space has been initiated."

My heart sank. "So they really are going to war with the Faction."

"It need not concern us. The Jorenians have no treaty with the League, so there is no question of involvement. Let them exterminate each other; the galaxy will be better off, and you'll finally be safe.

"Don't tell anyone, but I'm not going back to Joren," I said. He eyed me. "You know the minute I do the League will come after me."

"I suppose you're right." He frowned at something on his scanner, then at me. "These readings are off the grid for a Terran. I need to perform a full hematological series."

"I won't match the database parameters," I said. "And I want a copy of the results when you're through."

His gildrells got stiff. "Eat the meals I've prescribed, and I'll think about it."

The subsequent celebration we attended in the galley lasted several hours. Xonea, Salo, and a number of other department heads made long, flowery speeches. The medical staffers and nurses had some things to say, too. Squilyp kept bugging me to eat.

I couldn't enjoy myself, though I put up a good front. As soon as I could get away with it, I feigned weariness and asked Xonea to escort me to my quarters. My old quarters, I was delighted to see, as they had never been designated for another crew member.

"It was a somewhat absurd promise I made to myself," the Captain told me as he left me at the door panel. "As long as your rooms were not reassigned, I convinced myself your path would come back to us." He pressed a large hand to my cheek. "Our House rejoices in your return, ClanSister."

I placed my hand over his. "Thanks for keeping the light burning, big brother."

Xonea departed, and Jenner emerged to demand some attention.

Where have you been? His rough tongue rasped over my fingertips. *I'm starving.*

"You're always hungry," I said, and put him down to prepare his evening meal.

I'm always being neglected. He attacked the syntuna fillet with delicate greed.

I found myself in front of the room console, hoping someone had intercepted a message from Noarr or Wonlee. A quick scan revealed nothing from either of them, but it was probably too soon to expect they'd drugged enough of the centurons to get to the main security grids.

My intership relay file was, on the other hand, packed with personal signals from the crew. Several other relays had been saved for me, as well. One of them, a lengthy signal originating from Fendagal XI, had been encrypted for my view only.

I signaled Ship's Operational, and Salo personally responded.

"Now that you've been promoted to second in command," I said, "you're supposed to get a crew member to handle the nuisance calls, you know."

He gave me a warm smile. "You are never a nuisance, Healer. How may I be of assistance?"

I identified the encrypted signal in my console to him by the routing tag, then asked if he'd pre-screened it. He shook his head.

"I but verified that the League did not code the

signal with tracking receptors, Healer. It is safe to decode."

I knew who'd sent it. The only person involved with the League who cared to signal a genetic construct. *His* genetic construct.

I used the encryption program and accessed the relay.

The image of Joseph Grey Veil appeared on the screen. The first thing I noticed was how much younger and healthier he was than the last time I'd seen him. Of course, the last time I'd seen him he'd abandoned me to the Hsktskt, and was headed back to Terra to create another victim.

"This signal is intended for the Terran female Cherijo Grey Veil, currently being held by the Hsktskt Faction on the slave-depot asteroid Catopsa."

"Not anymore, Joe." I sat back and studied my father/brother's face. He'd had some microdermal work done around his mouth and eyes, I decided. The man looked almost as young as I did. He'd also dyed his hair. Absently I fingered the lock of pure silver in my own.

"I have no doubt you will endeavor to escape from the Hsktskt, my child, which is why I am sending this entreaty."

"An entreaty," I said to the screen. "That's a switch."

"I want you to see this for yourself." He stepped to one side, and a strange-looking apparatus came into view. My hands clenched when I recognized what it was—and what was in it. "This is the thirty-ninth trail specimen I have created since returning to Terra. Unfortunately, like the other trials before it, the experiment proved completely unsuccessful."

An unsuccessful experiment. That was what he called the grotesquely deformed baby, suspended in his synthetic embryonic chamber. Fabric tore under my nails.

"I have no choice but to appeal to you now, Cher-

ijo. Of all my trials, you remain the only viable proto-
type specimen in existence. I have failed."

I couldn't quite grasp that. After all, my creator
had never failed before.

"By now you must know the unique qualities af-
forded by your enhanced immune system. I have discovered that I cannot replicate the triumph I achieved
with you. I am certain that will give you a great deal
of satisfaction."

I would have settled for a gun. Or a chair with
tougher upholstery.

"I have convinced the Allied League to engage the
Hsktskt, and hope that will provide an opportunity
for you to escape your current predicament."

I snorted. "Oh, so that's why you signaled the
Hsktskt and told *them* all about it."

"The Jorenians will provide aid, and doubtless
offer you sanctuary again. I advise you think carefully before accepting it."

"You're not going to get another shot at Joren,
Joe."

"Secure sanctuary on any world will be at a pre-
mium, my dear." He chuckled, but it was a strained,
fake sound. "We are both in dire straits, are we not?"

"*You're* in dire straits. *I* have friends."

"I have sent a drone-manned ship to the following
coordinates." A series of numbers flashed across the
screen. "I consider it a gesture of good faith. Here is
the blueprint of the vessel."

The schematic replaced the coordinates on the vid.

"Mother of All Houses." He hadn't sent me a ship.
He'd sent me the largest and fastest Allied star transport in existence. And if this was a simple I'm-sorry-
for-experimenting-on-you gift, I was a Yturi. "Gee, I
feel terrible. I didn't get you anything."

"Use it to go wherever you want, but I hope you
will consider returning to Terra. I will not compel
you to take part in my research. My goal now is
understanding, and reconciliation."

Understanding. Reconciliation. In a pig's eye. "Sure you don't want to harvest some cell samples?"

"I look forward to the day I can apologize to you in person. Until then, I bid you farewell, daughter."

The signal terminated. I sat there for a long time, staring at the blank screen. I wasn't buying his change of heart, of course. Surely he realized I wouldn't. Just what was he up to now?

I returned to Medical the next morning, and pulled my chart before Squilyp came on duty.

Adaola, who was primary for the shift, hovered nervously around the desk as I reviewed the laboratory series.

"The Senior Healer will be glad to discuss your test results as soon as he arrives, Healer."

"I *was* the Senior Healer, Adaola. Stop pestering me." I looked up and gave her a wink. "Besides, that Omorr could probably use a good fight about now."

"Or a syrinpress." Squilyp hopped in through the door panel. "As I expected. All is well, Adaola. You may prepare your shift notes while I deal with our impatient intruder."

"Thank you, Senior Healer," Adaola said with sincere relief, then departed.

"I'm not impatient." I found the blood profile and studied it in silence. "I'm . . ." A protein level caught my eye, and a faint buzz began ringing in my ears. "Oh, boy. I'm in trouble."

"No, you are not." Squilyp took the chart out of my numb hands and tossed it aside. "We will deal with it, Doctor."

He might be able to, I thought as I got to my feet. I was petrified. The buzz grew louder. A moment later I was sitting back in the chair, with Squilyp pushing my head between my knees.

"Breathe slowly. You have had quite a shock."

That was the understatement of the century.

CHAPTER NINETEEN

The Last Captive

Squilyp and I argued for an hour after I nearly fainted, then decided on a course of action to our mutual satisfaction.

"I expect you to report to Medical as I've indicated." The Omorr handed me a copy of my treatment schedule. "Or I will have you restrained to an inpatient berth."

"Yeah, yeah, I'll be here." I climbed down from the exam table. "I bet you're going to enjoying ordering me around."

"Of course I will." He finished his notes and switched off my chart with a snap. "You certainly enjoyed being my supervisor when you were Senior Healer. Actually, this has a sort of poetic justice to it."

His smirk really annoyed me. "Oh, go jump in a pressure lock!"

Later that day, the Jorenians began bombarding the surface again, and dodging the reflected sonic fire. Since my condition wasn't anything that would slow me down for a while yet, I'd convinced the Omorr to let me work a shift. Good thing, too, since the few crew members reporting with minor injuries soon became a steady stream.

"We've received a signal from the stockade," one of the communications officers told me as I splinted his sprained knee. "League captives have been effective in taking control of several tiers."

So Wonlee's plan had started to work. "What about the rest of the compound?"

"It remains under Hsktskt control." The officer didn't want to tell me the rest, but I harassed him until he did. Less than optimistic reports had also come in, that the centurons had begun methodically executing prisoners inside Hsktskt-controlled areas.

I signaled Xonea, and requested that I be transported back to the surface.

"That is impossible, Cherijo. We have ground forces preparing to invade the compound."

"Then I'm going with them." When he would have yelled at me, I shook my head. "I have friends down there, Captain. And you need someone to head the medevac team. There will be plenty of work waiting for me."

Reluctantly Xonea granted my request. That made Squilyp throw his own temper tantrum, and upon hearing I was returning to the surface, half the inpatients in Medical began verbally threatening to mutiny and throw me into detainment.

"I know the compound better than anyone on the assault teams," I said, crossing my arms and looking down the row of grim faces and emerging claws.

"In your condition—"

"Space my condition," I told the Omorr. "There are over fifteen thousand prisoners down there—the Hsktskt are shooting them, and I left a first-year resident in charge of the infirmary."

He glowered at me. "Just remember, Doctor, you have other responsibilities."

Before I reported to the launch bay, Salo relayed a

direct signal from the Hsktskt Central Command, sent by OverMaster HalaVar.

"Reever?" I took a medevac pack and slung it over my shoulder, then accessed the signal. "What's your status down there?"

"OverSeer FurreVa and a portion of the guards have deposed SrrokVar and placed me in charge of the compound." He looked sweaty, and grime streaked his hair, but other than that, he could have been having tea with the Hanar.

"Why'd they do that? I thought you weren't a member of the Faction anymore."

"Upon arrival on the Hsktskt homeworld, TssVar officially reinstated my rank. The order to depose SrrokVar came from the Hanar himself."

"That was nice of him." I checked to make sure I had enough suture packs. "Tell FurreVa to stop executing the prisoners."

"I have. There are still some centurons loyal to SrrokVar, however, who have disregarded my orders." He turned away for a moment to consult with a waiting centuron, then addressed me once more. "Stay with the Jorenians, Cherijo."

"Uh-uh. I'm on the way."

"You will not be safe."

"You've got wounded down there. I'm coming back. Tell the guards not to shoot at me or the launch."

"They won't." He paused. "As long as you officially surrender to me."

There was always a catch. "Fine. I'll be there in an hour to give myself up."

The surface was littered with shattered black crystal and the smoking remains of Hsktskt launches. I insisted the Jorenians stay out of firing range as I went into the main compound entrance.

Xonea didn't like that, and told me. At length.

"I'll keep you informed as to what the situation is

in there. Keep monitoring this." I tapped my slave collar, which had been removed, altered, and refitted to transmit audio signals directly to the launch and the *Sunlace*. "For now, you're going to have to sit tight and wait."

Reever and a detachment of centurons stood just inside the compound pressure locks. As soon as I stepped through, rifles were activated, and my pack was confiscated.

I held out my empty hands. "I'm unarmed. I surrender."

One of the guards grabbed me by the collar, but Reever stepped forward and ordered him to release me.

"You will return to the infirmary and treat the injured," he told me. His voice may have been as flat and cold as ever, but there was an edge to it that made me look at him sharply. "Come. I will take you there myself."

He sent the centurons to work riot control in the tiers, and marched me down the corridors. Once we were out of sight of the beasts, he released my arm.

"Half the guards have been drugged and disarmed by the prisoners," he said.

"I know. Have you convinced them to surrender?"

"The Hsktskt do not relinquish their territory to inferior species." He turned a corner, then stopped me in the middle of an empty corridor. "This may end with a fire fight, Cherijo."

"Not if Wonlee has distributed enough of his quills." If only we had an extra edge . . . of course, the *pel*! I felt like smacking myself in the forehead for forgetting about them. "See what you can do to talk them into it. The Jorenians are starting to get tired of orbiting this rock."

The infirmary was in complete upheaval. Wounded prisoners lined the passages for hundreds of yards leading to it. A couple of them I stopped to check before I entered and yelled for Vlaav.

He yelled back from a treatment room. "Over here, Doctor."

The next several hours were devoted to emergency care and restoring some partial order to my facility. The nurses had become overwhelmed, and the renewed orbital attack did nothing to calm the prisoners. In addition to that, several centurons had reported with serious injuries, and got nasty about priority.

I'd just cleared the last serious case when someone gestured to me from the back of the infirmary. It was Wonlee. I hurried back and saw him point to a section in the wall.

"Noarr?" I asked, and he nodded. I pulled a privacy screen over and dodged behind it. The passageway opened to reveal the silhouette of a tall cloaked figure.

"God." I ran, threw myself shamelessly at him, and groaned as his arms closed around me. "I was so worried." I lifted my head and then thumped him on the chest. "Are you trying to make me go insane?"

"I am glad to see you, too, woman." He drew me back into the passage and closed the entrance. "It is time we liberated the population. I will need your help."

I grinned. Good thing I'd remembered about the one ally we had that no one else knew about. "Not just mine."

I turned and placed both hands against the wall, and concentrated. A minute passed, then a clear, gelatinous glop oozed down from the tunnel's ceiling. It dropped between us and collected itself into an amorphous, shimmering form.

*pel*here*

"Pel, this is Noarr." I looked at my lover's astonished expression and bit my lower lip before continuing the introductions. "Honey, meet the rock."

Once we'd managed to communicate what we

wanted to the pel, the Jorenians, and the Aksellans, Noarr left to attend to freeing the prisoners in the tiers still controlled by the Hsktskt. I went back to the infirmary to get things ready there.

Zella and the nurses handled triage, while Vlaav and I prepped the patients for transport.

"The Aksellans have landed outside the compound," one of the prisoners told us. "We saw their tethers through the walls."

I briefed the inpatients on what we planned to do once the liberation forces took control of the compound, then sent every staff member to put together field packs of supplies. Wonlee appeared briefly with instructions on where to go and how to find enough envirosuits to outfit the patients.

Everything was going well when a detachment of battered-looking centurons burst through the door panel, led by a very unamused former-OverLord SrrokVar.

"I expected to find you here, Dr. Torin." He came at me, and I grabbed a syrinpress. He knocked it away with one flick of a limb. "Your misguided sense of compassion will be the death of you, my dear."

"Zella," I called out, never taking my eyes from the madness gleaming down at me. "Clear the infirmary. Evacuate the patients. All of them. Now."

"You have proved resilient and resourceful. I particularly admire your Terran survival instincts. I had thought releasing FurreVa's brood in HalaVar's chambers would be the end of both of you."

So he was the one responsible. "I heard you got fired by the Supreme Lizard," I said, hoping the taunt would keep him from firing on the fleeing patients. "Guess TssVar was pretty convincing, huh?"

I didn't have a chance against a psychotic Hsktskt, so I dodged SrrokVar's next blow and dove around him. Dropping and crawling under an unoccupied berth gave me a few seconds to collect my wits. I rolled out just as SrrokVar lifted the berth and tossed it out of his way.

"You cost me my research, my mate, and my command. Now we will settle accounts, Doctor."

I didn't have time to get out of the way. Three limbs began descending with lethal force. I closed my eyes.

Because I did that, I missed watching the displacer pulse burst behind SrrokVar.

"You harmed my brood!"

He turned, and lunged toward the door panel. That's when I propped myself up and saw FurreVa fire her rifle again.

The thermal uniform he wore seemed to dispel most of the blast. He pulled a weapon from his lab coat, aimed, and shot the big female directly in her chest. The impact sent her crashing into a diagnostic array.

The closest thing to hand were two of the largest bonesetters, the ones we'd used on Devrak's guard. I disabled the auto-adjust clamp, ran up behind SrrokVar, and shoved one around his thick neck. After knocking the pistol from his claws, I jammed the other around the center of his skull.

Bonesetters normally contract until the clamp unit aligns the broken bone. Since I'd disengaged the sensor, the device kept contracting. SrrokVar tried to come after me, for a few seconds. I danced away as he stopped and started clawing at his neck.

"Now we'll see how much you enjoy physical tolerance ranges," I said, and stayed out of strike range to watch.

SrrokVar managed to wrench the bonesetter from his throat, but the time he spent doing that was a mistake. The one around his face was now cutting into the tissue, forcing his kinetic skull to bow out.

"Take it off!"

For once, I ignored my calling. "No."

He bellowed with agony as he stumbled past us, then disappeared down the corridor.

Too bad. I would have liked to watch his brains pop out of his eye sockets. I went to examine FurreVa.

She was in bad shape. A huge pulse burn smoldered on her chest; there was a deep gash in the side of her neck. I tried to drag her out into the corridor, but she was too heavy to move. Zella and Vlaav had already evacuated everyone, so there was no help in sight.

"You didn't have to defend me, you know," I said as I pressed a sterile pad to the spurting wound. "I was doing just fine."

FurreVa's lungs rasped as she tried to breathe through the blood. "I was wrong about him. Wrong about you, Terran."

"No talking." I managed to control the bleeding and ran a scan over her abdomen. Her vitals were dangerously weak. "You're hemorrhaging, so no moving either. Somehow I've got to transport you up to the *Sunlace*."

"No time." She coughed up more crimson fluid, then reached and took my hand. "My young are safe. You are safe. It is enough."

"Shut up." I infused her with adrenalysine, hoping to trigger the hibernation process before she bled to death internally. "You're going to live."

"SsurreVa." Two claws traced the invisible path of her former injury, then touched my cheek. "Friend . . ." She surrendered to the drug, and went into the beginning stage of natural suspended animation.

She wasn't dying on me. Not after all the trouble I'd gone to. I sat back on my heels and activated my wristcom. "Xonea. I need a medevac team to come to the infirmary, as soon as you breach the compound."

I went over to the wall, and placed my hands against it. *We need your help now, pel.*

The wall undulated beneath my palms, then melted between my fingers.

*pel*help*

I left FurreVa on life support (rigged around her on the floor, since she was far too heavy for me to move to a berth), and convinced one of the centurons to watch over her. Then I went to Central Command.

Reever and a large group of Hsktskt were gathered in the prisoner reception area. Dozens of rifles clicked on and pointed at my head as I walked into view. I displayed my empty hands and waved at Reever.

"I hate to interrupt, but I was wondering if I could evacuate the compound now."

Reever ordered the centurons to stand down. Several of them hesitated, and I wondered just how much control he had over his troops.

"You heard the transmission from the homeworld," Reever said to them. "OverLord TssVar's orders were clear."

Reluctantly the last of the centurons lowered their weapons.

Reever walked over to me. "The liberation forces have not breached the outer security grid. We have time."

"Actually, no." I leaned against a wall, and pointed to another. "You don't."

The wall opposite the group shattered, spilling shards all around us. The pel poured through the new opening and collected itself just in front of the aghast Hsktskts.

"Shoot it!" one of them shouted, and a few of them started firing their weapons into the transparent mass.

"It absorbs energy," I said in a helpful tone, when it became apparent the displacer blasts were having no effect. "It can also reflect them at will, so I suggest you knock it off."

The pel flowed around the beasts toward me,

where it formed a barrier protecting me from the rifles.

"What do you propose, Doctor?" Reever asked me.

"I propose you pack up what you can carry and you get out of Dodge," I said, running my hand over the undulating pel. "Because in exactly one hour, the pel is taking over the compound."

"She's lying," someone yelled.

I rubbed a hand over the back of my neck. Why hadn't I put the man in traction when I'd had the chance? "Shropana. It would be you. Someone want to lend me their rifle for a minute?"

"She's staged this hoax with that slave-runner lover of hers." The League Commander limped out into the Central reception area, carrying a Hsktskt pistol, and aiming it at me. "I know where he is. Give me back my ships and I'll take you to him."

Shropana hadn't a prayer of getting his fleet back, but he could railroad the evacuation and possibly get Noarr killed. I turned my head, and concentrated.

Hundreds of Lok-Teel crawled into the reception area, and encircled Shropana.

"Filthy creatures!" He fired at one of them, but it avoided the blast. The pel shot out a solid stream of its mass and enveloped the pistol and Shropana's hand completely.

I walked over, pulled the syrinpress from my tunic and pressed it to his neck. "Say goodnight, Patril."

He fell to his knees, then over onto the waiting Lok-Teel. Obeying my silent command, they quickly carried him back out of the area. I was tempted to tell them to eat him, but decided against it. The Lok-Teel shouldn't have to consume waste *all* the time.

"Gentlemen." I swiveled and addressed the beasts. "Shall we get this evacuation underway?"

Wonlee found me during the next hectic hour, and informed me that SrrokVar had escaped from Catopsa on a small scout ship he'd apparently hidden outside the compound.

"He is badly injured, according to witnesses. Some kind of severe head injury."

He'd finally gotten that last bonesetter off. I wondered how pretty *his* face was now. "Pity. I planned on turning him over to his victims and let them finish the job."

A few of SrrokVar's loyalists continued to fire upon the prisoners, but Wonlee and the Kevarzangian engineers took care of them in short order.

Reever and the remaining Hsktskt surrendered in the prisoner commons on tier nine, just as the Jorenians and Aksellans breached the last of the security barriers and entered the compound.

"I don't want these guards, or the unconscious ones, killed." Reever said to me as he watched the advancing arachnids swing in through the door panels on their silvery tethers. "Talk to them, Cherijo."

I did. It took a few minutes, but I managed to convince the Aksellans and former slaves not to execute the Hsktskt.

"They harmed our femalez," Clyvos said, acidic poison dripping from his leg fangs.

"They can help us transport these prisoners to the launches." The floor rumbled beneath our feet, and I sensed that the pel had begun gathering for its final assault. "We're almost out of time, pal."

"Very well. Let uz make hazte."

There was a lot to do. Since the surface bombardment had destroyed all the conveyance units, envirosuits had to be distributed and fitted. Litters were brought for the severely injured prisoners and unconscious Hsktskt.

"Did you bring the grav-lift I ordered?" I asked the former League crew when they came to the infirmary to help me with FurreVa.

"No, Doctor, the only one available is being used."

That meant I needed someone very strong and dexterous enough to avoid hurting the Hsktskt female. "Get Geef Skrople over here, then."

The small, wiry engineer appeared a few minutes later. "Doc, you've got something for me to lift. . . ." He eyed FurreVa. "Oh. Her."

"Yes, her." I finished sealing the envirosuit over the Hsktskt's unconscious form. "Don't worry, she's in a state of hibernation. Be careful and try not to jog her too much."

"Will do." Demonstrating his tremendous strength, Geef hoisted the big female carefully into his upper appendages, then turned to me. "Where should I put her?"

She needed to be stabilized before I sent her up to the *Sunlace*. "Out to the surface, for now." We were going to need shelters to house the prisoners until they could be transported up to the liberation fleet, I thought, and made a mental note to request it.

Geef managed to move FurreVa without difficulty, but there were simply too many other Hsktskts for him to handle. The sheer weight of the reptilian beings proved a problem, until Major Devrak appeared with a huge cargo storage container strapped to his broad back.

"I can carry ten of them at a time," he said.

I checked his injuries to see if he was in any shape to try. "No more than ten at once. If you get hurt, I know we won't be able to move you out of here."

The spiders silently watched the Hsktskt as they all moved through corridors toward the surface access hatches. I watched the spiders, and hoped they would hold on to their tempers.

We guided the continuous stream of happy ex-slaves through the tiers, releasing the locking mechanisms as we went to free the last of those in lockdown. Once we reached the access hatches, Paul and Geef organized the evacuees into manageable groups and started sending them out to the launches.

I followed the last group out to the pel crystal

plain, and gasped when I saw the massive collection of Lok-Teel eating away at the tul growths they could finally reach.

"Soft auld day, isn't it, *dote*?"

Gael's green eyes glowed through the plas face-plate of his helmet, and I nearly dropped the patient I was helping to the launch in astonishment. "Gael! I thought you were—"

"Gone? Takes more than a thick to get rid of a jackeen like me, *dote*. Let me help you now."

He got on the other side of the prisoner and sup-ported some of the weight. I started to demand to know what had happened to him, when a terrifying crash made us both stop and look back.

Streams of the molten pel punched through Catop-sa's surface, all around the borders of the compound. Like huge sprays of water, the streams shot hundreds of feet into the air, then curled over the highest of the prison towers. The ends met with such precision that in the blink of an eye the pel had formed an enormous cage over the tiers.

"Wait." After all we'd suffered here, it seemed ap-propriate to stick around and witness what would happen next. "Watch."

The pel cage slowly began to collapse in on the compound. The guard towers were the first to shat-ter. The weight of them in turn collapsed the lower structures. And still the pel kept shrinking, tight-ening, until the individual streams began to meld together at the top of the cage.

A yawning sinkhole formed all around the com-pound, and the streams solidified into a solid bubble of pel, still descending and contracting with the same inexorable force. We could see through it, and watched as the entire compound was rapidly re-duced to shards. The pel pulled the engulfed, shat-tered structures down into the crater, and filled in the hole with itself.

The end result was a featureless, smooth stretch of

crystal. As if the compound had never existed. The Hsktskt wouldn't be using Catopsa as a slave-depot ever again.

Moving more than twenty thousand beings from an asteroid couldn't be done in a day. I instructed the liberation force pilots transporting the prisoners to bring down emergency shelter units on every return trip. After being allocated their own, the Hsktskt sullenly provided their silent assistance in setting up the other temporary habitats.

I used one strictly as a primary-care unit and continued to treat prisoners and Hsktskt alike. Since she was too critical to move, I kept FurreVa there, too.

Vlaav stuck by me like glue.

"Doctor, you should take a rest interval."

"I will." No, I wouldn't. I gestured to Zella. "Next patient, please."

"What are your plans, when you leave this place? Will you resume your position on the Jorenian vessel?"

"I'm not sure what I'm going to do." That was the truth, and it surprised me anyway. I looked over at the Saksonan. "Why?"

The red nubs on his face glowed brightly. "I have learned much from working with you. I would appreciate the opportunity to finish my residency under your tutelage."

I knew he had a bit of a crush on me, but I wasn't going to encourage it. "Don't you want to go home, Vlaav?"

"No. Not if I can learn to be half the surgeon you are. Will you teach me?"

"Flattery won't get you any slack." I'd helped train other interns and residents in the past, but I'd never been asked to be a primary instructor before. If I'd possessed hemangiomas, they would have been popping like champagne corks. "Are you sure you really want to be *my* student?"

"Yes."

The other problems I had to deal with made my grin fade. "Let's get off this rock, then we'll talk about it."

Vlaav happily performed rounds for me after that, and came back to report on the half dozen prisoners we'd kept in the shelter for observation.

I listened, and imagined once more teaching this kid to be a cutter. I could do that, I thought. If everything else worked out. "How's the OverSeer doing?"

"She cannot remain in artificial hibernation much longer," he said as I finished medicating yet another former prisoner suffering from mild hypothermia. He gave me a rundown of scan results from her chart.

He was right. If we didn't get her up to the *Sunlace* and on an operating table soon, she'd never come out of it. "Keep close monitor on her vitals for me."

The massive transport operation slowly came to a close. Salo and a warrior party arrived as we were loading the last of the prisoners into the Akesellan launches, and I had saw their collective reaction toward the remaining Hsktskt.

It wasn't a desire to hand out Jorenian kisses of peace.

"Salo, the compound has been completely destroyed."

"A pity." The big warrior removed a large, bladed weapon from his sojourn pack. "I would have decorated it with my ClanSign."

ClanSign was what Jorenians did with the bodies of their enemies after they disemboweled them. I saw Wonlee join the Jorenians. Beneath his envirosuit, his spines flexed. He was carrying a Hasktskt pulse rifle in each hand.

"Stop right there, Lieutenant."

My prickly friend's voice transmitted his rage and fury over my comunit. "They enslaved us. They killed or sold thousands here."

"Which was my fault, remember?"

No one seemed to care. The lizards collected in a tight mass, ready to defend themselves. HouseClan Torin started swinging their blades in what looked like massacre warm-up exercises.

Time for me to play referee again.

"Hold it." I placed myself between the two groups, and held up my gloved hands. I'd already gotten the Aksellans to back off, and knew how to stop the Jorenians. "Salo, I shield these Hsktskt."

"You would protect these monsters, Healer?" Salo asked me.

"Yes. That's exactly what I'm doing." I walked over to the largest of the Hsktskt. "I want you to tell your people to stand down. Now."

"Hsktskt do not surrender to slaves," the centuron said with chilling conviction.

"The Hsktskt are going to end up as fodder if you don't back down and let me negotiate a compromise here."

It took a few more minutes, but I convinced the lizards to stop putting on the aggressive act. Finally, I had to deal with Wonlee, who didn't care what I shielded.

"Lieutenant." I intercepted him as he started toward the group of Hsktskt. "Don't do this. This slave-depot is useless now, and the pel won't let them build another one. We can let them go."

"They killed my wife."

"A lethal mineral called the tul killed your wife." I put my hand on the barrel of one pulse rifle, and hoped he wouldn't shoot me just to get at the lizards. "Wonlee, we've been through so much together. If I can let them go, so can you."

"You are a physician. You do not understand the need for justice."

Oh, but I did. "You were a medic. You know how fragile and brief life is. Let the violence and hatred end, here and now." I glanced over at the Hsktskt, and thought of the coming League invasion. "Believe me, they'll get what they deserve, soon enough."

Another round of negotiation convinced the Jorenians to allow the Hsktskt survivors to take a ship and return to Faction space.

"This was not the end I envisioned," the Jorenian said as we watched the Hsktskt launch lift off. "Releasing the beasts was never a consideration."

"They're not all beasts." I thought of FurreVa. They were—what they were. "Come on, big guy. We'd better get off this rock and back where we belong."

Zella met me halfway down the entrance ramp. "Continues to weaken, the Hsktskt female. In critical condition now, she is."

It was time to go home.

CHAPTER TWENTY

Masks Off

The last jaunt up to the *Sunlace* seemed to take forever. I couldn't stay in my harness, not with FurreVa stretched out on a litter, so I planted myself beside her for the duration of the trip. Her monitors didn't look good.

The surgery couldn't wait any longer.

"Signal Medical for me," I asked the pilot when we were halfway to the ship. "Tell them I need a thoracic team scrubbed and ready for us."

By the time the pilot docked in launch bay, I stood at the hull doors with the OverSeer, and pushed her out onto the docking ramp the moment the panels opened. Once off the shuttle, I had the Jorenians load her onto a gurney, and signaled Squilyp.

"Are you ready to go?"

"We're prepared, Doctor," the Omorr said. "What's the patient's condition?"

"Bad. Direct displacer blast to the upper torso. Multiple internal trauma, definitely cardiac and liver, God knows what else. I had to induce artificial hibernation just to keep her alive." I checked her infuser lines, then nodded to the crew members helping me. "Have the team in the suite. We'll be there in a minute."

I paused long enough to snap out orders for the injured to be taken to Medical, then accompanied FurreVa's gurney into a gyrlift. Every step made my stomach clench. Every glance down at the motionless Hsktskt female made me move that much faster.

Adaola, who was wearing a first-year intern's tunic, manned the gurney from the moment we entered the bay. "Go and scrub, Healer. I will prep the patient."

"Where's Squilyp?" I stripped off my outer garments as I headed for the cleansing unit. "I need him to assist."

He hopped out of the surgical suite, already scrubbed and gowned, and lifted his gloved membranes. "As I anticipated, Doctor."

"Mr. Wonderful. Still as exemplary as ever." My mouth hitched as I thrust my hands under the biodecon port to sterilize. "As soon as she's under, get her chest open. I'll be there in a second."

My eyes went to the monitors as I entered the suite, and waited for a moment as Squilyp lowered the sterile field. FurreVa's heart rate was erratic, and she'd lost too much blood. I was pleased to see Adaola had already initiated the synplasma infusers and had the heart/lung array standing by.

"First-year intern, huh?" I studied the instrument setup with approval. "So you were serious about becoming a physician."

"Senior Healer Squilyp has been an inspirational instructor," Adaola said, her white-within-white eyes crinkling above her mask. "He has encouraged me to pursue a surgical residency."

Squilyp had once treated nurses with the same compassion he would a lascalpel: to be used until they no longer functioned. He'd grown up a lot since those days. "Couldn't help infecting her with the bug, could you, Squid Lips?"

He winced at the old nickname. "I feel certain Adaola will make a competent surgeon."

"I always thought she was wasted as a nurse," I said as I went around the table and took my position opposite the Omorr.

The big Jorenian female made a modest gesture. "My thanks, Healer."

Squilyp had already made the initial incision and opened FurreVa's thorax from her neck to her pelvis, and was now clamping back the subdermal layers to expose the chest cavity. I pulled the primary laser rig down and activated the lascalpel, then leaned over to have a look.

"Son of a bitch." The Omorr lifted his head, and I shook mine. "No, not you, Squil. The one who did this to her." And had gotten away with it, which still infuriated me.

Squilyp ran an organ series as I performed the visual and probe assessments. "Significant vessel damage to both chambers of the heart. Right kidney is compromised, and there are dozens of perforations in the superior colon.

"She never could do anything the easy way." I couldn't get a clear take on the central region of the chest cavity—there was simply too much blood and tissue occluding the area. I ordered more suction. "What about the liver?"

The Omorr scanned the female Hsktskt a second time. "Elevated bilirubin, serum alkaline phosphatase, serum aminotransferase, decreased serum albumin and prothrombin time."

SrrokVar had known exactly where to shoot her to cause the maximum amount of damage. "What else?"

"I'm reading no organic cohesion. Liver cellular loss stands at . . ." Squilyp scanned her again, before he gazed at me with solemn eyes. "It's ninety-seven-point-four percent."

That meant—"No. You're wrong."

I thrust his scanner aside and took the suction tube from the nurse using it. Blood and body fluid swamped the cavity. I'd simply evacuate it myself.

"Cherijo—"

"It's displaced from the impact. I'll find it, it has to be here."

A moment later, I pulled the tube from her chest, and the Omorr cleared his throat. In the old days, when we'd been competing for the Senior Healer slot onboard the *Sunlace*, he would have gloated over this. Now all he offered was a silent gaze of sympathy.

"You were right. Okay. I'll harvest viable cells and clone her a new one." I pulled a specimen tray, and began to search for a shred of the organ. "We'll keep her going until I have a replacement organ."

Membranes took the probe from my hand. "Doctor."

I grabbed another one from the tray. "No, Squilyp. I've put her back together twice before. I can do it again."

"If there were no other injuries, I would agree with you." The Omorr came around the table and pushed the tray aside. "Cherijo. She took a full burst, at point-blank range. You have to accept the facts. Her liver has been destroyed."

I stopped probing the chest cavity and pulled the laser rig down. "Then we'll keep her in sleep suspension until I can locate a transplant."

The monitors went off, and Adaola gave me a despairing look. I began resuscitation, biting into my lower lip with each compression. She couldn't die on me. We'd been through too much together. Echoes of her low, rough voice pounded inside my skull.

Angry. *You are called SsurreVa?* Suffering. *Let me die, Terran.* Wistful. *Reconstruct . . . this?* Determined.

There will be no more arena games. Dying. *My young are safe. You are safe. It is enough.*

The monitors slowly flat lined.

We tried electro-stim. More drugs. Nothing worked. The Jorenians stayed out of my way. Squilyp and I worked on her body for a half hour before I finally straightened and slowly stripped off my gloves.

"I'm calling it. Time of death is"—I glanced at the wall console—"oh-nineteen, twenty-two hours."

The Omorr looked down at the dead Hsktskt. "I'm sorry, Doctor."

"Thanks." I gently pulled the surgical shroud up over the peaceful face I'd worked so hard to repair.

Adaola and the nurses intoned a solemn Jorenian chant of passage. I couldn't seem to move away from the table. It was as if I expected FurreVa to yank aside the linen and shout at me for giving up.

A warm membrane touched my arm. "You did everything you could for her," the Omorr said. "There was simply too much damage."

"Yeah." I tugged my wet mask from my face. "There was."

Adaola paused in her chant to ask me, "What was her name, Healer?"

I remembered how I'd called her Helen of Troy, and caught a sob before it emerged. "FurreVa. Overseer FurreVa."

Treating the injured prisoners kept me busy for the rest of the shift. My adopted family, while having no love for the Hsktskt, expressed their sincere sympathy for the loss of my friend.

Squilyp let me work until there was nothing left to be done, then asked if I would do rounds with him in the morning.

"Sure." I had nothing to do, nowhere to go. "See you then."

"Cherijo." I stopped at the door panel. "You told

me never to . . . *mess* with you over a patient you just lost, but if you need someone to talk to—"

I smiled wanly back at him. "You'll be the one, Squil. Thanks."

I couldn't face my empty quarters. Xonea had signaled from the helm that the last of the launches from Catopsa were arriving, so I decided to go down to the launch bay and see what I could do there.

The final shuttle hull doors parted, and the Jorenian team brought two men out. Both were in envirosuits, but their hands had been secured in detainment bonds. I started to ask why, then one of the crew removed their helmets and I saw who they were.

Gael Kelly and Noarr.

"What's going on here?" I asked one of the Torins. "Why are they tied up like that?"

"We discovered them fighting near an alien vessel."

"Blue-arsed mentallers! If you'll not give me a weapon, for pity's sake, shoot this sleeven before he gets loose." The Irishman strained at his bonds, then fixed his gaze on me with relief. "*Dote*, tell 'em to stop acting the maggot!"

A security guard glanced at me. "Our vocollars are not translating what he says, Healer."

"I know. Gael, you have to speak stanTerran, please."

"This gouger—this *collaborator*—tried to kill me, *dote*. I told you, he's been spying for the beasts, and I've got proof."

I glanced at Noarr, who stood in his usual brooding, silent stance. "Is that right?" I motioned for their bonds to be released. "Is what he's saying true, Noarr?" Not that I believed it.

"Part of it." The alien slave-runner rubbed the joints above his flippers slowly. "I tried to kill him."

My eyes widened. "Why?"

"He was attempting to remove prisoners from Catopsa."

"That's sort of the general idea, at the moment."

"He did not intend to bring them here." Noarr pulled off his hood and turned to Gael, who was visibly seething. "Will you tell her now, or shall I?"

"I will in me ring," the Terran said, and spat on the deck.

"I think that means no," I said to the confused Jorenians. "Gael?"

"His name is not Gael." Noarr folded his arms inside his cloak and regarded the Terran with an expression akin to pity. "It is GaaVar."

"Aye, right." The Irishman let out a sputtering laugh. "You're addled, that's what you are, sleeven." He continued in stanTerran. "I was born in Clare, in the Celt Republic, on Terra. Check the database, if you like."

"I am sure you were." Noarr pulled his cloak around him. "Your family took you from Terra to immigrate to a new colony. When you were a young child, did they not?"

"I've told you all this, *dote*," Gael said to me.

Noarr stepped closer to the Terran. "How old were you when the Hsktskt attacked your ship?"

"I was but a wee lad."

"You were an infant. The Hsktskt do not take children hostage. Why did you survive?"

Gael exploded. "I don't know what the gammy thicks wanted with me! They took me!"

"And adopted you, the same way they adopted me." Noarr turned and gazed at me. "He was raised by the Hsktskt from infancy. By Lord SrrokVar."

Before anyone could move, Gael pulled a Hsktskt pistol from the inside of his tunic and lunged in my direction. A moment later, he had me in an armlock, and the business end of the weapon pressed tightly against my cheek.

"Don't do this, Gael." I looked at the Jorenians, who had formed a deadly ring around us. White eyes narrowed, claws emerged. "They'll kill you."

He pointed the gun at Noarr. "In the shuttle. Now. Or this scanger bitch dies."

I warned the Jorenians to stay back as we entered the shuttle and Gael shoved Noarr toward the helm.

"Fly this gammy crate out of here."

"They'll come after us." Gael's shove made me fall against the harness rigging. I clutched it to regain my footing. "You don't have to slave for the Hsktskt anymore. Give yourself up, and I'll help you get back to Terra."

"Terra?" He laughed. "You're off your nut."

"I think you can drop the dialect now," I said as he tied me into the harness.

"It took me years to learn. Still, you're right. I don't need it anymore, do I?"

"Not anymore," I agreed.

Gael watched Noarr pilot the shuttle out from the launch bay. "Input these into the navigation array," he said, and rattled off some coordinates.

The slave-runner hesitated. "That will take us directly to the Hsktskt homeworld."

"My homeworld," Gael said.

"No, it isn't," I said.

He turned to me. "He was telling you the truth, Doctor. I was captured by the Faction when I was six months old. Lord SrrokVar adopted me, raised me, trained me. You're the first Terran I've ever seen in my life." He spat at my feet. "And the last, I hope."

"You were the spy all along," I said slowly.

"And you are supposed to be so bright. Yes, I provided inside intelligence on the slave population to my parent." He fingered the pistol in his hand. "I'm relieved it's over. Warm-bloods are disgusting, sniveling creatures."

"You're warm-blooded, too."

"I am the son of a Hsktskt Lord." Gael gave me

an eerie smile, one that reminded me of SrrokVar. "He taught me well."

"I'll bet he did." I saw some movement out of the corner of my eye and blinked. "So you're going to take us back to the homeworld, and . . . what? Sell us as slaves?"

"For the crimes you committed against the Faction?" Gael laughed. "I'm going to have you tortured, then publicly executed."

Lieutenant Wonlee emerged from a cargo hatch behind Gael, and I kept my gaze fixed on the Hsktskt spy. "I know what SrrokVar must have done to you as a child. Let me help you, Gael."

"I wouldn't—"

Wonlee jumped on Gael's back, knocking the pistol to the deck and sending the Terran into an interior hull panel. Noarr immediately steered the ship around, sending both men to the deck, while I fumbled with the clips on my harness.

It was over so quickly that Gael was bleeding and tied up by the time the launch landed back on the *Sunlace*. An angry Xonea entered the shuttle, carrying one of his multibladed weapons, and dragged the Terran out onto the deck. I hurried after them.

"Don't hurt him, it's not his fault—"

Before I could stop him, Gael got to his feet. "For my father!" he screamed, then thrust himself upon the eight blades in Xonea's hands.

Noarr and I rushed over, but the Irishman was already dead.

"He chose his path well," Xonea said, and wiped the blood from his blades on Gael's tunic.

"He hid behind the mask of his own face," I said, kneeling beside him and closing his eyes. What kind of father had SrrokVar been? I wondered, then shuddered instinctively. "And was probably abused most of his life."

"Not everyone who is abused chooses to betray," Noarr said.

"You should know." I got to my feet and faced him. "You can take that mask off your face now."

The Jorenians made sounds of astonishment as Noarr stripped off his flippers, then inserted his thumbs under a concealed flap, and slowly peeled away the false face. When he revealed his features to the crew, several of them appeared to be staggered by his true identity.

I folded my arms, eyed my adopted family, then shook my head sadly. "Don't tell me he had *all* of you fooled."

The mask, to my own surprise, turned out to be a Lok-Teel. It rapidly changed from Noarr's face to its natural blob state and happily trundled over to clean Gael's blood from the deck.

"When did you know?" the man I loved asked me.

"I don't think you want me to describe what we were doing when I figured it out." I lowered my voice for his ears alone. "Using a voice manipulator and not kissing me were clever moves, but you forgot, I'm very familiar with the rest of your anatomy, too."

His mouth twitched. "I see."

"I also thought it was odd when you boarded *Noarr's* ship, and yet still knew where everything was." I clucked my tongue. "Sloppy. Very sloppy."

Duncan Reever removed the concealing cloak and shook out his damp hair. "Yet you never confronted me with your knowledge."

"I knew it was you," I said. "But what I didn't understand was why you didn't trust me enough to tell me yourself."

"That requires a rather lengthy explanation."

"We've got plenty of time." I took his arm. "Come with me."

After the tragic scene with Gael, neither of us was hungry, so I settled for servers of hot Jorenian tea and the privacy of my quarters.

"Okay," I said as I sat beside him on the sofa. "Spill the beans. *All* the beans this time, if you please."

Reever told me what I had only guessed at—that he had been a slave to the Hsktskt, after they raided the world his parents had been studying. Both his mother and father were killed in the massacre. The adolescent Duncan had been tall and strong enough to pass for a mature adult, so he was taken along with other survivors to Catopsa.

"I was compelled to serve as an arena fighter for nearly a revolution, before the accident. An Over-Master pushed his young commander into the ring, and my opponent tried to kill him. I shielded him and saved his life."

"That would explain the blood-bond between you and TssVar."

"Yes. He was grateful enough to adopt me, and trained me to take the place of the OverMaster who had attempted to kill him."

"That's why you said Gael had been adopted, like you."

"Yes. As SrrokVar made Gael his son, TssVar made me his brother." Reever rubbed a hand over the back of his neck. "What he didn't know was I had no intention of ever serving the Faction, even when he sent me to infiltrate the Pmoc Quadrant colonies."

"You *spied* for them?" With a jolt I recalled the delivery of the quints. "You brought TssVar to K-2?"

"I had been sending false reports back to the Faction, making them believe the colonies were too poor to merit raiding. However, TssVar decided to recall me to Catopsa. On the jaunt to retrieve me, UgessVa went into labor, and the rest you know."

"Why did you come onboard the *Sunlace*?"

"I wanted to escape the Hsktskt, as much as you wanted to escape the League."

There was one thing that still bothered me. "You

told me you signaled the Hsktskt to come to Varallan. If you were trying to avoid them, why would you do that?"

"It seemed the only way I could protect you, and stop the League from destroying Joren. I didn't betray you, Cherijo."

"So you signaled them and played traitor again. And as soon as we reached Catopsa, you became Noarr, the slave-runner."

"Yes." Reever picked up the Lok-teel, which had followed us from the launch bay. "I realized what I could do the first time I established a telepathic link with these creatures. I used them to disguise the slaves before I took them from the compound."

Reever went on to describe the secret nature of the fungus. From what he said, they could also merge together and use their united bulk to assume the shape of a larger object, like a console or storage container. As Noarr, he had often smuggled prisoners out of the compound right under the snouts of the Hsktskt, in what they assumed were nonorganic waste receptacles.

"We'll debate your methods, and your penchant for camouflage later." Jenner jumped up between us, and chose Reever's lap to curl up in. The ingrate. "Where do we go from here?"

"I've dreamed of liberating Catopsa for many years. Now that it is realized, I have nothing more planned." He stared at the viewport. "The prisoners will want to return to their homeworlds and be reunited with their families."

"*Nothing* planned?" He didn't get it, and I smiled. "Tell you what. I have an idea." I filled him in about the drone vessel Joseph had sent out into deep space for me. "We can use that."

"We?"

"You're going to need a ship's doctor, aren't you?"

Troubled eyes met mine. "Only if she comes as my bondmate."

"No problem." I fumbled in the pocket of my tunic, and pulled out the ring I had thrown across the interrogation chamber onboard the *Perpetua*, all those months ago. He gave me an amazed stare when I placed it in his hand, and I scowled. "Okay, so I'm sentimental. Problem solved."

I got up and went to the console to signal Xonea with the details of our plan, and the coordinates of the drone ship. By my reckoning, it would take a few weeks to get there, so Reever and I would have plenty of time to work out the rest of our unconventional relationship.

"Cherijo."

I paused at the control pad.

"The League and the Hsktskt are going to war. It will be dangerous."

I snorted. "At least."

"We will be chased by mercenaries, out for the bounty the League still offers for you."

"We've been chased by mercenaries before. I wasn't impressed. Anything else?"

"Yes." He came up behind me, turned me around. His ring slid over the fourth finger on my left hand. "Squilyp told me you have a medical issue that must be treated immediately. Space travel may interfere with that."

"Did he tell you what it was?" If that Omorr had ruined everything, I was going to strangle him.

"No."

"Good. He's right, I do. But space travel won't be a problem. Eating will. I expect I'll have some problems keeping food down. Then there's all that nasty fluid retention—"

"Is it your stomach?" Duncan went pale. "You never eat properly. Is it serious?" He was so upset he didn't wait for me to answer. "You will do exactly as the Omorr tells you, Cherijo."

"As long as I agree with him, sure."

"You *will* agree with him." My bondmate's face darkened. "If I learn you have done otherwise—"

"Oh, settle down." I grinned. "It's not that big a deal."

"Do not make attempts at humor. Not about your health." One of his scarred hands cupped my face. "After everything we have been through, I refuse to lose you now."

"You won't lose me." I took pity on him and pressed a kiss into his palm. "You may even enjoy this"—I guided his hand down and placed it flat against my abdomen—"Daddy."